NOWHERE NICE

Rick Gavin

Minotaur Books ✖ New York

This is a work of fiction. All of the characters, organizations, and events
portrayed in this novel are either products of the author's imagination or
are used fictitiously.

NOWHERE NICE. Copyright © 2013 by Rick Gavin. All rights reserved.
Printed in the United States of America. For information, address
St. Martin's Press, 175 Fifth Avenue, New York, N.Y. 10010.

www.minotaurbooks.com

Library of Congress Cataloging-in-Publication Data

Gavin, Rick.
    Nowhere Nice / Rick Gavin.
        p. cm.
    ISBN 978-0-312-58319-4 (hardcover)
    ISBN 978-1-250-01600-3 (e-book)
    1. Drug dealers—Fiction.   2. Theft—Fiction.   3. Revenge—
Fiction.   4. Delta (Miss. : Region)—Fiction.   I. Title.
  PS3607.A9848N69 2013
  813'.6—dc23

                                            2013024713

Minotaur books may be purchased for educational, business, or promotional
use. For information on bulk purchases, please contact Macmillan
Corporate and Premium Sales Department at 1-800-221-7945, extension
5442, or write specialmarkets@macmillan.com.

First Edition: November 2013

10   9   8   7   6   5   4   3   2   1

NOWHERE NICE

ONE

Me and Desmond were wrestling a gas range out of a hummocky tangle of fescue. The people who'd bought that stove on time from K-Lo had left it in their yard. They were Arkansas Guthries who appeared to have abandoned their trailer home but not before they'd pitched their major appliances out the door. Their refrigerator had crushed a gardenia bush. Their washer had half demolished the pump house.

Desmond wasn't surprised. He had some repo history with Arkansas Guthries. He explained to me, "Their way of saying, 'Take your damn shit back.'"

Kendell rolled up in his county police cruiser. He climbed out and smoothed his trousers. Tugged his belt and adjusted his gear. Checked the safety on his Ruger. Gave his handcuff pouch a slap.

"Boys," he said and wandered over.

"Gone already," Desmond informed him. He jerked his head toward the trailer home with its storm door standing open.

But Kendell hadn't come about Guthries. He just told us both, "Walked off."

"Who?" I asked.

"That Boudrot."

I knew enough to shiver and twitch.

"What Boudrot?" Desmond wanted to know.

"What Boudrot you think?" Kendell asked him.

Desmond groaned. He said, "Shit," and let go of the stove. Back into the fescue it went.

We both waited for something further from Kendell who spat with his usual tidy precision.

He said nothing for long enough to cause me to say to him, "Walked off how?"

Thanks to me and Desmond, that Boudrot had been serving twenty years in Parchman, not the sort of place the inmates are usually suffered to walk off from.

"Out by Beulah," Kendell told us. "Had a gang mowing and cleaning culverts."

Prison work crews in their striped coveralls are a common sight in the Delta. Green and gray stripes, probably eight inches wide. You can see them a mile away. They have escorts, of course. No-neck guards in campaign hats with shotguns. The sort of boys who, but for some luck and restraint, would all be inmates too.

"He went in the bayou," Kendell said. "Back in some cypresses. Disappeared."

"They didn't chase him?" I asked

"Or shoot him?" Desmond wanted to know.

"Gators around," Kendell told us. "They must have figured he'd swim back."

"Which bayou exactly?" I asked.

There's a huge one up past Beulah where a man who hated Parchman more than he feared the gators and snakes could likely lose himself without much trouble.

"Out toward Mound City," Kendell said, and both me and Desmond groaned.

That was the big one. It went on for miles, probably even clear to the river. I did some spitting. I wasn't tidy and didn't try to be precise.

"Well, that's it then," I said.

"Just hold on." Kendell made a bid to reassure us. "They've got a whole crew up there. A couple of flat boats, an air boat too. They're bound to flush him out."

For a county cop in the Mississippi Delta, Kendell was awfully optimistic. It probably helped that he didn't know an awful lot about that Boudrot. The man was just a nasty lowlife on a booking sheet to Kendell, but me and Desmond had tangled with him in the flesh. We'd made sure he got incriminated by all the harm he'd done. When we knew him, he was a Delta meth lord with a vile sadistic streak, and he'd sworn vengeance on me and Desmond from the moment he got arrested. We'd heard he'd kept it up in Parchman like a catechism.

"What's he doing on a work crew anyway?" Desmond wanted to know.

Talk was he'd sliced up a couple of cons with a filed-down bunk stay, and there he was out in the regular world cutting grass and cleaning culverts.

"Guess they figured he'd straightened up a little." But Kendell didn't seem persuaded. "If they don't find him, he'll just keep on running, get as far as he can. I wouldn't fret much about it. Just thought you ought to know."

That Boudrot wasn't remotely the typical lowlife spouting

off, rattling on about all the harm he'd never get around to doing. He was a first-class Acadian fuckstick, the pride of Cut Off, Louisiana, and he was too eaten up with making us pay to back off it now.

"Who do we need to tell?" I asked Desmond.

He thought for a moment. "All of them."

"Why don't you start with me," Kendell suggested.

Desmond gave Kendell a snort in reply. The one that meant "Like hell."

We'd broken a few laws when we tangled with that Boudrot, and I'd been out of policing long enough to not be clear on what they were. Arson for sure. Assault most likely. More than a little felonious menacing and probably some grand theft too. It was all in a bid to put that Boudrot in prison where he belonged, but the whole enterprise had ended up with the bunch of us keeping his money. That had to be the thing Guy Baptiste Boudrot was most put out about. It didn't matter that he could sell more meth and make another fortune. We'd messed with his shit, and he wasn't the sort to tolerate something like that.

We couldn't tell Kendell the shiftless details because he was sure to haul us in. Kendell was about the straightest arrow I'd ever run across. It wouldn't matter to him that I was his friend and Desmond was his cousin. Kendell was a Baptist absolutest. You either broke laws or you didn't. He was never terribly interested in why.

Desmond informed me, "Sonic," once we'd finally packed up those Guthrie appliances and I'd pulled into the road.

"Sure about that?"

"Uh-huh." He jerked his head toward the truck route. Desmond needed to think, and he did his best thinking over a Coney Island or three.

The trouble was Desmond had been on a righteous Pentecostal diet. He'd been seeing a girl from his church, and they'd been losing weight together as a sign of their devotion to the Lord. Of course, he'd been in an evil mood for some weeks. Nitrate withdrawal, I guess.

I lingered at the truck route junction to give Desmond the chance to reconsider the Sonic. He pointed west toward Indianola. "Ain't telling you again."

Desmond's favorite Sonic parking spot happened to be available, well down the lot in the shade of a pine, away from the range hood exhaust. Desmond was ordering over the intercom before I'd even stopped entirely.

"Maybe they'll catch him," I said. "Might even have snagged him already."

Desmond was usually the sunny one, but he had a nephew who worked up at Parchman, so Desmond was personally acquainted with the brand of halfwit the prison employed.

"Won't," he told me. "They'll spread the word and wait for somebody else to do it."

"Swamp might have got him. Ever been out there? Snapping turtles a foot across."

"The man had a pet gator," Desmond reminded me.

I'd tried to forget about that.

Desmond took his usual quarter hour dressing his Coney Islands. Truth be told, I think he preferred the ritual to the hotdogs. Marshaling the relish and the ketchup packets, applying his condiments just so. I knew he wouldn't suffer questions while he was fixing his Coney Islands, so I just sat and ate my cheese tots and picked at my burger until Desmond had rolled up his condiment packets and had taken his first bite. He made a neck noise. He nodded. He could tolerate me now.

I fished out the golf pencil I kept in the ashtray and my phone bill envelope from the glove box. I licked the lead. "Start with Percy Dwayne?"

Desmond nodded.

"Any idea where he is?"

Desmond shook his head.

"And Luther," he said, "and those swamp boys."

"Tommy and Eugene." I scribbled all the names down.

"Dale for sure," Desmond added.

Dale had been the one to arrest that Boudrot after we'd told him where he'd find him. Dale was off the force these days and working repo like us.

"Might tell Pearl to keep an eye out."

Pearl was my dizzy landlady.

"I'll need to tell Tula something," I allowed. "This shit'll chap her pretty good."

Tula was my girlfriend, and I'd half been trying to tell her about that Boudrot. She was aware that me and Desmond had gotten up to some shady business, but she seemed content to let me lay it out for her as I pleased.

It was a simple story if you could tell it without cross-examination. A wiry white-trash specimen named Percy Dwayne Dubois had bought a rent-to-own plasma TV from K-Lo, our boss. He stopped paying on it, and I went to get the thing or come away with the money he owed. Percy Dwayne had another idea altogether and brained me with a fireplace shovel. Then he stole the car I was driving, which wasn't even mine. That was the trouble really. If it had been my Chevy heap, I could have left it all to county police. I couldn't do that with a car I didn't own. So me and Desmond went after Percy Dwayne, and things got complicated.

That's the leading problem with cracker lowlifes. They can't do anything straight. One of them steals your car, and you end up taking down an Acadian fuckstick meth lord you didn't truly have a thing against. It all just cascades into a gaudy heap and jumbles up together. Once you get in with white trash, there's no such thing as clean and neat.

So whenever Tula or Kendell or anybody asked me about that Boudrot, I was tempted to just tell them, "Percy Dwayne Dubois hit me with a shovel and stole a car that wasn't even mine." That seemed explanation enough to me, but people crave elaboration.

Desmond polished off his second Coney Island. He chewed and thought. He thought and chewed. "First off, you and me might go have a look," he finally told me.

"At what?"

"Bayou," he said and pointed in the direction of Beulah, I had to guess. "Went in this morning, right?"

I nodded.

"He might want to want to come out before dark."

TWO

Desmond didn't care for swamps and bayous. He didn't like the woods. Truth be told, he was never at his ease over by the river either.

"Might fall in," Desmond informed me once when we were standing on the Greenville levee. "Then where would I be?"

"Probably Vicksburg for supper."

"Funny," Desmond had said in a way that reliably meant "Shut the fuck up."

So we didn't do much vigorous poking around on the banks of that bayou by Beulah. There were roads enough in the vicinity to let us ride beside it instead. It was a big, sprawling thing as Delta swamps go, part marsh and part oxbow lake. The water was black, and every fallen log and limb was covered up with turtles. Big ones. Snappers. I'd blow the horn, and they'd tumble into the water like an avalanche with feet.

We were a week into October, so the bugs could have been a lot worse. It wasn't nearly as Indian-summer sweltering as it usually gets in the Delta.

"Where do you figure they're looking?" I asked Desmond. There was no sign of another human. Just crows and cranes and gulls and a dead fox in the road.

Desmond shook his head and grunted.

I shaded my eyes for a good look around. We'd been riding along the swamp bank for three-quarters of an hour and had seen one old leathery black guy fishing with a bobber and pole and a kid pushing a bike with a flat tire and no seat. No county four-by-fours. No state police prowlers. No bug-encrusted crew-cab Chevys from the fleet they keep at Parchman.

"Maybe Kendell heard it wrong," I said to Desmond. "People talk a lot of junk. Maybe nobody went anywhere. Try Rejondo?"

Desmond sighed and nodded. He didn't have much use for the boy. Rejondo was Desmond's sister's son, and he worked as a guard at Parchman. He sold yard statuary as a sideline and wore godawful cologne. It smelled like a piña colada a Tri Delt had already thrown up.

We drove straight to Parchman, and I pulled up to the guardhouse. I recognized the guy inside. We'd repossessed his bedroom suite. Bedstead. Nighstands. Bureau. Dressing table. The whole outfit. His wife had made him buy it all, and then she'd run off with a Tunica pit boss. He'd been happy enough to see us come and haul the stuff away. We'd ended up having a beer with the fellow sitting on his back porch steps.

"Hey, bud," I told him as we rolled up to the gate.

He squinted at me, came out of the guardhouse, and had a

look at Desmond as well. "She come back," he said. "Told you she would. Made her buy her own damn dresser."

We all had a laugh.

"What you need?" he asked.

"Heard you lost one out by Beulah," I said.

He nodded.

"Went in the bayou or something?"

"That's what I'm hearing."

"Find him?"

He shrugged. "Ain't my end of things."

"You know his nephew?" I jabbed a thumb Desmond's way. "Rejondo?"

That fellow nodded. He checked a clipboard with his roster on it. "On at eight," he told us. "Probably home."

"Thanks." I shifted into reverse. "Hope everything works out with the missus."

"Won't," he assured me and went back in his guardhouse to plop onto his stool.

Rejondo lived maybe eight miles from the prison. He had a couple of acres on 49 down by Sumner where him and his girl-friend shared a manufactured home in the middle of the property which was otherwise occupied by cement birdbaths, assorted sec-ular lawn statuary, and a three-foot-tall cast-concrete version of Jesus sitting on a stump. It was popular in churchyards and fam-ily plots all over the Delta, probably because it was cheaper than a tombstone and very much in the spirit of the place. The Lord and Savior taking a load off. Desmond called it "Shiftless Christ."

We pulled up to find Rejondo out in his yard talking cement donkeys with a woman. She was a wide white lady in stretchy velour pants with her hair piled up on her head and a Salem be-tween her lips. Me and Desmond threaded our way through the birdbaths, the geese, the deer, the gnomes, the peeing boys, the praying hands. We drew up short and waited while Rejondo conducted business.

That woman wanted a bulk discount on a pair of cement donkeys. Rejondo was of the view two didn't constitute a bulk.

"What do you even do with one of them?" Desmond asked me in a Desmond baritone whisper, which meant people could probably hear him in cars along the road.

"You put your goddamn geraniums in them," the wide white woman told us. She didn't even turn full around to do it or take the cigarette out of her mouth.

That woman offered Rejondo half of what he was asking.

"Got more in them than that," he told her.

She went up, and Rejondo gave the impression of coming down. But there was the stocking fee to consider, the yard-art tax, the hauling charge. Every time she thought she had him, they'd be lurking where they'd started. Then he gave her a break on delivery—knocked a ten spot off.

"Thirty usually," he told her, "but they'll do it for twenty." He eyed us across the way.

"Bring them right now?" she asked him.

"Follow you home," he said.

"Figures," Desmond muttered.

That wide white woman swiveled around to take the two of us in. We didn't appear to inspire much donkey-delivery confidence in her.

She shook her head. She flicked her butt. She told Rejondo, "I guess."

"Boys?" Rejondo said and pointed at that pair of cement donkeys.

I looked at Desmond. He shrugged. That was Rejondo all over. He'd calculated we'd come for something from him, so he'd get his something first.

That's how we came to be hauling cement donkeys for a wide white woman in a Suzuki. She spent the whole time we were carting her purchases over to my Ranchero squeezing herself under the wheel of her Samurai. Rejondo gave us some cardboard to protect the paint on my Ranchero bed. He chucked a box at us, anyway, that we could flatten or not.

"Where do you live, ma'am?" Rejondo asked the woman.

She pointed at her headliner and told all of us, "Memphis."

I was just beginning to sputter when she went on to explain that, for donkey-delivery purposes, she had a weekend place near Grady.

Rejondo stepped over to my Ranchero just as me and Desmond were settling in.

"Here about that Boudrot?" he asked.

We nodded.

"I'll get on the horn and try to have something for you when you get back."

When Desmond finally spoke, we were about halfway to Grady. He shook his head and said, "Ain't this some shit?"

Naturally, we toted that woman's donkeys all over what passed for her yard. She had a miniature windmill in it already, a canopied glider, a wishing well, a lawn tractor with a broken front axle, a flatboat on a trailer, and I think I counted three derelict barbecue grills. In her defense, it was hard to find a spot cement donkeys might improve. They ended up in her front yard either side of her stoop.

By way of thank you, that woman told us, "Don't be looking for no tip."

We were barely out of her driveway when Tula called me.

"Got something you'll want to see," she said.

"Right now?"

"Yep." Then she shifted away from her phone to tell somebody, "Why don't you back the hell on up."

Tula was out by the river, off Highway 1 just north of Legion Lake, about halfway between Beulah and Rosedale. By the time me and Desmond arrived, Kendell was on the scene as well, along with a no-neck deputy I knew only by reputation. He was a bad one to tap on folks with his nightstick as a first resort.

There were maybe a dozen civilians as well—neighbors and passersby—who'd gotten wind of calamity and had swung over to have a look. They were all gathered in a sun-baked patch of open ground between a ratty trailer home and one of those corporate tractor sheds, a steel and tin monstrosity about the size of an airplane hangar.

An EMT truck pulled in just behind us, so me and Desmond walked over toward Tula and Kendell in the company of a couple of techs who were arguing over what constituted a college football fumble and kept at it—barking back and forth about whose damn knee was down—until Kendell plugged the pair of them up by saying one time, "Hey!"

That's when me and Desmond saw the body. A white guy in his underwear. Maybe forty and on the stout side. His head was a sticky bloody mess, and he had what looked like a wooden chair leg jammed into his chest.

"Stole his car," Kendell told us. "Yellow Gold Duster with lifters and mess."

"Who?" Desmond asked, and Kendell pointed us to Tula.

She was squatting by the corpse taking photographs. She rose as me and Desmond approached. The mineral stink of gore was thick in the air, and what bugs there were had gathered.

"Show them," Tula said to her no-neck deputy colleague who used the tip of his nightstick to lift a shirt off the ground. Green and gray stripes, like an awning. Baggy, scratchy twill. Parchman garb.

THREE

"Why are we even here?" Desmond wanted to know.

We were parked by then with Tula and Kendell in what passed with the Greenville PD for an interrogation room. It had been somebody's office once. They'd left a credenza in it and had brought in a stout steel table and a half-dozen plastic chairs. There was a sheet of knotty plywood where the one-way glass should have been and boxes of files stacked head high full across the back wall.

"Whatever you got up to with that Boudrot—" Kendell started.

"Didn't get up to nothing *with* him," Desmond said.

"Fine." Kendell settled back and showed us his palms. "All I'm telling you is we don't care. You did what you did."

Tula wasn't entirely on board with that, which she made plain in a glance.

"You tell him," Desmond instructed me.

"Tell him what?"

"About that gator of his and shit."

"Gator?" Tula asked us.

I didn't quite know where to start, so I wound all the way back to where it began. "Percy Dwayne Dubois owed on a TV. Instead of handing the damn thing over, he hit me with a fireplace shovel. They took my Ranchero, him and his wife. Pearl's Ranchero at the time. And somehow the wife and the baby and the car all ended up with that Boudrot."

"Somehow?" Kendell asked me.

"I wasn't ever clear on why. I guess that Boudrot liked the car. Liked the wife a little too. Took them to a place he had down by Blue Hole."

"Burned down, didn't it?" Tula asked. It was more of an accusation than a question.

I nodded. Desmond shifted and groaned.

"A lot of fire in his life for a few days there." Kendell gave us that smile of his that looks primarily like a wince.

"Meth houses, you know," Desmond told him. "Damn things go up all the time."

"You didn't help?" Kendell asked, looking from me to Desmond.

"Could have been more careful probably," I allowed.

Tula, as it turned out, had a snort for that.

"Kind of tangled with him, didn't you?" Kendell asked us. He tapped on that Boudrot's booking sheet. "Concussion. Broken collarbone. Thirty-two stitches altogether."

I glanced at Desmond, and he was the one who nodded and

said, "Scuffed him up. He sort of made us. Knife and all. Right?"

I nodded. "Yeah."

"We figure he's coming after you," Tula told me and Desmond. "That's what we're hearing out of Parchman anyway."

"We heard he'd been stewing," I said. "Doubt he's the sort to let shit go."

"Crazy fucker," Desmond added. "Don't need to be after you to kill you. Guy with the chair leg in him didn't do nothing but own a car."

"Any idea where he might be headed?" Kendell asked us.

We shrugged.

"Does he know where to look for you two?"

We shrugged again. Who were we to say what that Acadian fuckstick knew.

"And the gator?" Tula asked me.

"Used to feed people to it once he'd whacked them into chunks. Down by Yazoo, back in the national forest. That's what we heard anyway."

Once me and Desmond were out of the station house proper and heading for my Ranchero, Desmond said, "Got to tell those boys right quick. Give them a chance to see him coming."

"In a yellow Gold Duster with lifters and mess? Shouldn't be much of a chore."

"Might ought to start with Dale," Desmond said.

Dale had been an overmuscled pinhead cop back when we'd steered him to that Boudrot. Now he was a flabby pinhead civilian working for K-Lo like we did.

"And let's hit Rejondo's on the way back," I suggested. "See if he turned up anything."

He hadn't. He claimed to have tried to. Rejondo told us about the phone calls he'd made to various of his Parchman buddies who didn't among them seem to know squat. An inmate was loose—they'd heard that much—and he'd stirred up some sort of trouble.

"Killed a guy already," Desmond informed him. "Needed his clothes and his car."

Rejondo took a moment to seem sorrowful on the corpse's behalf before saying to me and Desmond, "Help me a second here, how about it?"

Desmond headed for my Ranchero and left it to me to tell him, "Nope."

We arrived back at the Indianola shop to find K-Lo irritated. Not uncommonly irritated, but just standard-issue ill. He was standing out front on the sidewalk polishing off a Pall Mall.

"Where the hell you been?" he barked our way.

Before we could even begin to tell him, Peabo came out of the store with a couple of questions for K-Lo. Peabo was six foot eight with the physique of a silo and the intellect of one as well. He had a knack for repo largely because he was comprehensively fearless, chiefly due to the fact he didn't have the good sense to be scared.

Peabo's hobbies were fishing and getting tattooed. As a giant pale-white guy, he made for a fine canvas. He'd just see stuff in the course of a day and run off and get it inked. He had a sunset over a pecan grove across his right shoulder blade. A Willys Jeep on his left forearm. A sturgeon on his biceps. The face of some girl he'd met at the auto auction on the back of his right hand. There were hounds all over the place—across his torso and down his legs—along with Peabo's aunt Judy's tabby cat, Buster, who occupied one entire calf.

Peabo had come out with his usual brace of questions for K-Lo: Would he get overtime if he worked past five and why exactly not?

K-Lo told him, like he always did, "No, dammit," and, "Because."

Peabo raised his big pink hand and rubbed his shaved head with it. He said to K-Lo, "Well, all right," which was what he always said.

"Where's Dale?" I asked Peabo. Since they were both big, hulking white guys, they kind of hung together.

"He was out back yesterday."

"We're sort of looking for him now."

Peabo shrugged and then asked K-Lo if he worked past five tomorrow could he maybe draw that overtime he wasn't drawing today.

Dale was in the toilet down the hall past K-Lo's office. The room was barely big enough for the commode and the sink, and a well-fed cat could have walked under the door. Dale stayed constipated from supplements and muscle enhancers and usually just leafed through his latest copy of *Muscle Pro* for a quarter hour. Then he'd flush and come out to tell everybody in earshot, "Didn't do no good."

I heard him flip a page over. "Hey, Dale," I said.

"Yeah."

"Got some news."

"All right."

"That Boudrot, the one you arrested . . ."

"Who?"

"Guy with the meth. You know."

"Oh, right."

"He ran off from a work crew. Still loose, as far as we know."

"So?"

"Talk is he's coming after folks. Everybody that did him wrong." I let that sink in for a moment. "Running buddies mostly but probably you too."

"That little fucker?"

"Killed one guy already."

"I guess I'm all right," he told me. "Got an AK under the bed."

Then he slid his *Muscle Pro* under the door, opened to an oily veiny woman in a bikini. She had massive deltoids, purple eye shadow, and the neck of a lumberjack.

"What would you do with something like that?"

"Outrun it, I hope," I told him.

FOUR

Tula already had plans to go see a cousin of hers in Baton Rouge, a guy with a couple of kids the age of Tula's own son, C.J. I decided to swing by and try to make sure she took her boy and went.

She poured us each a glass wine, brought out some cashews, and we parked together on her sofa.

"So?" she said.

"Hasn't turned up?"

Tula shook her head.

"Kill anybody else?"

"Not that I've heard."

Tula took a sip of wine and eyed me hard. "Tell me about the money."

Me and Desmond had never spoken to anybody about the

money. I have to think now it was mostly because we'd been
raised that in this world you needed to earn everything you got
or it probably wasn't worth having. We might have worked for
that cash a little but not in any ordinary way.

"He had this closet in the back of his house," I told Tula.
"That place down by Blue Hole. The cash was all in there. Three,
maybe four hundred thousand."

She shook her head and invoked the Lord.

"We'd promised all those boys they'd get a cut."

Tula shot me a sour look.

"Not that I'm blaming them," I assured her. "But the money
wasn't going to get left there, and what else were we going to do?"

"Where's yours?"

"Pearl's basement. Desmond's too."

"How much?"

"I think me and Desmond split about half. The rest went to
Percy Dwayne Dubois, his nephew Luther, and a couple of swamp
rats. They've all burned through it by now."

"Not you?"

"You see how we live. I bought Pearl's Ranchero. Desmond
bought his Escalade. Got his mother to a doctor. We lend out a
little every now and again." I shrugged. "I've tried to feel bad
about taking it, but . . ." I gave her a wince and a shrug.

Another snort from Tula, but it was more contemplative than
emphatic, like she couldn't quite figure how she might feel about
taking that money either.

"All right then." Tula got up from the sofa and shouted toward
the back of the house, "C.J., let's eat."

"What's for supper?" I asked her.

"Depends," she said. "Where are you taking us?"

We ended up at Lilo's where we had steak and shoestring
potatoes and where me and Tula even danced a little. Near the

end there, when the band was playing "The Tennessee Waltz" for about the fourth time, my phone started buzzing in my pocket. I wouldn't have bothered with it if it hadn't turned out to be Desmond calling twice. Once was usually nothing special. Two times always meant "Oh, shit."

Somebody had busted into K-Lo's store again. That was not so uncommon a thing. By the time I got there, K-Lo had very nearly left off swearing. A car had driven into the front glass, which was the usual technique. Then the perp had passed five minutes looking for cash and merchandise worth stealing. This fellow had broken into K-Lo's office—had kicked in K-Lo's lauan door—and had made off with K-Lo's .38 revolver and K-Lo's twenty-gauge shotgun. He'd also busted K-Lo's pencil cup, which K-Lo was livid about.

"Shit," K-Lo told me as he showed me and Desmond the pieces of what had been a cheesy Graceland mug.

When I finally got Desmond off to the side, I asked him, "Why'd you call me on this one?" K-Lo had break-ins like most of the rest of us had gas.

Desmond motioned for me to follow him back out to the front of the store where he showed me a piece of the twisted aluminum channel the glass had been in. It looked to have dragged along the fender of the car that had busted the window. Desmond pointed out some yellow paint.

"Him," Desmond said.

"He hasn't got the only yellow car around."

Desmond chuffed the way a bear might and told me another time, "It's him."

We knew we'd find out for certain soon enough. K-Lo had installed surveillance cameras after he'd had his front glass broken out a solid dozen times. His underwriter had insisted on it, and K-Lo had squawked about the price, but he'd finally called in a guy from Jackson to come out and do it up right. K-Lo had four high-resolution cameras and a DVR in a hardened cupboard, so the ritual was that we'd sit down with whichever deputy finally arrived and show him precisely who'd gotten up to the crime we'd called him about. You could usually make out the tag number. You could always make out the fools.

I can't say why thieves on the lowlife circuit never seemed to get the word that everybody who broke into K-Lo's got arrested straightaway. They just kept coming, and we kept sending the law to snatch them up. Worse still, aside from the guns, there was hardly anything worth stealing, and you could get firepower in the Delta almost anywhere.

K-Lo kept talking about putting up roll-down shutters, but that felt a little too much to him like a hoodlum triumph. So he put off buttoning the place up tight, and the thieves kept on breaking in.

One of the new Indianola female deputies got the call that night and came out. A big girl named Wanda.

Wanda took some photos of the damage with her phone and started in on her report while K-Lo switched on his computer and cued up the surveillance footage. We watched black-and-white video of the rent-to-own storefront for about a quarter hour at quadruple speed.

We'd seen enough of this sort of footage to know what the method usually was. Some guy, almost always in a hoodie, would walk up to the front double doors and jerk on the handles a time or two. He'd see that the throw bolt was plated over, which ruled out a saw or a torch. I don't know why they never went around to the back. You could buck open *that* door with your hip.

That Boudrot must have made up his mind back down the road in Leeland or somewhere, because that yellow Gold Duster he was driving just appeared at full tilt and rammed straight through the glass. That Boudrot climbed out of the car and actively looked around for cameras. He followed the co-ax over to the unit in the corner. He smiled up at us, ran his palm along the side of his head to slick back his greasy hair. Then he pointed his finger at the lens and made like to shoot it out.

"Look familiar?" Wanda asked us.

"That's the boy that broke out of Parchman," I said.

"The one today?"

"Yep," Desmond told her.

We eventually watched Guy Baptiste Boudrot climb back into his stolen Plymouth and wave as he backed out into the lot.

We didn't know where Percy Dwayne Dubois might be, but we had a pretty fair idea where we could find his nephew. Luther sold oxy out of a roadhouse down near Yazoo City. He'd spent his cut of the Boudrot money on a new Ford diesel truck, had gone in with a cousin on a steakhouse that had closed, and had pissed away whatever was left on lizard boots and big belt buckles. Luther had gotten away from the drug trade for maybe eight months tops.

He'd worked for years out of a place called Tootie's, down toward Yazoo in the middle of nowhere much. We pulled in to find it had changed hands and was Lurleen's anymore.

Tootie's had always been strictly a cracker roadhouse, the sort of place Desmond would just have to walk into to end up in a fight. So I went in alone, stepped inside to discover that Tootie's had been renovated and transformed. It was still a jackleg roadhouse with a chipboard bar, a bunch of mismatched tables, a row of booths against the back wall with more duct tape than vinyl. The jukebox was blasting out some shitty Eddie Rabbittesque country song, and the patrons were dancing and smoking and

drinking Bud tallboys all at the same time. But there was a bou-
quet of flowers at one end of the bar—gladiolas mostly—and I
spied a patron eating something. It looked like an honest to God
order of ribs served on an actual plate.

There'd been no food at Tootie's. There'd been no gladiolas.
And the bartender had looked like Popeye after the meth had
taken hold. Now there was a girl behind the bar, and not one of
these girls you had to squint at to help convince yourself she was
an actual female. This one had on a tube top and was justified to
wear it. She had a smart spiky haircut and a sunburst tattooed
around her navel. Each of her stubby fingernails was painted a
different color. She could well have been an art student who'd
wandered way off the interstate.

"Hey, sport," she said when she saw me.

The girl slapped an actual printed cocktail napkin down on
the bar. According to what I read on it, Lurleen's was a lounge. I
noticed the chipboard bar was now under about six coats of ma-
rine varnish. "What'll it be?" The bartender smiled at me. She
had what looked like all her teeth.

"Bud, I guess."

She jabbed her thumb toward a half-dozen beer cans on a
shelf. "There's better if you want it," she told me.

Damned if there wasn't—and no more skunky Iron City like
Tootie used to drink. I ordered up a Molson and asked her,
"Where'd Tootie get off to?"

The girl behind the bar put a finger to her temple and made a
dumb show of blowing out her brains.

"Jesus," I told her.

"Unlucky in love," the bartender said.

"We're talking the same Tootie, right?" I tried to approxi-
mate Tootie's bulk, stretched out my arms and puffed up my
cheeks.

She nodded. "He had a girl in Jackson. I hear she threw him over."

Then I couldn't help but think of Tootie in the altogether. Many folds and tufts and hanging bits like an overstuffed Chesterfield couch.

"You ought to ask Lurleen," the bar girl told me. "They were cousins."

She pointed, and I glanced. Lurleen was sitting in Tootie's old spot down at the end of the bar. She was sipping a diet Pepsi straight out of the can with a soda straw. Lurleen had a pile of yellow hair, less a beehive than a termite mound. She had a ledger open before her and was toting up some figures. No matter how she twitched and swiveled, her hair never let on that she'd moved.

I eased down the bar to speak to Lurleen. I was standing next to her a good half minute before she left off with the bookkeeping and looked up.

"Hey, sugar," she said.

"Just heard about Tootie." I gave her my wince of condolence.

"Can't never tell what's going on in here." She tapped her sternum with a blood-red lacquered nail.

"I'm looking for a fellow named Luther Dubois. Used to be kind of a fixture in this place."

She laid her pencil down and eyed me hard. "You the law?"

"No, ma'am," I told her and snorted, tried to look offended.

"Why do you want him?"

"Just need to tell him a thing." I had the poor sense to add, "It's personal."

Lurleen had a hell of a pinched smile, which she treated me to for a good quarter minute.

"A boy busted out of Parchman," I informed Lurleen. "He might be after Luther."

She eyed me again in a comprehensive way and must have decided that I was all right.

"Got a regular office anymore," she said and pointed into the depths of the lounge. "I'll buzz him." She reached for a doorbell button at the end of the bar.

Luther's office was hard by the crapper, in a ratty little room where Tootie used to keep his busted furniture. Tables and chairs the patrons had wrecked that Tootie kept meaning to fix. Luther opened the door about the time I reached it. He grinned when he saw who it was.

"Shit howdy," Luther told me and gave me a shake and awkward hug. "Where's that nigger of yours?"

I drew a deep breath and country pointed in the general direction of the lot. "Don't let him hear you say that."

Luther laughed. He told me, "Fuck."

He stepped aside to let me pass into his office, followed me in and shut the door. The place was tidy and clean. Luther might have sold oxy, but he had a certain sense of style. Luther had a desk with a copy of *Barely Legal* open on the blotter and nothing else. There was a straight chair just beside the desk for "clients" (Luther told me), and he had a map of something or another taped onto the wall.

"Park it," Luther said as he slipped out of his blazer. He'd put the thing on just to answer the door.

Luther was wearing a proper suit. Proper except that it was purple and shinier than a regular everyday business suit should be.

"How the hell you been?" he asked me. "Figured you'd own an island or something by now."

"You and Lurleen some kind of item?"

Luther glanced around like he wanted to be certain there was nobody in his office but us. Then he shrugged and told me, "Got its perks."

I think he mostly meant the room we were in and the blind eye to his business.

"That's some pile of hair on her."

"Comes right off," he said. "She leaves it sitting by the sink."

Luther took a tug on his Rolling Rock pony, and I knocked back the rest of my Molson.

"Got some bad news," I finally told him. "That Boudrot busted out."

"Fuckstick?"

I nodded.

"They'll round him up, won't they?"

"Haven't yet, and he killed a guy already."

"Shit!" Luther got up and did a little stalking, though there wasn't truly much of anywhere to go. "Who?" he asked me.

I shrugged. "Civilian. Needed his car."

"Where do you figure he's headed? Away from here, right?"

"That's what we were hoping, but then he broke in at K-Lo's."

"Looking for you boys?"

"Made off with a couple of guns."

"I don't like the sound of this."

"Us neither. That's why we're here."

"Percy Dwyane know? Tommy? Eugene?"

I shook my head. "Know where we can find them?"

We followed Luther up 66. He had one of those tandem-wheeled diesel trucks that contractors and timber men drive. It was new and shiny and had some pop to it—as far as diesels go—and Luther left us straggling near Belzoni when he went roaring up the four-lane. By the time we caught up with him, Luther was in cuffs and getting marched to a trooper's sedan.

Me and Desmond said together and harmoniously, "Shit."

We rolled on by the radio car with its blue beacon going and its headlights pulsing. All of that was bouncing off the lavish chrome of Luther's truck. Desmond pulled into the lot of the day-old bread shop about a quarter mile up the road.

"Did you see who it was?" I asked Desmond

"White boy. Maybe that Cooper."

I shook my head. "Too fat for him."

Me and Desmond said "Shit" again.

We both knew by then it had to be Augustus Polk Benbow. A. P. Benbow was what it said on his name tag, but everybody called him APB. The law enforcement boys got an everlasting hoot out of that. As cops go, APB did one thing with reliable devotion: He arrested Delta motorists for just about anything at all.

He needed an audience, as it turned out. A man in bracelets in the back of his cruiser couldn't do a thing but hear him. So if you were driving above the posted speed or going over forty on your doughnut or riding with a light burned out or changing lanes without your blinker, then you were a candidate to suffer through what that Benbow thought about this world.

The day he stopped me he had a weed up his ass about the electoral college, was of the opinion that it was spoiling democracy mostly for people like him. He had all sorts of theories about the whys and the wherefores but not too many details and most of the facts he trotted out were ones he'd cobbled up.

"Here's the thing," he said about twenty times. That was All Points's chief rhetorical device. He'd tell you he was unloading the pith of the business about two dozen times. If I had to put him in a slot, I'd say A. P. Benbow was a libertarian under the color of authority and hampered by a partial lobotomy. After you heard him talk for about ten minutes, you'd wonder that he could drive.

"Now what?" I asked Desmond.

He'd been stopped plenty by APB. That Benbow didn't like your coloreds, so Desmond had gotten an earful about entitlement society, that and all the goddamn money wasted on those fucking rims when there were babies to raise and proper goddamn English to learn to speak.

"Bring the truck, I guess," Desmond said.

That was another Benbow feature. If he picked you up for a violation, he left your keys on the driver's seat. All Points insisted on it in the off chance you'd get a further lesson by having some lowlife come along and drive off in your car.

I followed Desmond to the barracks up by Leland in Luther's truck. The place had been a lodge hall once or something, and was a barracks in name only. Nobody slept there. It had a few cubicles and a kitchen, a tiny room for holding miscreants instead of a proper cell.

"I'm staying out here," Desmond told me in the lot.

I couldn't much blame him. The Mississippi State Police employed an overabundance of pinhead crackers, and you never knew what they might get up to, especially there inside their clubhouse.

It was a skeleton crew, given the hour. Just a desk trooper, a fellow name Cobb who was mostly a farmer anymore.

"Hey here," I told him.

He squinted at me like he was trying to place me on some bulletin he'd seen. "I know you?"

"Doubt it."

"What's doing?"

"Come after a guy. Just got hauled in."

"Ain't this some shit?" Luther shouted my way.

That Benbow was walking him down the hallway. Luther was still in bracelets and had twisted around to look at me over his shoulder. A. P. Benbow punched him in the kidney to steer him.

"Ow, dammit," Luther told him. That just got him hit again.

"What did he do?" I asked that Cobb.

He glanced at the charge sheet on his desk. "Ran a light."

"No lights out there. I was right behind him. Not a damn thing but road."

"Take that up with A.P.," he said.

We both watched Benbow slam Luther hard against the wall. Luther grinned like a man who'd been slammed around before.

"Come on now," he told that Benbow, which earned Luther a backhanded slap.

"Him?" I asked Cobb. "That cracker fuckwad back there?"

Cobb whistled through his teeth. "Boy talking shit about you," he shouted toward that Benbow.

That Benbow shoved Luther one time further. He told him, "Stay," like you'd tell a dog.

APB came swaggering up the hallway, his holster creaking and his keyring jangling.

"So?" that Benbow said to me. "I'm right here. Spit it out."

"You want to write him up, do it. But you've hit him your last time."

That Benbow grinned. At me. At Cobb. "That right?"

I nodded. I grinned right back.

He whipped around and caught me with the back of his hand. Just a slap really, more knuckles than meat. I stood there and took it. I winked at that Benbow. I fixed my mouth and blew him a kiss. It had just the effect I'd imagined it would.

"That fucking tears it," that Benbow said as he reached to loosen his buckle.

I guess he was aiming to take his gun off and lay it aside on the desk so he could go about the lively pleasure of beating me with his fists. I didn't allow him to get that far. I punched him in the throat.

Cobb said, "Hold on here!" He stood up and got a blow to his windpipe as well. They both lurched around the place wheezing and fighting for air.

"What did you go and do?" Luther asked me.

I pointed at that Benbow. "I don't like him much."

"Hell, who does? They'll be on you now."

That Benbow dropped into a plastic chair and made a string of whooping noises. He was bluer than I'd hoped for him to get.

"Want to stick around?" I asked Luther.

He held out his cuffed hands my way. "Fuck no."

I unlocked him with that Benbow's key, and I kind of told those two boys I was sorry. Then me and Luther went out the door and found Desmond in the lot.

"That was quick," he said.

I gave him the shrug I give him sometimes when things have gone all shitty.

Desmond had seen it enough already to know to tell me, "Awwww!"

FIVE

We headed for Pearl's with Luther behind us. It was half past ten by the time we pulled into her driveway. It looked like just about every light in Pearl's house had been switched on. There was a car parked in the pullout beside Pearl's dinged up Buick Regal. It was a BMW with Tennessee plates, a car I recognized. The thing belonged to Pearl's sister's daughter, Angela Marie.

We'd had kind of a fling a few years back. It never came within sight of torrid. We just had some laughs. She'd come to the Delta. I'd go up to Memphis. It didn't so much end as peter out. Angie met a guy at a conference in Denver. They were both in hospital administration. He wasn't a vegan or a teetotaler or even a Presbyterian, which made him the sort of creature Angie Marie felt she could tolerate. He was better for her than I'd ever be. You can't just have laughs forever.

I hadn't seen her since this then, so this was a sort unexpected, awkward reunion.

"Oh," I managed. "Hi," once Angie had answered my knock.

She looked past me to Desmond and Luther. She'd met them both a few years before, back when we'd tangled with that Boudrot the first time around.

"Hey, boys," she said.

"Evening, ma'am," Luther told her. He had the habit of getting old West courtly in the presence of any woman who wasn't palpable cracker trash.

"Everything okay here?" I asked her.

She nodded. "Why wouldn't it be?"

"Just saw all the lights."

Angie glance into the kitchen where Pearl was prattling on about something. She stepped out across the threshold and shut the door behind her.

"Problem?" she said.

"Remember that Boudrot?"

"Fuckstick?"

I nodded. "He's loose."

"Released?"

I shook my head. "Kind of busted out."

"And he's looking for y'all?" She took us all in.

We nodded like a clutch of shamed schoolboys.

"What do you want me to do?" Angie asked me.

"Take Pearl home with you. Only be for a couple of days."

Angie stood and digested the prospect in silence.

"He'll kill any damn thing. Got one body already."

"All right," she said and exhaled profoundly. "I guess I can stand to get earfucked for a week."

"Thanks," I told her.

I got a grunt. A corrosive nod.

As she was turning to lay her hand to the doorknob, I tried to make nice with Angie. "How's . . . uh . . . Donald?"

"Wife in Orlando, as it turned out."

"Oh. Sorry," I said. "Guys, huh?"

She lingered to cut us all three with a look. "Yeah," Angie told us. "Guys."

A trip to Memphis for Pearl was like going to Paris for most anybody else. She was uneasy driving anywhere but locally anymore and so made regular excursions to the Sunflower Market, to the Dollar Store, and the Rack Room—all of them on the truck route. She played canasta in the neighborhood. Drove to the Presbyterian church, and had lunch sometimes at the catfish place in downtown Indianola. But that was about as wide as Pearl's orbit got anymore, so she didn't need to be asked twice to go with Angie up to Memphis.

We all hung around there in the house while Angie helped Pearl pack. Me and Desmond cleaned up Pearl's dinners dishes while Luther found him a topcoat in Gil's closet. Pearl was keen to let Luther have anything of her dead husband's that would fit. It was a fine specimen as topcoats go, beautiful caramel-colored camel hair with only one mismatched button. Luther went on at some length about the skirting and hang of the thing. He talked about clothes the way most guys in the Delta talked about fishing.

We promised to lock up, and I assured Pearl I'd take care of her flowers, by which I meant that I'd try to avoid crushing them with my car. We all stood there in the driveway waving as they reached the road in Angie's beamer. Then she gassed the thing, and they rolled off into the night.

"There's Pearl safe anyway," I said.

Luther shoved his coat sleeve my way. "Smell that."

I didn't. "Put your truck in the pullout," I told Luther, "in case any troopers come around." My Ranchero was already buttoned up in Pearl's car shed.

Desmond had left his phone, like usual, in his Escalade cup holder. His "Satin Soul" ringtone started in before we could get back into the house. It was late, but Desmond was a night owl and his mama was the same, so there was nothing odd about Desmond getting a call in the small hours. It was probably after midnight by then.

Desmond opened his door and fished out his phone. He checked the screen and groaned a little. "Kendell," he said and answered.

Kendell wasn't a night owl, and Kendell worked the day shift. If he was up and about, it had to be for something catastrophic.

Desmond listened without comment for long enough to make me squirm. When he finally spoke, he only said, "Sweet Lord."

"What?" I asked him.

"Cut up?" Desmond said into the phone.

"Who?" Luther had even quit sleeve sniffing.

"Yeah, he's here," Desmond told Kendell. "Luther too."

He listened.

"Doing that now but hadn't caught up with any of them but him. Just sent Pearl off with her niece."

Desmond listened some more before he said, "All right," and dropped the call.

"Must have been going after Dale," Desmond told us. "Ended up at Patty's."

Dale and Patty had been married back when that Boudrot went to prison. They had a little house and a garden plot up by Boyer that Patty had kept in the divorce. When Dale went inside for taking bribes and beating a few boys up, Patty decided that he wasn't worth redeeming after all. She served papers on Dale in the lockup and presented him with the key to his self-storage unit where he could find his collection of tracksuits and his free weights and his dumbbells and his dietary supplements and his big chrome commercial-grade juicer.

He tried to win her back once he was out, but Patty's restraining order made that kind of tough.

We all rode out to Patty's together. It was a handsome little place a few miles north of town in the middle of nowhere much. Patty's nearest neighbor was on the far side of a wheat field, probably half a mile away.

Kendell met us out in front. There were two cruisers and an EMT wagon parked in the yard. The doors of the wagon were standing open and Patty was sitting on the back ledge wrapped in one of those scratchy rescue squad blankets and holding an oxygen mask to her face.

"She all right?" I asked Kendell.

He nodded. "Lucky."

Kendell motioned for us to follow him, meaning me and Desmond. He didn't have much use for Luther. "What's with the coat?" Kendell asked him. It was a warm October night.

"Smell that." Luther offered his sleeve.

Instead, Kendell led me and Desmond up into Patty's house.

I'd never quite seen a house turned upside down like Patty's was. The front door was kicked in, and the room it gave onto was torn all to pieces, looked about like a herd of cattle had passed through. The settee was upside down. The coffee table was busted in half. The TV had gone out the side window. There was kettle corn all over the floor. *Guideposts* and *Upper Rooms* scattered here and there. A secretary against the back wall had been broken all to bits. The glass was shattered, and the framing was splintered.

All of Patty's pictures of Jesus—and she had several dozen of them—were torn or burned. A few looked like they'd might have even have been chewed.

"We sure it was him?" Desmond asked.

Kendell nodded. "Pretty sure."

He led us along the hallway to Patty's bedroom and then stepped aside so we could see the mess.

That Boudrot had sliced up Patty's bedclothes, her pillows, her nappy stuffed donkey. She'd had a bolster with a Bible verse on it—the fruit of the righteous is a tree of life. It was in the sort of scraps and tatters only a madman or an enraged bear would make.

"Did she see him?" I asked Kendell.

"Heard him," he said.

"What did he say?"

"Sang," Kendell told us.

"Sang what?" Desmond asked him.

"Patty wasn't too clear on that. She was in the freezer by then."

Again we followed Kendell. He led us through the kitchen. The cabinet doors had all had glass in them, but it was shattered on the linoleum now. The microwave was in the sink. The refrigerator had been laid over. There was busted crockery and flatware all over the place.

Kendell opened a door that gave onto the cellar steps. We followed him down. The basement was half cement and half dirt. Somebody had hit rock and given up. There wasn't anything down there but a shelving unit made of rough-milled poplar and, off in a corner, an old chest freezer. It didn't appear to be plugged in.

"She was in the kitchen when he kicked the front door in. She said she threw open the back door and ran down here, got in the freezer and waited."

"Wanted him to think she'd run outside?" I asked.

Kendell nodded. "Must have worked."

Kendell walked us out to Patty's car shed. Once he'd finished with the house, that Boudrot had torn it up as well. He'd sliced up the upholstery in Patty's Chevy Biscayne. Front and back-seats. He'd stomped on the hood.

"That boy's gotta be amped up on something," Desmond said.

"I sure hope so," Kendell told us as he played his flashlight beam on a pen at the back of the lot. There was something that looked like a mound of hide laying on the ground.

"What the hell is that?" I asked him without venturing over to see.

"Patty's goat," Kendell told us.

"Did you send somebody after Dale?"

"Tula."

"I thought she was going to Baton Rouge."

"We decided to put that on hold."

That didn't thrill me any. I certainly didn't want Tula hurt, but mostly I didn't want her around to see what me and Desmond might get up to once law enforcement had failed to run that crazy Boudrot to ground.

I knew they'd do the usual stuff that local police seem to favor—visit that Boudrot's old haunts and talk to that Boudrot's old buddies, swamp rats and lowlifes and Acadian blood kin who would tell them collectively shit. They'd only find him by chance or once somebody had wounded him or killed him. It wasn't like any civilian would have the stones to turn him in. The chances seemed good that he'd be loose until me and Desmond tracked him down since we knew everybody he'd probably go after and we knew exactly why.

"What if he goes for Tula like he went for Patty?" I asked Kendell. "You've got to figure Dale's what brought him."

"She can handle herself."

Kendell seemed surer of that than I was. This wasn't a cracker traffic stop. That Boudrot was out for blood, and judging from Patty's goat, nobody and nothing was safe until he went back to Parchman or into the ground.

"He still driving that yellow Duster?" Desmond asked.

"She never saw the car. Didn't hear him pull up."

"And he was singing?" I said to Kendell.

"Some zydeco thing, she thought." As Kendell led us back around the house, he told us, "I think she was a little too rattled to listen."

Patty was recovered enough to be indignant by the time we reached her.

"You!" she said and threw her oxygen mask my way in a fashion that wasn't strictly Christian in the traditional sense.

"You all right, Patty?" I asked her.

"Germaine's dead!" she said as she sloughed off her blanket and blubbered a little.

Kendell leaned in and told us, "Goat."

"I'm sorry," I said to Patty. "Must have been that guy Dale put away."

"Sorry!" Patty told me and spat on the ground. "And he's no better." She was talking about Desmond who just dropped his head and exhaled instead of bothering to reply.

There wasn't anything we could say to her. You didn't placate Patty with talk. The only way me and Desmond could make her happy was to burn in hell together. Patty's was a hateful and vindictive sort of faith. She was happiest being righteous and wishing suffering on the wicked, and the wicked usually seemed to be everybody who wasn't her.

"The sweet Lord saw me through," she told us. "He put me in that freezer." She shook her head. "Dale," she told us, spat the name out. "This is all him and you."

It galled me to hear myself lumped in with Dale, even if it was coming from Patty. Me and Desmond could get up to some stupid business, but we were sensible most of the time while Dale was just a nimrod in the regular course of things.

"Anything in there with Dale's address on it?" Kendell asked her.

"Something he might have seen?" I said.

She was about to say no but she took a moment to think about it and said to us, "On the magnet. You know. When Dale had his business."

Before he'd taken work with K-Lo, Dale had tried to farm himself out as some kind of private eye. He'd been a state trooper and a county cop, but mostly he was a juiced-up weight lifter with all the sound investigative instincts of a raccoon. That didn't stop him from hiring out to look for runaway spouses mostly, the sort to owe on mortgages and child support and a couple of trashed sedans. The trouble was Dale had a talent for menacing the wrong folks, wailing on cousins twice removed, innocent colleagues of one stripe or another, and never quite laying his hands on the boys he'd been hired to go after.

So Dale tended to stay in bad odor with his customers and with Delta cops as well. Through the run of his business, Dale got brought up on charges more often than he got paid. But that didn't keep him from having some of the trappings of a successful business, like pocket calendars, notepads, and refrigerator magnets. The magnets had Dale's picture on them. His phone number. His address.

I went back in Patty's house with Kendell. We could see where the magnet had been. There was a space right above Patty's cottage cheese coupon and right below Patty's daily affirmation.

"That was two houses ago for Dale, wasn't it?" I said.

"Think so," Kendell told me.

"Wonder who's living there now?"

We followed Kendell over—me, Desmond, and Luther—in Desmond's Escalade. On the way, Luther told us about a pair of boots he had his eye on.

"Boa constrictor or something. Seen them on TV."

"Live it up," I told Luther. "Make it easy on that Boudrot. I think even Dale could find a guy in boa constrictor boots."

That shut Luther up for almost five whole minutes before Luther got going on a shirt he'd had his eye on. "Be-fucking-spoke," he told me. He dredged some phlegm and said, "That's right."

The guy in the house where Dale had lived two addresses back was sitting in his yard when we pulled up. He was in his underpants. It wasn't much of a house. A shack, more like it. Dale had only rented it month to month. He just knew Patty would take him back, so he hadn't much cared where he lived or how graciously he did it. Dale had decided he'd be forgiven because he had no idea at all of just what sort of Christian his wife was. She wasn't in it for the forgiveness. Brimstone was more her thing and after she'd caught Dale naked with a bottle blonde from Clarksdale, there was nothing even Jesus Himself could do to make that right.

The guy in the yard didn't know the first thing about Dale. He knew nothing of Patty. He had little cuts all over him from the sort of knife sharp enough to lay you open from just a touch.

It helped that he was drunk, helped him anyway. That Boudrot wasn't the sort you'd want to get sprung on you sober.

"What the hell's going on?" he asked us.

His TV was screen-down on the sidewalk. His sofa was

halfway out the front door. There were articles of clothing all over the place. Shirts and blue jeans and undershorts. Kendell walked over and played his light on the boy so he could assess the damage. The cuts were all clean and shallow, seeping a little at worst.

"That all you got?" Kendell asked him

"Ain't that enough?" he said.

That boy moved like he wanted to stand up.

"Stay there," Kendell told him. "Got somebody coming to patch you up."

"I'm all right." He shifted and one of his slices gaped open.

"Got to give it to the fuckstick," Luther announced. "He knows how to sharpen a knife."

"Got any beer?" the boy in his undershorts asked us.

I glanced toward his house and said, "Let's see."

Me and Desmond went in. We had to move that boy's ratty sofa to do it and stepped inside to find a front room that looked like a landfill under roof. Everything that could be upended was, and the windows were all busted out.

"What the hell's he on?" Desmond asked as we soaked in the destruction.

"Getting even's probably enough to charge him up."

"If he's doing this to people he's got no call to hurt, you've got to figure he'll go flat wild on us."

We hadn't come right out and talked about hunting that Boudrot down. I'm sure it had been in the back of Desmond's mind like it had been in the back of mine from the moment we'd found out he'd jumped in the swamp and gotten away from his keepers. We'd seen what that fool could get up to. We'd watched him beat a man to death with a pistol, an employee who'd irritated him and who'd only marginally deserved a punch. That Boudrot had throttled the boy into gravy, kept hitting him after he was dead, and then had taken him apart like a fryer and fed his pieces to a gator. We'd only heard about that last part, but it sure fired the imagination.

Me and Desmond didn't just know that Boudrot on paper, the way Kendell and Tula did. He was a madman on a mission, and the mission appeared to be us. It seemed sensible, instead of sitting and waiting, that we ought to go after him.

"So?" Desmond said.

"I guess we need to find Dale."

"Uh-huh."

"And then Percy Dwayne and the rest of them."

"Right."

"Then we ought to go get that asshole."

"That's what I'm thinking. What about Kendell and Tula?"

"One way or another," I said to Desmond, "Tula's going to Baton Rouge."

By the time we got back outside, the EMT techs had come and were examining the victim in the lighted bay of their truck. Kendell was at the bumper suffering a disquisition from Luther on the assorted virtues of worsted wool.

"Do something with him," Kendell told us both.

Desmond pointed at his car.

Luther knew he was beaten but that didn't keep him from muttering about gabardine as he walked across the weedy lawn and climbed into the Escalade.

"Same as the other?" Kendell asked us of the house.

"A little less Jesus, but yeah. Has Tula checked in?" I asked him.

He nodded. "Went out to that place Dale's renting near Moorhead. No sign of him."

"He's got some girlfriend in Jackson. Probably over there with her."

"Dale?" Kendell asked me with appropriate skepticism. Dale had no charm, and ever since he'd given up the steroids, he didn't have a physique to speak of either, unless you counted lumps of flab in unexpected places.

"Hey!" the cut-up boy from the yard shouted from the back of the rescue squad truck.

"Think you can find him?" Kendell asked us. He glanced toward the busted TV in the yard. "Like . . . soon?"

"Yeah," Desmond said.

"Hey!"

"Bring Tula in," I told Kendell. "Let her go to Baton Rouge."

"She can take care of herself."

"Let her get C.J. safe down there. Me and Desmond'll see to that Boudrot."

"Hey!"

"Should have finished him the first time," Desmond said.

I gave him my usual look. The two of us had had this quarrel before.

Usually Kendell would have chimed in with how he didn't want to hear about lawlessness. He'd throw up his hands and shake his head, make a point of walking away. This time, though, he stayed where he was and said to us, "Maybe you should have."

A guy dead from a chair leg and a couple of houses laid to frenzied waste can have a way of reordering a man's priorities. Even a man like Kendell.

"Make her go," I said to him. "And it has to come from you."

"Hey!"

Kendell nodded. He said to me, "All right."

"Hey!" that cut-up fellow shouted again. This time I headed for him. "I'm talking to you!" he said.

I mounted the bumper and stepped inside the bay where one of the techs was cleaning and suturing a cut on that fellow's arm while the other played a game on his phone with near Talmudic devotion.

"What?" I asked that boy. His underpants were staggeringly filthy in the bright truck light.

His bottom lip curled like he might cry. "Where's my goddamn beer?"

SIX

We ended up waiting for Dale at K-Lo's. If we didn't know where his lady friend lived, it stood to reason that Acadian fuckstick wouldn't have any idea either. Luther passed the time trying to get in touch with Percy Dwayne Dubois, which meant he used all our phones to call lowlifes and blood kin and see if he could get any of them on the line. He couldn't, as it turned out—the practical downside of universal caller ID. They didn't want to talk to Luther, and they didn't know from us.

K-Lo was emphatically unhappy. He was still mad about the damage that Boudrot had done to his storefront, and he seemed upset in a general way that he had hothead competition. K-Lo preferred it when he was the only loose cannon in greater Indianola, the one guy in a sputtering rage for no good reason at all.

"Can't last," I told him. "That Boudrot's wound too tight."

"I too am wound tight!" K-Lo informed me. He went all proper and vaguely foreign when he got excessively irritated.

"He'll blow a gasket or we'll catch him," I told K-Lo.

Desmond nodded. "This kind of bullshit never lasts."

K-Lo spat. He was an accomplished spitter. Even better at it than Kendell. More enthusiastic anyway.

"He'll go somewhere he ought not to be," I assured him, "and somebody'll plug his sorry ass."

K-Lo liked the sound of that. He smiled my way and said. "Let's hope."

So me and Desmond and K-Lo stood together hoping in front of the store while Luther (we thought) kept trying to track down Percy Dwayne on the phone. It turned out he was playing blackjack on Desmond's Motorola, which Desmond noticed before I did and gave Luther a slap about.

He staggered Luther. "What!"

"Give me that," Desmond told him as he took back our phones. "Where's Dale anyway?" he asked K-Lo.

K-Lo plucked a Pall Mall from the flattened pack in his shirt front pocket. He shrugged. He shook his head.

"Tell him we'll be back," Desmond said and then told me and Luther, "Let's go."

We drove straight to the Sonic where they thought they weren't quite open until Desmond pulled in, blew his horn once for service, and then informed them through the speaker they were more open than they knew.

"I'm thinking we go back and pick up Dale," I said. "Take him with us down to Yazoo and round up Eugene and Tommy."

Desmond and Luther could agree about one thing. Neither one of them wanted Dale in the car.

"We've got to look out for him. The man's let himself go. He's in no shape to look after himself."

They still weren't persuaded we needed to suffer his company and haul him around.

"So he gets cut on a little," Luther said. "Maybe he's got it coming."

"If that Boudrot goes at him," I assured Luther, "he'll turn Dale into gator-sized chunks." I let that sink in and then asked Desmond, "You ready to let that happen?"

Desmond grunted. Desmond fingered his relish packet. "Not if you say it like that."

Luther whined and grunted.

"What exactly did Dale do to you?" I asked him.

"Said I was shoplifting," Luther informed me with no little indignation. "I might have stole all manner of shit, but I ain't never stole nothing that way."

That was the leading trouble with Luther's ilk. They were all criminal shitheads with standards, and you'd tie up with them if you accused them of something lower than they'd do. Of course, it was always hard to know exactly what they'd consider lower.

"He take you in or just wail on you?" Desmond wanted to know.

"Both!" Luther told him. He was still indignant about it.

Dale was on the loading dock when we got back to K-Lo's, and he was looking awfully rough, even by Dale's standards. He had a black eye and a puffy lip. He was showing a colleague his stitches as me and Desmond came out the back door with K-Lo and into the loading bay. Luther was back in the Escalade trying to track down Percy Dwayne.

"Come here," K-Lo told Dale. He pointed at us. "Listen to them."

The new Dale was a slight improvement over the old juiced-up, weight-lifting Dale, but not enough of an improvement to make Dale sensible and savory. Back when he was fit and musclebound, at least we could covet Dale's physique, but now he was just a pile of flab, and we had some of that already.

"What?" Dale asked us.

"That Boudrot's on the warpath," I told him. "Looking for you."

"Fine by me," Dale said, but when he tried to grin, he winced. The inside of his bottom lip was all black and brambly with stitches.

"What happened to you?" Desmond asked him.

"Got in it with a boy." Dale shrugged the way he always did, like getting beat to a bloody pulp was a manly sort of thing to do.

"Talk to Patty?" I asked him.

"Naw."

"That Boudrot went to her place first."

Dale didn't get alarmed exactly, but he finally displayed some genuine human interest. "Didn't hurt her, did he?"

I shook my head.

"She hid in the freezer," Desmond told him. "He tore up every damn thing in the house."

"Then that's one fucker that's done for." Dale pulled a face and winced again.

"Come on with us," I told him. "We're going to hunt him down."

Dale shouted across the way to K-Lo, "Boss man?" He pointed at me and Desmond.

K-Lo shrugged by way of excusing Dale for the day, and then K-Lo spat. That was about as close to a "Yeah, go ahead," as you'd ever get from K-Lo.

Naturally, Dale wasn't pleased to see Luther in the Escalade.

"Shit," Dale said when he laid eyes on him. "Ain't got no use for this dirtbag."

"We need him," Desmond told Dale in the low, rumbling

declarative way that Desmond had of ending debate before it ever started.

"Shotgun," Dale said.

I'd expected as much. I shrugged and said, "Go on."

So I rode in the back with Luther as we headed south toward Yazoo. The plan was to locate Tommy and Eugene back in the swamp in the national forest. They'd given that Boudrot up when we were hunting him down before, and it stood to reason he probably knew it somehow.

"You might call Patty," I suggested to Dale.

He got all shirty at the suggestion. He turned half around to tell me he guessed he knew who he ought to call when.

That must have been the first good look that Luther got of Dale, because that's when he chose to ask him, "Who beat the living shit out of you?"

Dale's initial impulse was to reach over the seat back and take a swipe at Luther. Luther dodged and Dale hit me. I would have popped him back, but the swipe itself had pulled a few of his stitches, so he was hurt already without any help from me.

Tommy and Eugene had a place they sort of shared in the national forest, which was chiefly massive cypress bog and reptile habitat. They had a house up on stilts made out of most anything that had come to hand. Lots of road signs for siding and bits of sheet metal from sheds they'd taken apart. Actual ownership of the lodge, as they called it, was disputed and unsettled. That worked well enough as long as they were both sober or both drunk. When just one of them got loaded, the other one always tried to steal the place. They had some kind of deed they kept shut up in a cupboard, and the sober one would trot it out to try to make the drunk one sign.

We left the highway at Silver City and went down through Midnight and Louise, got gas at Spanish Fort, and then headed

straight into the forest. Desmond tensed up behind the wheel.
Luther got a little antsy as well. Delta boys weren't used to standing trees in any concentration. The national forest was all that
was left of what the entire Delta had once been. A heavily wooded
thicket, swampy and marshy by turns. The Delta had mostly
been cleared for farming, canals cut and swamps drained. There
was nowhere much to find leafy canopy overhead. You had to
come clear to the national forest just to go into the woods.

"Dark in here," Luther said.

Desmond made a neck noise.

Dale was from Little Rock and wasn't generally the sort to
much care where he was.

"I might ought to been there. I don't know." He was still
thinking about Patty and how if he hadn't cheated on her with a
string of tramps from Memphis to Meridian, then the two of
them might have been sharing a roof, and he could have locked
horns with that Boudrot.

Nobody cared, particularly Desmond and Luther who'd
moved on to how little they liked being in the woods.

We passed the big sheltered corkboard with the map of the
forest on it and the specimen cypress just down from it surrounded by rail fencing.

"You know where you're going?" Dale asked Desmond.

Desmond told Dale a form of "Yeah." It came out sounding
like "Shut the fuck up."

"There's the pipeline." I pointed.

Desmond and Luther nodded. We all remembered that thing
as a landmark from before.

"There it is." Luther pointed to a track off to the left.

Desmond turned in. He did it gingerly and at a crawl. "Ain't
got no four-wheel drive," he told us. "Switch went out or something."

I couldn't blame Desmond for leaving that particular repair undone, given his love for hard roads and civilization.

"Muddy up there." I pointed. "This is probably far enough."

We climbed out and the bugs descended on us. The chemicals kept them at bay in the open, but back in the woods they were thick in the air and hungry. Gnats and flies and mosquitoes—we were all wearing a layer of them straightway.

We did what most sane people would do. We got back in the Escalade.

"Don't usually need nothing," Desmond said as he rooted through his console after something with Deet in it. He turned up four tubes of Cruex and a roll of antacids.

"Try this," Luther told us. He stuck his hand down his shirt. He swabbed his armpits for some stink and then rubbed his fingers across his face. That was enough to convince us we'd rather be carried off by the mosquitoes, so we bailed back out of the Escalade and into the buggy woods.

Eugene's place was maybe a quarter mile ahead. Dale charged along the track, and me and Desmond and Luther followed at enough of a distance to guarantee that any snake Dale stepped on would have just him to bite. Dale reached the clearing and was waiting there swatting flies while I was still slogging out way up through the woods.

"I don't hear any dogs," I said. Ordinarily, Eugene kept a half-dozen hounds. He was a fanatic coon hunter and didn't think anything of tromping through the big woods in the middle of the night.

"You been out here lately?" Luther asked me.

"Been three years probably."

"Maybe he moved."

"Or died," Desmond said.

It was hard to tell at the corner of his yard if the place was abandoned or not. The thorny thicket that bordered Eugene's yard was as full of snagged shopping bags and impaled pouch chew boxes as it had been the first time me and Desmond had dropped in on Eugene. The same junked cars were still clotting up the lot along with a muddy Nova that looked like it hadn't seen the highway lately. No tags. No stickers. No nothing. And two of the tires were flat.

There was a paper sack full of paper sacks floating at the edge of the bayou that lapped at the pylons holding up Eugene's house, but no fresh garbage that we could see. Nothing in the yard or in the swamp that looked the least bit recent.

Desmond pointed at the soft ground to the right of where we were standing. Tire tracks, and they looked like fresh ones.

"Might just be off running around," Desmond said.

"Maybe. Who's going up?" I asked.

Dale told me, "Hell, I will."

Eugene's place was so slapdash and rickety that we all couldn't go up at once. One guy on the swamp-rotted stairs at a time and one on the jackleg cantilevered walkway. The house would probably hold us safely enough, but there wasn't any chance of us getting up there in numbers all of a sudden.

"Hold on," I told Dale and shouted out for Eugene.

Luther chimed in behind me with a "Hey here, buddy."

I thought I heard some kind of whimper but laid it off to the swamp and woods. There were all kinds of creatures around us making every variety of noise.

"Go on," I said to Dale.

Dale bent over with a chorus of grunts and groans and made of show of producing a .38 he carried in an ankle holster. He spun the barrel to check his load and then tried to spit in a manly way, but his stitches confounded him, and Dale ended up just dribbling down his shirt.

"Just shout down what you find," Desmond told him.

Dale nodded and dribbled again.

Then he climbed to the landing, paused for breath, and headed up to Eugene's deck proper.

"Probably off in Arkansas stealing shit." That was Luther's suggestion, and I stood there hoping to hell he was right and fearing that he wasn't.

I'm not much of a believer in things being too quiet or feeling somehow all wrong. I like to go by what I see, but something definitely felt off at Eugene's. The place was too damn quiet.

Eugene's door was standing open to judge from the way Dale peered in through the screen.

"Hey," he said. When he heard nothing back, Dale turned our way and shrugged. He knocked on the door rail and said, "Hey" again. Another shrug. Dale checked his .38 load again. "Going in," he told us.

From inside, and almost immediately, we heard from Dale, "Sweet Lord!" The screen door swung open violently, and Dale came lurching out and laid hard against the deck rail. It's a wonder it didn't give way and drop him at our feet.

"What?" I asked him.

"A human lives here?"

"Any sign of Eugene?" Desmond shouted up.

Dale shook his head. "Just all his shit."

"Busted up?" I asked him.

"Hell," Dale said, "who can tell?"

Luther had set out toward the stairs by then. "I'll go." He was wiry and light, and the whole place only vibrated some as he climbed.

Luther pushed his way past Dale and drew the screen door open. "You coming?"

Dale nodded. He dribbled again and followed Luther inside.

Me and Desmond could hear just the noise of Luther and Dale talking back and forth. Not the words, only the racket. Desmond pointed toward the swamp.

"What's that?"

There was sure enough something floating. I couldn't quite make out what it was, not from down where we were. I was about to call for Luther when he came out of the house on his own.

"I don't know," he shouted down. "Looks like shit, but it always did."

"What's out in the water?" I asked him and pointed.

Luther followed the deck around the side of the house and over toward the bayou. He was fifteen feet above us and so could see what we couldn't see.

"Dog," was all he said.

SEVEN

Dale moved around to join Luther. He was holding on to the railing. The whole platform was shaking now. Dale and Luther looked like they were riding a swamp rat parade float down the street.

"Yep," Dale told us, by way of confirmation. "Dog all right."

"What kind?" I asked them.

Luther turned our way and shook his head. "Coonhound."

Me and Desmond said together, "Shit."

Desmond followed me across the yard. Around the thickets anyway and hummocks of fescue, and past the junked overgrown Ford station wagon and the partly disassembled state-body truck. The dog pen was still and quiet. I stopped short once I could see it. Desmond came up beside me.

"He didn't, did he?" I said. "Shit, man, they're just hounds."

"Once you'd kill a guy for a Plymouth," Desmond told me, "I guess you'll do about anything."

We went over together. Being Eugene's, it wasn't a proper pen. The kennel was made from roofing tin and road signs. The "fencing" was mostly pallets on end. The dogs were white and liver colored. I don't know how many Eugene had, but there were six or seven of them in a pile. Shotgunned, from the looks of them.

"That fucker," Desmond said.

We were out to get that Boudrot already for what he had done and was doing to people, but things took a turn once we'd gone back there and found that pile of dogs. People did wretched things to other people all the time, but a guy who'd shoot down a bunch of hounds—a guy who'd killed a goat already—had surrendered any claim on mercy. Unlike with humans, a dog never quite knew what he'd signed on for in this life. I can't imagine a hound ever woke up thinking, *I guess I've got it coming.*

"He's a dead man," I told Desmond.

"Reading my mind," he said.

Just then that pile of dead dogs quivered and shook. Me and Desmond fairly levitated. I circled around to what passed for a gate and let myself into the pen. I whistled. I called. Nothing.

"Say something," I said.

"What?" Desmond asked me, and the pile quivered again. Desmond stepped back. "Damn," and I heard a distinct whimper from the heap.

"Got a live one, and it's hearing just you."

"What do you mean?"

That raised another quiver. I didn't see that I had much choice but just to dive on in and start sifting. They were big hounds and bloody. I dragged the top two off to the side by their back feet.

Pulled another one away and was reaching for a fourth when the leg that I grabbed on to twitched and quivered. The pup let out a yelp.

"What are you doing?" Luther wanted to know. Him and Dale were up on the end deck looking down on us at the dog pen.

"He shot them," I said. "Probably with the shotgun he took from K-Lo's."

Luther, to his credit, got indignant straightaway. He might have been a roadhouse oxy dealer and lifelong Delta cracker, but he'd about as soon shoot his mama as a hound.

"That son of a bitch," he shouted to us. "I guess we're chewing him all to hell now."

Dale didn't get it. He'd probably been one of those kids who just killed stuff for sport. Frogs and lizards. Ants by the thousands. A kitten if he could lay his hands on one.

"What's the deal?" Dale asked.

"He shot the damn dogs," Luther told Dale. He said it in the spirit of explanation and instruction, like he harbored hope that Dale had misunderstood the circumstances and would get properly enraged once he'd come to grips with things.

Dale just said, "Yeah." The "So?" was implied.

Luther looked our way and pointed at Dale.

"We know already," Desmond told him.

I reached back into the dog pile and brought out the survivor. She was a runt and bloody all over, but little of it turned out to be hers. She'd gotten skinned by a few shotgun pellets across the ridge of her back, but she must have been shielded by the rest of the pack as they took fire and fell onto her. I couldn't help but picture that Boudrot standing at the makeshift fence, leaning in over one of the pallets firing point-blank at those dogs.

I handed the live one out to Desmond who took her but held

her at arm's length. Desmond didn't have much use for dogs. It wasn't Dale's strain of indifference but rather a healthy fear of the creatures by having more a few turned loose on him.

"Why don't you rinse her off. See where she's hurt?"

Desmond looked at me like I'd asked him to make me a pair of shoes.

"Just dip her in the water," I told him and pointed at the bayou. So there I was trying to marry Desmond's natural fear of canines with his thoroughgoing distaste for swamps.

I attempted to get Luther to come down, but he didn't want to mess up his clothes. Dale, for his part, couldn't figure why we didn't finish the job, just kill the live dog and leave them all to the gators and coyotes.

"They'll pick them clean," he told us. Then he started making noises about lunch.

I was going to explain to Dale that it was only half past ten, but I decided instead to go with, "Shut the fuck up."

"Just keep her there," I said to Desmond. "I want to make sure she's the only one."

I shifted the rest of the dogs around. There were eight of them altogether, including the lone hound that had lived. I left the pen and took that creature from Desmond, carried her down to the edge of the swamp, and rinsed her off in the brown water. She was complaining all the while.

Luther and Dale came down from the house to stand by the swamp and watch me.

"What are you going to do with it?" Luther asked me.

I hadn't quite decided, but I knew one thing. "Can't leave her here," I said.

Luther surprised me by making noises like he could stand to have a dog, a companion to sit in his truck and wait for him while he was doing business at Lurleen's—hardly a fit pastime for a hound but maybe better than Eugene's pen. As Luther was talking, that wounded creature licked me on the wrist. A long, slow lick that she undertook as she rolled her eyes up at me. If a dog could ever tell me, "Thank you, brother," that hound was doing it then.

She was as clean by then as the swamp was going to make her, and I could see that she'd gotten away just skinned raw along her spine. There was a spot on her back where the shot took the fur off, and it was seeping a bit.

"Look in the shed," I told Luther and pointed at what appeared to be a glorified pile of lumber with a rusty corrugated roof. "See if there's any grease in there. Maybe a shovel."

Luther came out with an ancient pint of some manner of machine grease and a garden shovel with the handle busted three quarters of the way up. I spread a little of the grease on that hound's raw skin, which she seemed to like a lot less than the swamp bath I'd been giving her. She swung her head around to lick my hand and gnaw on it a little too.

"Let's bury the rest of them," I said.

Dale told us all, "Shit. Let the gators do it. I'm going back to the car."

That's exactly what he did, swatting bugs as he went, which left us little choice but to talk about him.

"Why's he with us again?" Luther asked me.

"Because that Boudrot wants to cut him up."

"Yeah," Luther said. "And?"

I looked to Desmond for support, but he just pointed at Luther. "I'm kind of with him anymore."

"We'll use him for bait if we have to."

Desmond snorted. He picked up the shovel and started digging a hole.

The deeper the hole got, the more it filled up with iridescent bayou seepage. The whole business began to feel less like burial and more like makeshift disposal. I had to guess Dale had a point about the bayou wilderness taking care of its own.

We buried those shot dogs anyway. Me and Desmond took turns digging while Luther comforted the surviving hound. Comforted her in his fashion anyway. He didn't touch her or anything. His clothes were clean, and he didn't want to get any swamp dog on them. So he just told that hound, "Hey, you," every now and again and made clicking noises with his tongue.

I asked Desmond to say something Pentecostal over the dog grave when we'd finished. He didn't want to at first. He quoted me a nugget about the beasts in the fields. But I kept at him, told him anyway, "For fuck's sake," a time or two. Either Desmond thought better of his misgivings or got tired of hearing from me because he finally mumbled a strain of doxology over that muddy ground.

Then he turned right around and pointed at the surviving hound over by Luther.

"Don't want no grease on my upholstery," Desmond announced. "Wrap her up or something."

That job fell to me, and I climbed up to the platform Eugene's house was perched on, pulled open the screen door, and went into a place that looked like it had tornado damage.

I stuck my head back outside to ask Luther, "This looks normal to you?"

He shrugged. He nodded. "Eugene ain't so tidy."

I called down to Desmond, "Place is busted all to hell."

Inside I was surrounded by the residue of that Boudrot's rage. He was hard on end tables and knickknacks. That stuff all looked like it had been through a chipper or some industrial pulverizer. The pitch of anger required to destroy household furnishing as thoroughly as that Boudrot did had to approach primeval.

The fuckstick had left a few of the heavy pieces pretty much where they'd been, but he'd been thorough about demolishing everything else. I didn't see any trace of human carnage, just filth and squalor mostly. I went poking around in the back of the house, looking for any trace of Eugene. That took me into his bedroom. I wouldn't have wrapped the body of Satan in Eugene's filthy sheets. The place smelled of socks and mildew, but at least there was no sign that blood had been spilled.

I had a heck of a time finding something clean enough to even wrap a coonhound in. I finally located a Barbara Mandrell T-shirt in the back of one of Eugene's drawers. It didn't look like it had ever been worn, though it was half rotted through at the seams. It looked pretty sporty once I'd finally gotten it on the hound.

"I'd do her," Luther informed me. I hoped he was speaking of Ms. Mandrell.

I had to carry the dog. She wasn't too feeble to walk, but she gave every sort of sign that she'd never worn a T-shirt before. Left on her own, she'd drop to the ground and bite at the thing and whimper.

Dale wasn't in Desmond's Escalade by the time we got back to it.

"Don't guess we can leave him," Desmond said, though he looked ripe to be contradicted.

"Blow the horn," I suggested.

Desmond did and Dale yelled at us from off in the viney scrub.

He was having a sit-down, as it turned out. Dale had helped himself to the stack of spare Sonic napkins in Desmond's console and had scrounged up a copy of *JET* from underneath Desmond's passenger seat.

"Let's go!" Luther shouted.

"Hold on." Dale was still fastening his trousers by the time he lurched into view.

He'd used all of Desmond's napkins, which Desmond wasn't pleased about. Then he tossed the copy of *JET* at Desmond and told him, "You goddamn people." Right after that, he told me, "I ain't riding with no damn dog."

I had to suspect a successful evacuation, even out in the woods, had a psychological effect on Dale. Made him confident and pluckier than he had any cause to be.

Desmond turned his head my way. He was leaving it to me.

"Aw, go on," I told him.

Desmond wheeled and swung on Dale. He caught him on the jaw Dale had scuffed already, and Desmond knocked the fool clean out.

"Now we've got to pick him up."

Desmond grunted and grabbed Dale's feet.

"Come help," I told Luther.

"I got a thing," he said and pointed at his back.

I put the hound down, and she collapsed immediately.

"She had like sisters and shit, didn't she?" Luther asked. "On TV and everywhere? One of them played like the banjo or something. And one of them played the piano."

The hound whimpered some more and gnawed at her shirt.

"Yeah," Luther told us, "I guess I'd do them."

As we tumbled Dale in the way back, Desmond shot me a look at the tailgate.

"Oh, all right," I told him. "You can't hit Luther too if you want."

EIGHT

By the time we got out of the forest, we were all pretty sorry we'd come. I finally had a cell phone signal again. Three missed calls from Kendell and two messages from Tula. Desmond stopped at a service station over by Big Eddy. Him and Luther went in to get something to eat while I stayed out with Barbara and Dale. There was so much groaning from the way back and whimpering from the hound that I had to leave the Escalade and wander the lot before I could hope to hear Tula.

In her messages, she just said, "Call me," so I did.

"Where the hell have you been?" She had that tone about her she got sometimes when me or her son or some man somewhere was on her last nerve.

"Down near Yazoo. Looking for a guy. Phone won't pick up much down here."

"Why's Kendell all over me about going to Baton Rouge?"

I knew where the pique was coming from now. It wasn't anxiety about my safety. She was steamed that I had meddled.

"Do what?" That was my typical stall, and Tula was close enough to me to know it.

"What did you say to him?"

"Now wait a second."

"What did you say?" She'd gone all low and determined, talked like she was gnawing on her phone.

"That Boudrot's running wild," I told her. "We just buried some dogs he killed. I don't know how I'd live with myself if he ever got his hands on C.J."

"Wouldn't be a problem," Tula assured me. "I'd fucking cut your heart out."

I didn't really know what to tell her back beyond, "Okay. Yeah. Well."

"Here's how it's going to be," she said. "I'm going to take him to his aunt's, but I'm coming straight back, and you don't get to say shit about it."

"Take the dog too," I told her. It was a beagle mix we shared. I'd ended up with him when his owner had screwed his plane into the ground.

That failed to strike Tula as meddling. She said, "All right."

"Going today?"

"Right after school. I'll be back tonight."

"Tomorrow would probably be—"

"Tonight." She was gnawing her phone again.

"Okay. Fine. Tonight. But check in, will you?"

She made a noise like she might.

We settled out and got back to normal after that. She and Kendell were doing what cops usually do, which is waiting for some fresh enormity to happen. This wasn't much of a whodunnit.

That Boudrot had killed a guy, had stolen a car, had trashed a few of houses, and now he'd wandered out of their jurisdiction and mowed down a half-dozen dogs. They'd put out their bulletins and raised their alarms and were waiting for him to get nabbed on the roadways or pop up doing additional mischief. Otherwise, they were keeping to their routines as if that Boudrot was just another thug.

That's the law enforcement way. Short of an outright manhunt—the kind with federal agents and troopers and guardsmen and helicopters—cops just do their usual stuff and wait for criminals to be stupid. It's a solid bet on their part, but that Boudrot would need to be stupid fast. He was amped up on rage and vindictiveness and doing such accelerated harm that a day in his life would be like a week for any other miscreant.

Just as Tula signed off, Desmond and Luther came out of the service station with something chicken fried on biscuits.

Luther jabbed a thumb toward the storefront. "Guy in there knows Eugene," he said.

"In jail in Arkansas," Desmond told me. "Couldn't remember if he stole something or maybe just burned something down."

"In for a stretch?"

They both shrugged.

"Where in Arkansas?"

"Eudora. Just across the river."

"We going?" I asked Desmond.

It was Luther who spoke. "A man heading home to that kind of mess needs to know what he's going to find."

I probably stared at Luther like he'd just dropped down from the heavens. Desmond gave him a hard once-over too. We weren't accustomed to Luther suggesting we do the decent thing or even knowing exactly what the decent thing might me.

"What?" he asked us.

"Eudora," I told him. "How do we get there?" I asked Desmond.

He pointed north and grunted. That was the trouble with being backed up to the river. It was always a hike to the nearest bridge.

Dale was awake by the time we all climbed into the Escalade while Barbara the coonhound was asleep stretched full across the backseat.

"She's getting grease on shit," Luther announced.

Desmond gurgled back in his throat.

"I'll get it all cleaned," I told him.

"You right." He started the engine and eased into the road.

"Where are we going?" Dale asked from the way back. He hadn't sat up or anything. He was still stretched out where we'd tossed him after Desmond had laid him low.

Luther, who'd shifted Barbara enough to clear him a spot by the passenger door, laid an arm along the seat back and said to Dale, "Eudora, Arkansas."

Dale was quiet for about a half mile. When he spoke again, he said, "Why?"

I think Dale must have dozed off shortly after that because he didn't seem to hunger for an answer. We were on the bridge just south of Greenville when the concrete seams woke him up. He sat up enough to look out the rear window and see we were over the river. Then he laid back down and asked in a general way, "We ever eating or what?"

There's not much to see in Arkansas. There's a delta on that side of the river too, but the well water on the Arkansas side runs to spoiled and brackish somehow. They grow peanuts and keep cows. They've got nothing like the scale of farming that's routine on the eastern side. There are trees and goats and pasture-land and not the first speck of soybeans or cotton.

Barbara got antsy near Eudora, so we stopped in the gravel lot of some business that looked to be a combination propane works and café. You could bring in your tanks and get them filled on the north side of the structure. Judging by the scent from the range hood, you could get gastric distress down south.

That café had a big weathered menu attached to the front siding, a sheet of plywood on which somebody had painted a catfish (as it turned out) and a half rack of ribs in a puddle of sauce. There was something called angel slaw available as a side, in addition to EVERY DAMN KIND OF FRITTER! and WHITE BREAD IF YOU WANT IT.

The aroma was enough to bring Dale entirely out of the way back.

"Lord, look," he said as he studied the menu. "Who's going to front me some cash?"

It ended up being me. Luther didn't let out money as a rule, and Desmond hated Dale, so Dale knew to wander my way. I was standing over by a weedy patch where Barbara was making her business.

I fished two fives out of my billfold and shoved them Dale's way.

Desmond was still digesting his chicken-fried thing, but Luther guessed he could eat again, so him and Dale went into the café. They were gone for maybe two minutes before Dale came back out trailed by a man he was planning to fight in the lot.

I was still over with Barbara. She was feeling fragile, I guess. Not confident enough anyway to just squat and get things over with. She was circling and sniffing and shivering a little. She'd look up at me every now and again and whine. Desmond was on the phone to his Pentecostal girlfriend. He was trying to explain what he was up to without actually telling her anything. So we weren't in any position to intervene on Dale's behalf, and Luther hadn't even bothered to come outside.

Dale and the fellow who'd followed him out had some words there in the lot.

Dale said, "The hell I did."

That fellow told him, "Shit."

Dale had something else on his mind and was casting around for the appropriate inflammatory language when the gentleman who had followed him out knocked Dale down with a punch. It wasn't a cinematic punch or even a bottom-of-the-ticket bloated heavyweight haymaker. The guy just lurched at Dale and hit him. I guess most anywhere would have hurt given that Dale had been beaten fairly thoroughly just the night before.

He went down like his bones had all dissolved at once. The guy who'd punched him said, "Shit," again and spat. His buddy was just coming out the door to see the fight by the time it was over.

He glanced at Dale. He asked his pal, "You want dark meat, right?"

The guy who'd punched Dale told him, "I guess," and the two of them went back inside.

Desmond had missed the whole thing. His back was to the action, and he was comprehensively preoccupied trying to explain to his Pentecostal girlfriend what exactly had carried him all the way to Arkansas.

I caught Desmond's eye and pointed. He turned around to see Dale piled up in the lot. The last Desmond knew Dale had gone in to buy a bag full of greasy lunch, and there he was tipped over and semiconscious out in the parking lot.

"Got to go," Desmond told his Pentecostal girlfriend. He

listened to her for half a minute and then added, "Yes, praise Him."

He shoved his phone in his pocket and looked to me for an explanation, which is to say Desmond showed me his upturned palms as he said my way just, "Huh?"

"I hate to call it a fight."

"He just went in, didn't he?"

I nodded. Barbara whimpered. Dale snorted up a puff of gravel dust.

"Guy punched him once."

"How do you piss off anybody that quick?" Desmond asked me.

I'd known Dale too long by the then to be qualified to say since he'd been a source of low-level antagonism for me for years. I couldn't remember if he'd chafed me the moment I'd met him or just very shortly thereafter.

Luther soon came out and explained it all to us. He was eating a catfish sandwich, which was shredded cabbage and about a half pound of fried fish between two slices of Texas toast. He took a bite. He chewed. He walked over to Dale and poked him with the toe of his snake-skinned boot.

"How the hell did he do it?" I asked Luther.

Luther jabbed his thumb toward the café-propane place. "Razorback fan," he told us. "Dale had a thing to say."

"You get him some lunch?" I asked him.

That was the sort of thoughtful gesture that didn't occur to Luther naturally. He looked at me like I'd asked him if he'd laundered Dale's undershorts.

"I'll go," I told Desmond. "Otherwise, he'll just start pissing and moaning again."

Desmond grunted and nodded. He instructed Luther to help him drag Dale to the car. Luther aired an objection or two about it before Desmond caught him on the cowlick with his open hand.

So I stepped inside the café on a mission just to get Dale some ribs, and without any provocation on my part, that Razorback fan got wolfy with me.

"Guess you want some too," was the first thing I heard.

Like Dale, he'd probably been muscular once but had fallen down on the upkeep. He was wearing a sky-blue dress shirt that he'd cut the sleeves off of, better to show off his Chevy tattoo on his left biceps and the scar from his polio vaccination (I guess) on his right.

"Some what?" I asked him.

He had a chuckle with his buddies. There were two of them sitting with him at a picnic table.

"Yeah, sugar," the lady behind the counter said. She was caramel-colored and had her hair all up and wrapped in a rag. I had to think she passed her life stinking of week-old fry grease and resenting the slights she must have suffered from the clientele.

"Ribs, I guess," I told her. "And all the trimmings."

"Half a rack?"

I nodded.

"You know what," the guy with no shirtsleeves said. "Asshole."

I don't mind getting called an asshole once I've actually been one. If I go into a house to repo a washer or take a sofa out from under Grandma and the family wants to vent about it, they can call me whatever they please. I'm not proud of that work, and I'm convinced this world's increasingly stacked against decent industrious people of low pedigree. So when "asshole" or "fuckwad" comes my way, I consider it the price of doing business.

But in a café in Arkansas when I'm only putting in an order and haven't been up to the first little thing to get called an asshole about, somebody's going to have to do a bit of explaining.

"Did I hear you right?" I said to that fellow.

He tightened up as best he could underneath his Chevy tattoo. He shifted his toothpick and grinned. "Asshole," he said. He nodded.

"You sucker punch a sack of shit, and you think you're Sonny Liston?"

He was grinning now. He set his toothpick on the napkin dispenser.

"How long on that order?" I asked the woman behind the counter.

"Five minutes."

I told that boy, "Let's go."

So out we came into the lot. All four of us. Desmond was leaning against his front grill enduring prattle from Luther who very nearly stopped talking when he saw us step into the lot. He still had a few points to make with Desmond about proper catfish-frying technique, but he turned his attention to me and my posse while he said what he had to say.

Dale was out of sight in the Escalade by then, and Barbara's head was hanging out the window.

"They ought to blow up all these goddamn bridges," the fellow with the Chevy tattoo told me. "Keep you Mississippi trash over where you belong."

He'd squared up on me by then and was making and unmaking his fists. He appeared to be looking for the chance to catch me with one of his lunging punches. I guess he thought, being Dale's friend, I'd probably fight like Dale. That was hardly the case given my long-held fighting philosophy of always being first and never taking pity. I'd learned the hard way that going easy on a guy out of some tender human feeling was almost sure to cost you in the end.

So I went ahead and made my move. I waited for him to

smirk at his buddies, and once he'd turned his head just slightly, I kicked him in the crotch. Hard and with full follow-through, like I was punting from the end zone. He tooted through his nose and bent forward. I swung on him with a right. Caught him flush and put him down.

One of his buddies said, "Fucker," so I laid into him as well.

The third one held up his hands and showed me his palms. He smiled my way. He told me, "Hey."

I very nearly eased off and relaxed, but then he went reaching for something, so I charged him and butted him over. I kicked him like hell once he was down. He had a pistol in his back jeans pocket, a little .25 caliber semi. It only held four rounds. You might kill a house cat with it if it was in your lap and you took dead aim.

I held the thing up and showed it to Desmond.

We liked our guns large and our calibers considerable. Desmond shook his head and told me, "People'll buy any damn thing."

Those boys were all twitching and groaning in the gravel at my feet. I pointed at the café and told Desmond and Luther, "Got to get Dale's ribs."

Luther shouted my way, "Can I kick them?"

Those boys were surely about to wish those bridges had all been blown to bits. I shrugged, reached for the screen door pull. "Do what you want," he said.

Luther yipped and yodeled with cracker joy. "I like Arkansas after all."

NINE

The Eudora, Arkansas, jailhouse had been a Big Lots once. It was off in a corner of what used to be a sizable shopping plaza. That store had been broken up into office space and modest shop fronts, and about half of them looked like they'd gone the way of the mother ship. Law enforcement, however, always loves a recession. There were new Crown Vic cruisers all over the place. People who've given over thieving for honest employment in boom times often find themselves laid off when things get tough and get back in the game.

If Eudora was much like Indianola—and it looked the same sort of spot, just smaller—the cops usually had an idea of who to pick up before even the choice goods got fenced. In terms of rank criminality, Eugene qualified as a sort of Eudora local. He'd shared with me and Desmond his crackpot theory of who had jurisdiction over what, and we'd been unable to shake Eugene from his abiding conviction that Mississippi was a sanctuary for thieving lowlifes like him.

Eugene primarily robbed Arkansas churches. "Shit, man," he'd explained to us once, "they almost all unlocked."

He'd started out stealing the bright brass liturgical bric-a-brac, but he'd soon discovered there wasn't much of a going market for it. So he'd shifted his focus to pews and chairs and altar tables and pulpits. At least he could tear that stuff down into lumber if he couldn't unload it whole.

Eugene drove a big junky truck he'd welded together from three or four other vehicles. During our first run-in with that Boudrot, me and Desmond and Luther had ridden around enough in Eugene's truck to recognize it straightway over at the far end of the parking lot. It had been left in what passed for the Eudora PD's impound yard, which was a weedy patch of shattered asphalt with two tractors and a backhoe in it along with Eugene's jackleg state body truck. The bed was piled with stainless-steel tables.

"Looks like Eugene found a kitchen somewhere," I said as we rolled up on the thing.

Desmond and Luther and Dale all told me together, "Methodists."

"Surely not around here. Look at that stuff." Desmond had stopped beside Eugene's truck, and I was sizing up the load.

Eugene had a Hobart mixer and what appeared to be a pizza oven. A commercial refrigerator. It almost looked like Eugene had thrown in the tables because they were handy and could be had.

"Pine Bluff maybe," Desmond suggested.

"Shit," Luther told us and pointed at some sort of fancy cooktop. "Little Rock probably."

Dale threw in with, "I doubt they're letting him out."

That was my opinion too from sizing up the swag. Eugene appeared to have stolen enough to qualify for genuine trouble.

"Who's going in?" I asked them.

They all pointed. They all said, "You."

I couldn't be sure I wasn't walking into a problem for myself. There I'd just been out in the open beating down some local pin-heads. Somebody in that café-propane place could have called the trouble in. Consequently, I made a kind of foray, went in through the station house door like I was looking for directions.

"Some propane outfit around here somewhere?" I asked the woman at the front desk.

She had on a uniform, but it looked like the kind a housekeeper would wear.

She told me, "Yeah." She pointed. She said, "Take 65. It's three or four miles."

"Open today?"

"It's Tuesday, sugar." She looked at me like I was dead simple and nodded.

If there'd been a call from the propane café, she sure didn't know a thing about it, and she was the only one I could see who was answering a phone.

The thing rang just then. "Hold on," she told me. "*Po*-lice," she said and listened to what sounded like somebody frantic on the line. "Uh-huh," she said every now and again—low and exasperated like Desmond was often given to saying. "Uh-huh." Then there came a gap in the chatter, and that receptionist announced, "I ain't sending nobody. You keep the lid on that septic tank of yours, and a cat isn't going to fall in."

A beefy deputy came wandering up out of the back of the place just then. He stopped in front of me, gave me a full and deliberate once-over.

"Help you?"

"Yeah, maybe. You got a guy in here named Eugene?"

"Where the hell you been?"

He motioned for me to follow him, and we headed into the bowels of the place. It was all unfinished wallboard and cubicles and smelly industrial berber carpet. We passed one cop playing hearts on his computer and another guy, a sergeant, who had the coffee machine apart. It was one of those double-eyed commercial things, and he'd taken it entirely to pieces.

"This him?" he said brightly to the guy I was following, hoping for the Bunn man.

"Swamp rat," my deputy told him.

Him and the guy playing hearts both clapped.

"I'm not his lawyer or anything," I told my deputy.

"Got twenty dollars?" he asked me.

I nodded.

"Then he's going with you," he said, "because he sure as shit ain't staying here."

"And that stuff in his truck?" I asked him.

"Said he traded for it. We'll sort that out later."

"You believe him?"

"Friend," that deputy told me, "right now I'll swallow whatever gets him gone."

With that he pulled open a big metal door and gestured for me to precede him into what proved to be the lockup. They had two cells—just cages in a big empty room—and Eugene was sitting on what looked to me like a shower chair in one of them. He had on a sky-blue county jumpsuit and a pair of laceless sneakers. His hair was combed. His face was shaved. He was so scrubbed his skin was pink. I'd never seen Eugene anything approaching that spruced up, and yet he stank like a barrel of black snakes. It was an intensely musty reptile reek. An aquarium odor but concentrated and hard beside intolerable.

I must have made a disgusted noise. A human couldn't help but grunt when met with an odor like that.

"See?" that deputy said. "And we flat scrubbed the son of a bitch. He's sweating it out or something. Maybe gator in the woodpile."

Eugene had stood up by then and had stepped to the front of the cage to gawk my way. There was wafting involved, and the swampy stink of the place got even worse for a time.

Eugene said, "Hey."

I hadn't seen him in probably a year or two.

"So what happens here?" I asked the deputy.

"You give me twenty dollars. I let him out, and he goes with you."

"His truck?"

"We keep it and all his shit until we get this sorted." He turned to Eugene after that to say to him directly, "Wouldn't surprise me much if he don't come back."

Eugene got immediately pitiful there with his arms hanging between the bars. "My truck?"

"Let it go," I told him.

He whimpered some more and said, "But I ain't done nothing."

I ventured over as close as I dared to Eugene and said, "Let's me and you get out of here."

He sighed and shook his head like this world was a trial and ordeal for him. "All right," Eugene told me. "I guess."

I turned and nodded at the deputy. He held out his hand, and I dug up a twenty and laid it on his palm.

"Paperwork?" I asked him.

He shook his head. "And he's going out the back."

He handed me the cell key and made me unlock the door.

Eugene stepped out 'where me and the deputy were. The wafting was tough to take.

"What about all the stuff from my pockets and shit?"

"Burned it," the deputy told him.

Eugene sighed again. He said to me, "Had all my numbers in there."

"We'll figure something out," I said.

The deputy pointed at a back door. "Straight through and out," he said.

"And he's clear?" I wanted to make sure.

That deputy nodded. He pointed at the door again.

"Let's go," I said, and I got in front of Eugene in a bid to avoid the wafting, but he gave off stink the way a bonfire gives off heat. It went all over.

"Thanks," I told the deputy.

He wouldn't hear of it. "No, thank you."

We came out on what had been once the Big Lots loading dock. It had six abandoned bays, and two of them were full of trash. Smelly trash. Rotting trash. But it couldn't compete with Eugene.

"What are you even doing here?" he asked me as I pointed to direct him toward the near corner of the building.

"Fuckstick's loose," I told him.

"Boudrot?"

I nodded.

"Turned out or busted out?"

"Busted. And on the warpath."

"Where are we going?"

"To find him."

"Hell. Why?"

"If it helps at all, I was hoping to leave you in jail. They wouldn't really let me."

"I don't know what their problem was. Kept washing me and shit."

"You've got kind of a funk," I informed him.

Eugene appeared surprised to hear it. "Naw."

We rounded the corner of the building. Desmond's Escalade was out of sight, parked down beyond the backhoe and the tractors and Eugene's truck.

"You do," I said. "Smelling snaky to me."

Eugene raised a forearm and sniffed it. He shrugged.

"What exactly have you been up to?"

"Selling skins."

"From what?"

He shrugged again. "Gators mostly. Snakes. Tried a few bullfrogs, but they don't work."

"Don't work how?" asked him.

We were closing on Desmond's Escalade by then.

"Never get proper dry," Eugene said. "Stay . . . juicy."

"You must have soaked some of it in," I suggested, "because you stink something awful."

Eugene sniffed his forearm again. Eugene informed me, "Naw."

Desmond saw us first, and he called my way to say, "How the hell did you get him out?"

Then we got closer, and Desmond found himself wafted at. Luther and Dale as well. Barbara clearly too.

"And why?" Luther asked me.

For her part, Barbara was happy to see Eugene. She got lively all of a sudden. She went squirming out the side window and jumped down into the weeds. She came wriggling around toward me and Eugene. She sidled up to him in a writhing crouch like she couldn't be sure if she was due for a pat on the head or a kick.

"Well, hey," Eugene told her and gave her pat. "What's she doing here?" he wanted to know.

"We stopped at your place," I said and before I could settle on how to continue, Eugene tugged at the collar of that Barbara Mandrell T-shirt.

"Why the hell's she wearing this? You go in my house?"

I looked to the boys in a way that drew them out of Desmond's Escalade. Luther and Desmond anyway. Dale stayed where he was in the way back. He didn't suffer from decent impulses and so had yet to tune in to the fact that I was about to have to break some painful news to Eugene.

"Hey here," Eugene told Luther.

Luther looked primed to say, "Hey here," back, but Eugene's aroma overcame Luther by the time he reached the front wheel well. So instead Luther invoked the Savior a dozen emphatic ways, covered his nose with hand, and told us, "Shit!"

"Frogs mostly," I explained. "Probably gators and snakes some too. Must have got in his pores or something."

Luther wasn't really interested. The stink had also hit Desmond by then, and he wasn't interested as well.

"Tell him about his dogs?" Luther asked me.

"What about them?" Eugene said.

"Come here," I told Eugene.

Me and him and Desmond took a stroll down across the weedy, ruptured asphalt toward the street.

"That Boudrot came looking for you."

"Why?" Eugene wanted to know.

"Why do you think?" Desmond asked him.

"Wasn't me that put him in the lockup."

Technically, Eugene had a point. Him and his swamp rat buddy Tommy had hung back when the rest of us had charged on in to take that Boudrot down. They were lurking behind a grassy hummock quarreling over wide-mouth lures. So they weren't exactly in on the action when me and Desmond and Luther and Percy Dwayne Dubois corralled that Boudrot and hauled him off for Dale to take in, but that was probably too fine a distinction for an Acadian fuckstick to make.

Eugene had helped us find that Boudrot, and that was likely all that mattered.

"I think he figures you did your bit," I told Eugene.

He was prepared to go on sputtering about it until Desmond informed him, "Went looking for you at your place. We just come from there."

Barbara, the lone surviving coonhound, had followed us down toward the road. Once we'd stopped walking, she'd flopped on the ground hard beside her master.

"Tear up the place?" Eugene asked us.

I nodded.

Desmond told him, "Yeah . . ."

"What else?" he asked us. He could tell there was something.

Desmond glanced over to as good as say he was leaving the hounds to me.

"He shot up your dogs," I told Eugene.

We watched the news sink in. Eugene seemed to shrink a little. His mouth dropped open. He squinted at me. "Did what?"

"He stole a shotgun from out at K-Lo's. Looks like he used that on them." I pointed at Barbara. "She was down on the bottom of the pile. Only got hit a little."

Eugene looked Barbara's way and gave her a fond nudge with his laceless sneaker. "The rest of them?" he asked me.

I gave him a wince and a slight shake of my head.

Eugene squatted right where he was and covered his eyes up with his hand.

We must have been some kind of sight for the few folks passing on the main road. Me and Desmond. A hound in a T-shirt. An inmate in a sky-blue police-issue jumpsuit, and him squatting there in that weedy Big Lots wasteland weeping like a child.

TEN

We couldn't put him anywhere that suited us all. We tried Eugene first in the way back. Desmond cracked the rear window. He had a theory about airflow in his Escalade that may or may not have been sound, but it surely didn't help with the reptile stink. That Escalade soon smelled like we were parked at the bottom of swampy hole.

"Can't we wash him or something?" Dale asked us.

"He's clean," I said. "Look at him. They scrubbed him half to death."

Dale might even have tried to look at him, but it hardly would have mattered. My eyes were watering up in the front seat. Dale's must have been in the back.

"Got a roof rack?" Luther wanted to know.

Desmond cranked the fan up another notch.

"Cut open one toad that was full of eggs," Eugene offered up by way of explanation. "I stank a little right there at first. Don't stink much anymore."

I think we all felt slightly relieved to gain the bridge and cross the river. Even if that crazy Acadian fuckstick was still loose in Mississippi, we were happy to be on that side of the water too.

Desmond stopped at an AutoZone just south of Greenville and bought some kind of car perfume. It didn't help much, just made it smell like our pregnant toad was on her way to the prom. We sat in the AutoZone lot with the doors flung open to do some strategizing. It was midafternoon by then, and we were all a little dazed from the canine carnage, the fisticuffs, the reptile stink, the abiding threat of that Boudrot.

We sat there breathing in what fresh air we could and catching up with the world on our phones like men just back from a lunar mission.

"Percy Dwayne called!" Luther announced.

"Leave a message?" I asked him.

"Uh-huh." Luther put the thing on speaker and held it up where we could hear it.

"I'm calling him, ain't I," Percy Dwayne said to someone. "Get the fuck off me."

Then there was a muffled clatter and shouting. Desmond grunted.

Dale said, "Shit. Somebody's sure got him."

"Pick up, pick up, pick up," Percy Dwayne said.

"Not quite up on voicemail, is he?"

Luther told me, "Naw. Don't even have a phone no more."

"Boudrot?" I asked Desmond.

He shook his head. "Fool would have just killed him outright.

He's on a tear, you know?" Desmond told me. "Thrill of the hunt and all that."

That kind of made sense to me in as much as any of this business did.

"Where was he calling from?" I asked Luther.

Luther pulled up his missed calls. "Three three five," he told us.

"That's Greenville," Desmond said.

"Try it," Dale instructed Luther. Me and Desmond nodded.

Luther called back the number Percy Dwayne had called in from.

The guy who answered just said, "Grady's."

Luther got out, "Grady's what?"

The guy was talking to somebody else already by the time he hung up the phone.

"Grady's?" I asked Desmond and Dale.

They both just shook their heads.

Eugene was out of the Escalade and standing ten yards off in the lot. It was a voluntary courtesy. We'd moaned enough to cause Eugene to come around to the opinion that he stank.

"Grady's?" I asked him.

Eugene squinted as a sign that he was thinking, and he still hadn't decided what he knew when a fellow came out of the AutoZone. He had on a filthy Delta State Fighting Okras cap and a Remington T-shirt that the collar had rotted off of. He fished a cigarette from behind his ear and lit it. He gave us the hard eye. We gave it right back.

"Grady's?" I said to him.

He pointed in the general direction of Alpha Centauri. "Mile or two. Just past the crossroads."

"What the hell is it?" Luther asked him.

He drew on his cigarette and blew smoke out his nose while he considered Luther from cowlick to boot heel.

"You looking for it," that fellow told Luther. "Guess you ought to know."

Ordinarily, his logic would have been unassailable, which Luther probably should have explained. Instead just Luther went with, "What the hell is it?" with a bit more volume than the first time around and appreciably more passion.

That fellow just laughed and spat. He drew his cigarette clean down to the filter, pulled on it so hard that sparks flew. He flicked the leavings into the lot and then squared up toward Luther and glared at him.

That was just the way in the Delta. You ask a guy a simple question, and you end up in a fight.

While it would have been no trouble much to draw back and slug the guy, I opted for the ambassadorial approach. We were in Tula and Kendell's territory after all, and I knew they had their hands full.

"His uncle," I said and jabbed a thumb Luther's way. "Wandered off. Kind of gone in the head. We heard he was at some place called Grady's."

Like all men who have to crawl down from a quarrel, he went about it slowly.

"Just worried. That's all," I told him in a bid to explain Luther.

Then I looked hard enough at Luther to cause him to throw in with a "Yeah."

"Body shop," that boy told us. "Turn left at the fruit stand. If you get to that silo with the creepers all over it, you went too damn far."

"We appreciate it, don't we?"

Luther passed a quarter minute working up another "Yeah."

"Where do you eat around here?" Dale asked that guy before he could get away.

He pointed again. Nowhere helpful. "Fruit stand's got tamales."

"Well all right, then," Dale said. He reached down and grabbed up a fistful of Barbara Mandrell. "Come on, dog."

My phone rang just then. It was Tula. "Pulling out of the driveway," she told me. "Happy?"

"Might get there later," I said back. "Just keep calling along the way."

"Right," was all I got back before she dropped the call.

We all piled out again at the fruit stand. A whiskery old black woman was running the thing. She didn't have much in the way of fruit. A few brown bananas. Some tired looking beans. Bright yellow hoop cheese. Chunks of smoked hog. She did have a stew pot full of tamales. They were submerged in greasy red juice as thin as water. She kept telling us it was gravy. She sold the things six to a bundle, and she was prepared to declare them whatever meat we wanted them to be.

Luther asked for beef. Dale requested venison. Eugene had a taste for chicken. That woman just dug the things out willy-nilly from the pot and dropped them all in coffee cans she'd laid in for that purpose. They came with packets of Russian dressing and saltines.

"What about you?" I asked Desmond.

We both watched that woman spoon iridescent "gravy" into a can.

"Coney Island," Desmond told me and shook his head.

I opted for a brown banana while Desmond informed Dale and Luther and Eugene, "Don't take them damn cans anywhere near my truck."

Those three went over and perched on a rusty fuel-oil tank

while me and Desmond chatted up that whiskery old black woman. She asked us where we were from. We told her, and she informed us she'd been to Indianola once.

"Nineteen sixty-seven," she said. "Bought a crown. For Easter."

"Haven't been back?" I asked her.

She told me, "Nome," her version of "uh-uh."

"Smell him?" Desmond asked her. He pointed at Eugene across the way.

"Couldn't much help it."

"Toad," I told her. "What can we do about it?"

"This here," she said and fished out from somewhere a chunk of something wrapped in wax paper. In addition to her tamales and her brown bananas and tired beans, she turned out to have a milk crate full of mixed goods sitting by her feet.

"Lye soap," she said. Then she acquainted us with how exactly Eugene ought to scour himself. "Dishrag," she told us. She had one of those too. It even looked very nearly new. Eugene was to scrub from his armpits to his fingertips. "Two times," she said. "A quarter hour apart. Then rinse him in a branch." She pointed. "One over there in them rushes." After that Eugene had to personally bury the dishrag under a rock.

"Any particularly kind of rock?" I asked her.

She looked at me like I was simple. She turned to wink at Desmond and then swung back my way to tell me, "Nome."

"Not going to burn him, is it?" Desmond asked her.

"Rinse him in the branch," she said and pointed at the rushes again.

She wanted six dollars for the soap and rag.

"I'm about out of money," I told Desmond.

"Tell me when you're full out. How's that banana?"

"Rotten."

I gave her a ten. She didn't have any change.

"Then how about some information?" I said. "You know Grady's?"

She said, "Lord, them boys."

She motioned me to her with one of her leathery fingers. I brought my face down close to hers. She sure had whiskers in odd places. At either edge of her upper lip and in tufts along her jawline. She smelled like snuff and applejack. She said in a whisper, "Rascals."

"How many?" Desmond wanted to know.

"Four or five of them today. Come through here this morning. Bought up all my biscuits and pickles."

"What are they up to exactly?" I asked.

"*Rascals,*" she said more emphatically this time around.

"What exactly do rascals do?" I asked her.

"Any damn thing they like."

Eugene turned out to be reluctant to get scrubbed down with homemade lye soap, especially after we'd explained who'd sold it to us and what we'd been instructed to do.

"I don't smell nothing," he kept saying. Then he said a hard thing about black folk, which Desmond objected to with a blow to the back of Eugene's head.

"Right," he said to Desmond, rubbing his cowlick. "You black, ain't you?"

That was the thing about Eugene in particular and Delta swamp rats generally. They had racial reflexes like everybody else had allergies or red hair. Eugene knew better than to run black folk down. It just came out of him like a sneeze.

"I wouldn't use that shit," Luther told us and made a show of glaring at that whiskery old black woman.

Dale didn't seem to have an opinion. He was drinking tamale juice from his can.

"Want to keep smelling him?" I asked Luther.

He told me, "Well" and "No."

So we escorted Eugene down to the branch, gave him his washcloth and his lye soap and suffered Eugene to strip down to his nasty underwear. They'd been tidy whities once but now the elastic was exhausted and the fabric looked like it had been steeped in tea.

"They didn't give you underpants?" Desmond asked him.

"Naw."

Luther groaned and shook his head like this world was a disappointment to him. He gazed off toward the horizon and said just, "Arkansas."

Eugene was a spectacle in his briefs. He was scarred all over, hairy in strange spots, and selectively discolored. He had more knife wounds and bullet holes and surgical incisions than most of us have fingers and toes.

"Lord," I said to him. I couldn't really help it. "What all happened to you?"

So there we all stood by that branch south of Greenville watching Eugene in his nasty underwear as he supplied us with his personal history of conflict and miscalculation. He'd point to a knife wound and tell us, "Some fucker down in Yazoo," or at a scar on his shin and say, "Goddamn mower went to pieces."

It went on like that for a quarter hour. We almost had to fight some boys. They came by in about the dirtiest pickup truck I'd ever seen. It looked like they'd parked it in a mud hole for a year. When they saw Eugene, they stopped in the road. The passenger cocked his head back to cackle and so showed us all fourteen of his teeth.

"Look at them faggots," he decided to say before him or his buddy either one noticed Dale closing in from the opposite side.

Sometimes Dale's useful. This was one of those occasions.

He had about a third of a coffee can of tamale juice left, and he shot it all over those boys, just doused them with it. That stuff was red and greasy from the cayenne and the chili powder.

It wasn't coming out, not even with lye soap, and the driver got all shirty. But he turned out to be the sort of boy who was leery even of Dale. Big blubbery Dale who told him, "Come on," and flung the empty can at him.

Those boys didn't quite have the nerve to pile out of that truck and tangle. They had instead a mutual swearing fit as they shot on down the road.

We didn't any of us say anything. That sort of passing confrontation was all too commonplace in the Delta. After a quarter minute, Eugene piped in again. He laid his finger to a scar on his lower abdomen. "Appendix blew all to shit."

We finally prevailed upon Eugene to slip down into the branch. There was an eddy right below us where the water curled and pooled. He stood shin-deep in the stream, glanced down at his briefs, and asked in a general way, "Who's going to hold my underpants?"

It was so quiet you could hear that fruit stand lady dribbling snuff juice into her cup.

"Why don't you start over," Desmond suggested. "We'll get you some new ones down the road here."

"Throw them out?" Eugene said. The wastefulness of such a thing appeared to offend him greatly.

"What with the toad and all," I told him.

"Well," he said. "All right."

So Eugene came out of his underwear. He had a ring around his waist where the band of briefs had laid, the sort of ring you might get in a bathtub if you washed a couple of donkeys. Eugene wasn't uneasy or embarrassed at all to be standing in a branch out in the open naked to the world. If anything, he was the opposite of uneasy and embarrassed, and rattled on for a little while about the prowess of his member and the sort of effect it had on "gals," as he called them.

"Makes them flat yell."

It was close to having the same effect on me.

"I might have to kick that Boudrot to death," Desmond informed me. "Wouldn't be seeing a thing I'm seeing but for him."

The worst part was the lye soap didn't rout the stink entirely. It sure made Eugene pink all over. He finally sat down in the branch, lathered up and rolled around to rinse himself off. The man had no modesty and kept showing us his bits and pieces before we could look away. By the time he was zipping back up into his sky blue coveralls, me and Desmond and Luther were all fully primed to make stew meat out of that Boudrot. It turned out there were some things even a guy like Luther couldn't unsee.

"This ain't the day I'd hoped for," he told us.

We didn't have much quarrel with that. Me and Desmond closed on Eugene so we could sniff him a little.

I sampled an elbow. Eugene smelled a bit like a river carp that had been power washed in Clorox.

ELEVEN

Grady's was about what me and Desmond expected it would be. It was a dump. A Quonset hut. A big galvanized tube sitting flush on the ground. They're common in the Delta. Farmers used to use them for tractor and equipment sheds before tractors and equipment got so oversized no Quonset hut could hold them. So the things got sold off and hauled away and used for other stuff. Like at Grady's where his Quonset hut appeared to be a cracker magnet.

There was white trash lounging every damn where. The surrounding lot was littered with cars. No few of them disassembled along with no end of stray cast-off parts. That included bucket and bench seats, so there were plenty of places to sit, and there's little trash likes more than lying around and jawing.

Luther, for his part, perked up like we'd finally reached the ocean after months of bouncing on a buckboard across the fruited plain.

"Well, shit howdy," he said a little too brightly for Dale to tolerate with grace.

"Which one's your daddy?" Dale asked him.

Luther pointed to a couple of boys. "Him, and maybe him."

Luther yipped as he piled out of the car. He got a fair amount of yodeling back.

"Goddamn reunion," Dale informed us.

"I'm on fire back here," Eugene said.

He showed me and Desmond his forearms. They were scarlet from the lye.

"Probably got some Gojo or something in there," I told him and pointed at that Quonset hut. "Wash them down with that."

Eugene rolled on out. Being a swamp rat, he was a natural link in the cracker chain as well and got welcomed like a brother. It would be a little different for me and Desmond and Dale.

"We're going to end up hitting somebody, aren't we?"

I was talking only to Desmond, but Dale couldn't help but pipe in with, "That's right."

I turned around to find him crawling over the seat back and angling for the door Eugene had left open.

"That's awful eager," I told him, "for a guy who got put down hard in Arkansas."

"Lucky punch," Dale said.

That's what Dale always said.

"I ain't staying in the car," he told us.

"Any trouble you make is yours," Desmond said. "And don't make any."

Dale grinned and raised his hands like we had no cause to worry. Like he was in control of his bile and his agitation. Like there wasn't a thing cracker trash could tell him that would serve to get him worked up.

Dale got out of the Escalade and made an exhibition of stretching, which included a spot of shadowboxing. Me and Desmond groaned in two-part harmony.

"I don't see Percy Dwayne nowhere," Desmond said.

I hadn't spied him either.

"Look at him." Desmond pointed.

There wasn't anything a soul on earth could do to Dale to keep him from strutting like a cock. He'd gotten punched in a roadhouse the night before and knocked down outside a rib joint in the middle of nowhere Arkansas, and yet there he was swanning around at Grady's like he was built to put fear in a man.

"I don't even want to get out," I said.

And Desmond told me, "Uh-oh."

Dale was to blame for everything that happened, but we could only hold it against him in a general sort of way. A few years earlier, Dale had arrested some of those boys at Grady's. Two of them when he was with the sheriff's department and three more with the state police. Dale had treated them badly, of course. He'd roughed them up once they were cuffed, had talked to them like dogs, had hauled them around where everybody could see them. Toured the county with them in his cruiser. Walked them three or four blocks to the lockup. Dale liked to think he was teaching trash a lesson in humiliation, but the truth was he was only making them mad.

The thing about Delta cracker trash is that they never forget a slight but have short memories for a favor. A good turn is wasted on cracker trash, but an insult lasts forever. Sometimes it's even handed down from one generation to the next. You could beat some fellow with a shovel in a fight you didn't start, and twenty years later his grandson might show up to kick you to pieces or, if you're not handy for it, any relation you have who's within reach.

Out of the ten or twelve layabouts hanging around Grady's, Dale had made enemies out of five, and three of them had relations lying around the place as well. So it turned out there were eight boys primed and ready to do Dale harm.

"Look who it is," one of them said.

"I know you?" Dale asked him.

"Got your pistol?" I said to Desmond.

He fished it out of the console for me. I checked the clip. It would hold fifteen rounds, but Desmond had found it would jam if you loaded it full. It looked considerably less than not full to me. The thing looked damn near empty.

I showed him the clip. "What's this?"

"Killed a snake. Wouldn't hold still."

There were only three rounds left.

"Who you going shoot?" Desmond asked me.

"Nobody much, I guess."

Truth be told, I wasn't hoping to shoot anybody at all, but Desmond's pistol had a lot more heft to it when the clip was loaded. You could hit a hardhead like Dale with the thing and earn his full attention.

"What about you?"

Desmond kept a Browning under the seat. A twelve-gauge his uncle had sawed off years ago. Desmond reached down and pulled it out.

"Riot readies," Desmond told me.

We'd fallen a little in love with a shell that was packed full of little rubber balls. If you didn't want to do a boy lasting harm and still wanted to make an impression, you could let him have a riot-ready load from twenty or thirty yards out. It was like shooting a swarm of hornets at him, and you could usually have your way after that.

The only downside was that they bounced about anywhere they wanted.

"Don't hit that damn Quonset hut," I told him.

Me and Desmond had known enough ricochets to leave him thinking the same thing too.

Desmond slipped out of the Escalade and eased over to flank the place. I got out and stayed wide, found a spot where I doubted even a sawed-off could spray to hit me. From what I could see, Dale hadn't tuned in at all to his peril. That was his style and his technique. He never seemed to quite know what was happening to him until it was too late to fix it.

Those boys were all reminding each other just who Dale was, but it turned out they didn't need awfully much refreshing.

Dale spat. Dale said, "You boys ain't ringing no bells."

I think sometimes Dale just forgot that he'd stopped lifting weights. Back when he was a muscle head, Dale's physique was a deterrent. He had enough sinews and bulges and oversized bits to persuade a man who didn't know any better that Dale could take him apart. You could see his biceps well enough, but you couldn't really make out his glass jaw or get much of a sense of Dale's feeble, girlish way of throwing a punch. Now he was blubber mostly and usually winded and shiny with sweat. The sight of Dale might make you reconsider your diet, but that was about it.

All of those boys were smiling now. Grinning at Dale, shifting around to grin at each other. There was a beat-down in Dale's future, and he still didn't know it yet.

"Seen Percy Dwayne Dubois?" I shouted out.

The whole pack of them looked at me. It was just Dale and them out in front of the place. Eugene and Luther had gone inside the big bay door. Barbara the coonhound had climbed out of the car and had come over to stand at my side.

"What the hell's that dog got on?" one of those layabouts asked me. He looked older than the rest. Probably a daddy to some there, an uncle to others. If anybody could keep this thing in check, it was surely him.

"T-shirt," I told him. "Boy shot her."

"What boy?" he wanted to know, more than a little peeved.

People might have been in favor of shooting each other every now and again, but only a lowdown snake of a man fired on a hound.

"Guy Boudrot," I said.

He asked me back, "What the fuck kind of name is that?"

I was going to go with Acadian, but I went instead with, "French."

"Shit." He fairly spat it.

France and the bowels of hell are nearly identical for some people. This guy outside of Grady's was clearly one of them. I decided to wander over to him, hoped to draw him into the sort of parley that might allow Dale to get scuffed up only a little.

The fellow was sitting in a bucket seat with ruptured vinyl upholstery. He had a Busch tallboy in one hand and a Case knife in the other. He was flipping the blade open and snapping it shut with his thumb.

Barbara followed me over. That fellow pointed at Eugene's coonhound with his knife. "Goddamn Mandrells," he told me. "I ain't thought of them in a while."

He took occasion to think of them as I stood there. He seemed gratified for the chance, judging by the way he reached down with his knife hand to work an adjustment on his member.

"I liked that little blond one," he confessed.

I was not personally competent to distinguish between Mandrells, but one of those other layabouts proved to be some sort of Mandrell expert.

He shifted around. He told his elder colleague, "Irlene."

"That's the one."

"Pretty girls," I told him. I wasn't about to play Mandrell favorites.

He sipped his beer. He fooled with his knife. He finally asked me, "What are you doing with him?"

We both studied Dale. He was standing over by a pile of battered car doors trying to look tougher than he was.

I didn't have a simple answer, not an honest one anyway.

"We're cousins," I told him and shook my head. If there was one thing everybody in the Delta understood, it was that you couldn't pick your kin.

That fellow pointed with the tip of his knife blade at a napping layabout. He was stretched out on the raw ground, was one of those twenty-something crackers who looked like he was maybe forty-five. Partly from the meth. Partly from neglect. Partly from the tattoos. His arms were covered in them. His neck. His ankles too.

"That boy," the elder layabout told me and sighed. "Cousin of mine." Even shiftless trash had standards a human could sink below.

I felt we had a bond now, so I tried to forge ahead.

"You seen a Dubois around here?"

My layabout pointed with his knife blade at Desmond. "What's he up to over there?"

"Standoffish?" I told him.

"Damned if that don't look like a sawed-off."

"Goes where he does. I can't break him of it."

"You'd think," that fellow told me and paused to finish off his beer, "being a gigantic nigger would be enough."

Phony cordiality can only carry a fellow so far. I'd hoped I could grease the way enough to find out about Percy Dwayne, but then that elder cracker had to take a swipe at Desmond, and I could never quite swallow hard enough to make that sort of thing all right.

"Well, fuck it," I said and turned toward Desmond. I raised a finger and twirled it. If Desmond had been driving a loader, he would have brought the bucket down. Instead he was packing a Remington and raised the sawed-off up.

"Can't do nothing with them," I told Desmond.

He leveled his gun. "Ain't that the way."

I found a pile of fenders to dive behind, caught up Barbara and took her with me. "Get down," I shouted at Dale, but Dale wasn't the sort to entertain orders. He just stayed where he was and gave me that look like *nobody* told him where to get.

Desmond squeezed off a riot-ready round, followed hard on by another, and the rubber pellets were straightaway on those boys like an Old Testament plague. Because Desmond didn't have any barrel much, the shot went everywhere, and because he was firing rubber pellets, they ricocheted like nobody's business. Those things were screaming all over that rubbishy lot and finding crackers where they sprawled.

That shot was about twice the size of BBs, and they'd leave you polka-dotted. Those boys couldn't figure out what to do to get out of the way.

They all fished out their weapons, so I got a good look at the sort of arsenal we were up against. Since Desmond kept firing, they couldn't take aim, were far too busy attempting to burrow. Everybody except for Dale, that is. He stayed where he was and got pissed.

"Hey!" he kept yelling Desmond's way.

I heard Desmond tell him, "Hey, yourself."

I think Desmond fired six shells altogether. He was loading up for another batch, when I called out to him, "Dog's getting nervous."

"All right," Desmond said. "Guess I'm done."

The elder cracker was trying to scrabble out from the crap he'd crawled up under when I mounted the pile, jumped up and down twice. That proved enough to raise a whimper.

"Percy Dwayne Dubois," I told him.

When I got nothing back, I jumped again. Desmond had closed on us by then to keep an eye on the rest of the cracker trash. They were still in throes of wonderment, didn't know what exactly had happened to them. They weren't used to such a steep transition from shiftlessness to anguish, and they were peeved and stung and waving around their rusty pistols and sheath knives.

"Hell," Dale said. "What the shit was all that?"

Dale looked like he had the measles. He'd done the thing he always does when trouble is coming at him. He'd turned around to see just what was headed his way.

"Should have ducked," Desmond told him. "Like him." Desmond jerked his head in my direction.

I jumped up and down on the pile again. "Percy Dwayne Dubois," I said.

My cracker finally suggested, "Talk to Grady."

"Why?"

"He got beef with Percy Dwayne. I don't know shit about it."

My cracker struck me as the sort who would make it a policy not to know shit about much. I got off his pile and told him, "I'd stay there if I was you. Mad gigantic nigger out this way."

He made an I-hear-you-brother noise, so I jumped on his pile one time more.

I was just heading into the Quonset hut when Eugene showed up in the big bay door. There was a compressor running back in the bowels of the place, so he hadn't heard a thing.

"Percy Dwayne problem," he said. Then he caught sight of polka-dotted Dale and the speckled layabout who'd been fool enough to lounge around without his shirt. "What happened to them?"

"Riot ready," I told him. We'd let one go in Eugene's house a few years back, so he knew from high-velocity rubber pellets on the loose.

"How's my hound?" he asked me.

Barbara had dropped to the ground a few yards behind me. She was trying to find her privates to lick underneath the hem of her shirt.

"She's good. I had her. What's the Percy Dwayne problem?"

"They hauled him off somewhere."

"Who?"

"Some of them." He jabbed his thumb back toward the garage.

"Why do folks think life out in the countryside's so damn simple?" I asked Eugene as I stepped onto the slab garage floor and pointed down at Barbara. "Might want to stay here with her."

I'm slow to exasperate anymore. It's probably age and metabolism. I'm hardly the wanton hothead I used to be. Now I build to agitation, do it slowly and over time. Desmond is even more deliberate, and we talk about our upsets. Frequently at the Sonic. We'll mull over our provocations and reason out what to do about them. So it's less like rage and more like slow, considered retribution. But that's all on our end. By the time we pop and swing on a guy, I'm sure he just feels like he's getting punched all at once and suddenly.

When we arrived on the scene at Grady's, I was hoping just

to talk. I've got kind of a balky shoulder, and my hip goes twingy sometimes. So I was just looking for Percy Dwayne Dubois, wanted to clue him on that Boudrot. I wasn't angling for trouble or hoping for a brawl. For his part, Desmond had gone semi-Pentecostal, but you can only give wall-to-wall crackers the sort of business they require.

So I was primed to a pitch as I mounted the slab and entered the body shop proper.

There at the first, I couldn't see anything. They had fluorescents overhead, but the place was so greasy and dark and massive—tractor hangar size—that gazing into the depths of that garage was like looking at the night sky. A lot of black pricked here and there with stars.

I sure couldn't see Luther and, because of the racket, I couldn't hear him either. A compressor was running just about constantly, and there were two air wrenches going.

Two guys came out of somewhere, told me, "Look out," and went blundering past with a bumper.

"Where's Grady?" I asked them

One of them flung his head toward the back of the place.

The deeper I got in, the more I could see. Luther was talking to a couple of boys near a workbench by the back wall. He was shouting at them really, waving his arms and prancing around. Luther was naturally expressive, so I couldn't be sure he was upset until I'd closed on the three of them close enough to hear him call those boys "cocksuckers." That wasn't Luther's style at all. He was vulgar by lifestyle and pedigree and probably disposition, but he wasn't one of those guys who swore and profaned in the general course of things.

When Luther spied me, he said, "These fuckers," and spat on the cement floor.

"What's the trouble?" I asked him.

"They got Percy Dwayne."

"Where?"

"Won't say." He glared at the homelier of those two fellows, though that was a close call.

They turned out to be brothers. Greers from Arcola who had claims on Percy Dwayne. When I asked them why they'd snatched him, they tried to explain their reasons to me. The prettier one said anyway, "He took some shit and stuff."

"We need him," I said. "You can work this out later."

Those brothers grinned and snorted.

"Which of you is Grady?" I asked them.

The homelier one said, "Him."

He was still pointing when I smacked him with Desmond's Ruger. I caught him just above the ear with the flat bulk of the thing. He had time for one offended glance before he dropped onto the floor.

"Like I said," I was talking to Grady now, "you can work out your Percy Dwayne problems later."

He weighed his options. Me and Luther watched him. He glanced at a mallet on the workbench. Looked around to see who was handy to help him. He might have even have tried to reason how much a pistol blow would hurt.

I guess it was pride and testosterone that caused him to ask me, "Who the fuck are you?"

I held the pistol whipping in reserve and punched him in the stomach. He doubled over and gurgled some. My shoulder ached like hell.

"Should have kicked him," Luther advised me. "Like this." Luther laid into the Greer with a snakeskin boot.

An audience was collecting by then. A dent puller. A paint guy. Some sort of female in a tube top. She lit a Lucky Strike. She had tattooed fingers and an angry cesarean scar.

She asked me and Luther, "What did he do?"

"Insurance company sent us," I told her.

I didn't even need to tell them to mind their own damn business. They appeared to figure an insurance company probably knew what it was about, so they all just sort of wandered back wherever they had come up from.

"Where's Percy Dwayne?" I asked that Greer.

He just drooled and mumbled.

"Bring him?" Luther wanted to know.

"Hell," I said, "I guess."

TWELVE

I couldn't blame Desmond for being upset about the state of his Escalade. When he'd divorced Shawnica and she'd laid claim to the first Cadillac he'd owned, Desmond had sworn he'd buy another one brand new off the lot and keep it precisely the way he wanted it kept. That meant shiny and thoroughly detailed on a regular monthly basis. The money we'd taken off that Boudrot had made all of that possible. Now that Boudrot was loose, Desmond was having to half trash his vehicle to find him.

"Funny, isn't it?" I said, and I touched on the particulars that made the whole business ironic.

I shouldn't have been too terribly surprised that Desmond had a snort for that.

We'd parked Grady from the body shop between Luther and

Dale on the backseat. Eugene was in the way back with his hound and smelling finally better than the dog. Partly because of the extra four feet between us and partly because of the caustic lye soap.

The Gojo in the body shop hadn't done much for Eugene. He'd tell us every now and again, "I itch."

Now we had to deal with Grady Greer who was as fragrant as a camel. Worse still, he was being uncooperative, had no plans to give Percy Dwayne up.

"You can have him back," Luther promised. "We've just got pressing business with him."

"Who's to say I ain't got pressing business?"

"Can I hit him?" Dale wanted to know.

Partly to frustrate Dale and partly because I wanted to be civilized, I tried instead to reason with that Greer from the body shop.

"We'll just need him for a day or two. Then we'll bring him right back to you."

"The hell we will," Luther informed me. "I ain't giving up Percy Dwayne to this shithead."

That Greer snarled at Luther and acquainted him with the harm he'd do to him in the wild.

"Can I hit him?" Dale asked me.

Desmond turned and informed me, "You're steam cleaning every damn thing."

"All right."

I was talking to Desmond, but Dale assumed I was turning him loose on that Greer. No harm much came of it, though. Dale couldn't throw a proper punch out in a bean field. In the back of an Escalade, he was good for even less. He caught that Greer with the sort of blow you might use to discipline a schoolgirl.

"And where the shit are we even going?" Desmond asked me. We were heading back east toward Leland and Indianola by then.

I couldn't say, was largely waiting for Grady Greer to tell us, and Dale hadn't hit him hard enough to tempt him to speak.

"Don't be stupid," I said to that Greer, but he pulled one of those Delta cracker faces that was meant to let me know he'd be as stupid as he pleased.

There wasn't much help for it. "Hit him again," I said, and Dale and Luther and Eugene all thought I was talking to them. I can't be sure how that Greer clung to consciousness after the battering he took. They all hit him about simultaneously from three different directions. It sounded like somebody had thrown a bag of rice down the stairs.

That Greer took a second to collect himself before telling all of us, "Ow."

"I half missed him," Eugene said from the way back as he swung on that Greer again. He caught him flush on the cowlick this time.

"Shit, buddy!" That Greer raised a hand to his head.

"Fucker shot my dogs!" Eugene told him.

"Percy Dwayne?" he asked.

Desmond was already looking for a spot to pull over before I could suggest he ought to. We had too much explaining and co-ercing to do to undertake it over the seat back, so Desmond eased off the road by a catfish pond, rolled up the bank, and parked on the levee. The place stank of guano and floaters, a ripe variation on eau de Eugene.

"Get him out," Desmond barked at Dale.

Dale looked like he was going bristle until Desmond pointed to a spot down the levee. "You can swing on him over there."

Dale liked the sound of that and dragged that Greer out of

the car by his collar. He tried to anyway, but that Greer had run
up on Dale before. It turned out Dale had written Grady Greer
a summons or two, had even pulled his sainted mother over up
at Metcalfe, a woman who'd never driven above forty in her life.
So that Greer had simmering resentment for Dale, which Dale
failed to factor in.

We hadn't bound him up or anything, given how thoroughly
outnumbered he was, so that Greer let himself get fished out of
the Escalade by his collar until he was upright on the levee, where
he felled Dale with a blow.

"Hey!" Dale said to him.

He was sprawled on his ass in the dirt by then. The "Hey!" was
mostly for us. Dale seemed to think we should have stopped that
Greer from hauling off and slugging him or, at the very least,
should have been beating him out of collegial indignation.
Instead we were all just standing there wondering what might
happen next.

"Don't remember me, do you?" that Greer asked Dale.

"I don't know you," Dale told him. Dale gripped his chin and
wiggled it some, just to see if all the parts and pieces were un-
fractured and connected. Dale did that like most people ream
their ears or pick their noses given how often civilians wanted to
hit him and how frequently they did.

"Ruleville," that Greer said. "2008. October. And I'll tell you
now what I told you then. I wasn't doing shit."

"Ticket?" I asked him.

Grady Greer nodded. "Sixty goddamned dollars."

That was enough of a scalding reminder to prompt him to
kick Dale hard one time.

"Hey!" Dale was talking to us again.

"Get up," Desmond told him.

That was no easy thing for Dale in ordinary circumstances,

given how thick and lumpy he'd become. With an indignant Greer flailing at him, he was slower even than normal.

"If we stand here," I said, "and don't do a damn thing, are you going to give us Percy Dwayne?"

That was closer to the kind of bargain that Greer figured he could live with.

Dale, of course, just told all of us, "Hey!"

"Daddy's got him. Him and Uncle Flo. You'll need to work it out with them."

"About money?" Desmond asked him.

"Ain't it always?"

"You'll take us?"

That Greer nodded my way.

"Well," I said. "Go ahead."

If Dale could have run, he would have. Instead he got knocked back down on the levee, and the fun was just beginning when my phone rang in my pocket. It was Kendell calling *me* this time. He usually got to me through Desmond.

"Yeah," I said to him.

"Where are you?" Kendell asked me.

"Over toward Greenville. You heard from Tula?"

"About an hour ago. On her way back from Baton Rouge. Around Brookhaven. She said for me to tell you everything's okay."

"Good to hear," I said to Kendell. "Anything new on Boudrot?"

"Nope, but there's a thing you need to see."

"We're kind of in the middle of something."

Dale said, "Hey!" He added, "Come on!" That Greer was laying on top of Dale and elbowing everything he could reach.

"Is that Dale?" Kendell asked me.

"Yeah. A guy's beating the hell out of him."

Kendell knew better than to be surprised by the news. "Once you're done," Kendell told me, "why don't you come on home."

"My home?" I asked him.

"Yeah," he said. "What's left of it."

Lucky for us, Dale and that Greer were too old to fight for long. They snarled at each other and punched and rolled around on the levee for a bit. After maybe ten minutes, they were locked in what would have looked like a loving embrace in lamplight on a queen-sized bed.

That's when Desmond kicked the heap and told them both, "Get up."

Naturally, they brought a bunch of levee filth into Desmond's Escalade, which Desmond reminded me about intermittently all the way to Indianola.

"What exactly did he say?" he finally asked me of Kendell.

"I got the feeling that Boudrot's been by Pearl's."

Had he ever, as it turned out.

Kendell's cruiser was parked in the road out front. Kendell was standing in the driveway between Pearl's house and the car shed. There was in imperial blue Nissan parked (I'll call it) in the backyard. The driver's door was standing open. The lid of the trunk was raised like whoever had rolled up in it had bailed out and fetched his stuff.

I glanced at Pearl's Buick in the pullout where she usually parked. Luther's truck was still alongside. They both looked untouched. I couldn't say the same about the side screen porch. All of the screen wire was slashed and ripped.

I was hardly out of the Escalade before I asked Kendell, "He bust in the house?"

"Busted in all over."

Kendell pointed toward the car shed. The bay doors were standing open, and I got a sick feeling that told me everything I needed to know.

That car shed bay was the tidiest part of Pearl's residential holdings. It had been her late husband's workshop and refuge. She'd honored Gil's memory by leaving it be. The cement was shiny. The tools were hung, ranked by size on Gil's pegboard. Even the yellow jack stands looked like they'd been simonized. But there was a big vacant slot right there in the middle where my Ranchero should have been.

"Stole it?" Desmond shouted to me from back by the Escalade. I nodded. I told him, "Again."

That's how I'd met that Boudrot the first time. He'd stolen Gil's calypso coral Ranchero. Or rather Percy Dwayne Dubois had stolen it from me and that Boudrot had taken it from him. The trouble was, I'd just borrowed it because my Chevy was in the shop, so it wasn't like it was up to me to let the thing stay stolen. I'd told Pearl I'd bring it back to her just like I'd driven it off, so I wasn't about to rest until I got that Ranchero back.

Since then, I'd bought the thing from Pearl, gave her cash for the title. So I guess I could have decided that I didn't need it back. I could have told Kendell, "It's just a car." I could have stood there before that empty bay and been philosophical about it. I could have reasoned that Boudrot stealing my Ranchero yet another time was a sign that I was due for a fresh set of wheels.

I could have done all of that, but I did something else instead.

"Motherfuck," I said, which earned me one of Kendell's Baptist glares. "That's a dead man."

"I didn't hear that," Kendell told me.

"Want him in a box or a bag?" I asked him.

"Didn't hear that either."

Kendell pointed to the stairway that led up to my apartment.

"What did he do?" I asked.

Kendell shook his head. "Some kind of human tornado thing."

That Boudrot had started with the door. I got up to the landing, thinking my apartment door was merely standing open, but it turned out the only thing left of it was some splintered wood on the hinges. He hadn't been satisfied just to kick it in. That Boudrot had busted it all to bits. The panels had all fallen out once he broken the styles and rails, and he'd taken the time and the effort to bust them all up into kindling.

Most everything else in my puny apartment was simply obliterated. Human tornado was about the size of it. He'd made confetti out of all my stuff. I stood in the middle of the carnage and tried to be philosophical again.

I heard Kendell behind me as he mounted the landing and lingered at the threshold.

"Got to figure," I told him, "that boy's been keeping his energy bottled up."

"Yeah," Kendell said. "Pretty impressive."

I'll admit to being awestruck. That Boudrot had been about as thoroughly destructive as a human could hope to be.

"What do you figure he did it with?" I asked.

Kendell directed me to a mallet on the floor by the far wall. It must have been Gil's and had one of those hard rubber heads that was full of shot.

"Knife too, I guess," Kendell allowed as we considered together the sofa. Most of the stuffing that had been on the inside was on the outside now.

"Pearl's house?" I asked him.

"Not so bad. Busted up her TV. It looks like he took some clothes."

"You got a roadblock up or something?" I toed a heap of

rubble with my boot. It turned out to be all my dinner plates and sandwich saucers gone to litter.

"They're talking about it."

"Who?"

Kendell shrugged. "Bosses."

I heard Luther climbing the stairs. He had taps on the heels of his boots. He stepped inside my destroyed apartment, didn't seem much phased by the mess.

"Grady's raising a fuss," he told me. "Got work and shit to do."

"Who's Grady?" Kendell asked him.

That's when Luther finally tuned in to the wholesale destruction.

"Flat tore it up, didn't he?" he said to Kendell.

"Who's Grady?" Kendell asked me.

"A Greer," I told him.

"The body shop guy?"

I nodded. "He's got some quarrel with Percy Dwayne Dubois. We're trying to sort it out."

I followed Kendell onto the landing from where we could look down on the crew. Desmond had his tailgate dropped and was sweeping out his way back with the whisk broom that he carried to keep his vehicle neat. Eugene and Dale and Barbara were watching him. That Greer was leaning on the Escalade, looking glum and mouthing off. They made for a wretched sight as far as clutches of people go. Eugene was scarlet from the lye soap. Dale and that Greer were both splotchy and swollen from various punches they'd taken. Their clothes hadn't been much improved by rolling around on the levee either.

Kendell looked on for a quarter minute. He said, "Hmm," through his nose primarily. He adjusted his belt, laid his hand to the hilt of pistol. When he finally settled on what to ask me, it was, "Why's that dog wearing a shirt?"

THIRTEEN

In Pearl's house that Boudrot had busted whatever he could reach on his route through the place. He'd kicked in the den door off the back screened porch and had knocked Pearl's TV onto the carpet. It looked like he'd broken the screen with Pearl's floor lamp. He'd pitched her magazines all over the place and had blundered into the dining room where he'd shattered Pearl's cake plate and both her pickle dishes. He'd broken the mirror on her sideboard and thrown her candlesticks into the kitchen. He'd even jerked her drapes onto the floor, had yanked the curtain rods out of the wall.

I had come inside with Desmond and Kendell to survey the destruction.

"What do you figure he has against curtains?" Desmond asked as he surveyed the damage.

We had to figure out how to lock up Pearl's house, no easy thing with the back door kicked in, but we found enough plywood to plug the doorway up and then gathered on the driveway to work out how best to proceed.

I know now it was along about then when Tula met with trouble. She called me, and I eventually got her message, but my phone never rang in my pocket, one of those cellular hiccups that seem to happen all the damn time. When I finally heard her voicemail, a good three or four hours later, it was Tula calling to ask me, "What are you doing way down here?"

The Delta's a fairly sizable place—a hundred miles long and seventy wide—but the people are all concentrated in pockets here and there. The humans are crowded around the edges to make room for the agriculture, to leave the arable land wide open for the crops to thrive and the planes to dust. So there are clumps of populated Delta like oases in the desert, and not so terribly many spots where people congregate.

On her way back up from Baton Rouge, where she'd dropped C.J. and the dog with her aunt, Tula had left the interstate at Jackson and headed north on 49. That took her straight up by Yazoo City and, as I understand it now, she was sitting at a light in the commercial clottage on the north side of town when she caught sight of my Ranchero in the lot of a shopping plaza. I knew the spot well enough myself. It was adjacent to the Yazoo Sonic, which me and Desmond had stopped at for lunch a few times in a pinch.

So I was acquainted with that shopping plaza. I'd sat and looked out on its lot. There was Kroger at the near end. A lady's boutique in the middle. Some kind of cut-rate drugstore just beyond it, and a payday loan place down from that. As I understand it now, my Ranchero was parked catty-cornered in front of the loan shop, and the sight of it had tempted Tula off the road and into the lot.

There weren't so terribly many calypso-coral Ranchero's around. Maybe only mine. I'd seen a blue one once, but it was half beat to pieces. El Caminos were far more common, but nobody kept them up.

So there wasn't much chance that Tula would fail to notice that Ranchero, and it was decidedly unlikely she'd doubt that it was mine. The way I heard it, she got out of her Honda and glanced in the cab of my Ranchero. Everything looked normal but for the bag of Cheez Doodles on the passenger seat and the skinny Red Bull can sitting on the console. Those weren't part of my standard diet, but Tula was ready to file them both under the heading of The Shit Men'll Do When They Think You're Not Looking.

That's just when that Boudrot came out of the payday loan store in one of Gil's seersucker sport coats. That Boudrot wasn't wearing the thing with any flare to speak of. It was just hanging on him like a cheap slipcover on a couch. He was carrying a freighted shopping bag in one hand and a pistol in the other. One of those thin white shopping bags with THANK YOU! printed on it. Tula noticed it was crammed full of loose cash money before she even saw the gun.

And there she was standing hard alongside that Boudrot's getaway car. They were both accomplished enough in their fields for things to come to a head dead quick.

Tula told that Boudrot, "Police," as she reached for the weapon she carried off duty. It was a .380 she kept in a snapped-down holster around in the small of her back.

So she needed to reach while that Boudrot had a revolver already at hand. My revolver as it turned out, a .38 I keep in my glove compartment. The way I heard it, he swung it on Tula and caught her flush on the side of the head. She toppled toward my Ranchero and fell half in the bed. That Boudrot popped her another time and tipped her in entirely. Then he tossed his bag of money in the cab, piled in behind it and took off. He stopped up the road somewhere. By then he'd found all the stuff that me and Desmond tend to use in the course of rough days on the job. I had a full roll of duct tape in the console along with a box of .38 rounds and a package of three-mil plastic sheeting. The kind you buy in the homewares store if you're thinking of painting your bedroom. Or if you're worried about some fool bleeding all over your area rug.

All Tula knew when she came around was that she was taped in place all over and wrapped up with a plastic drop cloth in the cargo bed of my Ranchero. That Boudrot seemed to be racing somewhere on an agonizingly bumpy road.

Back at Pearl's, right at that very time, we were working on Grady Greer to see how we might free up Percy Dwayne. Desmond and Kendell were in agreement that Percy Dwayne was safer where he was than out with us in the Escalade riding the roads and looking for trouble.

"What about that wife of his and little P.D. Junior?" I asked them.

"She's a Vardaman," Luther and Desmond and even Kendell told me all at once. They said it like being a Vardaman was like being a Tyrannosaurus.

"I know she's mean as hell," I told them, "but she's not bulletproof. And at the very least we need to let Percy Dwayne know that Boudrot's running free."

I finally convinced them the decent thing to do was locate Percy Dwayne, tell him that Boudrot was loose from Parchman, and let him do what he wanted after that.

Even Luther, Percy Dwayne's nephew, decided that was fair enough to suit him, and he immediately closed on Grady and said, "All right, then. Where's he at?"

"I told you. Daddy's got him. Him and Uncle Flo."

"Where?" Kendell asked.

That Greer country pointed nowhere much. "Farm," he said.

"Why?" Kendell asked him.

"They didn't go into it much. Sounds like that Dubois beat them out of some cash."

"You going to show us where?" Desmond asked.

That Greer just nodded. He said, "All right, but I ain't got all day."

With that he piled onto the backseat of Desmond's Escalade. That Greer told us, "Come on, dammit," like we'd been ballast all along.

We left Kendell at Pearl's, and I probably would have checked in with Tula along about then, but I didn't want to tell her what I was up to and who with exactly. She didn't approve of Dale and wouldn't have had much use for Luther. Throw in that Greer and Eugene and a hound in a Mandrell Sisters T-shirt, and I was riding around in her idea of shiftless hell on earth. And she didn't like to be checked in with anyway in the general course of things, always took it somehow as constricting and more than a little nosy.

At least that's how I've worked it out in my head ever since that afternoon. I let myself off for having not called her because she didn't like getting called.

I thought we'd never get to that Greer's daddy's farm. It was way up the hell in the middle of no damn where. That's saying a lot in the Delta where most every place is nowhere much. But this spread was well off the paved road, no asphalt near it for miles. It was up in Bolivar County somewhere in the vicinity of Rosedale. We rode right by that house in Beulah where we'd hauled that woman's donkeys.

I was about to point it out when Desmond grumbled my way, "Shit."

It didn't help that Grady Greer didn't seem to know where his daddy lived. He sent us down a road that ended in a hedge-row.

"All right now, wait a minute," was all he said.

"Want me to hit him?" Dale asked us.

"Ain't you wasted enough time," Eugene asked Dale, "getting your sorry ass kicked?"

"There they are," that Greer told us and pointed.

We could see a tin roof through the scrub.

"Got to go around," that Greer said to Desmond. "Back to the junction and over. I had you turn a little short."

A good four miles later we were easing up the track that passed with that Greer's daddy for a driveway. I think his house had a trailer in it somewhere, one of those stubby single-wides that was probably the core of the entire structure. He'd just added on rooms and wings and breezeways as the mood struck him and the need arose. He had Tyvek instead of siding and blue tarp where there wasn't tin.

That Greer's daddy and his brother, the Uncle Flo we'd heard about, came out on the front porch when they heard us rolling up. Uncle Flo had a Buntline revolver shoved down in his pants. That Greer's daddy was holding a rifle that looked for all the world like a musket.

"I ain't getting out," I heard Luther say.

"I'm all right back here," Eugene told us.

We actively wanted Dale to stay in the car, but he had his door open before we'd stopped. He was a tip-of-the-spear sort of guy without the feel or capacity for it.

"What the hell's all this?" Dale shouted toward the house.

Our Greer, of course, was still in the car, so those gentlemen had no earthly idea who we were or why we'd come. It wasn't the Greer way to call ahead or to even have a phone. So there was an

Escalade with a bunch of guys inside it and Dale out as our mouthpiece, and he looked as rough as a fellow could look. His face was scarlet and puffy. His knuckles were all skinned up, and he was filthy from rolling around on the ground while getting punched and scuffed.

Those Greer brothers did about the only thing gentlemen of their vintage could do. They both leveled their guns at Dale and warned him that they'd shoot him about a half a second before both of them fired and missed. Uncle Flo put a round in one of Desmond's headlights while that Greer's daddy scattered shot all over the place. It sounded like sand on the windshield and the hood. It might have been salt by the racket of it, but that didn't make much difference to Desmond.

He threw open his door and rolled out of his seat to tell those fellows, "Hey!"

So now, in addition to Dale, there was a big black guy in their yard. Naturally, they trained fire on him as well. These were hardly the sort of men to much trouble themselves with consequences. This time the Buntline bullet hit the bumper, and that Greer's daddy's rifle smoked when he pulled the trigger. There was a fizzle somewhere back in the works, and then the thing caught fire.

"Throw it!" our Greer bellowed from the backseat.

His daddy did just that. He flung that rifle into the yard where it went off and hit the pump house. Then the stock fell off the barrel, and the whole thing came apart.

"Just hold on here." I was out by then. I turned and told our Greer, "Come on."

He stuck his head up over the open back door, "Hell, Daddy," he said.

It looked for a second there like Uncle Flo might draw a bead on our Greer. There wasn't much doubt he wanted to.

"Shit, it's Grady," he told Grady's daddy.

"Let him be," Grady's daddy said to his brother with weary resignation. He shook his head at the sight of his son. He dredged some phlegm and spat.

"What did you do?" I asked our Greer.

"We kind of fell out," he told me.

That was a going local trend, as far as I could tell. Families went to loggerheads over every damn thing in the Delta, from "Why's my wife in your house naked?" to "Where'd my pack of Old Golds go?"

"Money?" I asked our Greer.

He shook his head and told me, "Martha."

"Don't you even say her name!" Uncle Flo shouted our way. "Best damn squeeze I ever had."

"You stole *his* girl?" Luther asked. He was out and standing by now.

"Wife," our Greer confessed. "I was kind of gone on applejack."

"Your aunt?" Dale asked him. There were lines Dale drew when it came to women, and apparently fooling with uncles' wives was a fairly bright one for him.

For Luther too, to judge by his squawking. "She as old as him?" he wanted to know.

Our Greer hung his head and nodded. "I told you," he said. "Applejack."

"Maybe you can work all this out later," I suggested to Uncle Flo.

He spat just like his brother had. "Ain't so sure," he said.

I could tell by the neck noises Desmond was making that he was building toward a conniption. The longer he got to study his car, the worse he felt about it. If I let him reach the point where he got indignant enough, somebody would have to die or at least suffer monumentally.

Desmond was sure to sail up onto the porch and grab

whichever Greer was handy and pitch him around the property until he was fit for stew. If Desmond had any energy left after that, he'd go get the other one, and there weren't enough muskets and Buntline revolvers around to even slow him down.

"I'll get you another one," I told Desmond, and I jabbed my thumb toward his Escalade.

"New off the lot," Desmond said.

"All right."

"Loaded."

Me and Desmond still had most of the cash we'd taken off that Boudrot the first time around. We kept it in a toolbox on a shelf down in Pearl's basement. I had to figure I had four or five Escalades worth of money left.

"You're on your own for rims," I told him.

"Using these," Desmond said and pointed at one of his current gleaming, faceted specimens. "Ain't nobody shot them yet."

"Keep all them down here," I said to Desmond as I moved toward the porch riser.

Dale made a move to come with me, but not a strident, decisive one. So all Desmond had to do was raise a hand and tell him, "Naw."

"You got Percy Dwayne Dubois in there somewhere?" I shouted up to those Greer brothers as I mounted the stairs.

"Who the hell wants to know?" Uncle Flo trained his revolver on me.

"I do, shithead." I cleared two risers.

"Far enough, buddy."

The sight of that Buntline pointed my way just made me hotter still.

"Lower that damn thing."

Uncle Flo chose otherwise. I heard the hammer click as he drew it back, like tumblers in a lock.

I'd had plenty of guns pointed at me through the years, in law enforcement and repo and even out in the natural world. A fellow with a gun usually felt like he was obliged to point it at something. If you'd shown up to arrest him or reclaim his Xbox, it might as well be you.

The worst thing I could do was stop or show even a hint of wavering. I couldn't let the likes of Uncle Flo cow me with a gun.

"I'm going to shove that thing right up your ass."

Among the threats I could have selected, that turned out to be a poor choice. I couldn't have known about Uncle Flo's history of hemorrhoids and various anal calamities. So I didn't imagine that he'd be especially sensitive about what got shoved and where. For me, it was just something to say. There's a world of places a Buntline revolver won't fit with ease or grace, and a man's bunghole is surely one of them.

Then I heard our Greer yell, "Don't!"

And damned if Uncle Flo didn't pull the stinking trigger. I heard the hammer hit the pin with a dull thunk. Then I just stood there and waited to die, but beyond the thunk nothing really happened. Uncle Flo, as it turned out, went around with an empty chamber for safety's sake, and the hammer just happened to come down on it after the several shots he'd fire. It was just dumb luck. That's the only thing that spared me. I was maybe four feet away from him. He would have been hard-pressed to miss.

I didn't give that fool the chance to squeeze the trigger again. I took the last two stairs in one bound and yanked the gun out of Uncle Flo's hand. It was shortly thereafter that I got to hear all about his rectal troubles because I kicked him so hard in the ass that I sent him sailing off the porch. There wasn't any shrubbery to break his fall. He landed on an ancient wheelbarrow carcass and a chunk of tractor tire.

"Hell, man," I shouted down his way, "what are you thinking?"

He just stayed where he was and whimpered. I turned and hurled that Buntline revolver out into the weedy side yard.

That Greer's daddy opened his mouth like he had a thing he wanted to tell me.

"Shut up," I said.

He reconsidered.

"Where's Percy Dwayne?" I asked him.

Whatever they'd been planning on, he knew it was all over.

"In here," he told me, and I followed that Greer's daddy into the house.

The place smelled like the inside of brogan in July, and the rooms were all piled up and heaped with clothes and junk and human litter. The whole place looked like the sort of nest a rat would build on a dare.

That Greer led me down his dingy hallway to what proved a closet door. He had a ladder-back chair cocked under the knob that he kicked out of the way. He flung open the door. That closet was in the shape of the rest of the house. There was one bare wire hanger left on the rod. Everything was down on the floor, including Percy Dwayne who was curled up asleep on about a foot and a half worth of junk.

"What's the story here?" I asked that Greer.

Percy Dwayne groaned and turned his back to us, snored a little.

"Stole from us."

"He steals from everybody."

"It was shit we couldn't have stole."

In my experience with Percy Dwayne, he had an unerring sense of stealing shit people simply couldn't have stole.

"You going to bring him back?"

"You really want him?"

"It's Flo mostly. I'd have just kicked him around and left it at that."

"You can kick him around now if you want to. I can give you a few minutes."

But all the spark had gone out of the enterprise by then.

I poked Percy Dwayne with the toe of my boot. He groaned and stretched and rolled.

He looked at me. He eyed that Greer.

"Come on," I said.

Percy Dwayne yawned and kneaded a shoulder kink. He asked me finally, "Why?"

We left our Greer at his daddy's house to help nurse on his uncle who was sitting up by the time me and Percy Dwayne came out onto the porch. I got a dose of news straight from Uncle Flo about his various posterior complaints.

"Anything broken?" I asked him.

"Hell, I don't know."

If Uncle Flo had said he was all right, I think I would have kicked him a time or two just because. Instead I let "I don't know" and a tender backside get him off the hook.

Me and Desmond and Dale and Luther and Eugene and Barbara and Percy Dwayne all piled in Desmond's Escalade and backed out of the yard at breakneck speed. That wasn't normally Desmond's way, but he'd moved on to his new car already.

"I'm thinking yellow this time around. You know, that creamed corn color they've got."

I didn't know what to say for a few seconds there. "We talking Cadillacs?" I finally asked him.

Desmond nodded. "Black's all right," he said. "But awful hot in the sun."

He was flat racing along the gravel road that led from the Greer farm to the blacktop. Rocks were pinging off the fender wells and dust was boiling up all over.

"Act like you still love her a little," I told him.

"Can't," Desmond said back. "Don't."

We arrived at the junction by the blacktop in pretty much a full skid.

"What's with him?" Percy Dwayne asked of Desmond. "And where are we going anyway?"

I swung around and told him over the seat back, "You're welcome all to hell."

He took a few seconds to consider what he might need to be grateful about. "Them?" he finally asked me and did a spot of country pointing. "I'd have gotten loose whenever I wanted."

"They had you shut up in a closet."

"They didn't mean no harm," Percy Dwayne insisted.

"One of them tried to shoot him," Luther said.

"But for an empty chamber," I told Percy Dwayne, "I'd be dead."

Percy Dwayne gave that some thought as well. He seemed to believe he ought to say something sympathetic and compassionate, but he was too much of a thieving lowlife cracker to know what that might be. "Yeah," he finally said my way. "Well."

Desmond short-circuited the niceties directly after that. "Boudrot's out," he barked at Percy Dwayne without letting his gaze stray from the road. A good thing since we were roaring down the blacktop toward the truck route at about ninety.

"What Boudrot?"

"Fuckstick," Luther told his uncle. "Run off from a road crew."

"So?"

Eugene piped in from the way back, "Killed all my dogs."

"What's that then?" Percy Dwayne pointed with his nose at Barbara.

"She's shot too, just not enough."

"Whatever went with the Mandrell sisters? They in Branson or somewhere?" Percy Dwayne wanted to know.

"Hit him," me and Desmond told Dale in two-part harmony.

Dale grinned and then winced because of his bruises and laid-open places. He drew back and punched Percy Dwayne in the ear.

We came out on the truck route over by Leland between Lusco's and the Kermit the Frog Museum.

"Where are we going?" Desmond asked me.

That was a fair enough question, and I was working on an answer when my phone buzzed in my pocket. That's when I got the voicemail from Tula. It was nearly three hours old.

"Which way?" Desmond wanted to know.

"Call Kendell," I said.

"What's up?" Desmond asked me.

"I think Tula found Boudrot." I played her message for Desmond.

Desmond was trying to reach Kendell when a call came buzzing in on my phone.

I checked the screen. "It's her," I said. I answered the call, said, "Hey."

There was only car noise there at first and shitty country music.

"Hey," that Boudrot finally told me, "fucker."

FOURTEEN

Now the cops got profoundly interested. That's the galling thing about police. They seem to hold back their fury and passion when just civilians are involved, but once an officer is in peril there's hardly anything they won't do.

"He's got Tula," was about all Desmond needed to say to Kendell.

"Let me make a few calls," Kendell told him, and he was off the line.

"Got your girl," that Boudrot had told me.

He was just guessing, as it turned out. Of course, I'd jumped right in and confirmed for him that Tula was something special to me. I'd described to that Boudrot in detail the way I'd take him apart if he caused her any harm.

He'd cackled. He had a heck of a cackle, an evil genius sort of thing. "Thought so," he'd said and had added, "Catch you later."

He'd cut me off in the middle of another animated threat. I'd been stewing ever since. I couldn't help but figure I'd ratcheted up the danger on Tula. It didn't help that Percy Dwayne was keen to tell us everything about that Boudrot that his wife had told him after that Boudrot had nabbed her a few years back.

"Sissy says he's a hound," Percy Dwayne informed us. "Always drinking them energy drinks. Got this Red Bull hard-on all the time."

Knowing Percy Dwayne, I imagine he thought he was being helpful. He probably felt sure he was telling us stuff about that Boudrot we needed to know. So I didn't hit him or even turn around and bark at him. I was consoled, to the extent I could be, by what I knew of Tula. She was just the sort of creature who'd snap a Red Bull hard-on off.

"Bag still at Junior's?" I asked Desmond.

He nodded. "Get it?"

"Yeah."

Junior was related to Desmond's mother in some complicated fashion I'd never quite puzzled out. He was a cousin by marriage or a step-in-law. I was only certain that he had a storm cellar where me and Desmond sometimes stored our accumulated armaments. We had a big duffel full of guns that I used to keep in my car shed apartment until Pearl saw me fooling with it one day when she showed up to drop off a cobbler.

She was such a helpless prattler that I knew she'd talk about it at canasta or garden club or ladies' circle at the church. Then word would travel, like word does, through various family trees, until it reached some shiftless far-flung lowlife down a branch somewhere, and I'd come home one day to find me and Desmond comprehensively unarmed.

So now we shifted that bag of guns around like an unpapered refugee. Since we wanted to keep Junior's cellar a secret, we stopped at a chicken place in Web. We bought those boys a bucket to keep them busy and left them there at the restaurant. Me and Desmond rode over on our own to pick our duffel up.

"Tula'll be all right," Desmond told me on the way. "She won't even be scared. She's a hard case."

I think I managed some nodding. "I let him know she's my girl. I should have known better than that."

"He won't hurt her." Desmond was just gassing now. "Sure won't kill her," he said. "He wants us, and he won't get us if he does a thing to her."

"Happy coincidence," I told Desmond. "I sure as shit want him back."

Junior was home, of course, playing some game on his TV. Desmond had set him up with a repoed plasma and a PlayStation we'd confiscated, so now Junior both collected disability from some vague lumbar complaint and sat around killing zombies and Nazis all day.

Desmond knocked on the door screen, and Junior told us (pretty much like he always did), "I ain't said nothing to nobody."

"Good," I told him through the screen wire.

Desmond opened the door and headed straight back into Junior's kitchen. We kept a key hidden in a cabinet Junior never cleaned or used. I stood there and watched Junior cut an undead Nazi colonel in half with a Thompson submachine gun.

"So sometimes they're zombies and Nazis both?"

Junior looked at me like I was stone-cold fool. He gave a little snort and said, "Yeah."

Junior's place had a proper root cellar out in the backyard by a ramshackle shed. It had been dug out by hand and then walled around with planks like a mine shaft. There were dusty jars of preserves down there from God only knew when. Just them and our canvas surplus duffel.

"Want them all?" Desmond asked me.

"I guess. How are we for ammo?"

He dragged the thing over to the block of sunlight below the open cellar doors. Desmond unzipped the bag, poked around, pulled out three full boxes of bullets and one that looked like about a third spent.

"If that won't do it, it shouldn't get done," I told him.

We swung back by the chicken place to pick up the boys.

"Where to?" Desmond asked me.

"Can't you track her phone or something?" Luther wanted to know.

"I can't," I told him. "Think Kendell can?" I asked Desmond.

"Probably. Maybe."

Desmond called Kendell and did quite a lot of listening.

"He's on it," Desmond said once he'd tossed his phone back into the cup holder.

"What's he want us to do?"

"He knew better than to say."

We ended up taking a kind of spontaneous vote on where we ought to go. Dale figured he'd head to Jackson if he was that Boudrot, but we didn't put any stock in that.

"And him with a hostage?" I asked Dale. "Lot of cops in Jackson."

Luther and Percy Dwayne were all for Vicksburg.

"Steak place down there," Luther told me. "Some buddy of that Boudrot runs it."

"Thought it was his cousin," Percy Dwayne said.

Eugene chimed in from the way back to tell us all, "Naw."

Eugene had actually worked for that Boudrot in the meth

cooking business. He'd hauled chemicals and Mexicans in his jackleg state-body truck.

"Boy at the steak house did time with him. They beat some guy near to death and got a couple of years in Rayburn."

"Know him?" I asked Eugene.

"Been to his place once or twice. Steak's all right."

"Think that Boudrot might go there?" Desmond wanted to know.

Eugene shrugged. "Only friend of his I ever heard about."

We didn't have any better options. "Vicksburg, I guess," I said to Desmond.

We all pumped Eugene for Boudrot details on the way down Delta. It turned out the guy who ran the steak place was an Acadian fuckstick too. He sounded to be a notch or two down from Boudrot volatility.

"He got shot or something," Eugene told us. "Eased off with shit after that."

"What if we snatch that boy?" Dale suggested. "Make some kind of swap?"

I'd never heard a good idea out of Dale, so I was ready to dismiss this one until Desmond grumbled in an approving sort of way.

"Really?" I asked him.

"Might could work," he said.

"Why would he care?"

Desmond shrugged. "Prison buddies. You know how they get."

That sure put an unsavory image in my head.

"That Boudrot," Eugene informed us, "don't give a happy damn about nobody."

Luther and Percy Dwayne chimed in with, "He don't."

On the way to Vicksburg, Luther and Percy Dwayne and

Eugene all reached a consensus that the Boudrot we were after was a southern Delta sort of creature.

"Up Delta for prison maybe," Luther said, "but down Delta for everything else."

"He got any houses left?" I asked Eugene.

"I think you burned them all down," he told me.

"Aside from this place in Vicksburg, anywhere you remember him hanging out?"

Eugene passed a half minute in fairly deep study. "Oh yeah," he said. "My house sometimes. Liked to shoot stuff off the deck."

"The way they tell it," Percy Dwayne started in, "he kind of tore your house to pieces."

"How bad was it anyway?" Eugene asked me and Desmond.

We hadn't truly gotten past the hounds with Eugene. That had seemed like trouble enough.

"Kicked your door in," I told him. "Sliced up your sofa. That big cabinet? The one by the window? He pushed it over on the floor."

"I kind of did that," Eugene said. "And I seem to recall I tore up the couch."

I waited for an explanation, and Eugene didn't disappoint.

"Got a new knife," he told me. "Bottle of Ancient Age."

"Did you happen to kick your door in?" I wanted to know.

He didn't seem to believe he had.

Kendell checked in when we were nearly to Vicksburg to share with us how little he knew. Tula's phone was shut off, as best as anybody could tell.

"The man's no fool," Kendell told me. "Where are you headed?" he wanted to know.

"Vicksburg. Going to check on some prison buddy."

"Desmond too?" Kendell wanted to know.

"Yeah."

"He tell you about his trouble down there?"

"What trouble?" I glanced at Desmond. He didn't squirm exactly, but he twitched.

"Had a girlfriend a while back. She's got a bunch of brothers and cousins angling to kill him."

"Haven't heard about her."

"Ask him," Kendell suggested. "I'll call you when I hear something."

"Girlfriend in Vicksburg?" I said to Desmond.

Boy did he have a snort for that.

The way Desmond explained it, she was a Purdy, and they were a large clan down in Vicksburg.

"Went out with her twice maybe," Desmond said. "Found out she wasn't right."

"Nuts?" Luther asked him. Luther had a nose for trouble, and he was sensing some ahead.

Desmond nodded. He showed us a scar on his neck.

"She get a new knife too?" I asked him.

"Fingernails," Desmond told me.

"What did you do to her?" Percy Dwayne wanted to know. His nose for trouble rivaled Luther's.

"Nothing. Took her dancing. She's just wired the wrong way."

"You dance?" I asked Desmond. I knew he glided everywhere he went, but I'd never known him to do it to music.

"Sometimes."

"Big fat white girl?" That was Dale. "That's all you coloreds seem to want."

Me and Desmond knew Dale well enough to hardly hear him anymore.

"White girl all right. A little dumpy," Desmond allowed.

Luther and Percy Dwayne and Eugene as well were all on board with dumpy.

"Plush," Luther told us. It turned out that was the word his Lurleen used about herself.

"So who's mad at you?" I asked Desmond.

"Her brothers. Her cousins. Whole pack of them, I guess."

"Why?"

"She told them all kinds of fool stuff. Said I made her do things . . . you know . . . in the bed."

"What things?" Luther and Percy Dwayne were halfway to the dashboard.

Desmond gave them a look. "Bunch of shit I'd never do."

"Like what?" Luther asked.

"Hit him," Desmond told me.

"I tied a lady up once," Eugene said from the way back. "She wouldn't have it any other way."

Somehow Dale was reminded of how very much he'd like the steak, and he chimed in from the backseat to tell us all about it.

After that we passed a dozen miles in relative silence. We were somewhere between Belzoni and Midnight when Desmond got back to his girlfriend's brothers. "If they get wind I'm in Vicksburg, we're going to have a mess."

"What kind of mess?" I asked him.

"The one with the eye patch," Desmond said, "ought to be locked up in Whitehaven. Rest of them are just mean and stupid, you know, in the regular way."

"Big?"

"Like Dale."

"Stupid like Dale?"

"I heard that," Dale told me.

"Yeah," Desmond said. "But with muscles. Dale's just fat."

"Heard that too."

"If we only go to the steak place, talk to that Boudrot's buddy, what are the chances we see any of them?"

"Purdys all over," Desmond said. "They kind of know my car."

"So she's recent?" I asked him.

"Remember when I told you I was helping my cousin with his shed?"

I recalled a week there a year or so back when Desmond had been scarce and shifty. "Her?" I asked him.

He nodded. "Didn't want to tell you."

"So you knew she was trouble."

"Had a sense," Desmond said. "Couldn't help myself."

"I like a woman who's all half cocked and shit," Luther informed us over the seat back.

"Is Lurleen a wildcat?" I asked him.

Luther moved some spit. He nodded. He told me morosely, "No."

FIFTEEN

Damned if it wasn't a semi-fine restaurant down on the far end of Vicksburg. Past the casino barges. Beyond the renovated downtown. The place had a half-assed view of the highway and the bridge over the river. It had a proper neon sign. The restaurant was just called Ricky's. It looked like it had been a diner or a meat-and-three-spot once.

There were only a couple of cars in the lot. It was around four thirty by then, and Ricky's apparently didn't offer a Golden Corral–style buffet. It seemed to hold itself out as a swanky sit-down place where you ordered off the menu and you gave the waitress a tip.

"Where'd he get that damn cow?" Percy Dwayne wanted to know.

It was a fair question. There was a massive steer on the roof of the restaurant. It looked to be fiberglass. It glowed all over, had some sort of light inside.

"Texas probably," Luther informed us. "They got shit like that all over."

Percy Dwayne just nodded. Now if anyone ever asked him about that steer, he'd say it was from Texas because that's what he'd been told by his nephew who didn't have any better idea where it came from than he did. In my experience, that was the usual pedigree of facts in the Delta. If a man made a confident declaration, then whatever he'd said was probably true. Of course, nobody knowing anything was the abiding chink in the process.

"We all going in?" I asked in a general way.

Everybody but Barbara nodded. The hostess seated us at a big round table in the back.

"Boss here?" I asked her.

She nodded.

"I'd like a word."

I could see across to a service window. She went over and raised him there. Ricky was wearing a chef's tunic and a Saints cap. She talked. She pointed. He looked. He told her something brief and curt and sent her back our way.

Dale and the boys had finished off our entire basket of breadsticks by then. Luther waved the empty basket at the hostess as she approached and told her, "Hey."

She ignored him and came straight to me. "He's a little busy right now. Maybe after you eat."

I saw Ricky the chef cross past the service window. He'd stripped down to just a T-shirt now.

"Kitchen," I told Desmond. "I'll go around back."

Desmond went gliding off toward the service window while I headed out the door. I circled around at a jog past the

Dumpster and intercepted Ricky about halfway to his truck. He spun around and tried to bolt back into the restaurant, but Desmond was coming out of the kitchen by then.

"Just hold on," I told him.

He had a look of desperation we weren't accustomed to inspiring. He was sweaty and twitchy, panting like a lapdog. He had on proper chef pants and green plastic clogs, a RICKY's T-shirt with a likeness of his plastic steer on the back. He looked a lot more like a chef than a felon, but he was sure acting like a lowlife for us.

"I ain't got it," he told me. Then he turned to Desmond and informed him, "I ain't." After that he reached into his pocket and pulled out one of the tiniest guns I'm sure I've ever seen. "I told you next week, and you said it'd be all right."

"We're not them," Desmond said.

Ricky told us, "Like hell."

He pointed his tiny pistol at Desmond. That was exactly the wrong thing to do. Desmond had been shot twice that I knew of and hadn't suffered much for it either time. Consequently, the sight of a gun barrel pointed his way had an eccentric effect on Desmond. His impulse was to glide on over and make it point somewhere else.

That's exactly what he did with Ricky. The man might have been a Parchman grad who'd done real time for assault, but he sure didn't look an awful lot like a killer. He certainly didn't behave like one. He was still only threatening to pull the trigger when Desmond took away his puny gun.

Ricky broke down. He wept and drooled. He begged us to let him take off his trousers because he'd bled already on his other pair and these were the last clean ones he had.

"Just don't break anything," he told us. "Can't do no cooking in a cast."

"What are you talking about?" I asked him.

He cowered as I closed. Cowered more anyway. He was already pretty much in a sniveling crouch. He just got a little smaller and shakier.

"We're not here for money," Desmond said.

"Don't bust up the place." Ricky was blubbering and pleading with us by now.

"We're here about that Boudrot you bunked with," I told him.

He looked from me to Desmond and back to me. "Guy?" Being the Acadian fuckstick version of the name, it came out as a mucousy "Geeee?"

I nodded. Desmond nodded too.

"You ain't down from Memphis?" he asked us.

We both shook our heads.

"Shit," Ricky said. He turned off the spigot and stood upright more or less like a man. "I thought you was them."

"Them who?" I asked him.

"Some fucker with his finger in every damn thing. Making me buy his lousy meat."

"Making you how?" Desmond asked him.

Ricky motioned for us to follow him past the Dumpster. At the side of building he pointed toward a row of shiny new windows.

"Three of them with ball bats. Busted every last window out."

"Wail on you too?" I asked him.

He pulled up his T-shirt. Ricky was wrapped around the torso. "Broke four ribs. Kidney hurts like hell. Don't know what they did to that."

The decent human in me didn't care for this sort of thing, and me and Desmond together could make for about one upstanding citizen between us. I looked at Desmond. He looked at me.

We embraced our civic duty by telling each other, "Well, shit."

"Expecting them today?" Desmond wanted to know.

Ricky nodded. "And I ain't got their money."

"How much?" I asked him.

"Two thousand a month."

"Sounds steep."

"Sure to put me out of business in a month or two," Ricky told us. "How damn stupid is that?"

"We help you with this and you help us with Guy?" That was my proposal.

"Help you how? He's up in Parchman."

"Not no more," Desmond told him. "Killed a fellow already. Got a friend of ours we want back."

"Who the hell let *him* out?" Ricky wanted to know. He said it like he was indignant, like there were people who deserved to rot in Parchman and his buddy, that Bourdrot, was surely one of them.

"Bolted from a work crew," I said. "We thought he might come here."

"Wasn't like that with us," Ricky told me. "I got straightened out up there. Got all that thug shit out of my system. Learned to cook and run a business. Guy just kept on being nuts. He isn't much like the rest of us. He ain't hardly human sometimes."

"Where do you figure he'd go?" I asked him.

Ricky looked from me to Desmond and back again. He started putting things together in his head. "You the guys who burned him out?"

We nodded.

"I heard all about you. He hates you fuckers. And he's got a friend of yours?"

We nodded.

"Wouldn't want to be him."

Once we'd followed Ricky into his restaurant kitchen, Desmond handed him back his gun.

"Get a real one or don't bother."

"Ain't got no bullets in it."

"Only a fool points an empty gun at a fellow."

"Like I told you," Ricky said, "I got reformed."

He fished an envelope out his freezer. "Here's their money. I've just got eight hundred." He offered the envelope to me.

"Just buy us all dinner," I told him. I jabbed my thumb toward the front of the house. "And those boys can eat."

"So what's going to happen?" Ricky asked us.

"You expecting them now?"

"Any time now," Ricky told me.

"We'll make them wish they stayed in Memphis," Desmond said.

It wasn't a plan exactly, but as strategies go it was all right. We decided not to tell Eugene or Percy Dwayne or Luther. We didn't even have to discuss not telling Dale. Me and Desmond were debating what to arm ourselves with from the duffel in the Escalade when a Grand Marquis wheeled into the lot and short-circuited the discussion. Two big guys in shiny suits climbed out and headed for the door. The three of us watched from the service window.

"Them?" Desmond asked.

Ricky sighed and nodded. "Must be."

They both had pistol bulges. Silk ties. Gold watches and rings. I could imagine the cologne before I had to actually smell it.

"Want to talk to them any?" Desmond asked me.

I'm sure he knew I'd tell him, "No."

One of the problems with Dale is he has antenna. He knows trouble when he sees it, but he lacks the instincts and the sound sense to know what he should and shouldn't get up to. So when those two mokes came into the restaurant proper and blew past the hostess without a word, Dale noticed the way the leading one shoved that girl aside with his forearm. He knew he didn't like it much and that it spoke poorly of those fellows.

Dale shoved his chair back and told those gentlemen both at once, "Hold on here."

Back when Dale had all his muscles, passed his evenings lifting weights and dining on supplement milkshakes with anabolic steroid chasers, it might have been enough for him to say, "Hold on here." You couldn't be sure that wasn't a prison-yard physique he'd cultivated. Even a couple of buff guys with pistols from Memphis might be tempted to tread with some care.

But Dale's muscles had all gone to fat in strange places, so the Memphis thug with the sandy hair, the one who looked like a gym-rat surfer, advised Dale, "Sit down, tubby," without even giving him more than a glance.

Of course, Luther and Eugene and Percy Dwayne weren't about to have Dale's back. Dale had far too much of a shithead history to hope for a fellow to throw in with him. Those boys were busy spooning cheese dressing and Bac-O bits over their shredded lettuce salads. They weren't about to give up dinner to help Dale.

"Hey!" Dale shouted at those two guys from Memphis.

They were nearly to the kitchen door by then, but surfer thug didn't like Dale's tone enough to make a detour to Dale's table.

Dale was primed to mouth off to the guy and looked to be putting some hard talk together when surfer thug arrived at Dale's table and knocked Dale over with one punch.

Me and Desmond watched from the service window.

"Brass knuckles?" I asked.

Desmond nodded. "Got them out of his coat pocket. Sure didn't need that shit with Dale."

"I might rethink this," I told Desmond. I hung my eight-inch skillet back up on the pot rack. I took a ten-incher down instead.

"Look," Desmond said.

I went back to the window. Luther and Eugene and Percy Dwayne were dividing up Dale's salad.

The only other customers was an elderly couple down front, and they didn't appear to think anything that went on in the back of the place was their business. Better that they should look out the window and snipe at each other instead.

Those two Memphis thugs pushed on into the kitchen where they came upon me and Desmond and Ricky and a couple of Mexicans who helped Ricky out. A wiry one who washed the dishes and a dumpy one who cooked. They were accustomed to making themselves scarce and disappeared behind the range.

"So?" the thug with the dark hair and the porny mustache said to Ricky.

The sandy-haired surfer thug sized up me and Desmond. He drew back his coat flap so we could see his pistol. "Who the fuck are you?"

Me and Desmond aren't like Dale. We've got no appetite for preambles. I glanced at Desmond. He glanced at me. We went at those boys hard.

When I hit the sandy-haired one with my ten-inch skillet, you'd have thought we were at Churchill Downs. That pan rang as clear and true as a starting bell. That boy considered being unconscious long enough to allow me to reach in and pluck his pistol free. I thought I might have to point it at his colleague, but Desmond had glided over at full speed and was raining blows on him.

Unlike Dale, Desmond knew how to throw a punch with all of his weight behind it, and that other thug had hardly lifted his fists before he was out on his feet. His nose was flattened and bleeding. Desmond had laid him open at both eyebrows. I watched as Desmond lowered his aim and caught that fellow in the gut.

The blond one moaned, so I kicked him.

"Want some of this?" I said to Ricky.

He looked from one heap of thug to the other and shook his head. Maybe he was reformed.

Ricky finally asked me and Desmond, "Now what?"

It was a fair question, and we hadn't worked out all the details. In truth, we hadn't worked out any details at all.

"We beat them or they beat you," Desmond explained to Ricky.

"Fine," he said. "I get all that. But what happens after you leave?"

"Hey." That was Luther from the service window. "Our damn steaks ready yet?"

Luther took in the boys from Memphis piled up on the kitchen floor. Me and Desmond had laid their guns on a cutting board next to the mushrooms that Ricky's assistant had been slicing before he'd evaporated. Luther eyed the pistols, went back to the thugs.

"That one put Dale down." He pointed at the sandy-haired one.

"He all right?" I asked.

Luther glanced back into the restaurant to take a visual reading on Dale. Then he swung back our way to give us a shrug like he didn't quite know and couldn't bring himself to care.

"I'd go on and cook Dale's rib eye," Luther suggested to Ricky. "If he can't handle it, we will."

Ricky said something in Spanish to his helper who came out of hiding and approached the stove.

Me and Desmond dragged those two Memphis enforcers out the back kitchen door. We spoiled their shiny suits in the process what with all the floor grease and the grit. It only seemed proper and decent to turn the hot hose on the pair of them after that. Ricky must have used it to clean his range-hood filters with.

The water that came out of it was tepid at first but scalding shortly thereafter. Once their clothes got wet and steaming, those two gentlemen woke up and did some impressive shrieking and scrambling before we saw fit to shut off the water.

"You're fucking dead," were the first words out of the porny mustache guy's mouth.

Desmond glided over for an editorial session. He popped the guy two good times hard by way of saying, "Think again."

The sandy-haired surfer dude must have been the brains of this particular brace of no-necks.

"What do you want?" he asked us. He didn't bother with bristling and threats.

"What the hell you doing way down here? You don't have business enough in Memphis?"

The surfer thug shrugged. "Tough times," he told me. "Think we like it? Hell of a drive for us."

"Who do you work for?" Desmond wanted to know.

Porny mustache guy told him, "Fuck you."

He must have been fooled by Desmond's girth and monumental stature, wasn't prepared to believe that Desmond was about as quick as a cobra. Desmond wheeled and caught porny mustache guy with a spinning backhand to the jaw. That guy collapsed straight onto the muddy ground in an ungainly heap. There was an elbow here and a wingtip there. A tie knot and pinky ring.

"Don't mind him," surfer thug told us in a low, conspiratorial whisper. "Chief's sister's kid."

"Got it," I told him.

Desmond said, "So you're the brains?"

"I guess," he said. "Here anyway."

I jabbed my thumb toward the restaurant. "You're putting him out of business."

He nodded. "I guess they were thinking we'd pull out four or five large, and that'd be worth all the miles."

"Isn't," Desmond told him.

"How much you getting?" he wanted to know.

"Only steak worth a shit in the whole damn county. Think you'd want to live on Arby's?" I asked him.

"So you eat here?"

We nodded.

"Oh," he said.

"Times might be hard," I told surfer thug, "but they can't be that hard. Take him." I pointed at his colleague who was moaning and wriggling a little now. "Get the hell out of here and don't come back."

"Chief might not like that?"

"You want us in Memphis?" Desmond said.

Surfer thug hesitated, so Desmond kicked his partner as a kind of visual aid.

"I'll talk to the chief. You boys make a lot of sense." He poked the porny mustache guy with the toe of his loafer. "Hey, Larry."

Larry groaned, rolled over, and made a sort of career out of standing up.

"Think I can get my gun back?" Surfer thug asked. "Ex-wife gave it to me."

I nodded in an altogether reasonable way. "If you don't mind carrying it up the road in your colon."

That qualified as advanced logistics for sandy-haired surfer dude. He gave the proposition some thought before he told me, "Keep it."

They both took off their suit coats and trousers out in the parking lot and left Ricky's steak place in just their shirts and briefs. Ricky came around from the back to join us as we watched them head up the road in their Ford sedan.

"They won't be back," I told him.

"Hungry?" Ricky asked us.

"Wouldn't say no to a couple of rib eyes," Desmond said.

"Got anything they didn't sell you?" I asked.

"Tenderloin," Ricky told us and held his finger and thumb three inches apart.

"Ruin his," I said and nodded Desmond's way. "I'll take mine rare."

As Ricky left us, I heard Desmond's Barry White ringtone from his pocket. He fished out his phone.

"Kendell," he told me. He raised the thing to his ear. "Yeah."

Kendell talked for about a quarter minute before Desmond told him, "Hold on."

He turned on his speaker and held the phone so I could hear Kendell too.

"Say it again."

"Got the phone company on the case. Thing doesn't even need to be on. They went through Columbus half an hour ago. Looks like they're headed for Tuscaloosa."

SIXTEEN

Dale had lost a tooth. Not a real tooth but a crown he'd paid good money for, so he was crawling around on his hands and knees when me and Desmond came into the restaurant. There were maybe three other tables by then, in addition to our gang in the back corner, and the other diners made it plain to me and Desmond as we passed that they'd come for a steak and some bad cabernet and not the shit show our boys were putting on. They said it all with frosty glares, but they said it plain enough.

So there we were both saving Ricky's restaurant and driving his customers away.

"Get up," I told Dale.

He showed me the stump where his crown had been before he went down.

I pointed at his chair. He sat.

Desmond dipped into the kitchen to pick up the pistols we'd left there and get Ricky out so we could have a word.

"Ever know that Boudrot to have business in Tuscaloosa?" I asked Eugene.

He was working on something. It turned out to be gristle that he dribbled straight onto his plate.

Ricky had arrived in time to see it, and he told us sadly, "Memphis beef."

"Alabama?" Eugene asked me like I'd figured he probably would.

I nodded. "'Roll Tide' and all that."

"Naw. Stuff in New Orleans. Baton Rouge, I think. Never heard nothing about Alabama."

I turned to Ricky. "Looks like Guy is headed for Tuscaloosa. Any idea why?"

Ricky thought on it for a half minute and then snapped his fingers at us. "This girl used to visit him in Parchman. I think she was from over there."

"What girl?" Desmond asked.

"We were locked up with her brother. She used to come over to see him and got to know Guy. They went conjugal after a while."

"Got a name?" I asked him.

He didn't. "Wasn't much to look at. Hard miles on her, but you can't be too picky in Parchman."

"What happened with her brother?" Desmond asked Ricky.

"Out. Beat a guy cripple. Did ten years. Back on his chopper by now."

"What was his name?" I asked Ricky.

"Bobbie something." Another shrug. "I kind of steered clear of him."

Just then the hostess carried over steaks for me and Desmond, which snagged the regard of Dale and Eugene, Luther and Percy Dwayne too.

"What the hell's them?" Eugene asked.

"Fillet," Ricky told him.

"Can I get one?"

I cut mine in half and forked a portion onto my bread plate. I offered it to Eugene.

"Might have cooked it," he said to me by way of "thanks a bunch."

A couple of boys came in along about then. Whiskers and dungarees and greasy seed caps. One of them had a word with the hostess while the other one just looked at us. Looked at Desmond, I have to guess now. He slapped his buddy on the arm to get him focused on Desmond too. Then they appeared to change their minds about dining and went out just like they'd come in.

"Know them?" I asked Desmond.

He shook his head.

"You?" I said to Ricky.

"The big one's Fred or Frank or something."

"Fred or Frank what?" I asked him.

"Purdy," he said.

"Let's go," Desmond told us, and he was gliding already toward the door before he'd finished talking.

"What about my tooth?" Dale wanted to know.

Eugene grabbed my baked potato.

"Can't we get pie or nothing?" Percy Dwayne wanted to know.

"Nick'll buy you a tooth," Desmond called out to Dale. He'd reached the door and held it open for us.

I drove our crew out ahead of me. They complained the whole way to the lot.

"I'm already buying a Cadillac," I told Desmond.

"So what's an incisor?" he said.

We'd just piled into the Escalade—all of us but for Eugene who'd lifted Barbara out of the way back to let her pee in the steak house lot—when Ricky came out with a pastry box.

"Shortcake," he told us, "for the road."

There were general hosannas from the backseat. Ricky reached into to shake Desmond's hand and then mine, and that's when the Purdys swarmed up from every damn direction they could.

The two who'd come into the restaurant were sitting across the way in their truck, and Purdy Neons and Purdy Geos, even a couple of Purdy Fiestas came flying into the parking, bouncing across the skirting.

Desmond told the bunch of us, "Hold on."

With that he dropped his Escalade into gear and left the steak house the way, I had to think, nobody had left the steak house before. We roared across a weedy patch and down through a ditch toward the blacktop. A Purdy tried to head us off in an orange Wrangler. He came at us off our right flank, and Desmond nudged him with the bumper. It didn't take much to lay that trifling piece of shit right on its side.

"Aw," I heard from Luther. "They going to be stirred up now."

And I was going to say to him, "Now!?" but Percy Dwayne set up a fuss instead.

All the bouncing had wrecked the whipped cream on the shortcake Ricky had supplied us, and Percy Dwayne treated the mess in the pastry box like an authentic catastrophe.

"Look at this," he fairly wailed, and he showed his seat mates the carnage.

"Fucking Purdys," Luther said.

We had Purdy's coming at us like star fighters on the road.

We'd gotten on the blacktop just in time, but they were all turning around wherever they could and chasing behind us.

"You sure you didn't hack her up and throw her in the river?"

"Didn't even get any regular sex."

"What kind of sex did you get?"

"Rather not say."

I didn't press him since Desmond was doing about ninety by
then.

Vicksburg is rather confining. The city is chiefly down by the
river with bluffs above it where all the batteries were during the
Civil War. Desmond raced up Washington Street to Clay and
swung east up out of the city proper. He'd managed to put enough
distance between us and the Purdy posse—those four-cylinder
heaps they drove could barely hold fifty going up hill—to let us
pull off the road at the battlefield without any Purdys seeing us.

The park was closed. It was just past sunset. A chain was up
beside the gatehouse, and Desmond rammed right through it.
The busted chain came whipping around and cracked the back
side window with enough force and racket to distract Dale from
his missing tooth.

He took his finger out of his mouth long enough to tell us,
"Shit."

"I was kind of hoping to trade this in," I told Desmond.

"Might still," he said and hit a speed bump at somewhere
north of forty. Desmond was the only one wearing a seatbelt, so
the rest of us levitated. Fortunately, the lid of the pastry box was
shut because Ricky's shortcake had to be getting close to soup.

Desmond pulled into an overlook with an obelisk and can-
nons. He left the engine running but shut off all the lights.

"Road just go around?" I asked him.

Desmond nodded.

This wasn't your standard Civil War battlefield park, like

Shiloh or Antietam, with treeless stretches of farmland that troops might have charged across. This was all close and wooded on a bluff above the river.

"Got to pee," Luther informed us all, and then the pack of them got out.

Even Barbara came out of the way back, and she followed the boys over to a handsome rock wall where they all drained their bladders. Then they came wandering back to where me and Desmond stood by the Escalade, all of them but for Dale who had a bashful bladder problem. He was still over against the wall when the headlight beams played in the trees.

"Purdys?" I asked Desmond, like he would know somehow.

Whatever car it was had stopped down at the gatehouse and was sitting. We could hear both the ticking of the engine and the racket of a couple of crackers in agitated conversation. The place where we were parked, a half-moon loop called Pemberton Circle, was the first pull out off the main loop if they decided to come in.

I said to Desmond, "So?"

"Could be a couple of boys out drinking."

"And if it's not?"

"They might stay right there," Desmond told me, "this being history and all."

I knew just what he meant. Those Purdys had passed their entire lives in and around Vicksburg, and you could about be sure not a one of them had ever set foot in the battlefield park. Exposure to actual history off plaques and brochures and from scale-built dioramas wasn't a thing they needed when they could just sit drinking forties and being dumb.

So I could imagine the sort of debate those boys were having at the gate. In the few minutes since they'd shown up another car had pulled up behind them. That second guy was playing his radio—some sort of twangy yokel bullshit. They all had to shout over it to be heard.

That helped us there at Pemberton Circle once we'd prevailed upon Dale to be quiet. He'd started in with his molar and the tenderness of his stub. I was going to suggest that he shut the fuck up when Desmond hit him in the stomach. Same result but with moist wheezing instead of the whining I would have earned.

"We can take them," Luther informed us. "Why don't you bust out some of your guns."

"Want to just mow them down?" I asked him.

There in the twilight I watched Luther and Percy Dwayne consult with glances. Then they both turned my way and nodded.

Percy Dwayne asked me, "Why the hell not?"

"You'd go to Parchman for these shitheads?"

"Ain't like we'd ever get found out."

I hadn't passed much quality time with Percy Dwayne and Luther's ilk since back when we'd first tangled with that Boudrot over my Ranchero. So I had pretty much forgotten about the inner workings of their cracker minds. The stew of self-pity and rationalization that passes with their sort for thought.

Here Percy Dwayne and Luther had been chased into a Civil War park by a bunch of guys they hadn't personally done a damn thing to provoke. So if they shot them all down and left them, they'd be well within their rights. Better still, nobody would think to look for them because they weren't down Delta creatures. They were Sunflower County Duboises after all. To their way of thinking, even Purdys should have known they weren't the sort to tolerate getting chased.

"We're not shooting anybody," I told them, "unless there's no help for it."

"Might ought to go ahead and give us a gun," Percy Dwayne suggested.

Desmond took over. He pointed at Dale who was sitting on the asphalt holding his stomach and laboring to breathe.

"Want some of that?" Desmond asked.

"Guess we'll shut the fuck up," Luther told him.

You could educate a Dubois in the short term. The trouble was that it never seemed to take.

It sounded to me like those boys at the gate had fallen into confounded silence. There was an outside chance that one of them was on the phone to Purdy reinforcements. Then they'd just sit there and wait until a whole flotilla of Purdys could swamp the place. More likely, though, they were mulling what a foray into the park might mean.

Desmond was surely correct in assuming they didn't know the territory. The chances were high that at least one of those boys had an outstanding warrant on him, so he wouldn't be at risk for trespass alone but probably some felony too.

"Wait them out?" I asked Desmond.

He appeared set to nod just as Barry White's Love Unlimited Orchestra chimed in from the Escalade cup holder. Desmond's ringtone had long been a snatch of "Satin Soul," long enough probably for a Purdy to have heard it a time or two before.

"Shit," Desmond said.

The Escalade windows weren't just all down. The doors were all standing open. We saw the headlights shift in the treetops as whatever Purdys had gotten out of their cars got back in them. Those tiny engines revved and whine. Barry White seemed to have provoked them. They were coming on in after us, fighting through both their fear of Desmond and their distaste for American history.

"Let's go," I said.

"I ain't running from them." It was Dale on the ground talking bold.

Me and Desmond found we lacked the patience to quarrel with Dale at all.

"Fine," I said. "Be sure and tell them about your tooth."

"I just might." Dale had gone all pouty. There wasn't a thing for us to do but leave him where he was.

The rest of us charged toward the Escalade.

"Go on," Dale said. He'd gone pitiful. Once Dale had made up his mind to do a thing—no matter how ill-considered—it was sort of like a vault door slamming shut. You could only undo his thinking with appreciable time and effort, and we didn't have enough of either to hope to sway him at all.

"They'll pound him," Eugene informed us all.

"Hell," Luther said, "wouldn't you?"

A bend in the loop road served to mask our escape. We pulled out of the north end of Pemberton Circle as those Purdys were pulling in from the south. They came in harder than they should have. A speed bump caught the muffler on one of their coups. Desmond stopped just a little ways up Confederate Avenue, and we sat and listened to what sounded like a Purdy conniption.

One of them set to clucking: "Fuckfuckfuckfuckfuckfuck."

We could hear at least two other Purdys laughing at that boy's distress.

"Touching, isn't it?" Desmond said. "Pack of shitbags," he added.

Then they turned their wholesale attention to Dale and blamed him for the mess they were in.

"Sounds like what? Four?" I asked.

Desmond nodded.

"Five?" Percy Dwayne said. "Listen."

We did.

"Four regular. And that one that sounds like somebody's squeezing his balls."

"You might be right." That was something I'd never said before to Percy Dwayne.

"Am," he told me. "Five of us too. Six with him." He country pointed with his nose in the general galactic direction of Dale.

"What the hell we doing back here?" Eugene asked.

I shifted around to take them all in—Luther and Percy Dwayne, Eugene and Barbara. It was hard to conceive of those boys as musketeers. Particularly where it came to Dale. He didn't inspire that kind of feeling in anybody who knew him even a little.

"You want to go back?" I asked them

"We can swarm on in and take those boys," Luther told me. Then he glanced at Eugene and Percy Dwayne and both of them gave me the dumb show version of "Fuck yeah."

"They're liable to kill him," Percy Dwayne said as if he thought that were a bad thing.

"Been in this damn car all day," Luther said.

I was about to tell Desmond to back on up when we heard the gunshot.

"Hmm," Desmond told me. "I'd feel kind of bad if they killed him."

"Sure hope that Purdy girl was worth it."

Desmond thought about her for a moment before he told me, "Naw."

SEVENTEEN

Instead of backing up, Desmond blew his horn. We could hear those Purdys scrambling.

"They coming," Desmond said.

One of them even squealed his tires a little through the lot.

"Was she as dumb as them?" I asked Desmond.

He nodded. "But built," he told me. "Torpedos."

"I guess you were taking a break from the Lord."

Desmond nodded. "Stray from the path, and see where it gets me."

"Me too, apparently."

We had to wait for those Purdys to finally come out on the north end of Pemberton Circle. I don't know where white trash finds the shit they drive. You've got to do some powerful looking to turn up a Fiat in Mississippi, but damned if the lead car wasn't a Lada Riva. So not even fine Italian craftsmanship but Soviet handiwork instead.

The thing was screaming our way. The duct tape on it caught the light of the rising moon. There was a Fiesta right behind it with its entire exhaust system dragging the ground. Sparks were shooting out like the tail of a comment. We were all a little mesmerized.

"Probably should go," I finally managed to tell Desmond.

He dropped the Escalade into gear and raced ahead about fifty yards.

"Don't lose them," Eugene shouted from the way back.

And there was genuine danger of leaving those Purdys struggling well behind. They had bald tires and tiny engines and busted muffler hangers. If Desmond went faster than thirty-five, he pulled away like they were dead stopped.

It wasn't much of a chase as far as velocity went, but it had its compensations. One of those Purdys kept firing a pistol at us. Some kind of nickel-plated revolver. We would have been more upset about it if he'd gone to the trouble to aim. Instead he just shoved his arm out the passenger window of the Lada Riva and kind of shot in the air like he was celebrating a West Bank holy day.

"Drunk?" I asked Desmond.

"Usually," he told me.

"All of them?"

Desmond nodded. "Didn't see them much, but I never saw them sober."

"Then what are we waiting for?" Percy Dwayne asked. "Let's kick the shit out of them."

That sounded sensible enough to Desmond to prompt him to say, "I'll pull off up here somewhere."

We were looking for a stretch of open ground where we

could take full advantage of our sobriety and enthusiasm, but the territory was so wooded and tight along Confederate Avenue that Desmond had cut east to the Union side. He made his way all the way up to the Illinois monument. It looked like a miniature version of the Jefferson Memorial and was perched on the grassy knob of a hill.

"This ought to work," Desmond said.

He'd been careful not to lose our Purdys, so it had taken us a good quarter hour just to get where we'd ended up. If Luther and Percy Dwayne and Eugene had been spoiling for a fight before, they were desperate to lay into some Purdys by the time we all piled out of the Escalade.

"Let's wait in there," I told them and pointed at the building itself.

It had a domed roof, a few columns out front, and an open doorway. I had to think the names of the Illinois dead were etched on the walls inside.

"What's wrong with right here?" Percy Dwayne wanted to know.

"In case they've got more than just the one pistol, a little cover might be nice," I told him.

"So where's our guns?" Luther asked me.

"Let's take the bag," Desmond said.

That's just what we did. We hauled that duffel up the hill to that chapel proper. That's how I started to think of it anyway once Eugene had told us, "I ain't going in that church."

"Ain't a church," Percy Dwayne and Luther said back both at once.

"Probably haints and shit all in there," Eugene said and than glanced down at his coonhound and asked, "Right?"

Barbara didn't appear to have an opinion. She just scratched at her T-shirt as if she'd grown weary of it.

Then the Fiat came rattling down the road with the Fiesta hard behind it. Those Purdys fairly hurtled into the parking lot, scraping off more undercarriage as they came. The boy who'd fired was the crazy Purdy with the eye patch. He tumbled out of the Lada Riva, took a little aim, and squeezed off another round. He hit the near granite wall of the monument, and the bullet ricocheted. We all crouched and ducked and puckered and then raced up the steps and in through the doorway.

The second round singing off granite caused Eugene to reconsider his fear of haints. He passed us on the landing and ran as far inside as he could go with Barbara right beside him.

That idiot fired off another round. It sounded like it hit a column, and I guess the fluting and facets served to turn that bullet back around. It zinged halfway across the parking lot and broke out Desmond's back passenger window.

"Well shit!" Desmond said, and he fished the TEC-9 out of our weapons duffel. Desmond slapped in a freighted banana clip and stepped full out on the landing. He fired a burst in the air. "Get on back," he told those Purdys, but they weren't the sort to take instruction. Especially from a boy who, to their way of thinking, had put their kin to such poor use.

So they just stood there while Desmond, because he could shoot, demolished their vehicles around them. That Fiat went to pieces. The near door fell off while Desmond was still riddling the fender. Two of those Purdys spread flat on the ground. The other three ran and regrouped and ran again.

Desmond emptied his clip into those two cars. The racket that gun made was deafening. He broke out all the windows and caused the Ford coupe to catch fire. At first I couldn't hear anything but a muffled roar. Then I could hear Barbara barking. I finally got to where I could hear Luther and Percy Dwayne and Eugene all screaming about how they couldn't hear.

"I guess you showed them," I said to Desmond.

He cleared his breach. He asked me, "What?"

Those Purdys were all infuriated now. Or they seemed to think anyway that they had ample cause to be infuriated, and the five of them came running at us, yodeling and shrieking all the way. The one with the pistol fired his last round in the air. He led the charge up the granite staircase toward the landing. It was just me and Desmond there to meet them. Our colleagues were inside carping about being deaf.

"What the hell you doing back here?" the lead Purdy asked just as he gained the landing.

I thought Desmond might tell him it was a free country and he could go any damn where he pleased. But I have to think Desmond had long since decided he was finished talking to Purdys. He grabbed this one at the throat and crotch, raised him over his head and threw him. That boy hit his brothers and cousins as they closed on the landing themselves, and they all went down together, toppling backward to the ground.

Falling down stairs is painful enough when it's wooden risers. Going ass over elbows down a granite stairway with a pile of kin proved enough to take the remaining starch out of that pack of Purdys. They ended up in a canna lily bed remonstrating with each other, which with Purdys took the form of saying "Jesus" and "Fuck" in equal parts and in turn.

Percy Dwayne joined us on the landing. He was reaming an ear out with his finger and working his jaw. He caught sight of the Purdys piled up on the ground. They were moving enough to seem alive but hardly enough to seem a danger.

"What happened to them?"

"Slipped," I told him.

"We going to stomp them or something?"

"Naw," Desmond said.

And that's about when the Fiesta blew up. It was feeble and half-assed as explosions go. You can be sure they only had about two gallons of gas in the thing. But the blast proved loud and gaudy enough to serve as a useful beacon to the other crew that was already looking for us in the park.

They came roaring up in proper four-by-fours. Two Park Service Chevys, a state police cruiser, a Warren County patrol car, and two Vicksburg city units.

"Ain't this some shit." Luther announced. "Got arrested once already today."

"Yesterday," I told him. It seemed like a year ago when I'd gone in and pulled Luther out of the Greenville lockup.

"I ain't going back in." That was Eugene. His Arkansas experience had clearly shaken him up. I guess if you'd gotten pitched in a cell in an Arkansas shopping plaza, you might decide you'd rather not be arrested again.

"Let's just tell them what happened," Percy Dwayne said. "It's all these boys' fault."

I heard Desmond sigh. We both a knew a life that depended on Percy Dwayne Dubois talking you out of trouble wasn't really a life worth leading on this earth.

Those cops and rangers and troopers all crouched behind their doors and pointed every manner of firearm at us—pistols and shotguns and rifles.

"Hands," one of them barked out. "Let's see 'em."

I heard the TEC-9 clatter onto the landing.

They didn't have enough handcuffs to go around, so we got zip-tied and all parked in a line on a length of curbing down where the sidewalk met the lot.

One of the county cops passed his time telling us all to keep our mouths shut while the trooper asked us what we were up to in the park at night.

"That boy right there," one of the Purdys said—the fat whiskery one with a snake tattoo on his neck—"had his way with our
Denise."

"Who's Denise?" the trooper wanted to know.

"His sister," a Purdy said and country pointed with his nose
at nobody much.

"Had his way? What do you mean?"

"Hell, you know." The Purdy with the eye patch was the one
who chimed in now.

"Tell me."

The Purdy's couldn't settle on a fit description of what they
meant. Consequently, they fell to arguing and got told by the
county cop, "Shut up."

Then one of the city cops found our weapons duffel, and they
didn't care about Denise after that.

"Any of those legal?" I asked Desmond.

I owned a couple of guns I'd bought outright, but I believed
they were back at home. The duffel was mostly full of stuff
we'd taken off people. Criminals primarily and drunken lowlifes who'd threatened to do us harm. We had a policy of claiming firearms once they were pointed at us, but we had no way of
knowing what those guns had been up to before we came along.

"Well now," one of the city cops said.

He was awfully proud of himself. Him and one of the park
rangers had hauled our duffel down the stairs, and they dropped
it clanking before us as he spoke.

"What's all this?" he asked us.

Me and Desmond were accomplished at telling police nothing
at all. I'd been a county cop in Virginia, so I knew all the dodges
firsthand. Desmond had them down by instinct and disposition.
We'd been in enough trouble together to know how to weather

the sort of bluster that cops were inclined to get up to once they thought they had us cold.

One of the Vicksburg boys had us doing a dime in Parchman right off the top.

Desmond gave him a neck noise, but that was as far as he would go.

Percy Dwayne had a different strategy. He'd probably been cuffed and zip-tied more times than I could count. He liked to latch on an absolving explanation and just ride it until either it was dead or he was free in the world again.

"Ain't even ours," he told those cops while dipping his head toward our duffel. "Took it off those boys."

"Like hell," a Purdy chimed in.

"Couldn't do much else," Percy Dwayne said in a more-in-sadness-than-anger sort of way.

Desmond swung around my way to steal a glance.

I shrugged.

"They was after him," Percy Dwayne told the three cops that had gathered before him. A city policeman. A trooper in his cocked campaign hat. A park ranger in twill so wrinkled and baggy he should have been hanging off a garbage truck.

"Why?" The trooper was taking the lead.

"Used to date one of them, didn't you?" Percy Dwayne asked Desmond.

"One of *them*?" the city cop said and sneered as he pointed at those Purdys.

They objected faster than Desmond ever could.

"Aw hell no!" they shouted out like some aggrieved cracker chorus.

Then the one with the eye patch up and declared, "He used my sister hard."

"What does that even mean?" the trooper asked.

I was being careful not to look him full in the eye. I couldn't say but that the trouble I'd had with A. P. Benbow at the barracks had followed me clear to Vicksburg and would do me in at last.

"You know," that Purdy told him, which didn't appear to lead to enlightenment in any significant way.

"His sister?" that trooper said to Desmond.

"Saw her once or twice," Desmond said.

"Tied her the fuck up," that Purdy brother told us all.

"That right?" The Vicksburg cop was getting interested now.

"Only way she'd have it," Desmond informed him.

"Like hell." The Purdy brother tried to stand up but got shoved back down. His Purdy colleagues grumbled.

"Wasn't even real rope," Desmond explained. "Wrapped in velvet and shit."

"Caught him beating her," the Purdy brother with the pitiful aim said.

"Ain't never hit a woman," Desmond said.

"But you'd tie one up," the trooper reminded him.

"Not before her. And not after," Desmond said. "That was all her kink. I just like them naked and upside down."

Luther and Percy Dwayne both said, "Amen."

"Whipped her," the Purdy brother declared.

"She asked me to," Desmond explained. "Damn thing was made out of foam."

"Where's your sister now?" the trooper asked the Purdy brother.

"Houston. With some boy."

"Like him?" The trooper pointed at Desmond.

That Purdy spat and blew a breath before he told him, "Yeah."

"Here's a thing I want to know," that shabby park ranger told us all. "What the hell's that dog doing in a shirt?"

There wasn't a lot for us to be up to after that beyond giving those guns to the Purdys. As pastimes go, we went at it with concerted energy. It helped that we had a gaudy assortment of firearms in the duffel. Those cops would pull out a Steyr or our M1A, our 93R, our Heckler & Koch, and all our regular pistols too, and those Purdys just couldn't seem indignant when we insisted they owned them.

Ours were finer firearms than probably any Purdy had ever had in hand to judge by the revolver the eye patch Purdy had been firing all over the place. Consequently, those Purdys couldn't help but admire them and probably covet them a little. I had to imagine they were thinking ahead to when this spot of trouble got sorted and they could haul off their bag of guns as they left the jailhouse all free men. That must have been what kept them from raging against us because they didn't put up much of a fuss.

"That one there like to mow us down," Percy Dwayne said and pointed at the Purdy brother.

He couldn't trouble himself to bark back how he'd never done any such thing. Instead he just sat there looking like the sort of hard man who might just use a machine gun.

"Shot out all our windows," Percy Dwayne said. "Went half wild. Even shot up his own damn car."

The cops all looked at that Purdy brother. He was so deep into being a machine-gunning bad-ass that all he could do was spit.

"Might even have shot a buddy of ours," Luther chimed in, sounding teary.

"What buddy?" the trooper asked.

I called Dale's name. "Used to be a trooper up by Indianola," I said.

That did it. That trooper snatched that Purdy brother up off the curb.

"What did you go and do?"

"Nothing!" He was finally wising up. "We just kicked him around a little."

"Where?"

That Purdy brother was so confused about where he was he couldn't say. Traveling in a Riva Lada was probably a lot like riding in a blender. You were so busy trying to stay between ditches that you hardly knew where you were going and surely couldn't tell where you'd been.

"Back where we came in," I told the trooper.

"Show me," he said. "You two." He pointed at me and Desmond and escorted us over to his cruiser.

As he was helping Desmond into the back, that trooper asked him, "Was she worth it?"

Desmond had hardly changed his mind since earlier on when I'd put the question to him. He dropped hard on the seat, made a noise in his neck, and said, "I'm still thinking mostly no."

EIGHTEEN

Dale wasn't shot. It was hard to tell if he'd been roughed up or not because he'd gotten kicked around so thoroughly for the past day and a half that he was a mess before those Purdys ever reached him.

He was crawling around the gritty lot where we'd left him, looking for another crown. Dale had a disposable lighter to help him see, but it was so hot he could barely hold it.

When we pulled in, the first thing Dale said to that trooper was, "Shine your high beams over this way."

That trooper opened our doors for me and Desmond but let us struggle out on our own. He squinted at Dale, pitched his head like a dog might, and gave Dale a thorough once-over.

"That you, Magnum?" he finally said.

Dale stopped scouring for his tooth and had a good look

instead at the trooper. I doubt he could see awfully much for the headlights.

"Who wants to know?" Dale was his usual cavalcade of charm.

"What the hell happened to you?"

Dale didn't like the sound of that. He glared full into the high beams and embarked on the chore of getting up.

That trooper turned and said to me and Desmond, "He was the one with the muscles, right?"

"Wife left him," I said. "Kind of went in a tailspin. Out of work for a while. Quit lifting weights. Couldn't afford to juice anymore."

"Had plenty of beer money, looks like," that trooper said.

Dale informed him, "I heard that."

Dale was full on his feet by then with his bulk illuminated in the high beams.

"Hate to see you like this," the trooper told him, and he sounded even to mean it.

Dale shaded his eyes. "Who the hell is it?"

"Tucker."

That was enough to get a desolate grunt of recognition from Dale.

"Hey, sarge," Dale said as he tidied up his clothes. "Didn't mean for it to come to this, but shit'll do what it does sometimes."

"You drunk now?"

"No, sir."

Dale was stumbling on his words, but that was likely due to the finger he kept plunging into his mouth. He had two nubs now and felt the need to touch one of them about all the time.

"Another crown popped out. Watch where you walk."

Sergeant Tucker unholstered his flashlight and played the beam of it across the pavement.

"Where'd you lose it?"

Dale would have told most people, "How the fuck would I know?" He must have held that sergeant in special esteem because he told Tucker almost politely, "Right around here, I think."

Soon enough that Trooper had freed up me and Desmond, and we were all crawling around in the lot. You'd have thought a molar would be conspicuous in among the grit and pebbles, but we were a good quarter hour finding it. It looked like half a kernel of corn. It was dinged and dented where somebody—Dale figured a Purdy—had stomped on it.

"Those fuckers," was all Dale said.

"Took a shot at you, didn't they?" I asked him.

Dale had been shot at so much and beaten down so often that he had to pause to think if he'd, in fact, been actively fired on lately.

"We heard it," Desmond told him.

"Oh, right," Dale said. "After *you left me* . . ." He did some glaring for effect. "The ugly one with the patch. Pistol of his just went off."

Dale didn't seem too interested in what had happened to the rest of us, or most of the rest of us anyway. He took his finger out of his mouth long enough to ask me and Desmond, "Barbara all right?"

We nodded.

"Barbara?" the trooper asked us all.

Dale gave him a finger-choked, "Dog."

"Funny name for a dog."

"She's a Mandrell," Dale informed him.

Sergeant Tucker chewed on that one for about a quarter minute before he adjusted his campaign hat and said, "All right."

Trooper Tucker seemed decent enough. That was my impression anyway, so I consulted Desmond with a glance, and he nodded that way he does when he's giving me the go ahead. We're like that, me and Desmond. Often a look and a twitch is enough.

"We've got kind of a problem," I said to the sergeant.

He turned his full attention on me in a no-fucking-kidding sort of way.

"This here," I said and gestured in the general Purdy direction, "isn't it."

It must have seemed like trouble enough to him because he got interested in a hurry at the prospect of me and Desmond being deeper in Dutch elsewhere.

"I guess you heard about the guy who escaped from Parchman."

The sergeant nodded.

"And the girl he's got?"

Tucker nodded. "County cop. It's on the wire."

Desmond pointed my way. "His girl," he said.

"His cousin's with the PD up there." I pointed at Desmond and called Kendell's name. The sergeant was acquainted with Kendell.

"We're working with him," Desmond said.

"Deputized?" he asked us and then looked us over hard. I'm sure we didn't appear to be fit law enforcement material at that moment.

It was Dale who said, "Yeah." He'd even pulled his finger out to do it. "That Boudrot's headed for Alabama. Probably over there already. We're supposed to bring him back."

"You're bounty hunters?" Tucker asked us.

I could tell he was groping for some way to be accommodating, but he needed a traditional, orthodox slot he could shove all of us in. Bounty hunting was semirespectable in the country anymore. There was even a pack of knuckleheads with a TV show.

"That's right," I told him.

"Kendell gave us a paper," Desmond said.

"And those other boys?" Tucker asked us.

"They've got history with that Boudrot," I said. "Know his habits and stuff. We need them along to help us smoke him out."

We were winning him over. I could tell. He lapsed into a study. Scratched his chin and looked at nothing.

"What do you mean that hound's a Mandrell?"

"You know," Dale told him. "Those sisters. The blond ones. Barbara and Betty or something."

Desmond followed up with an account of the carnage we'd come across back at Eugene's dog pen in the swamp.

Sergeant Tucker looked moved by the idea of what some people'll do to dogs. That's what I thought anyway until he told us, "She played the banjo or something, didn't she?"

"Who?" Dale asked him.

"That Mandrell," the trooper said in a wistful sort of way like he was remembering his first car or his prom.

It didn't take nearly as much explaining as it should have to get us loose. Not just me and Desmond and Dale, but the rest of the crew as well. It was only once those Purdys saw Luther and Percy Dwayne and Eugene getting cut from their zip ties that they decided to raise a fuss about the guns we'd said they owned. Naturally, it was too late by then. Those cops had all decided, the way cops do, who they'd like to see locked up and shut away for what exactly and who they didn't much mind running free.

To Sergeant Tucker's credit, he'd required a telephone conversation with Kendell before he would let us go. Kendell must have vouched for us emphatically enough, because that sergeant spent the bulk of his energy being down on Purdys after that.

Those Purdy boys raged and hollered and threatened. They

most especially wanted harm to come to Desmond, but they had enough hard things to say about all the rest of us as well to ensure they'd be sitting in the Vicksburg lockup for a while.

One of the park rangers even gave us enough Visqueen to cover the hole where that Purdy's ricochet had busted Desmond's back passenger window. Then we had to suffer the quarreling among Percy Dwayne and Luther and Dale about who'd sit next to the plastic and for how long. Luther even tried to worm his way into Eugene's way back before Eugene made noises against him like he was ready to come to blows.

"Don't be a stranger, Dale," Sergeant Tucker shouted as we were heading out of the lot toward Union Avenue.

Dale made the sort of noise he had to make with half a hand shoved into his mouth.

"What happened over there?" Luther asked us. It seemed next to a miracle to him that we were leaving unarrested while those Purdys were in a fix.

"Found my tooth," Dale told him and showed the thing to Luther.

"What are we going to do now?" Percy Dwayne wanted to know. He held up his hands and showed them to me. "I ain't fighting that crazy fucker with just these."

"We'll find something," I told him. I wasn't about to go at that Boudrot empty-handed either.

"Damn straight." I think they all said it together.

"Tuscaloosa?" Desmond asked me.

"Shouldn't we talk to Kendell first?"

Desmond knew we should and nodded, but he wasn't about to do it himself.

"Your turn," he said. "If you use my phone, he'll start yelling before you even open your mouth."

I fished Desmond's phone from the cup holder, found Kendell's number, and placed the call. Sure enough, he answered in a full-fledged dudgeon.

It mostly boiled down to Kendell asking three or four times, "What in the world are you boys up to?"

"It's me," I said once I'd found a spot for it.

"They cut you all loose? Even the Duboises?"

"Yeah. It turned out those Purdys were running around with a whole bag full of guns."

Kendell had seen our duffel, knew our practices and methods.

"Big green thing?" he asked me.

"Might have been."

"What have you got left for that Boudrot, just in case he won't come easy?"

"The love of Jesus and about fifty knuckles."

"I know a guy in Columbus. He owes me."

I picked up Desmond's gazetteer off the floorboard, which was actually my atlas that Desmond had helped himself to like usual and never given back. I was flipping through the thing to find the county we were racing through, I asked Kendell, "Heard anything else from that Boudrot?"

"Not directly," Kendell said. "Techs are on him. He hit Tuscaloosa about an hour ago."

"Where exactly are we?" I asked Desmond.

He pointed straight ahead. "Jackson in maybe half an hour."

"Never had a girl in Columbus, did you?" I asked Desmond.

He gave the question more thought than I'd hoped for before he told me, "Nope."

NINETEEN

Dale needed to eat again, and he started talking about some chicken that he'd had once in a place near Jackson.

"Kind of on the way," he told me. "Out by Bradie."

"Didn't you just have a steak?" I asked him.

"My tooth came out," Dale said. "The first one."

"I guess I need an ATM," I told Desmond. "We're going want a pile of money."

"For chicken?"

"Guns mostly. Chicken a little too."

Desmond grunted. "I know that place Dale means."

"You too?"

"We get a bucket for the car, maybe we don't have to stop anymore."

I knew that was a fantasy, given our crew. We had five bladders with five different calibrations. Six if you counted Barbara's, though she was the least trouble of the bunch. Except that— according to the boys in the back—Barbara broke powerful wind.

"Money first," I said.

Desmond nodded.

Near Clinton, he pulled off the highway at a shopping plaza. The neighborhood looked about as down-at-heel as a civilized place can get. There was some kind of shitty dollar store anchoring the place. A day-old bread shop and beauty parlor. Everything else was vacant. The ATM was a CashPoint out in the middle of the lot.

There were two pickup trucks parked nose to tail closer to the cash machine than I would have liked and what looked like two guys in the cab of each—yokels in greasy ball caps. They stopped talking to watch us come.

"Want me out too?" Desmond asked.

I shook my head and told Percy Dwayne, as he was reaching for his door handle, "Stay where you are."

"Got to bleed it."

"At the chicken place," I told him. "I don't want you setting these boys off."

"What boys?"

That was the trouble with Percy Dwayne and his ilk. They never saw anything coming. Instead they'd blunder into trouble and have to figure some way out. I tilted my head toward the pickups.

Percy Dwayne told me, "Oh."

I stepped over to the machine. The light above it was full of bugs. They'd all died in the globe and were blocking out the light. I could barely see what I was up to. I withdrew all that machine would give me, four hundred dollars in twenties, and I was pulling the cash out of the slot when I heard one of those truck door hinges creak. I stole enough of a glance to see one of those boys out and heading my way.

"Damn thing worked for you?" he said as he closed.

"Did."

"I couldn't get shit out of it."

"Try it again."

"Ate my damn card."

"That's too bad," I told him.

"Just need maybe forty."

"Friend," I said, "go need it somewhere else."

He snorted like he was entertained.

Desmond's window came down. "You all right?"

"Yeah. This boy needs forty dollars."

"Fuck him!" It had to be Luther. Him or Percy Dwayne or maybe both together.

Then I heard Desmond say, "Don't!" one time, but Dale still swung open his Escalade door and joined me in the lot.

If I'd been beat down as much as Dale had, I do believe I'd have learned a thing from it. I would have known enough anyway to stay where I was with my finger in my mouth. Not Dale. He clearly still thought of himself as a menacing muscle head even though he was just some blubbery guy with a tooth in his shirt pocket and two uncrowned nubs in his mouth.

"Back in the car," I told him.

That didn't even slow him down. Dale came lumbering over my way.

"What's the trouble?" he said.

Another boy got out of one of the pickups. Evening up the odds, I guess.

"You want forty too?" I asked him.

He grinned and spat. He said, "All right."

I was actually considering trying to buy my way out of mischief with a twenty when Dale closed off that avenue for me by telling those two boys, "We ain't giving you shit."

"Want me?" Desmond asked.

I shook my head. Those boys looked like loggers or something on that order. They were rough and dirty and tapped out and probably getting low on beer. I imagined they'd driven over to the ATM half thinking they'd bust it open, and then we'd rolled up and they'd decided to strong arm me instead.

I doubt they were evil. Just stupid and thirsty with sawdust in their pockets instead of folding money. A twenty probably would have done it for them right up until Dale chimed in. The second one who'd wandered over reached to his belt and unsheathed his knife.

It was one of those tactical items with a flat black finish. It was all angles and facets and oddly placed serrations. It looked like it had been forged by a Romulan three hundred years from now.

"Might just want all of it anymore," the one without the knife informed me.

"Back in the car, Dale."

"Uh-uh," Dale said.

"We don't have time to get you sewn up."

Dale plunged his finger into his mouth to lay the tip of it on one of his nubs. He told me around his knuckle. "I'm good right here."

"Hold what you got," I said to those boys, particularly the one with the knife.

I stepped over to Dale and grabbed him by the nearest piece that was handy, which turned out to be his left ear. I kicked him in the backside and then shoved him toward the Escalade.

"Get back out and I'll kill you."

Dale was long enough acquainted with me to know when I'd quit fucking around.

"You can still leave," I told those boys as I turned my attention back to them.

"Let's have it," the one with the knife said and did some flashy thing with the blade. He spun it around and was right in the middle of tossing the thing from one hand to the other when I closed hard on him and punched him in the throat.

That knife hit the pavement, and I kicked it under the Escalade. Those last two boys came piling out of the trucks.

"Need me?" Desmond asked again.

That first yokel charged at me. He bored straight in but punched well wide. I caught him a hard, sharp blow directly in the nuts. There were no rules of order when it came to a Mississippi parking lot fight.

He made a feeble noise in the back of his throat as he toppled onto the ground.

"Think I've got it," I told Desmond.

He helped me anyway. He rolled hard forward and knocked the other two boys over with the car. I only had to kick one of them to persuade them both to stay down.

Luther shouted over the seat back toward me, "See what they've got."

Another sensible Dubois idea. While those boys didn't have anything worth taking on their actual persons—just empty wallets chained to their belt loops and multitools and knives—they had a fine little twenty-gauge shotgun under the seat of one of the trucks and a .25 caliber pistol held together with tape in the glove box. I got it halfway back to the Escalade before the slide broke loose and fell off.

I kept the shotgun. Handed the thing to Luther over the seat back.

"Chicken place is just off Twenty," Dale informed us all, as if stopping at that CashPoint had gone off exactly as we'd hoped.

"You good?" Desmond asked me as I buckled in.

"This world's making me a little tired," I told him.

Desmond had a snort for that.

The chicken place was an ancient dump. Less the result of ne-glect than the wages of thirty years worth of fryolating. But the chicken was exceptional and the joint was hopping. By the time we got there, it was closing on midnight, and half the crowd was rolling in drunk, the other half coming off work.

They fried gizzards. They fried livers. They fried everything but beaks. We sat for a half hour at a picnic table on a slab down by the ditch waiting for our chicken to get cooked and our number to be called. Even without a dog in a T-shirt, we would have looked like refugees. We sure smelled like a boatload of month-old socks.

"We going to stop somewhere or something?" Eugene asked us.

Desmond shook his massive head. I was right there with him on that.

"Two hours or so from Columbus?" I said.

Desmond nodded. "About," he told me.

"We head over there. Wait for morning. Go see Kendell's guy and get some guns."

That sat well enough with Desmond, but Eugene didn't like it much.

"I was kind of hoping to wash up a little."

"Didn't take you for the particular sort."

"What's that supposed to mean?" Eugene asked me.

"You live in the swamp," I told him.

"Been in jail!" Eugene reminded me. "In goddamn Arkansas. Washed in a creek with lye soap. Stuff's still burning like hell."

I guess that was enough to make even a swamp rat crave a bath.

"Why don't we do this: We'll stop up by Columbus and get a room somewhere for a couple of hours. We can all clean up. Better than sitting in the car."

"We finish this thing tomorrow," Desmond informed us all. Then he turned to Dale and raised a finger to shake at him for effect. "When we tell you to stay in the goddamn car, you stay in the goddamn car."

Dale was feeling his nubs. He nodded and said, "Arlwpp."

We decided to eat our chicken right where we were, went at it at the picnic table. It was glorious stuff. The iced tea was treacly sweet, and the potatoes were drowning in white gravy. The biscuits seemed to be about equal parts flour and lard.

"They got pudding," Luther announced when he was still on his first piece of chicken. Culinary strategic thinking was the only strategic thinking Luther did.

We'd ordered enough chicken to take some with us, but we ended up eating it all at the table. Barbara ate hers twice. It went down. It came up, and she gobbled it down again. By the time we'd gathered at the Escalade, we were all speckled with grease from biscuit crumbs and chicken bits, and we smelled like yesterday's Crisco. We were so rank as a group that none of us climbed in the car with any zeal.

"Let's stop at the Walmart," I told Desmond. "Bound to be one around here somewhere."

Two exits over we found one, and it was open all night. We were well on the wrong side of midnight by then, but the parking lot was still half full. Third shifters and insomniacs were populating the store, and I went in and bought each of us a pair of coveralls. Got a couple of packages of undershorts as well. I even bought Barbara a fresh T-shirt. It was between Kyle Petty and

Miley Cyrus. I thought Kyle was more in the theme of things, and the red and blue looked patriotic. Most especially with the head of a coonhound sticking out of the collar.

We argued about which route to take over to Columbus. I was all for heading up 55 and cutting over at Winona, while Dale took his finger out long enough to suggest we head east to Meridian instead and then north on the four-lane through Scooba and Macon and over to Columbus. The rest of the boys in the back were all for a cross-county jaunt on a goddamn mule track that the state of Mississippi calls Route 25.

That was all Desmond needed to hear. He hates a proper highway. So we headed up the interstate one entire exit and then struck out on that wretched blacktop through the Mississippi wild.

Living even in a modest-sized town like Indianola, you can forget how monumentally empty the state of Mississippi is. The Delta is chiefly farmland, but the Delta has always been chiefly farmland with cities and towns around the edges for housing the workers and shipping the crops. The rest of the state is mixed-use countryside. Scattered communities and the odd modest town with vast stretches of nobody much but cows.

Route 25 was *that* Mississippi but in two in the morning darkness. Nobody anywhere. No traffic to meet. The odd mercury light way off at a house or hard by a tractor shed. We'd hit two possums and six armadillos before we'd gone twenty miles.

"Don't know whether to trade this car in," Desmond said, "or barbecue it."

Everything was shut, of course. Aside from twenty-four-hour Walmarts, casinos on the river, and the odd gas station on the interstate, there's not much in Mississippi that stays open after nine. And boy was it dark. It was like driving across the bottom of the ocean. We went north of Carthage and south of Kosciusko.

We didn't hit anywhere flush, so it was just the odd light pole and stray grocery mart and occasionally the sickening crunch of a creature under wheel.

Desmond was steering with one finger, which I asked him not to do.

"What's your trouble?" he wanted to know.

"Say you run in the ditch or hit a deer—there's no help for us out here."

As a big black man in among cracker pinheads, I guess Desmond was accustomed to the idea of no help anywhere.

"What's your point?" he asked me.

"Just go easy," I said. "Look sharp and all."

He had a double-barreled snort for that.

Percy Dwayne came up over the seat back to ask me, "You scared of the dark or something?"

"More people where I come from," I told him. "Not used to all this nothing."

"Where do you come from?"

"Virginia."

"I robbed a boy from Virginia once. Went to some college up there. Was trying to find New Orleans."

"Where did he run into you?" I asked him.

"Shit. Way the hell over by Rosedale. Wasn't going to get to New Orleans from there."

"Beat him?" I asked.

"I ain't like you," Percy Dwayne told me, insulted. "I got me some finesse."

"You ever had a proper job?" I asked Percy Dwayne.

"Depends."

"Ever drawn a check? Like that?"

Percy Dwayne was giving the question a spot of serious

consideration when Luther joined him on the seat back to say, "Fuck no."

"Icehouse. Remember?"

"You didn't last a day."

"Drove that lady to dialysis."

"That was more like a 'got to,' wasn't it?"

Percy Dwayne sighed and nodded by way of concession. "I was kind of plugging her," he confessed.

"You?" I asked Luther.

"Aw, hell yeah," Luther said. "I used to farm."

That got Desmond interested. Back when he was tractor-seat size, he did quite a lot of plowing and planting all over the Delta.

"Whereabouts?" he asked Luther.

Luther named three or four plantations.

"Sharkey County, aren't they?"

"Most of them."

"I worked down there."

Then we passed a half hour listening to Luther and Desmond talk about tractors they'd driven. Harrows and seeders they'd had good use from. Harrows and seeders they hadn't.

"Sweet Jesus," Eugene finally shouted at them from the way back. "Ain't that enough of that shit for a while?"

Dale seemed to be of the same mind. He told all of us, "Uhlerp."

"Why do you keep pawing?" I finally asked him. "Those nubs hurting you?"

He did me the courtesy of withdrawing his slobbered-up hand. "Naw," Dale said. "Ought to be though." Then he filled his mouth again.

The good thing about driving in the middle of the night in

the wilds of Mississippi is that you can just stop in the road and get out and pee. There's not a damn soul to see you, if you don't count armadillos. Me and Percy Dwayne were standing just about on the center line, when an armadillo came shooting up out of the roadcut and scuttled across to the far ditch.

"I hear they give you the mumps," he told me. "Or maybe chickenpox."

"How does it feel to know nothing?"

Percy Dwayne spat. He shook and zipped. He shrugged a little and finally said, "All right."

TWENTY

At about four in the morning we pulled in at a motor lodge near Columbus. It was one of those places where some people live for months and others just pass through. I had to wake up the desk clerk by ringing a bell. From the pitch of the grumbling that earned me, it sounded like I woke up some guests as well.

Eugene didn't help things any.

"Cigarette machine?" he shouted at me from the car.

"Pipe down," I told him.

He couldn't hear me because I was trying to whisper at him back.

"What!?"

"He said shut the fuck up." Luther didn't have any volume control to speak of.

Somebody yelled, "Jesus!" from one of the rooms.

"Cigarette machine?" Eugene shouted at me another time from the car.

I nodded and pointed nowhere much, but the damage was done by then. The whole place was awake, the owner included. He came out of a room off the shabby lobby still fastening his pants.

"Quiet, Mr. Sir," he told me once he'd unlatched the door.

He was Pakistani, I think. He was slight, brown, and irate but still passably polite about it.

"The guests are sleeping," he said. He country pointed. "It is dark."

"Sorry."

I was surprised and gratified he'd thrown back the bolt and let me in. I got a glimpse of myself in the mirrored wall on the far side of the lobby, and I looked like a guy who might have dropped by to remove the clerk's head with an ax. And that was without even factoring in the smell. The man stink from the Escalade and the food stink from all over. I was in such rough condition, I would have given a sheet rocker pause.

That clerk barely paid any notice to me. He had his ledger to swivel around my way, his computer to wake up.

"A room?"

"Yeah."

"Week, month, night?"

"Just for a couple of hours," I told him.

"Same rate," he said and tapped a laminated card taped to the countertop.

I looked over the menu of charges. The nightly rate was sixty-nine dollars. Swanky Alabama prices there on the Mississippi border.

"I'll give you forty."

He made a show of shutting his ledger.

"We'll be out by eight."

"We who?"

Now I country pointed.

That gentleman peered around me, through the glass and into the lot. Dale was leaning against a fender with his hand in his mouth up to the knuckles. Percy Dwayne was explaining something to him with far more volume than four in the morning called for. Eugene was standing by scratching his nutsack with Barbara at his side.

"Two rooms," the clerk informed me. He tapped his laminated rate card again. "Triple A?"

I shook my head.

"One thirty."

"How about a hundred?"

The ledger was closed already, so he yanked it off the counter entirely.

"Fine. One thirty." I fished out my wallet.

"And no pets." He pointed toward Barbara. "Even with . . . clothes."

I came into the lot with two keys. I gave one to Percy Dwayne for him and Luther and Eugene. I kept the other for me and Desmond and (as much as I hated it) Dale.

"Paid retail," I told them. "Use all the towels, and don't pick up shit."

As it turned out, they didn't truly need that sort of instruction from me. Our rooms were next door to each, down at the far end by a weedy lot and a Dumpster. The first thing those boys did was crank up the TV. They found an episode of *T. J. Hooker* down the dial, tuned it in. The installment was mid-shootout. Bullets were flying. Music was thumping. William Shatner was emoting at full pitch.

I went over to tell them to crank the thing down and found

Luther and Percy Dwayne stretched out buck naked on the beds. Somebody had yanked off Barbara's old T-shirt, and she was rolling around on a pillow. Eugene was in the shower. Steam was boiling out of the bathroom. I heard him hoot and swear as he slipped in the tub and took the curtain rod to the floor.

Luther and Percy Dwayne both said just, "Hey," as I stepped into the room.

I suddenly couldn't locate the gumption to give a happy damn about them. I handed over the slate-gray coveralls I'd bought for them at the Walmart and fresh underwear as well.

Luther and Percy Dwayne's neighbor popped over soon enough, and me and Desmond sat in our room and listened to the yelling and the threats.

Dale had claimed our bathroom. He'd taken the phone book in with him. The sound of Dale riffling pages was the only human noise he made. Everything else he got up to could have been the work of a cow.

"Got any matches?" I asked Desmond.

"Air strike probably wouldn't help."

We heard Luther and the fellow from the room on the other side yelling at each other about what they might get up to, the brawl they might have, and the harm they might do if they could even begin to stir themselves to fight.

I stood up and peeled off my nasty clothes down to my clammy undershorts. I tore the tags off my new coveralls and slipped them on. They were scratchy but clean and smelled like dye.

"I think I'd rather wait in the car," I told Desmond.

He grunted and followed me to the door.

"You're not going to change?"

I pointed at the coveralls I'd selected especially for Desmond. They were slate gray like the rest of them but about the size of a weather balloon.

"Things make me look chunky."

"Give them a try." I stood at the door and waited.

Desmond stripped down to his shorts and stepped into his coveralls. Dale started whistling what sounded like a Sousa march from the toilet.

Desmond zipped his coveralls shut. He turned full around to model them for me. I saw what he meant. They made him look plumper. Wider through the beam and rounder in the front.

I kept it all to myself and told him, "Looks all right to me."

Desmond seemed inclined to debate the matter. There was a mirror on the far wall that he eyed himself in. But then Dale groaned and went pure feedlot. We could hear the splashes from where we were. Me and Desmond didn't so much leave that room as escape it into the dawning.

Instead of just sitting in the car, we went for a ride around greater Columbus, Mississippi. The place was all shopping plazas and burger joints on the outskirts and vacant storefronts in the heart of town. They didn't get much traffic in downtown Columbus along about half past five in the morning, so me and Desmond alarmed a deputy just by driving past his cruiser. He could have been Dale's little brother for all his doughy bulk and smarts.

We were just in front of the Lowndes County courthouse when he pulled us over. There wasn't much me and Desmond could do but groan at each other and sigh.

That deputy had his pistol in hand by the time he closed on us. His flashlight was up at his shoulder. He played the beam of it in on me and Desmond in our matching coveralls.

"Who you supposed to be?"

Desmond reached for his wallet. Desmond was big enough and black enough to know to avoid all sudden motion, but Deputy Dale junior was far too antsy for anybody's good.

"Uh-uh," he said and raised his service revolver. He pointed it at the pair of us.

That's hardly the kind of thing I can tolerate with grace. I'd been a cop myself. I knew to aim my gun at people who needed shooting. You didn't bring your barrel to bear on two guys just sitting in a car.

"Put that away," I told that boy. "We haven't done a thing."

He keyed his mike with his flashlight hand and called his buddy Gary in.

"Out," he said and motioned with his pistol for us to join him at the curb.

We rolled out of the Escalade and let Dale Junior herd us to the sidewalk. Desmond had an old sun-faded county sticker on his windshield. The deputy played his light beam on it.

"Sunflower County. Where the hell's that?"

"Delta," Desmond told him.

"Well now," Deputy Dale Junior said, "that ain't nowhere around here, is it?" Deputy Dale Junior keyed his mike again. "Gary, where the hell are you?"

Gary came back entirely as static.

"We going wait on him," the deputy told us.

"Wait on him for what?" Desmond said.

The deputy pulled a face to let Desmond know that the very last thing he wanted was lip from a big Delta nigger in coveralls. It's a law-enforcement look that still prevails in the South. All you have to do to provoke it is be black and say anything.

"You got a plan, Homer?" I asked him.

That got him off Desmond right quick. He pointed his flashlight and gun both my way.

"I'm searching this damn car," he said.

"On what grounds?"

"Who you? Fucking Matlock?"

NOWHERE NICE   197

We had a shotgun in the Escalade we'd taken off those CashPoint boys and God only knew what else was in there. With six grown men—and two of them Duboises—there was sure to be incriminating detritus.

"You're going to need a warrant," I told him.

"Like hell," he said and came my way.

Thinking back, I probably taught that deputy a valuable lesson in policing. Chiefly: Don't let some mouthy wiseass in coveralls make you forget what you're about.

He laid the bore of his pistol against my gut, and I took that gun away from him. It wasn't a plan on my part. I hadn't laid a trap. I'd been well trained in both the army and at the police academy. If I got threatened with a gun and was close enough to lay hands on it, I knew how to flip the thing around and make it end up with me.

So he had that pistol—a Remington revolver—until I shoved my finger in the trigger guard and wrenched it out of his hand. Then he was on the bore end, and I was looking at the hammer.

He didn't do anything for a couple of seconds. They must not have trained their cops up much in Columbus, Mississippi. He reached for his Taser but only in a slow halfhearted way.

Desmond just told him, "Uh-uh," and took that away from him too.

A city cruiser pulled onto the main drag a few blocks east of where we were standing. Gary, we had to figure. There was the real chance this whole business would go even further sideways and probably go there fast.

Deputy Dale Junior swallowed hard. He'd half raised his hands by then.

I was hardly at my sharpest, and I couldn't think just what to do. Fortunately, Desmond came up with an out.

"We're federal," he said.

The deputy was anxious to believe it. That was the sort of news that meant he might just live. He nodded in a twitchy way and sucked air through his mouth.

"Bureau," Desmond informed him.

"Tell him." I pointed at the cruiser.

"Gary?"

"Yeah." I tapped on his mike.

He keyed it. "You there?"

"I see you," we heard through his belt speaker.

"These guys are federal."

"Under cover," I told him.

"They're under . . . ," the deputy was saying when Gary's cruiser rolled up to the curb and lurched to a rocking stop.

Gary popped out. He was wiry and was sporting some sort of Flowbee haircut, the style of do a man would have instead of a girlfriend or a wife. His uniform shirt was oversized and fit him like a jumper. He pulled his gun as he approached us.

Deputy Dale Junior told him, "We're good."

"Don't look good," Gary said.

He lurked a little ways off, pointed his gun at nothing much. Besides us, the town was entirely vacant. I could just hear the clatter of a train down to the south.

"They're FBI," Deputy Dale Junior told Gary.

"They show you badges or something?"

"We're under cover," I said.

"Doing what?" he wanted to know.

Since I wasn't quite sure what we were doing, I decided to leave that one to Desmond.

"Got yourselves a gunrunner," Desmond told those boys.

"Where?" Gary asked him.

"Right here in the county," he told them.

"Ain't Dewey, is it?" Gary asked Desmond.

"Not at liberty to say."

"You got paper or something?" Gary asked us. "Ain't like we can just take your word."

Deputy Dale Junior exhaled and deflated a little. Gary didn't just have bad hair. He was officious too. His colleague knew it well enough, and we were finding it out.

"Under cover," I told him. "We've been on this guy for a year."

"Give me a number. I'll call somebody."

"Don't work that way," Desmond said.

"I'm all right with it," Deputy Dale Junior announced.

"You would be." Gary spat. He still had his pistol in hand and looked half inclined to aim it.

Me and Desmond said what we needed to say between us in a glance.

"All right," I told Gary. "I'll give you the number, but you make the call on a landline from the precinct house."

Gary spat again and nodded. I reached into my coverall pocket and fished out my billfold. That seemed to satisfy Gary that we were all heading in the right direction. He holstered his pistol and stepped over my way. With my free hand I grabbed a fistful of Gary's mop of Flowbeed hair and slammed his face against the door rail of Desmond's Escalade.

Gary grunted one time and lost his will to be upright. I let him down easy by his collar.

"This fucking guy," I told Deputy Dale Junior. "Can't let him spoil a full year's worth of work."

Lucky for us, Deputy Dale didn't have much use for Gary. "Still lives with his mama," he said. "Always doing shit like this."

"We're taking our boy down today," Desmond said it lowly and on the sly to let Deputy Dale Junior know this was privileged information. "Can't have any trouble from him." He poked at Gary with the toe of his boot. His smock of a shirt was all bunched and out of place, but Gary's layered hair was sitting just right.

"I'll tell him."

"Might need more than that," Desmond said to Gary.

Desmond fished a fresh roll of duct tape out of the spare tire well of his car, and we instructed Deputy Dale Junior in proper trussing technique.

"For your country," was all we had to say.

He'd heard enough of that sort of thing from gasbag nimrods in D.C. to leave him open to acting on it once he'd heard it from Desmond and me.

We helped Deputy Dale Junior lay Gary out on the backseat of his cruiser.

"We'll make sure," I told him, "you get properly cited once this whole gunrunning shit goes down."

"That'd be all right. I kind of was thinking I might sort of aim for the Bureau."

"We'll do what we can," Desmond said.

A call came in for Desmond just then, and we heard a snatch of "Satin Soul" from Desmond's Escalade.

"I guess we're on," I told Desmond.

He nodded and gave me a neck noise. Desmond told Deputy Dale Junior, "Stay frosty," as he climbed into the car.

We left him there on the sidewalk, eased out into the empty road.

"Stay frosty?"

Desmond showed me the screen of his phone. Kendell was who had just called.

We rode in silence for a few minutes.

"Here's a question for you," I finally said to Desmond. "You figure we're going to hell or Parchman?"

Desmond told me, "Yeah."

TWENTY-ONE

There was something close to a riot underway at the motor lodge by the time we got back to pluck our colleagues free. Dale had stopped up the toilet in our room and had gone to see about a plunger. Since the little guy who ran the place did all the toilet plunging himself, he'd came back to the room with Dale and had gotten an earful from his lodgers on the way. They were offended by all the racket Percy Dwayne and Luther were raising. Eugene was wandering the property by then looking for a cigarette machine. He had Barbara with him all decked out in her new Kyle Petty T-shirt.

They were what we saw first when we pulled into the lot.

"Is there some kind of rule?" Eugene asked me straightoff. "Now we got to call her Kyle?"

"No," I told him. "What are you up to?"

"Can't find the cigarette machine."

"When did you start smoking?"

"Hell, way back. Quit for a while. Starting in again today."

"Why?" I asked him.

"Nervous," he told me.

I figured that Boudrot was the root cause. The closer we got to him, the edgier Eugene grew. Out of all of us, he was the one who'd seen that Boudrot operate over time and up close. He knew what the man could do to people and how very much he enjoyed it.

"We'll get you a pack somewhere," I promised him.

That's when the yelling ratcheted up. The little brown desk clerk was screaming at Dale about how badly he'd plugged up the toilet. Apparently, in Pakistan you always break up a massive stool with a stick, which was not the brand of activity Dale had ever contemplated. You sit on the ring. You flip through a magazine (a phone book in a pinch). You do your business. You flush. You go out of the bathroom and warn off your loved ones.

"Who the hell's got a stick?" Dale asked the guy. "Ain't no damn stick in there."

Dale sort of had him on that one. You could hardly expect people to travel with a stick they'd bust up their bowel movements with.

That motor lodge clerk knew he was caught out, so he did what most people do. He started yelling at Dale about the general mess he'd left the room in, all the racket he'd made along with his buddies, all the people they'd woken up. It fit right in with the general tone of the lot. Everybody else was screaming already.

Desmond never got out of the Escalade. He whistled from the driver's seat. Desmond had a powerful whistle. It was piercing and arresting. Everybody quit what they were about and turned to look our way.

"Let's go," Desmond shouted in his baritone rumble at full volume.

By then, Luther and Percy Dwayne and Dale were all looking to bug out anyway.

"Pile in," I told Eugene and lifted the back gate for him.

Barbara was feeling sprightly enough to leap in and Eugene followed hard upon her.

Dale and Luther we're already halfway across the lot by then, but Percy Dwayne had hung back to suggest to some woman, "Why don't you shut the fuck up."

Percy Dwayne must not have noticed that she had some kind of stick in her hand. Probably not her toilet stick. It looked like an old broom handle that she half used for a cane and half used for flogging shitheads like Percy Dwayne. She was leaning on it until suddenly she wasn't, and Percy Dwayne was getting tattooed.

He covered up there at first and swore, but she kept whacking him with a fury, and Percy Dwayne was just the sort to swing on a woman after a while.

"Quit it!" he told her.

She didn't.

I hustled over to do what I could. We were already leading a fairly delicate existence in Columbus what with Gary trussed up in the back of a cruiser and Deputy Dale Junior about four shades of dumb. We didn't need any more police interaction, and I could tell by the way the desk clerk was stalking toward his office that he was either off to fetch a bazooka or dial 911.

"Come on." I grabbed Percy Dwayne's coverall sleeve and yanked him.

That damn woman caught me flush on the wrist bone with what proved a shovel handle. It stung like hell. She swung it on me again. I raised my hand and grabbed the thing. I tried to break it over my knee, but it was stout and ash and didn't do a thing but hurt like hell. So I threw it instead, flung it out into the weedy patch of ground down from the parking lot, and *that* was the thing that served to set the crowd off. You would have thought I'd impaled her with it. Now they were all yelling at me.

"Let's go," I told Percy Dwayne.

"Fuck it," he said. "We can take them."

"Let's go!"

I about had to drag him with me. Not that Percy Dwayne wanted to fight. He just didn't want to seem like the sort of guy who'd walk away from trouble. I could see the desk clerk on the phone in the motel office.

"Who you looking at?"

Percy Dwayne had stopped to shout back at some fellow. A big ugly guy in his undershorts and a pair of dingy tube socks. He had a tattoo on what must have been his six-pack some years back. A spiderweb originally, but now the thing was so stretched and blown out it looked like a cargo net.

"Looking at you," he told Percy Dwayne. "You got a problem with that, boy?"

"Aw, fucker." Percy Dwayne laid his hands to his hips and spat.

"Come on," I told him.

"Let me see to this asshole first."

The guy in the undershorts spat as well and readied himself for battle. There wasn't a lot he could do, given the little he was wearing, so he tried to take off a sock. His belly got in the way, though, and he ended up shouting, "Mama!"

A bony woman in curlers and a housedress closed on him. She bent over and raised his foot up like she was fixing to shoe a horse.

"Let's go," I told Percy Dwayne.

He shook his head. He wasn't budging. That woman peeled

off one nasty sock and let that be enough. Percy Dwayne and that fellow looked ready to ram together like mountain goats.

Desmond had sized up the situation from over in the Escalade. He wheeled the thing around between Percy Dwayne and that fellow and had Luther throw open the back door.

"Get in," I told Percy Dwayne.

He fixed his mouth like he had an objection, so I punched him one time hard in the gut and then tossed Percy Dwayne into the car myself.

I climbed straight in, and off we went. We weren't a quarter mile from the place when we passed three police cruisers, rolling full tilt. Desmond watched them in his rearview as they swung into the motor lodge lot.

"We might want to get on out of Columbus," Desmond suggested to me. He said it that way that let me know he'd made his decision already.

"What about the guns?" I asked him.

"They got guns in Alabama."

"They who?"

"I know a boy," Desmond told me.

"Where?"

"Gordo," he said. "It's right on the way. Just this side of Tuscaloosa."

"How about some waffles or something." Dale had taken the nasty hand he'd wiped his ass with out of his mouth long enough to talk.

"Yeah," Luther threw in. "Ought to be a Waffle House out here somewhere."

It turned out there was one just off the truck route. We could see it from the road. The noise that crew made when Desmond failed to pull off approached caterwauling.

Luther laid up on the seat back. "What the hell's up with you?" he said.

He meant mostly Desmond, since he had the wheel, but Desmond was in his getaway mode. Just trying to clear out to safety. He left me to explain things to Luther.

"Alabama first," I said.

I knew all those boys—probably even Dale too—had a queer sense of police jurisdiction, so I played on that. I made out like we'd be like Nazis in Brazil once we'd hit the Alabama line and broke out of Mississippi.

It turned out to be about twenty miles or so to the Alabama state line. We finally hit a place called Reform. The town didn't have much—a shabby grocery store, a lumber yard, a Fred's, a Magic Wand, a Kangaroo gas station. On the far end of the clutter, when we'd just about given up hope, we rolled up on a Jack in the Box, and Desmond wheeled into the lot.

There was a state police car and two county four-by-fours already parked in a back corner. The sight of them gave me and Desmond pause, but the rest of those boys piled right out. We were in Alabama after all where none of their misdeeds had followed.

We watched them parade on into the place like they were untouchable.

"Don't you wish sometimes you could be like them?"

Desmond turned full around to gaze upon me like I was daft.

They didn't have waffles exactly. Didn't have waffles at all but instead burritos and biscuits and something called the Hearty Breakfast Bowl. It looked like a meal a collie would make if a collie could half cook.

The boys were up at the counter ordering by the time we went into the place. They were getting the hard once-over from two deputies and a trooper who were sipping their coffee and munching their hash brown sticks in a far corner booth.

I heard Luther tell the girl at the register, "Yeah, this is all together." Then he glanced my way and pointed. He told her, "Him."

"You talk to Kendell?" I asked Desmond.

"You know I didn't."

"Want me to?"

"You know I do."

I gave Desmond my wallet. "Just get me some coffee." My chicken had gone in fine as well, but it was still right where I'd put it.

I went back out to the Escalade, fished Desmond's phone out of the cup holder, and called up Kendell while I wandered around the Jack in the Box lot.

"Where you been?" he said instead of hello.

"It's Nick. We're in Alabama."

"Alabama where?"

I looked around like that might help me. "Nearly to Tuscaloosa. Hour or so away."

"You talk to her?"

"No. Did you?"

"Yeah," Kendell told me. "Last night."

"You talked to Tula directly?"

"Uh-huh."

"How'd she sound?"

"Mostly pissed."

"But she's okay?"

"Define 'okay'."

"He hasn't hurt her or . . . you know, messed with her."

"I can't see Tula standing for that. She said she was fine. I believed her. But she's spent more time with that nut than any human ought to have to."

"What else did she tell you?"

"Nothing much. Just proved she was alive. Then that Boudrot got on and yammered at me."

"Where do you figure they are?" I asked him.

"Tech guy here says they're in Tuscaloosa. South of the river, north of the interstate. That's the best he can do."

"That'll work," I told Kendell. Not that I'd ever been to Tuscaloosa and knew what we'd be up against between the river and the four-lane.

"Get you some firepower?" Kendell asked me.

"Wrinkle," I told him.

Like his cousin Desmond, Kendell had an assortment of snorts as well. He deployed one my way.

"Wasn't anybody's fault."

He had a snort for that too.

"Hold on."

I opened the way back of the Escalade and let Barbara out to pee. Two guys came out of the Jack in the Box just as she hit the ground.

The one without the toothpick said, "Hey!" to me twice. He pointed at Barbara, who was squatting, while he informed me it took a goddamn faggot to think Kyle Petty was worth a shit.

"Nick . . . Nick!" Kendell was calling to me over the phone.

I raised the thing to my ear again. "Yeah."

"You can't fix Alabama," Kendell told me. "Let it go. Maybe you can beat him up on the way back."

I paused to salute those gentlemen as they pulled out of the lot in their camo pickup.

"Yeah. I'll keep a good thought."

Desmond came out of the Jack in the Box with my cup of coffee.

"Still getting armed, right?" Kendell asked me.

"Desmond says he knows a guy."

"Not that fool over there in Gordo."

"I'll let him tell you."

I tried to put Desmond on, but he wouldn't take the phone. He just shook his head, said, "Uh-uh," and stayed just out of reach.

That was Desmond's way with Kendell, his usual technique with rectitude. If somebody was keen on him doing something he knew he ought to do, something there was no earthly chance of him doing, Desmond preferred to make himself unavailable to advice. His arms got short and his fingers useless. His ears became obstructed, and you couldn't ever find his front side because he was always turning away.

"He's doing that thing," I said to Kendell, and it was all I needed to say.

"That Gordo boy?"

"Yeah," I said.

"Don't eat anything he gives you."

"What's he going to give me?"

"You'll see." Kendell must have been at the Greenville station house already. I could hear somebody yelling about his rights and liberties. He sounded drunk or maybe only toothless. "Got to go."

"All right."

"Call me from Tuscaloosa. I might know a little more by then."

"Pull your pants up, fool!" I heard Kendell shout. It made do for "good-bye."

"That buddy of yours in Gordo," I said to Desmond. "He some kind of chef or something?"

Desmond took his phone back from me. "He ain't no buddy of mine," he said.

TWENTY-TWO

It turned out we were less than half an hour out of Gordo, which was kind of someplace, unlike Reform that hadn't been any place at all. Gordo had a water tower and four actual blocks of downtown. Two of them going east to west and two of them north to south.

We stopped at the Marathon station so Percy Dwayne could use the bathroom. The Jack in the Box Jumbo Breakfast Platter wasn't agreeing with him.

"Likely the bacon," Luther explained to me. "Maybe the hash browns. Could be the pancakes. Eggs were a little greasy too."

"That's all on one plate?" I asked him.

Luther nodded. "Jumbo," he explained.

Eugene bought some cigarettes. He smoked one and grew

dizzy. He sat down on a curb stone over by the air hose. Barbara closed on him and laid her head in his lap.

"Used to settle me out," Eugene told me, waving his pack of Merits.

"Jumbo Breakfast Platter?" I asked him.

He owned up in sadness. "Yeah."

Desmond didn't have a current number for his guy. He checked his phone for the time.

"Not but eight thirty," he said. "He won't be up for a while."

"Can't we get him up?"

Desmond grunted. Desmond nodded. "Probably going to have to."

Dale had gone into the minimart and bought an *Iron Man Magazine*. Without intervention, I could see us spending our forenoon parked right there while Dale perched on the ring in the men's room and did more monumental business.

"No sir," I told Dale and pointed at the Escalade. "When Percy Dwayne comes out, we leave."

"Ain't like I can control it."

"Try."

I shut him in the backseat.

"Time to wake up your buddy," I told Desmond. I shouted to Percy Dwayne, "Come on!"

He said something from the toilet. He sounded like a mouse behind a wall. I went over and kicked the door twice. Percy Dwayne came out pulling up his pants.

"It was that last hash brown." Percy Dwayne had been doing some powerful analyzing. "I've seen cleaner Dumpsters," he told me of the Marathon men's room. "Got a good mind to write a letter." We both knew he never would.

Desmond couldn't precisely remember where his friend in Gordo lived. It was out in the Alabama wilds just north and east of Gordo proper. In Desmond's defense, they looked to have logged half the county since he'd last been through there. A lot of bald red dirt and stumps and lap wood and ugly unchecked erosion.

"Who'd want to live here?" Luther asked us about every ninety seconds, right up until Dale distracted him with a picture of a woman from his magazine. A gatefold photo of an oily bemuscled creature holding up the front end of a truck.

"Is that even a girl?" Luther asked Dale.

That was enough to make Dale quarrel. "Hell, I'd do her," he told Luther. It came out sounding like a challenge.

Luther grabbed for the magazine and studied her some. "Yeah," he said. "Maybe. If I could use your dick."

Dale made his aw-fuck-I'm-going-to-hit-you noise, so I reached around and grabbed his ear again. He squealed at such a pitch that he stirred up Barbara in the way back. She warbled and harmonized with him.

"Swallow your knuckles," I told Dale. "And you," I said to Luther, "pipe down."

"Could you get wood with that in the room?" Luther asked as he showed me that oily creature. From the collarbones up, she looked like Johnny Mathis in a wig.

"Think we're here," Desmond told us all and pointed up a track.

The roadway was lined with yellow pines, but the territory on either side had been logged and picked over to a fare-thee-well.

"You sure?"

Desmond nodded and turned in. "Used to be woods. Threw me a little."

Percy Dwayne had drawn up to the seat back. "Sure looks like a shit hole now."

That was impossible to argue with. The surrounding landscape had that ruined postapocalyptic feel to it. It was all dead limbs and red clay gullies, stumps and viney thickets. The standing trees along the roadway made the scene seem odder still, like somebody had hoped we wouldn't notice the devastation beyond them.

"Who's this guy?" Percy Dwayne asked Desmond.

Desmond groaned and shifted. He said, "Lance."

Up until then I thought I knew everybody Desmond knew.

"Lance?" I asked him.

Desmond winced and nodded. Whenever he did that I could be sure I was about to meet a stone-cold freak.

"Worse than Manny?"

I could see the house by then, a ramshackle federalist heap that hadn't been painted in several decades. The tin roof was rusted and two of the portico columns were holding each other up.

Desmond winced. Desmond shrugged. Desmond knew Manny from some Pine Bluff roadhouse back when Desmond was courting his ex, Shawnica, who hailed from Arkansas. We ran into him in Memphis once where Desmond was forced to introduce us. Manny talked and twitched like a tweaker, was tattooed from his cowlick down, and wore a cap with a leathery thing attached to the brim. A dried pig's vulva, he informed us.

Manny told us about a guy he'd killed and a woman friend he'd maimed. He laughed all the while, showed us his nasty broken teeth. Desmond had to give him money to get him to leave us alone.

"Colorful," I told Desmond once we were finally free of Manny.

Desmond said, "Shawnica," in a mournful sort of way.

Lance, as it turned out, was colorful too. We didn't have to wake him up after all. He hadn't gone to bed yet. He answered the door when Desmond knocked like he was expecting somebody else.

I wasn't quite ready for the spectacle of Lance since I was still soaking in the carnival's worth of crap in Lance's yard. Two ice cream trucks. A life-sized camel made from brown shag carpet. A row of theater seats—still bolted together. A hot-air balloon basket. A World War II–vintage antiaircraft gun. The sort of boat Robinson Crusoe might have made if he'd had no end of epoxy. A DeLorean, I think (the weeds were kind of high). One of those painted canvas sideshow banners you see at the county fair. It wasn't entirely unfurled, and I could just make out the face of a man with snake scales down his neck.

Our crew was wandering the property like they were walking the streets of heaven. They moved from item to item, marveling at each in turn and saying with wonderment, "Shit!"

Consequently, they were preoccupied when Lance threw open the door. I was on the front porch with Desmond still half dazzled by the yard crap but focused enough to keep myself away from the holes in the porch planking.

Lance was Mick Jagger skinny. Not an ounce of fat on him and a mohawk for a do. He was wearing what turned out to be a tangerine crepe tube top and a pair of tartan Bermuda shorts. Black watch, I have to think.

At the sight of Desmond, Lance shouted, "Honey!" and threw open the screen door. Kicked it open actually since it was swollen stuck in the jamb. There was no harm to be done. It was just a warped frame with no screenwire in it. Lance burst across the threshold and all but leapt into Desmond's arms.

That got the crew's attention. Percy Dwayne said, "What the fuck . . . ?" Now the wonderment was tempered with disgust.

Lance was wearing leopard flip-flops. The toenails on one foot were painted blue, and the nails on the other were pinkish red.

"Cherry blossom," he told me later.

Lance gave Desmond a prodigious kiss on the cheek. Desmond proved to have a snort for that. He then uncoupled himself from Lance as delicately as he could manage. Desmond didn't fracture Lance's bones anyway as he took his arms off his neck.

"Sorry to just roll up," Desmond said.

"I thought you were Jason." Lance slapped Desmond's chest fondly as he spoke. "His medicine day. Ought to be here shortly."

"Jason from Meridian?"

"Don't you know it!"

Desmond jabbed his thumb my way. "Nick," he said.

"Well now." Lance laid his hands to his hips and treated me to an exhaustive once-over. He said, "Hmmmm," as he gave me a hard scour down and a hard scour up.

I wasn't offended or uneasy. Lance seemed mostly otherworldly. Unless, of course, you were Percy Dwayne, Luther, Eugene, or Dale. I could hear them all breathing past their adenoids at the base of the porch stairs. Lance must have heard them too. Once he finished with me, he stepped over to the lip of the porch floor and gave our colleagues the once-over.

"What are you looking at, Betty?" Percy Dwayne asked him.

"Splain!" Lance said to no one much, but Desmond knew he was talking to him.

"We're in kind of a fix," Desmond told Lance.

"Yes, and . . ."

"We're chasing a boy. They're helping us. Need a few things."

"Want to go way up? Want to go way down?"

"Guns," Desmond explained. "Holding maybe five hundred, but we're good for whatever it takes."

"Then come on." Lance waved us toward his front door. "You boys too if you want," he shouted down to Luther and Percy Dwayne, Dale and Eugene. He'd turned full around to do it, and Barbara, naturally, caught his eye. "Hey, sugar," he told her, and then he said to me and Desmond, "I've got a better shirt for your dog."

Lance collected antlers and tusks along with brown mottled Charles Chips cans, the big tin canisters they used to deliver to customers straight out of trucks. He had deer antlers and moose antlers and what looked to me like ram horns. They were mounted on the walls. Laying on the tables. Piled up on the floor. There were two elephant tusks standing up in a corner and what I had to guess was a hippopotamus tooth on the mantelpiece. Lance also had a stuffed and lacquered python on his hearth. It was diamond patterned and pale pink underneath.

Dale saw it first. He pulled his hand from his mouth and alerted the rest of the crew with, "Fucking hell."

That parlor was like the front yard only better.

"Ain't for sale or nothing is it?" Eugene wanted to know of the python. He was a bit of a reptile buff himself.

"No, sweetie," Lance said.

Eugene shivered involuntarily. He'd probably never been called sweetie, even by a woman.

"Park yourselves," Lance told our crew. "Nibble." He pointed at an open Charles Chips canister on the coffee table. It was half full of pale, mishapen cookies. The table itself was a slab of glass held up by a thicket of ibex antlers or something. Not deer anyway. They were black and ribbed and curled all over the place.

"Jack in the Box," Percy Dwayne said and patted his dodgy stomach. Then he reached straight down, plucked up a cookie, and popped it in his mouth.

"Back here," Lance told me and Desmond and led us through his kitchen. There were three empty half-gallon vodka bottles on the dinette table and a heap of sheet pans and pots and mixing bowls in the sink.

Lance caught me gawking at the mess. "Got a woman who comes in," he told me.

"To do what?"

He wagged his finger my way. "Don't get sassy."

There was a narrow back hallway off the kitchen, so tight Desmond could barely fit through it. Lance tugged on the light cord for the fixture overhead, but the socket was empty, so nothing came on, and we stood there in the dark.

I heard Lance pawing for a key. He knocked it off the door ledge and then scrabbled around for it on the floor. When he grabbed the doorknob to steady himself, the door proved to be unlocked, and the thing swung open.

"Isn't this a fine how-do-you-do," Lance said.

The place looked tossed to me, but disheveled and upended seemed to be standard Lance décor.

Lance parked himself in the middle of the room. He planted his hands on his hips and whistled through his teeth.

"Problem?" Desmond asked him.

"Look!" he told us.

We did. It was just another messy room in a house full of them.

"Something missing?"

Lance rolled his eyes at Desmond. "Ain't sweet fuckall left."

There were no antlers or tusks anywhere, but I couldn't imagine that was the problem.

Lance stalked over to the lone closet door—he was quite a spectacle in a snit—and yanked the door open. Lance glanced inside and said, "Hmmm."

"What?" Desmond asked him.

He pointed at a naked bit of floorboard. "Took all my weed." He pointed again. "Had four AKs and an M1. All the shoulder-fired shit's gone." Lance kicked a pile of paper grocery sacks aside. "Pistols too."

"Who?" I asked him.

"Boys last night. Had to be. Curtis brought them."

"Tupelo Curtis?"

Once Lance nodded, Desmond groaned. He turned my way to fill me in. "Piece of shit," he explained.

"So no guns?" I said.

"We'll get them," Lance assured me.

Then he went sifting through a pile of clothes under a window on the floor. He came away with a T-shirt. It was brown-and-white spotted like a Guernsey cow. Lance held it up so we could read the back. Just two words: MOO, GODDAMMIT.

"For your dog," he said.

We thanked him. What else were we going to do?

"Get him out of that NASCAR shit. What's his name anyway?"

"Barbara," Desmond told Lance.

"I had a coonhound once," Lance said. He crossed the room and lingered for a pensive moment in the doorway. He tugged at his tube top. He scratched his nose. "Rusty or something," he told us. Then he was out in the narrow back hallway and gone.

Desmond actually let me glare at him hard before he told me, "Don't say it."

"I'm not going back to Columbus. I'll go in the Walmart and buy us another a shotgun."

"We'll figure it out."

That's when Lance yelled, "Hey! You ought to come see this."

So it was back up the hallway for me and Desmond, across the kitchen, and into the front room. Our gang was piled up on the sofa in a semi-conscious, lethargic heap. All but Luther. He was stretched full out on the nasty rug. The cookie tin was empty. Barbara was chewing on an antler.

"What the hell happened?" Desmond wanted to know.

"Honduran hash," Lance told us. "Probably should have said."

I poked Luther with my foot. He giggled.

"Yeah," I told Lance. "Probably.

Desmond grabbed Dale's arm and pulled his hand out of his mouth. He was well past feeling his nub, had swallowed his hand up to his wrist.

Drool dripped off his chin as Dale grinned and told Desmond's left leg, "Hey."

Eugene and Percy Dwayne and Luther all cackled. Barbara gnawed on her antler.

"Truth is," Desmond informed Lance, "they weren't too much good straight."

TWENTY-THREE

Fortunately, Tupelo Curtis didn't live in Tupelo anymore. He'd migrated to Alabama and rented a trailer at the head of a gully, a convenience for Curtis whenever he wanted to pitch out an appliance or trash.

We left the crew at the house, and me and Desmond rode with Lance over to visit Curtis in Lance's Hummer. We had between us the sawed-off shotgun I'd taken off those CashPoint boys.

"Never fired it," I told Lance. "Might not work."

"I wouldn't worry about that." Lance drove all casual, with his left foot on the armrest. "We'll probably just beat him with it."

"You sure it was him?" Desmond wanted to know.

Lance nodded. "When he came over with those guys last night, he was acting like a goddamn hostage. I can see it all now." Lance shook a finger at us. "I was full of cookies yesterday myself."

"How did he know about your guns?" I asked him.

"How did you know about them?" was all Lance needed to say.

That's about when Lance reached a gravel pullout off the hard top. He pointed across the hilly terrain at a trailer perched on the rim of a gully. Just like at Lance's house, the trees had all been harvested, and the scrubby vines had grown in where the limbs were littering the ground.

"What's with all the timbering?" I asked Lance.

"Times get hard, the pines go to the mill."

"Looks like hell."

"Does," he told me. "Wouldn't you be high?"

We rolled right up in Lance's Hummer on Curtis's shabby trailer.

"Don't want to slip up on him?" Desmond asked.

"Aw, honey. He's asleep."

He was too. So asleep, in fact, that we needed a solid quarter hour just to wake him up. But for a bed and a loveseat, Curtis didn't have any furniture. He must not have had any bedclothes either because he was stretched out on a naked mattress under a sleeping bag.

"Hey," Lance told him while tugging on one of Curtis's filthy big toes.

Curtis considered us all with one eye open and then went back under for a bit.

He didn't much look like the sort of hick who'd live in a trashy trailer at the head of a gully in nowhere Alabama. He had a square jaw and handsome features, what looked to me like a professional haircut. He had no tattoos that I could see—not anyway of the ill-considered, disqualifying sort. The amateur kind on his neck or his hands, the sort of ink that screams out, "I give up!"

He looked fit and clean as far as it went and reminded me of an actor.

"Who?" Lance and Desmond both asked me.

"Tony Franciosa. Played a blind detective once."

"A blind detective?" Lance asked Desmond. It didn't ring a bell with either of them.

"Had a dimple like that." I pointed at Curtis. "I'm just saying he doesn't look local."

We stood there in silence for a moment, watching Curtis go on sleeping.

"Do I look local?" Lance finally asked me.

"You mean," I said back, "from earth?"

Lance cackled and tugged on his tube top. He picked up a half-empty liter of Popov vodka from the floor beside the bed. The top was already off, so all he had to do was pour it.

Curtis didn't even wake up in the local way. He stayed where he was and got soaked through with spirits before he told us in just a flat and regular voice, "All right."

Even after that, he just laid there for a while. He turned over on his back and looked up at us. He rubbed his eyes. He dozed and woke.

When Curtis spoke again, all he said was, "What?"

"Who were they?" Lance asked him.

You had to admire the efficiency of it all. Curtis didn't bother to pretend he didn't know what Lance had come for, and Lance didn't let standard-issue backwoods fury get in his way. This was more in the way of a transaction. Freak to freak was the sense I got. A handsome boy in a trailer above a gully probably had to go every which way.

"Lucy brought them," Curtis said.

Lance told me and Desmond, "Women!"

"They had some shit in mind for me I didn't want to do." I had to imagine Curtis probably said something like that a lot.

"So you brought them to me?" Lance asked with an air of wounded disappointment.

"Sorry, sweetie," Curtis told him and reached out a hand like he was seeking absolution.

Lance told Desmond, "Hit him," and Desmond did.

I have to think that was all part of the process for Lance and Curtis, and Desmond knew enough of Lance to do just what he asked. There certainly wasn't any whining from Curtis. He had a punch coming, and he knew it.

"I guess we'll need to find them," he said to Lance as he finally threw back his sleeping bag and rolled out of his bed.

Curtis picked a cigarette up off the floor, a stray Chesterfield laying against the baseboard. It was only torn and broken in a couple of places. Curtis mended it with his fingers. Lance produce a lighter and lit it.

"Coffee?" Curtis asked Lance.

"On the way."

Curtis got dressed after a fashion. He wore a yellow belly shirt with E TU? screen printed on it and a pair of clam diggers that were still primarily white. The sort with a rope for a belt and calf buttons shaped like anchors. The Reeboks without any laces confused the whole effect.

Lance wanted Curtis up front with him, so me and Desmond rode in the back. Lance told Curtis about some waistcoat he'd seen on the Bravo channel.

"With lapels," Lance said.

"They work?"

"Stunning!" By now Lance had his left foot out the window. "And big buttons. Bone, it looked like."

Curtis said, "Oh my."

I'd barely started looking at Desmond in a meaningful sort of way before he made it plain he had a snort for Lance and Curtis both.

We stopped for coffee at a Kangaroo mart. Lance parked against a far curb where he pumped Curtis for details.

"It was some guy Lucy dated and a cousin of his. They'd heard about all the shit you had."

"From you?" Lance asked him.

Curtis shook his head. "Lucy handed them off to me because she knew I could get them in your house."

"Where are we going to find them?"

When Curtis made like he was about to shrug, Lance smacked him hard. It was more of a slap than a punch, but he caught Curtis flush on the cheek and left the outline of his hand there.

"Lucy knows," he said.

"She working?"

"Probably."

"Bear with me," Lance told me and Desmond as he drove us away from the Kangaroo Mart and back down the road the way we'd come.

Lucy worked at a sawmill. She was perched in a puny shack up above the scale, which gave her the perfect vantage point to see a Hummer coming. Worse still, it was a yellow Hummer, so we couldn't hope to go unnoticed.

The woman had to know who was in it and suspect what he'd come about, so she went ahead and radioed up a few of her lumberyard friends to meet us. Roughnecks in hardhats, all four of them, and those boys were armed with log pikes. They stood four abreast by the truck scale looking surly and pissed off.

They appeared to think Lance would draw up short before he ran them over, but what was the point of having a big yellow

Hummer if you couldn't run roughnecks down? Lance never so much as touched the break. He caught three of them flush with his bumper and threw his door open to clip the fourth and knock him over. Then he leapt out right onto that boy's midsection. Lance jumped up and down like he was a bratty child on a settee.

I told Desmond, "Man, it's tough over here."

By then Lance had shifted to give hell to the other boys he'd hit. That was a bit more of a challenge since they were largely under the Hummer, but Lance managed to drag one mostly out and make an example of him. Lance threw what qualified as a violent hissy fit.

"That's right, honey," he kept saying as he jumped up and down on a burly guy in a nasty T-shirt. Then he pointed at the scale house and told the Hummer windshield, "Get her!"

"Talking to us, isn't he?" I said to Desmond.

Desmond made a neck noise.

"I don't want to get arrested in Alabama," I told him as I threw open my door.

"You coming?" Desmond asked Curtis.

He shook his head and said, "I'm all right."

We crossed the truck scale and climbed the steep steel stairs to the scale house door. A woman I had to take for Lucy was by herself inside. We eyed her through the door glass. She was a woman of some girth with strawberry-blond hair and no end of freckles. She was built like a doorstop—shapeless and dense— and she was waving a claw hammer at us.

"Go on!" she shouted.

I tried the door. It didn't have a proper bolt to throw, just one of those knobs with a privacy latch like you'd install in your bathroom. There was a hole in the knob on our side. I knew I could unlatch it through that.

"You got a toothpick?" I asked Desmond.

He always had a toothpick. Desmond went feeling through his pockets.

"I kill you!" Lucy told us. She waved her hammer around with such vigor she just about knocked herself in the head.

"Get her!" Lance shouted from the front Hummer bumper. He was bouncing on a third guy by then.

"I don't think I like his tone," I told Desmond.

He groaned and offered me a cellophane-wrapped peppermint toothpick.

"We're coming in," I told Lucy. "Might as well put that hammer down."

She made a feral noise back in her throat and did some more hammer brandishing. That scale house was puny to start with, and the door opened in, so I could tell that we'd all be right there in the same puny spot together.

"Come on!" Lance shouted from down at the Hummer.

"He's pushy," I told Desmond. I didn't need to unwrap that toothpick. I just shoved the entire business in the doorknob hole. It popped the button on the far side. I pushed the door full open, and Lucy got so worked up and brandished that hammer with such violence that she finally succeeded at hitting herself in the forehead.

"Ow. Shit!" she said.

I took half a stride and grabbed the hammer handle. I yanked the thing out of her hand.

"Come on," I told her.

"I kill you!" She swatted at me with the hand she wasn't nursing her forehead with.

I looked to Desmond for help, but there wasn't room for him in the scale house. I managed to work my way behind Lucy and shove her toward the door. She smacked at the door frame. She slapped at Desmond.

"I kill you!" she told him as well.

Desmond gave her one of his gentle, openhanded shut-the-fuck-up blows. It rang her bell enough to make her docile for a time.

He walked her down the scale house stairs. I could hear enough radio chatter to know that we needed to leave that sawmill straightaway if we had any hope of getting out.

"Better go," I shouted down to Lance.

He looked winded from jumping on roughnecks. He gave over those fellows on the ground so he could wag a finger at Lucy. He had Desmond put her in the backseat, and then Lance shouted up at me, "Come on!"

"Jesus, man, I'm coming," I told him.

He backed the Hummer up and whipped it around. I had to sprint to the back door and jump in before Lance, who was revving that Hummer engine, could tear out of the yard.

"You're welcome," I told him.

Lance shot me a wink in the rearview. "Don't be like that, honey," he said.

"I kill you." Lucy was training her animosity exclusively on Curtis now.

"Who and where?" Lance asked her.

She pinched her lips together and shook her head.

"These boys'll do you all kinds of wrong," Lance said of me and Desmond. "They're from goddamn Mississippi, and not even nowhere nice."

Lucy was a spitter. She hit Lance's headrest.

"Tell her," Lance said to Desmond.

"Delta," Desmond rumbled at Lucy. "We'll do any damn thing."

I hadn't really ever considered what people elsewhere thought of the Mississippi Delta. I knew it had a reputation for being hardscrabble and damned, but that was prevalent among the residents of hill country Mississippi. I didn't know they'd have a Delta opinion in Alabama at all. Then Lucy went and gave us a look like me and Desmond were both assassins. She calmed right down. She even reached over and wiped her spit off the headrest.

"Sorry," she said.

Desmond winked my way. This was a Delta virtue I'd never even suspected. It was a help, in the general course of things, if people thought you'd make them dead.

"Why you want to steal from me?" Lance asked Lucy.

"Didn't," Lucy told him. "Those boys come to take my shit."

"So you helped them take mine instead?"

That seemed to capture the thrust of the thing well enough. Lucy nodded. Lucy told Lance, "Yeah."

"How are we going to get it back?"

"Ask him." She pointed at Curtis.

"I don't know them boys," Curtis said to Lance. "She brought them over. It was all like I told you before."

"You took them to his place," Lucy snarled and indicated Lance with her lumpy forehead. That hammer had raised a welt that was going more purple by the minute.

"They wanted to party," Curtis said to Lance. "They would have tore me up."

Lance didn't appear to doubt him. He nodded like a man who guessed Curtis would have been pulling splinters from his lower intestinal tract.

"So you took them to Curtis. Curtis took them to me. I got that," Lance told Lucy. "Where are we going to find them right now?"

"Pooky's probably," Lucy said. "Only place I ever seen them."

"Who we talking?"

"Big one's J.J. Little one's Odell."

"They got people around?" Lance asked Lucy.

"Not that I know about."

"Watch that Odell," Curtis told us. "That little fucker's mean."

Curtis showed us a human bite mark on his shoulder. It was angry red and the teeth had broken the skin in a couple of places.

"What was that for?" Lance wanted to know.

Curtis shook his head. He shrugged.

"Up on your shots?" I asked him.

That raised a cackle out of Lance. He wagged a finger at me. "Aw," Lance told me, "honey."

TWENTY-FOUR

Pooky's looked about like it had to. A low cinder-block road-house with no character at all. Weeds were growing everywhere they could. A prickly thicket was fairly strangling an abandoned harrow near the ditch, and the hollow core of a pile of tires at the far corner of the building was overflowing with beer cans and trash.

The door of the place was standing open. There was one state-body truck and two muddy little coupes parked nose in out front. Instead of music pouring out the door there was Fox News morning banter and the intermittent clack of billiard balls.

Lance parked at the far end of the building. Since the windows were all painted over, there was little chance that we'd been seen. Even in broad daylight and even in a yellow Hummer.

"Let's hear it," Lance said to Lucy.

She didn't need any more prompting than that. "Melvis must have sent them. You know how he gets."

Curtis turned out to have a snort for Melvis. "Figures," was all he said.

"They knew all about you," Lucy told Lance. "The guns and the weed and shit. Nothing special. A couple of hicks. Cousins, I think, or something."

"Knives? Guns? What?"

"The little one has a hunting knife. A big one." Lucy described a blade about the length of a paint stick. "Likes to whip it around and shit. Other one had some kind of pistol but no telling what he's got now."

That was true enough, given all the guns they'd stolen.

"Live around here?" Lance asked.

Lucy nodded. "Motel down toward Eutaw. Work in timber most of the time. Got a wild hair or something, I guess."

"I guess," Lance said. "Which of them's theirs." He pointed at the vehicles in the lot.

"Blue one," Lucy told him.

That was the muddier of the coupes.

"Look back there," Lance said to Desmond. "Wonder Bar in the box."

Since Desmond had precious little room to maneuver there on the backseat, I did the swiveling for him and found the pry bar straightaway.

"Probably hadn't been home yet," Lance informed us. "Take a look." He pointed at the muddy blue coupe. He was clearly talking to me.

"Pop it?" I asked him.

"Yeah, honey," he said, like he was talking to a toddler or a goat. "He ain't from the Delta, is he?" Lance asked Desmond, the implication being that Delta natives popped trunks as a matter of course.

"Give it to him," Lance pointed at Curtis.

"Think I can manage," I told him.

I was getting a feel by then for Alabama where everything you got up to and everything you didn't was a test of your manhood and your local standing.

I rolled on out of the Hummer and eased over to that coupe. I had to pass before the open roadhouse doorway to get to it, but the balls kept clacking and the morning Fox News crew kept being irate about something. I squatted behind that filthy little Nissan and waited, but nobody came out of the place.

The Wonder Bar didn't prove to be much help because the trunk lid was clothesline-wired shut. The latch had been punched out a great while ago, judging from the rust, and some anal-retentive hoodlum had thoroughly lashed that trunk lid down. I had to think the swag would be in there. Otherwise they would have just done a loop through and left it at that.

I didn't have anything to cut the wire with, so all I could do was unwind it. That didn't sit too well with Lance, who kept hissing, "Honey!" my way. I'd hold up a finger to buy me a minute and then wait to get honeyed at again. I was starting to have mixed feelings about Lance. He was part good old boy, part disco diva, part Victorian dancing master.

I stayed busy unspooling the clothesline wire while Lance kept pestering me about it. When I'd finally worked it all loose and lifted the lid, the hinges made a hellacious squawk. One of them was bent, and it moaned so that a guy came out of the roadhouse. He'd emerged partly to see what the racket was but partly as well to pee.

"Hey, champ," he told me. "What's doing?"

He wandered over my way. He was unzipping as he came. I
glanced toward the Hummer and saw Curtis shaking his head.
Whoever this fellow was, he wasn't one of ours.

"Trunk's busted," I told him.

He was reaching in to pull out his member about the time he
passed me. He walked a stride or two beyond the Nissan bumper and started sluicing into the lot.

"Toilet broke?" I asked him. I shrugged toward Lance and
awaited instructions.

"Ain't one," that fellow said.

I could see a big faux-leather bag in the trunk. The zipper on
top was busted, and the thing was laid half open. Lots of gun
metal and pharmaceutical bottles. Plenty of Cryovacked weed.

"Do I know you?" my peeing buddy asked me.

"Naw," I told him.

"Know that ain't your car."

It seemed to me like an ill-considered approach to say something provocative to a stranger while you were draining your
bladder. If I were going to accuse a guy of messing with a car that
wasn't his, I'd be ready in case he decided he wanted to do something about it.

I had time to enter into a sort of consultation with Lance and
Desmond. I shrugged in their direction. Lance drew a finger
straight across his throat. Desmond pitched his head in that way
that usually meant, "Go on and hit him."

It didn't quite seem fair. Then the guy turned to me so I had
to watch him shake.

"Want to tell me what the fuck you're up to?"

"Go on and zip," I said.

"When did I start working for you?" He spat. He grinned.

I grinned right back. "So long."

I slugged him hard.

He went down like he'd been pitched off the roof. His belly spilled out from under his shirttails, and I could see the handle of a pistol shoved in the waistband of his jeans. I had to think it would take him a quarter hour just to draw it out. I tried to pull the thing, but I couldn't budge it.

Lance left the Hummer with Desmond and came over to join me by the Nissan.

"Would you look at that." Lance pointed at the guy I'd slugged. "He's not even put away."

Lance stooped down and carefully tucked away that fellow's privates. Most of them anyway but for a flap of skin he snagged in the zipper when he did that boy the courtesy of closing his blue jeans up.

Me and Desmond twitched and convulsed. We couldn't help ourselves.

"That ought to give him something to remember us by," Lance said. He glanced in the trunk. "Yep. All mine."

Lance reached into the bag and drew out a TEC-9. He fished around for a loaded clip and found one. He slapped in the clip, jacked in a round, and tossed the gun at Desmond.

"Shoot them if I say."

Then Lance struck out for the roadhouse door. He was a sight going away in his tube top and his plaid shorts and leopard flip-flops. He had a bit of a prance to the way he moved, especially now that satisfaction was at hand.

"Doubt he even needs us," I told Desmond.

Desmond grunted as we followed.

"Don't shoot shit," I added.

Desmond had a snort for that.

It was so hard to keep up with how much trouble we were in already that I was holding it in my head as just "a lot." I had to think shooting up an Alabama roadhouse would only compound all our problems. There's only so much of a toxic mess we could hope to make and skate.

"Why don't you stay out here?" Desmond said.

"Yeah, right," I told him and went in.

I've been inside more shitty roadhouses than I can even begin to count. Through the mid-South and the deep South, and I worked a month in Ohio once where I passed evenings in some of the most run-down, bedraggled taverns I've ever seen. But I had never come across a more disreputable and slovenly excuse for a place of business than Pooky's.

There was a trash can full of greasy paper plates and beer cans hard beside the door. There looked to be about as much trash on the floor as there was in the barrel itself. The place stank of grease, spilled beer, and cigarettes. I wasn't half a yard inside before I was sticking to the cement floor.

It was dark but for the TV screen and the light over the pool table.

"Help you?" a guy said from behind the bar. It sounded more like a threat than an offer.

"You Pooky?" Lance asked him.

"Maybe."

"Might want to get the fuck out."

The fellow who maybe was Pooky produced a ball bat from behind the bar. He slapped the business end on his fleshy palm, which got a rise out of Lance. Probably not the rise Pooky had hope for. Lance giggled and stomped his feet.

"Wrong," Lance said and glanced at Desmond who leveled his TEC-9 at a Fox News blonde and blew up the TV.

Now the three boys at the pool table were paying full attention to us.

One of them was wearing a uniform—deep green twill—like a janitor or a plumber might. Lance pointed his way.

"You," he said. "Go."

That was not the sort of talk that fellow had any reason to want to hear twice. He set his beer down on the pool table rail, made a few cowardly noises to the fellows he was leaving. Something about his wife and his daughter and his need to go on living.

"Go on then," the little one told him as he pulled out the knife we'd heard about.

It was a massive shiny thing with plenty of facets to catch the light. Unless he was hoping to deflect bullets with the blade, I don't know why he bothered.

"Hello, boys," Lance said. "Know why I'm here?"

The big one laid his cue on the table. "Thirsty maybe."

He went reaching for something.

"Uh-uh," Desmond said his way.

There in the gloom, I think Desmond intended to make enough racket with that TEC-9—beyond the racket he'd already made destroying Pooky's television—to discourage that boy from pulling out whatever pistol he had tucked away. Desmond was primed to shoot our Boudrot but not some stray Alabama pinhead, but somehow in racking that gun around, he hit the clip release by mistake.

His full banana clip dropped out of the slot and went clattering across the cement floor. Desmond made his "uh-oh" noise. He tried to corral the thing but kicked it. Lucky for us, those boys at the pool table were so used to being unlucky that they didn't straightaway see the mishap for what it was. Instead we all just stood there for about a quarter minute looking at each other.

"What are you holding?" Lance asked me out the side of his mouth.

I didn't have shit. I told Lance, "My breath."

"Hey," I heard the little one say to the big one. Then he pointed at us with his knife.

He must have been the brains of the duo. He seemed to suspect we'd screwed up somehow. He didn't know how exactly.
He'd heard all the racket from Desmond and only knew that
him and his buddy weren't actively getting shot.

"Come on, then," he told us. I guess just to see if we would.

His partner muttered something at him, and the two of them
quarreled there for a bit. That gave me occasion to ease up toward
a stool by the roadhouse wall. Not a metal upholstered bar stool
but a rickety oak one. That suited Pooky's.

I heard the little one tell the big one, "Pull."

The big one was reluctant. "He'll shoot me," he said of
Desmond.

"Dropped his bullets." That boy with the knife was too ob-
servant for his own good. "Go on," he told his partner, and his
partner reached back for his gun.

Now I was wishing I'd shifted aside that fellow's belly out in
the lot. His was just a .22, but that was better than a bar stool.

Lance stayed with the script while he could, even though his
supporting cast had failed him.

"The way I hear it," Lance said, "you boys made off with some
shit that wasn't yours."

"Ain't done it," the puny one told him. "Hell, princess, we ain't
never laid eyes on you."

"I remember you," Lance told him. "Don't see a damn munch-
kin every day."

That sure did it. The puny one appeared to have no patience
for getting reminded that he was puny.

"Fucker!" he said to Lance and then told his partner, "Pull,
dammit!"

The big one brought his gun out. He juked and cringed like
he was sorely afraid of getting shot. Desmond just had one bullet
in the chamber, and he let that one fly. It dug into the block wall

between those boys. You can't really aim a TEC-9, and I don't think Desmond was hoping to shoot anybody anyway.

He certainly wasn't hoping to get shot in return or sliced open by a runt. The big one leveled his pistol at Desmond.

"Better know what you're doing," Lance suggested.

Truth be told, that boy didn't look like he'd known much of anything for a while.

There weren't too many options left for me. I just about could only do what I ended up doing. I had ahold of that bar stool by the legs and flung it at those boys. I followed hard behind it, and Desmond glided over from where he was. The idea was to get on top of that big one before he could squeeze off a round. That was Desmond's job. He was on the flank for it. I had to take care of the little mouthy one with the hunting knife.

Lucky for me, those boys had thrown their pool cues on the table. I grabbed one up and started swinging.

The little one called me, "Fucker!" now.

He tried to close on me. His blade was long, but it was no match for a pool cue, so I caught him once on the shoulder and once just above his ear. That only made him madder.

He gave me a louder "FUCKER!" and came charging at me through the blows. He got close enough to be a danger to lay me open, but I just let his momentum carry him past me, and then I wailed on him from behind.

I finally caught him flush on the cowlick. The thud even made Lance say, "Oooohhh."

I heard the knife hit the cement floor. It was followed straight-away by its owner. I wheeled around to help Desmond, but he'd managed to smother the bigger one by then. He had him in one of those Desmond bear hugs. That boy's pistol was down at his side, but that didn't keep him from firing the thing. He had no more sense than that.

He squeezed off four or five rounds straight into the concrete floor. It was a wonder a ricochet didn't drop him and Desmond both together. Those bullets were singing all over the place. Me and Lance both flopped down flat, and the floor in Pooky's was only barely fit for well-shod feet.

"Sweet Lord," I heard Lance say. "I'm throwing all this away."

I knew instantly he meant the tube top and the black watch tartan shorts. My brand-new coveralls were built for abuse, but that slab felt like a fly strip, so I knew I'd be throwing them away as well.

The large boy ran out of bullets, and me and Lance pried ourselves off the cement. We watched as Desmond flung that fellow around. That was his preference in a fight. He'd punch who he had to, but he'd always rather toss a cracker pinhead if he could. Pooky's was perfect for that. No end of hard surfaces to bounce that boy off of.

"All right," Lance said once he'd finally decided Desmond wasn't about to wear out. "Let him be."

Desmond pitched him one last time against the back block wall, and we all watched as that boy sank to the nasty slab floor with a groan.

"Who put you up to it?" Lance asked him.

That boy had started dumb and had gotten addled. He tried to raise a hand, but it was stuck to the floor.

"Was it Melvis?"

"Who the fuck's asking?"

We all turned around to see who was talking at us now. The voice was high and phlegmy, a little on the wheezy side. It seemed to have come from a guy over by the roadhouse door. He was sitting in the shaft of light just aslant the open doorway. A bony old coot with stringy white hair and an oxygen tank on his lap.

He had a tube running under his nose and a cigarette between his lips. He was parked in a wheelchair, appeared to be wearing just a housecoat.

"Goddammit, Melvis," Lance shouted at him and went tearing across the place. He lost his flip-flops early on, and he hit Melvis at a dead run. Lance knocked the wheelchair over sideways, and the oxygen tank went bouncing and ringing across the floor.

Judging from the hard things they said to each other as they grappled like jungle cats, I got the impression Lance and Melvis had a volatile history between them.

The bartender told the both of them, "I'm calling the damn police." Then he threw an empty vodka jug at them. It was plastic. It just bounced.

"Jesus," I said to Desmond.

He sighed and told me, "Alabama."

TWENTY-FIVE

Desmond drove us back to Lance's house in the yellow Hummer, mostly because his hands had never touched the roadhouse floor. Worse still for Lance, Melvis must have lived with a half-dozen cats. The man had shown up nappy with cat hair, and Lance had functioned like a human lint brush. Lance was so sticky from lying down on the floor that most of the fuzz on Melvis had transferred once the two of them had grappled and rolled around.

Lance had crawled into the Hummer way back where every now and again he'd let go with a pitiful, "Shit."

Of course, Lucy and Curtis were anxious to find out what Lance had in mind for them, but Lance was too fuzzy and upset about it to know what he might do.

Lucy kept saying, "I'll get fired and all."

Curtis would occasionally point toward the Hummer headliner and say something on the order of, "Got this thing I ought to do."

But they couldn't seem to make much headway with Lance. He was too tacky and disgusted to fix on anything but getting clean and proper.

"Think the hose'll do it?" Lance asked me.

I was all gritted up as well. That roadhouse floor had been covered in beer and bourbon, both reduced to a syrup. Most of mine was on my coveralls. It felt like molasses. I told Lance, "Nope."

"Can't get these no more," Lance told us while plucking at his tangerine tube top.

I tried to look sad as I shrugged Lance's way.

Lucy told him, "I'll get fired and all."

"I ain't done with you," Lance informed her. "Take them to the house," he told Desmond.

Dale and Eugene and Percy Dwayne and Luther were all parked on the roof of a horse trailer out in Lance's yard. It was dented and unusable. Its tandem tires were rotted and flat. Barbara was sitting by the near wheel well in her MOO, GODDAMMIT T-shirt warbling at the boys up on the roof. I had to guess she'd had some cookies too.

"What are you doing up there?" I asked them as I climbed out of the hummer.

They all looked at me like I'd washed in with the tide and was the last thing they'd expected see.

"Hey," Luther told me. He gave Percy Dwayne the elbow.

"Hey," Percy Dwayne told me too.

"What are you doing up there?" I asked them again.

"Snake in the house," Eugene told me.

"Where?" Desmond had planted one foot on the weedy ground. He hated reptiles in a helpless, spastic sort of way. He drew his leg back up and shut the Hummer door.

"Cobra," Dale said and pointed toward nowhere much.

Lance and Lucy and Curtis were all out of the Hummer by then. Lance pointed at a rusty glider in the yard. It had a sack full of Romex wire and junctions boxes on it. "Sit," he told them. "I'll get to you."

"Cobra?" I said to Lance.

He nodded as he hooked up the hose to his spigot. "Stuffed python," he said. He gave me the nozzle. "Go on and squirt me," he said.

So there I was somewhere in Alabama hosing down a guy in a tube top. He wriggled when the cold water hit him and fairly squealed, "Lordy!" a few times.

The roadhouse floor syrup and cat hair appeared to be impervious to wet. I would have needed a power washer to do any good against them and might have had to take off a layer of skin.

The boys on the trailer roof found the whole spectacle hypnotic. When Desmond tried to get out of the Hummer again, Dale and Luther both told him, "Snake."

"It's stuffed," I shouted.

Desmond wasn't taking chances. He decided to stay in the driver's seat until his options improved.

"Get the 409," Lance told Curtis. "It's in the kitchen somewhere."

Dale started going on about the cobra in the house. Dale high was a lot like Dale drunk, only his tongue still seemed to work. He held forth about cobras. He'd seen a show on cobras once. Apparently, he'd seen a show on sloths once too because he kept getting them all mixed.

"And it'll come out of its tree about once a month," Dale told us all, "just to take a dump."

"Had an uncle like that," Eugene announced, and Luther

and Percy Dwayne hooted and hollered so I feared they might pitch to the ground.

"And bring that damn snake," Lance told Curtis.

Lucy stood up to say, "I'll get fired and all."

"Squirt her," Lance instructed me. I did.

The 409 did the job on Lance. He stripped naked in the yard and scrubbed himself clean with the back of a kitchen sponge. I made a halfhearted attempt to wash the filth off my coveralls.

"Leave it," Lance said. "I got clothes for you."

Curtis stood and watched us with Lance's lacquered python in hand. It was worse than just stuffed. It was ratty and broken and covered in a quarter inch of dust.

"Cobra!" Dale shouted from the trailer roof.

"How much pot was in those cookies?" I asked Lance.

He stood there naked and dripping. He shook like a spaniel. Lance eyed our crew on the trailer roof. "Too damn much."

When they wouldn't come down, I pitched the python up there with them. The way they bailed, you would have thought that trailer was on fire.

The only clothes Lance had around that would fit me was a full set of navy whites. Not dress whites but the Village People kind with the jumper and the baggy pants.

"Had a . . . friend once," Lance told me by way of explanation. He eyed me in a way I found unsettling. It didn't take much. Lance was wearing paisley boxer shorts and a jet-black sports bra by then. "The shit we got up to," Lance added and leered.

"Yeah, well," I told him. "I'll bring them back."

Lance shook his head and shot me a sour smile. "Ended funny," he said, and I tried not to imagine what that could possibly mean.

If our crew hadn't been stoned to the gills, they would have given me no end of shit on my outfit. Instead they'd piled in Lance's Hummer because that's where Desmond was.

When I came out of the house onto the porch in my navy whites, only Lucy ventured to make a remark.

"I'll get fired and all," she told me.

"Let's go," I shouted at my crew.

Desmond got out of the Hummer and made his way to the Escalade. Snake fear wasn't a rational thing with him, so there wasn't much point in talking to him about it. He just glided to his car as quick as he could and buckled up under the wheel. The rest of gang didn't seem much interested in going anywhere. The hash had made them chatty and a lot more cordial than they were in straight life.

"Come on," I said, but they stayed where they were and continued their round table on catfish they had caught and ways they preferred to cook it, all variations on "fried."

"Buttermilk, ya'll," Percy Dwayne said ten times if he said it once.

He was going on about cornmeal when I yelled at them all one time further. They hardly seemed to hear me, though Barbara looked my way and barked.

I went over the horse trailer and picked up Lance's ratty stuffed python with the flaky hide and the punctured tail. I pitched it into the Hummer, and that did the trick straightway. All of those boys came boiling out, but they scattered all over the place.

I tried to get Curtis to help me herd them. He pointed and said, "Got this thing."

I finally picked up a tomato stake and drove those boys into the Escalade and climbed right in behind them.

"Go," I told Desmond.

He did, and we were down at the end of Lance's dirt track before me and Desmond realized we'd not picked up any guns.

"Go back," I said.

He did that too. Desmond pulled up by the Hummer. Lance

had brought out a tennis racket from somewhere and was chasing Lucy around the yard.

"What are you looking at?" he said to me as I circled around toward the Hummer.

I pointed at the yellow tailgate. "Forgot something," was all I said.

I took the TEC-9, a .308, and a Sig with tape on the handle like it had done duty in a gangland hit and gotten down to Dixie somehow.

"How much?" I asked Lance.

"Go on, honey," he told me.

So I climbed back into the Cadillac and we set out again.

I checked the time on Desmond phone in the cup holder. It was already past eleven.

"You missed two calls."

"Who?" Desmond asked me.

"Kendell, looks like. Both."

"Call him."

I did. He picked up on the first ring and demanded to know where we'd been and what the hell we'd been up to and where exactly we happened to find ourselves at this very moment right now.

"Kind of complicated," was all I could come up with.

"You can believe I'm going to tell Tula to have a good rethink about you."

"Talk to her again?" I asked him.

"Yeah," Kendell told me. "About an hour ago."

"She tell you where we ought to go?"

"You to Tuscaloosa yet?"

"Nearly."

"When you cross the river, you call this number." He gave it to me. I repeated it back. "For godsakes, write it down."

I found a receipt and a gnawed-on ballpoint deep in Desmond's console.

"Two-oh-five what?"

Kendell gave me the number again.

"The law doesn't know we're coming, right?"

"Not from me," Kendell said. "But it's not like I can say what you got up to between here and there."

"Nothing much," I told him.

"He means to kill you. You know that don't you?"

"Kind of counting on it," I said.

"Why don't you call me if he doesn't?"

"All right," I told him, and then he was off the line and gone. Kendell might have been a devoted Christian, but he wasn't sentimental.

"Remind me to call him if we're not dead."

Desmond said, "I'll do it."

After twenty minutes of countryside, we finally rolled into a string of shopping plazas and traffic lights.

"Northport," Desmond announced. "About there."

"Where exactly?" Luther asked.

I shifted around to find out just how high our gang still was.

"You good?" I asked them in a general way.

They nodded, and then they giggled.

"Just me and you," I told Desmond, but then it was usually just me and him.

Desmond shrugged like he'd never expected anything else all along.

"Here we go," he said as we cleared the last light, passed one final CVS and an adjacent Taco Casa. We rolled onto a bridge high above the Black Warrior River and soon gained the south bank that put us in Tuscaloosa proper.

"Where are we heading?" Desmond asked me.

"Let's get down the road a little and park."

By then we were passing under University Avenue at what looked like a corner of the campus, and we'd arrived down around a major commercial intersection when everything went to shit. Not for us so much but for Tuscaloosa generally. There were stunted trees and blank cement slabs where stores and service stations had been. Right in the middle everything was a towering steel pillar that looked to have once held a billboard. It was twisted and bent and sheered off at the top.

"Big tornado," Desmond reminded me.

"That was like a year ago, wasn't it?"

He nodded.

"You'd think it'd all be tidied up by now."

It wasn't even close to tidied up. That town was scarred straight through the middle. Aside from the scoured concrete, there were still houses with their roofs half off and churches reduced to piles of brick.

"What the hell are they waiting for?" I asked Desmond.

He couldn't say and shook his head.

"This place ain't much to look at," Dale announced, and those boys in the back all giggled again.

I'd seen the videos. Who hadn't? A big honking tornado tearing straight through Tuscaloosa. It came in at the southwest corner and went out at the northeast. It chewed up everything in a mile-wide track directly through the city. Since it missed the football stadium and the hospital, everybody felt a little spared.

Desmond turned right off McFarland and onto Fifteenth Street. The twister had passed squarely through that intersection. Aside from tidying up the rubble and building a brand-new

Church's Chicken, everything had been left as it was. All of it swept clean.

Desmond eased off into what had once been a service station but was now only asphalt, bare pump islands, and cement.

"Call him," Desmond told me.

I punched in the number Kendell had given me. I got eight or ten rings, and then a recorded phone company lady came on instead of a personal message. I hung up and was in the middle of telling Desmond that I'd shortly try again when "Satin Soul" started in. It was Tula's phone calling me back.

"Where you been, scooter?" that Boudrot asked me. "Don't like just hanging around."

"Long way over here," I told him. "And we had to pick up your money and shit."

He didn't even bother to pretend like he believed me. This wasn't about money we'd stolen from him. It was far more primitive than that. That Boudrot paused to take a drag on something. Knowing him, he was smoking crack or meth just to get himself amped up.

"So?" I said.

That Boudrot coughed. He moved the phone away from his mouth. I heard him tell somebody, "Give me that."

I waited.

"You there?" that Boudrot asked me.

"Yeah. Let me talk to Tula," I said.

"Not here," he told me.

"Where is she?"

"Around," he said.

"Nothing happens until I talk to her."

"Listen at you," he told me. Then he laughed, all phlegmy and wheezy.

I'd been thinking he might survive the day until I got him

on the phone. Something about the sound of his voice, the pitch of his human indifference, caused me to know if he ended up in a gristly puddle, that'd be all right with me.

I waited. He toked. I could hear the coal of whatever he was smoking crackle by the phone.

"I could eat a rib." Dale had come around enough to talk out loud.

"Who's that?" that Boudrot asked me.

"Nobody."

"Got that big nigger with you?"

I glanced at Desmond. "Yeah."

"Just you and him. None of that cracker trash you brought around last time."

He meant Luther. He meant Percy Dwayne. Probably Eugene a little as well.

"Tula first."

That Boudrot toked and wheezed. "Where are you?"

I looked around. "Some four-lane road. In the middle of a bunch of tornado shit."

"Kicker," he told me. "Around Tenth. By the railroad tracks. Half an hour." Then he was talking to somebody else again as he hung up on me.

"Did you hear me?" Dale said. "I could eat a rib."

Eugene made some racket in the way back to let us know he could eat a rib too.

"All right," I said and then told Desmond, "It's just you and me. Let's drop them off somewhere."

Desmond pulled back out into the road. We had another half mile of scoured concrete, chewed-up buildings, and splintered trees before we crossed out of the tornado zone into untouched Tuscaloosa.

Desmond eased over into a service station so I could ask a big guy in surgical scrubs where a fellow could get a decent plate of ribs in Tuscaloosa.

"Where you from?" he asked me.

I told him, more or less.

"Then Archibald and Woodrow's." He explained where to turn. "Send all the Yankees to Dreamland. It's like goddamn Disney World."

Archibald and Woodrow's was a clapboard shanty with a brick smokehouse attached. There was hickory smoke pouring from the chimney and the smell of charred pork in the air.

I fished three twenties out of my wallet and held them up. "Who wants it?"

Dale grabbed first.

"We're going to run see Tula. That's the deal," I told them all as they were bailing from the Escalade.

"Leaving her," Eugene said of Barbara and clambered over the seat and out.

"But you're coming back, right?" As he talked, Percy Dwayne checked himself in my sideview mirror. "I mean, we all get to fuck him up some, don't we?"

I lied and told him, "Sure."

"Where?" Desmond asked me. He was a checking a map on his phone.

"Kicker and Tenth."

He found it. "Back that way."

Desmond dropped his phone in the cup holder and gave me a thorough look up and down. All this riding around was getting my sailor suit a little wrinkled.

"What?"

He shrugged. He groaned. "You wearing that?"

TWENTY-SIX

Desmond turned onto Kicker off Fifteenth, and we rode past the junction at Tenth. Desmond didn't slow down. We only reconnoitered. That was easy enough since the neighboring eight or ten blocks was tornado blighted. There'd been houses up on the rise to the south, and there were pieces of some of them left. Three or four were even habitable. One had a demolished carport. One a blue tarp on the roof. And one was down to Tyvek and tarpaper but still had cars parked in the yard. The trees were all splintered and wind-blasted. Big oaks just trunks anymore with stubby, fractured limbs that had some autumn foliage on them. I saw more than one tree with siding or roof tin snagged in its busted branches and crooks.

"Water oaks," Desmond told me. Trees were one of Desmond's

things. "They call them druid oaks around here. Call the whole
place Druid City."

"How do you know so much?" I had a fair idea of what Desmond would tell me before he did.

"Had a girl from here a while back."

"Figures."

"She was living in Greenwood. Homesick, you know. She
talked me half to death on Tuscaloosa."

We passed under a cross street, beneath a shabby fractured
bridge.

"Did it ever used to be anything?"

"Better than this," he told me.

We pulled into the parking lot of what had been a big brick
church. The wooden steeple had gotten unscrewed by the wind,
wrenched off and dropped into the churchyard. It lay on its side
all busted to pieces. The sanctuary was awaiting demolition. It
had a chain-link fence around it. The near wall was cracked and
half buckled. The graveyard was littered with roofing shingles
and colorful scraps of hand fans.

"Driving past this stuff every day can't do anybody much
good."

Desmond grunted. He nodded. He pointed. "See her?" he
asked me.

I looked to where he was pointing, back in the direction we'd
come. Beyond the bridge we'd passed under and up on that
storm-ravaged hill that had once been a suburb. There were
people standing on a cul-de-sac we'd gone by coming down.
Three or four of them. I might have had early-afternoon glare to
contend with, but I had no trouble seeing my calypso-coral
Ranchero parked by the curb.

"Yeah," I told Desmond. "I see somebody."

"I think one of them's her," he said.

"Tula?"

Desmond nodded.

I shaded my eyes and looked again. There was one person standing apart from the others. "That one out there?"

Desmond nodded.

I squinted and looked again. "Wearing a skirt, right?"

Another nod. Odd though since Tula wasn't the skirt-wearing sort. I mentioned as much to Desmond.

"Might have put her in it," Desmond said. "That Boudrot be-ing a kink and all."

So Desmond made me think about all the possibilities I'd decided to leave unconsidered. From the moment I knew that Boudrot had nabbed Tula clear through to standing in that church lot, I'd not let myself dwell on the untoward stuff that Boudrot might get up to. He was a puny rat terrier of a guy, hinky and dangerous in his way, with straight-to-video movie star looks if you could take your actors stunted. But I'd only ever known him to brutalize men, and that's what I'd decided he'd get up to. A woman like Tula he'd want to romance, and that sort of thing takes time.

I'd decided he'd need probably three full days before he told himself, "Fuck it," and went at Tula like the beast he was.

Tula was barely twenty-four hours in as I stood there squinting at her in Tuscaloosa. Her skirt hem shifted in the light autumn air as she stood on that cul-de-sac in that storm-scoured suburb.

Together me and Desmond watched Tula raise her arms above her head and wave them at us.

My phone buzzed in my pocket. I fished it out. The call was coming from her phone.

"Yeah."

It was that Boudrot on the other end. "You looking?" he asked me.

"You know I am."

The line went dead, and me and Desmond watched the guy we took for that Boudrot. He looked like a child from where we were as he left the boys he'd been standing with and stepped over toward Tula. He must have told her to put her arms down, because that's just what she did. Then he raised an arm himself and pointed at the side of Tula's head. She suddenly dropped in a heap onto the ground and was already piled up on the pavement before the sound of the pistol shot reached me and Desmond where we stood by that ruined church.

I didn't know what to do, could hardly believe I'd seen what I saw. That Boudrot and his crew got into my Ranchero. Two in the cab and one in the bed. Off they went onto Kicker and up out of sight. We only heard the squeal of the tires after they had vanished.

"No," was all I could manage.

"Come on." Desmond was half in the Escalade.

I imagined Tula's son without a mother. I heard in my head what Kendell would say, shot through with the flinty disappointment he had a talent for. I did that thing where I wondered what life would be like if Tula and me had never met. If she'd never pulled me over and written me up for speeding. If I'd never made it my sole romantic purpose to wear her down. Now I'd piled her up on a barren road in storm-blasted Tuscaloosa. Even there in that littered church parking lot, I already couldn't live with myself.

"Come on," Desmond said.

I moved. I climbed in. We went tearing out of that church lot, under the shabby overpass, and back up Kicker to that cul-de-sac. The whole business took us maybe a minute and a half, and I remember wondering at all the people around us going on with their regular lives. A woman had been gunned down in the broad October afternoon in a city in Alabama, and nobody seemed to have noticed it but us. It was like we were operating in a different dimension from the regular world at large.

Desmond whipped into the cul-de-sac. Barbara bounced around in the way back. I could hear her clawing for purchase on Desmond's rubber matting. Desmond stopped by a power pole so snug to the curb that I almost couldn't get out. Some guy had recently put up a Day-Glo flyer with tabs fluttering across the bottom. He was offering mandolin lessons. Two people had torn off his number. I remember wondering how you'd come through here and think about shit like that.

Desmond got to her first. He was in full glide, but I was hardly trying to keep up with him. I didn't think I had the nerve to see Tula dead, bloody in the road.

Desmond shook his head. "Not her," he told me.

I didn't believe him at first. "What?"

Desmond pointed. I finally brought myself to glance down at the body. I saw a muddy sneaker and a tattooed calf.

"Blew half her head off," Desmond said.

Even disfigured and bloody, she didn't look like Tula at all.

I was too relieved to be disgusted. "Who you figure it is?" I asked Desmond.

"Prison girlfriend probably."

One of the cars that passed by on Kicker was a Tuscaloosa police cruiser. It went down under the overpass, and we saw brake lights at the church.

"Come on," Desmond said. Not that he needed to. We were both heading back to the Escalade by then.

Desmond zipped around the cul-de-sac, turned south, and raced over the rise. He went left on Fifteenth and kept on going, finally eased off at a road that led into the university arboretum.

"We need a think," Desmond told me.

I was perfectly fine with that. I needed to stand up and breathe for a minute or two while I contemplated the savage harm I intended to visit on that Boudrot. Then I wondered if he'd just keep toying with us until he ran out of people to shoot and so finally got down to Tula proper and made me lose her all over again.

I'd only been to an arboretum once. That one was a forest with signs on the trees, hardly the sort of place we rolled up to in Tuscaloosa. Their arboretum was an old golf course that they'd largely let grow wild. The clubhouse windows were boarded up, and the golf cart shed was empty. We parked directly behind the first tee box. The fairways was knee-deep with weeds. People were strolling along the cart paths, most of them with their dogs.

"This is a hell of a thing," Desmond said. He climbed out and went around to get Barbara.

When she hit the ground, an English setter came over to tell her how do you do. A pug soon joined them. A beagle. Some kind of curly-haired retriever. They all sniffed Barbara's spotted T-shirt while she squatted and tried to pee.

She would have been the strangest sight out there but for a girl across the way. She had dreadlocks, was wearing what looked like a kilt and a grimy tie-dyed wife beater. So she would have been conspicuous already if she hadn't been walking a goat.

"Like some weird dream," Desmond said.

I nodded. I told him, "So far."

We wandered over to a sand trap with pine trees growing in it. Barbara followed us partway before she got distracted by the goat. She'd probably never seen a whole one. Eugene used goat chunks for gator bait. She went straight up and had a good snout-to-snout with the creature. It was long eared and spotted and seemed, for a goat, vaguely aristocratic. The creature had little use for a hound in a T-shirt and communicated as much by grunting that way goats will and lifting its snout in the air.

Its owner was a lot less haughty. She told Barbara, "Moo, goddammit."

"Call Boudrot?" I asked Desmond.

"I guess."

"What do you figure he's up to?"

Desmond shrugged.

"I thought maybe he'd meet us to get his money, and we'd kick the shit out of him."

"Yeah," Desmond told me. "But when's it ever as easy as that?"

"Got a string of bodies on him. I can't see him back in Parchman."

"Naw," Desmond said. "One way or another, he's done."

End times for that Boudrot fit right in with everything I had in mind.

"Call him," Desmond said.

I pulled up Tula's number. That bloodthirsty little fucker was laughing when he answered the phone.

"How do you like me now, brother?" he wanted to know.

"You're a funny little twitch," I told him. I knew that Boudrot hated getting reminded he was an abject runt.

"Ain't all that little," he said. "Ask your girlfriend."

"Put her on. I will."

"Can't," he told me. "Got a mouthful right now." He laughed. He added, "Ooohhh, baby."

I just stood there and took it. He made rutting noises. He pulled away to have a laugh with a lackey. I glanced at Desmond, shook my head and waited.

"She's a pistol," that Boudrot finally said. "I don't know but I should keep her."

"So you don't want your money?"

"That's the shit of it, isn't it. I do want it, brother. I do."

"Then work it the fuck out," I told him, "before the cops get all over you. Not but so many people a man can shoot, even in Tuscaloosa."

"Don't you worry about me."

"Trying hard not to."

"Where are you?"

"Standing here looking at a goddamn goat and talking to you."

He laid the phone aside again and told his buddies what I'd said. They laughed like guys who were hoping to keep unshot for a little while longer.

I pointed down the fairway we were overlooking and asked the girl with the goat, "What's down there?"

"A lake," she said. "The dogs swim in it."

"Straight down that cart path?"

She nodded.

I told that Boudrot, "Here's how it is."

That got his attention the way it was meant to. You can only float along with head jobs like that Boudrot until they start dithering on you. Then you have to take charge and let them know you're done with their nutty shit.

"Listen," he started.

"Uh-uh," I told him. "You've got twenty minutes to get here or we're gone."

"The fuck you say. I've got your—"

"You've got shit. World's full of women."

By then Desmond was looking at me like I was giving him powerful gas.

"Maybe I'll do her right now."

"See you," I told him. I waited. I waited some more.

I heard that Boudrot exhale. "Let's do it then," he said.

"You know where the arboretum is?"

"The what?"

Desmond showed me the map on his phone. I gave directions to that Boudrot once he'd come up dry with his lackeys who weren't nature lovers, I had to guess.

"Old golf course," I told him. "Walk straight down the cart path off the parking lot. There's a lake at the far end. We'll do it all there."

"You ain't running nothing," that Boudrot sputtered at me.

"Bring her along if you want your money."

That was just the kind of talk that Boudrot had a taste for. I knew his work. He knew ours. We didn't respect each other exactly, but there's a certain pleasure attached to dealing with people who deliver on what they promise. We knew that Boudrot was bloodthirsty enough to gun down about anybody, and he was aware that me and Desmond had pulled a trigger or two ourselves.

"I'm going to tell *you* what's happening," that Boudrot said. "Half an hour. You be at that lake."

"Got it," I told him and hung up before he could keep explaining to me everything I'd already told him that we'd do.

"So?" Desmond said.

"Doing it here," I told him.

TWENTY-SEVEN

It was probably a four- or five-acre pond in between an old par three tee box and an overgrown green on a hilltop. The water was low, and the pond was stump riddled over by the dam end. There was a clearing on the near side that sloped straight down to the bank, a grassy ramp the dogs made use of while their owners stood and chatted.

We'd seen plenty of cars in the arboretum lot but not terribly many people until we got our first view of the lake. That's were everybody was.

"This'll work," I told Desmond.

It was a happy accident really. There was a solid dozen civilians down there and probably twice as many dogs. Too many witnesses for even that Boudrot to get homicidal in front of. He wasn't the sort who'd think to bring enough bullets to mow everybody down.

Barbara quivered and warbled as we headed down the hillside toward the water.

Desmond checked the clip of Lance's TEC-9. He shoved the gun down in his waistband. Desmond's shirt was baggy enough so that he almost looked unarmed. Massive and menacing certainly but not ripe to shoot the place up. I'd gone for a Kimber .45. It had come oiled and loaded out of Lance's bag and had enough weight to crack a skull.

Barbara stopped to gaze at the lake and yodel. She looked up at me and Desmond. If she could have spoken, she would have told us both, "Get me out of this nasty shirt."

She licked me in gratitude when I started pulling at the collar. Barbara gave a hard shake once she was entirely shirtless. The wounds on her back had mostly scabbed over. She was only seeping a little.

"Go on then," I said.

She spun around twice and lit out for the water.

"Where?" I asked Desmond.

Desmond was a natural master of open-field strategy.

"I'll get back behind those bushes there." He pointed at a lush bit of leafy scrub growing on the dam. "You mix in with the folks."

I held out my arms in a looking-like-this? sort of way. They probably didn't get too many seamen at the pond.

"They'll just thank you for your service," Desmond told me.

So we split up. Desmond followed the cart path that curved around toward the dam while I walked down the foot trail toward the bank of that stumpy pond. Barbara was nose to asshole with some ugly wire-haired dog that looked only mostly Airedale. He had a head shaped like a doorstop but the ears of a basset hound.

Most of the people were on their phones. A few had their
earbuds in and made it clear they were preoccupied listening to
their music or something. I soon found out why. There was a
woman down there laying for a victim like me. If I'd not been
actively worried about that crazy Acadian fuckstick cresting the
hill above the pond and shooting me in the head, I might have
noticed that woman earlier and seen her for what she was. A
plague and a torment and a sack of ceaseless tedium in a skirt.

"Hey, sailor," she told me.

"Ma'am."

"Don't you 'ma'am' me. What you doing way out here?"

I pointed at nothing the way Tupelo Curtis would have.
"Got this thing," I said.

It didn't matter. She was finished listening before I'd even
started. She was one of those creatures with no proper use for her
ears. They were something to hang her earrings from and to rest
her glasses on.

"My Larry's in the Coast Guard," she told me.

"Oh yeah?"

I'd judged her straightaway and had made my decision about
her. I'd eased around to put her between me and the crest of the
hill I'd come down. She probably wouldn't stop a bullet
entirely—she was too bony for that—but the chances seemed
good that she could slow one down.

"He's in Budapest," she said.

"Larry?"

"My boy." She plucked up a fold of my white sailor's top. She
rubbed the material like she was a tailor or some GSA functionary.

"What's the Coast Guard doing over there?" I asked her.

"Oh, silly," she said as she tugged at my tunic. "He's on some
kind of leave."

I caught a few of the other people glancing my way with what looked like pity leavened with relief. They clearly didn't want to be me, but they could still feel sorry for me.

"Constantinople." She was tidying up my collar now. "That's what it used to be."

"Right." I eyed the hilltop. It was like waiting for a Cherokee war party to show up in silhouette on the ridge line.

"Him and that wife of his," she said. "New one. First one, died, you know?"

"Sorry to hear it."

I tried to spy Desmond, but he was well concealed behind a big viney clump of shrub. It looked like a blend of wisteria and honeysuckle.

"Killed in a wreck," she said. "Drunk, if you ask me, but nobody asked me."

"Sad thing." I told her. "Which one's yours?" I made a show of taking in the canines swarming about. Eight or ten of them were running around on the grassy slope. The rest were in the water, or down at the edge of the pond anyway. That's where Barbara had ended up. She wasn't swimming exactly, but she'd flopped in the shallows and was wallowing and rolling around.

That lady shook her head and informed me, "I'm allergic. Just come out to walk."

"Don't want to keep you from it," I told her.

I watched some guy come over the hill. Not our Boudrot. Some willowy sort with a French bulldog behind him.

She kept pawing at my sailor top. "My Larry's in the Coast Guard."

I told myself some version of, "Uh-oh."

Just then a black retriever came over to rub his nasty wet self against me. He was a leaner, the way some dogs are. He pitched himself against my knee and gazed up at me with his tongue hanging out as if to say, "Hey, buddy. Sorry for the mess."

His owner came over to save me from him. Some student type, and she pulled out an earbud in order to tell me, "Whoops."

I paid her back by tipping my head toward my friend and saying, "Her Larry's in the Coast Guard."

Right on cue, that woman said, "Budapest," as she closed on the girl with the lab.

Earbuds wouldn't save her now. She glared at me like I'd given her ebola.

Then I heard Desmond make a neck noise over in the shrubbery. I glanced his way and then back to the hilltop, and that crew was already there.

It was hard to miss that Boudrot, as puny as he was. He had a couple of colleagues with him, a pair of beefy guys with bad haircuts and bellies hanging over their jeans. Cons, I had to figure, that Boudrot had run with back in Parchman. He wasn't remotely the sort to have any unconvicted friends.

Tula was standing between them. There wasn't any question about it this time. She was in her civvies. Jeans and a sweater that was stretched and pulled and sagging like she'd been dragged around and mussed up. Even still, I could tell she wasn't scared. Furious, more like it, and anxious for a chance to put all that fury to some use.

That Boudrot looked the whole crowd of us over. It took him a while to pick me out. Hell, I probably wouldn't have picked me out. Some guy in sailor whites? He finally laughed and pointed, and those buddies of his had a good hoot about it as well.

He left Tula and those boys on the hilltop and came sauntering down toward me. He tried to saunter anyway, but his gate was too damn short, so he bounced more than he meant to and came faster than he would have liked.

Larry's mother was easing back my way just as that Boudrot closed. They both reached me at about the same time.

"Shit howdy," that Boudrot told me. "Look at you."

"Larry's in the Coast Guard," Larry's mother said.

That Boudrot treated her to his shut-the-fuck-up glance and grabbed a handful of my top, a fair clump of chest hair too. "You look like a faggot," he said.

A few of the dog owners heard him and took the kind of offense that civilized people take. They made disapproving faces at that Boudrot, but he wasn't remotely the sort dialed in to give a happy shit.

"He's in Budapest."

"Shut it, sister," that Boudrot told her.

I tried to steer her away, but she was no more the sort to get steered than that Bourdrot was the sort to get chastened.

"Constantinople," she managed to get out before that Boudrot swung on her with his open hand.

You probably could have heard the racket of it way up in the deserted clubhouse. She went down without further commentary, just laid down on the ground. The civilians around looked torn at first between being appalled and grateful. Since they were fundamentally civilized, they went with appalled in the end.

One of the guys said into his phone, "Gotta go," and stalked directly over. Big guy. Linebacker type.

"Don't," I told him, but it didn't help.

That Boudrot pulled out a pistol, a shiny Smith & Wesson. He caught that boy on the jaw, never hesitated at all. The skin parted. The blood gushed. That fellow staggered back and stumbled. Before that Boudrot could wind up and hit him again, he sat down on the ground.

Now there was general consternation.

"Ya'll go on," that Boudrot said, and he waved his pistol to help them decide. It seemed to do the trick.

There was a lot of dog calling and frantic noises. While all those people moved away across the hillside from me and that Boudrot, it wasn't like they were going to leave their dogs behind. The dogs, of course, didn't seem too alarmed by the runty guy with the pistol, so they just kept darting and playing the way they'd been before.

"Where's my money?" that Boudrot asked me.

"I've got it."

"I don't fucking see it."

"It's around."

Out of the corner of my eye, I noticed Desmond's bush was doing some shaking. Not I'm-trying-to-signal-you shaking but something closer to there's-a-hornets'-nest-in-here.

"Where?" that Boudrot asked me and poked me on the breastbone with the barrel of his gun.

"Girl first."

He laughed. He didn't sound happy.

"Up in the car isn't it?"

I gave him a shrug.

"Or it ain't anywhere," he said. "Burned through it, didn't you? You and all them boys."

I guess I grinned a little more than I should have. That Boudrot raised his pistol a foot from my head and pointed the bore of it at my right eye. It was just the sort of move I'd seen from him earlier, back on that hilltop off Kicker.

"Didn't I tell you it'd all end up like this?"

I made like I couldn't say, but I did sort of remember that Boudrot yelling at me and Desmond in the courthouse. The bailiffs wrestling with him and him still screaming about how we were as good as dead.

"Your money's up there," I said and pointed with my cowlick mostly toward the hilltop while I waited for Desmond to go on and shoot that Boudrot somewhere or another.

I looked toward his bush. The limbs were lurching and pitching. Then Desmond started singing out. In agony, it sounded like. That Boudrot heard the racket, and me and him watched the bush together as Desmond came fighting through it and flung himself into the pond.

"Ants!" he shouted. He ducked under the water and came up swatting himself all over. The dogs that hadn't been gathered up yet all stopped where they were and barked. Even Barbara. Desmond went wild scraping ants off himself, big red ones from what I could see. His TEC-9 was either back in the bush or down with the golf balls and the eight irons.

I probably would have told myself, "Uh-oh," but that Boudrot said it for me. He still had his pistol pointed at my eye. I turned my head enough to see Tula between those lackeys on the hilltop.

"Wasn't ever about the money," that Boudrot said and pulled the trigger.

I think I just had time enough to wish I was wearing something else. I doubt Popeye would have wanted to die in a sailor suit on a derelict golf course in Tuscaloosa. I sure had things I'd rather be doing and garden spots I'd yet to see.

I remember going rigid as the pistol hammer fell. I heard the dull metallic thud and waited for the explosion. Waited a little further. Waited a bit more. Then I stopped squinting and looked at the gun. That Boudrot broke out laughing.

That was twice in a day I'd been on the business end of an empty chamber.

"Next one's for real," he told me, but we didn't get that far.

I shoved his wrist aside and grabbed him like I'd been trained in the army. He screamed when I dislocated his shoulder, just grunted when I broke his arm. He didn't make much racket at all when I busted his nose with a Glasgow kiss. I tossed his Smith & Wesson in the pond.

He'd given over entirely to whimpering by the time he stag-gered out of my reach. I caught a glance of Tula up on the hilltop stomping one of those lackeys' knees. He pitched and over and collapsed. Even from where I was, I could hear his pitiful shriek. She slugged the other one and bolted. He had too much gut to catch her. He didn't even bother to chase her and, what with all the people, failed to pull out his gun.

"Fucker!" that Boudrot informed me. It came out primarily as nose blood.

Barbara had wandered from the lake by then. She jabbed my knee with her snout, and then—being a hound and all—she got distracted by a scent.

She alerted, that way hounds will sometimes, and she closed hard on that Boudrot. She sniffed his trouser leg for a good quar-ter minute and then chuffed once like a bear.

I was about to advise that Boudrot to either run or drop and cover, but he chose the first one before I could even speak. He was holding his bad arm with his good hand, and his nose was dripping all over his shirtfront as he struck out across the dam with Barbara hard behind him. She'd surge up to bite the back of his thigh, let him run some and close again.

There wasn't much doubt she knew just who he was. When a guy mows down your littermates—point-blank with a shotgun—there's little chance you'll forget him. Even if you're just a hound.

I went over to see to Desmond. He was still wallowing around in the pond.

"Go on," he told me. "I'm all right." Desmond showed me his lumpy forearm.

I just had to follow the sound of that Boudrot. He was visiting hard talk on Barbara. I heard her bay a couple of times. From sheer joy, I had to think. For man or animal, there's nothing quite so sweet as retribution.

I walked across the dam and up a root-ruptured cart path. I didn't want to arrive on the scene too soon and cut short Barbara's fun.

I finally found the two of them back in some piney scrub that had once been a sand trap. Every time that Boudrot twitched, Barbara took a little skin.

"Do something with him," that Bourdrot told me.

"Her."

He whined. She bit.

"Call her off."

"She's part of that pen of dogs you shot. Was it . . . yesterday?"

Shooting dogs was like breathing for that Boudrot. If he could have shrugged at me, he would have.

"Get him," I said, not that Barbara needed egging on.

That Boudrot squirmed and Barbara laid full into him all over. I'd seen hounds go after foxes and rabbits like that but never an Acadian fuckstick from Cut Off, Louisiana.

I made him beg me to get her off him, and I let it go on for a while.

"All right," I finally said as I grabbed Barbara by her back legs. She turned to snap at me couple of times before she settled down. Then she whimpered once and licked me. I told her, "Stay," and for some reason she did.

I eased over to where that Boudrot was and pointed my Kimber at his forehead.

"Let's see if mine'll go off," I said as I pulled the trigger. That Boudrot shrieked like a maiden aunt. I showed him the clip in my other hand and then caught him hard across the jaw with that heavy .45.

Barbara wanted me to kill him. I sure wanted to kill him too, but I also had a nagging need for that Acadian fuckstick to suffer.

I'd decided he'd do more of that in Parchman than six feet under ground.

So I made an executive decision, but I didn't tell that Boudrot.
I took Barbara aside and explained it to the hound.

TWENTY-EIGHT

Me and that Boudrot and Barbara met Tuscaloosa SWAT as they swarmed toward us over the dam.

"DOWN!" If they all said it once, they said it a dozen times.

I grabbed Babara and took her to the ground with me. Those boys were all Kevlared and helmeted up. They were primed to shoot something, and with hair-trigger cops, a dog will always do.

I left that Boudrot to fend for himself. He was all dog bites and busted bones and parted skin. He just stayed where he was and launched into a tirade. He seemed chiefly disappointed in the state of Alabama as a fit place to get up to the sort of mischief he tended to be about. He was partial to the Delta, out by Greenville most especially, and he rattled on in a mucousy way about the failings of Tuscaloosa until a couple of SWAT boys closed hard on him and slammed him to the ground.

Another pair charged over to see to me.

"Go easy on the dog," I told them.

"Shut up," one of them suggested as he crushed my neck with his knee.

There's a reason people don't like cops, and it's chiefly cop inflicted. They too often operate with the attitude "I'll treat you like shit until word comes down I shouldn't anymore."

These guys were accomplished at that sort of thing. They gave me a pretty rough time. I'd thrown down my pistol as soon as I'd laid eyes on those boys, and I only had two pockets and not a thing in either one. So there was nothing to find, but they kept searching until I was scuffed up all over.

Then one of them fetched my gun off the ground while the other one jerked me upright.

"Maybe you ought to . . ."

I was going to suggest they put some kind of leash on Barbara, but the SWAT boy at my elbow wasn't feeling suggestible. He leaned in and hissed, "Shut up, dirtbag."

If anything, they were treating that Boudrot worse, and he had actual broken bones. I drew some consolation every time that Boudrot screamed.

They walked us along the weedy fairway to the parking lot. When I'd cluck to keep Barbara coming, one of those cops would shake me hard.

There was an armored truck, like a minibus, parked in with a bunch of squad cars. I could see Tula talking to what looked like a captain alongside three guys laid facedown on the gritty asphalt. Two of them were Boudrot's lackeys. Desmond was the third.

When we reached the lot, one of my guys handed my pistol to the captain. The other one gave him the spotted T-shirt he'd pulled out of my waistband.

The captain held it up by the shoulders for inspection.

"Moo, goddammit," he said.

"You all right?" I asked Tula.

The guy on my elbow jerked me and look prepared to escalate until his captain told him, "Cut him loose." He pointed at Desmond. "That one too. Let's make some sense of this."

That fellow pulled out a big tactical knife and sliced off my Flex-Cufs. I was still standing there rubbing my wrists to get the blood flowing when Tula slugged me.

She had a hell of a punch, and I wasn't looking for it, so I didn't dodge or shirk. I just stood there and took it flush on the jaw. I saw stars and tasted iron and half wanted to drop down on my knees and cry.

"Ow!"

"Where the hell have you been!? And what the hell's that?" She had my sailor suit in mind.

Both fair questions. I should have been armed with decent answers. Instead I just said, "It's complicated." And I was meaning to tell her how.

But Tula exhaled hard through her nose and drew back and hit me again.

"Quit it."

"That little asshole could have killed me."

"We knew he was waiting on us," I told her.

"You didn't know shit," she said back.

Desmond had been cut loose as well and was lifting his wet self off the ground by then.

"And you took your sweet time," Tula informed us both. Then she spat with the sort of vigor K-Lo would have found beguiling.

I looked to Desmond for some help.

He turned and said to Tula, "Yeah. I guess. All right."

She didn't do a thing but stand there.

"Why don't you hit *him?*" I asked her.

"I don't sleep with him," she said. "You either. Probably. Now."

That got everybody's attention. The cops all looked at me and Tula. That Boudrot wheezed at us through his broken nose. Even his lackeys on the ground had a chuckle between them about it. The one with the dislocated kneecap was handy, so I kicked him one time hard.

"I'm sorry," I told Tula. "We ran into some trouble, what with Luther and them. For what it's worth, I didn't know what I'd do back there when I thought he'd shot you."

"Shot who?" the captain asked.

"Some girl."

"And you saw it?"

I nodded.

"You too?"

Desmond nodded.

"Everybody goes," the captain announced to his officers. They gathered all of us up.

"Her too." I pointed at Barbara. When the captain balked, I said, "Hell, she caught him."

Tula said, "I'll get her." Then she asked us, "Where's the rest of your crowd anyway?"

"Over at a rib place somewhere." That was the best Desmond could do.

"Shack," I said the captain's way. "Next to some sort of car lot."

"Archibald and Woodrow's," the captain said. "Take them with you. Pick them up," he told one of his officers. A tubby blond boy with a toothpick in his mouth.

Tula caught me sizing up the state of my Ranchero as me and Desmond followed that officer to his four-by-four.

"You and that damn car," she said. She troubled herself to spit again.

Naturally, we rolled up on a brawl at that rib place in Tuscaloosa. Luther and Percy Dwayne had gotten into it with a trio of frat boys. Big guys. Athletic scholarships probably. Strapping and clean-cut and very likely decent and dumb. Untutored certainly in the ways of Delta cracker trash. That was easy enough to see straightaway because Luther and Percy Dwayne were flogging those boys to a fare-thee-well.

Luther was beating one of them with a galvanized bucket while Percy Dwayne was kicking at a second one and half standing on the third one. That boy was trying to crawl under a flatbed truck, but Dale—who wasn't otherwise fighting—kept pulling him out by the ankles and telling him, "Naw."

Our cop asked us, "Yours?"

"I guess," Desmond told him.

"You've got two minutes to crank them down, or I'll have to call it in."

Eugene saw us first. He was watching the fun while gnawing on a rib bone.

"Hey," he said. He jerked his head by way of pointing toward the barbecue joint. "Ought to get you a slab. Them boys know what they're doing."

"Ribs and chopped and every damn thing," Dale told us as he pulled that crawling frat boy out from under the truck again.

"What's all this?" I asked.

Luther left off swinging his bucket long enough to say, "Got all mouthy with us." He drew our attention to the boy Percy Dwayne was kicking. "Him especially."

"Yeah," Percy Dwayne said. He caught that boy in the backside with some sort of half-cocked judo stomp.

"Going to have to leave it," I told them all, "or he's going call his friends."

I think that was the first notice any of them had taken of that city police four-by-four.

"Where's Barbara?" Eugene wanted to know.

Desmond told him, "Tula's got her."

"Come on," I said. "Let's go."

Those frat boys became an instant afterthought. Our crew shifted across the lot toward the Blazer.

Percy Dwayne jabbed a thumb toward the restaurant. "They probably want you to pay them something. I think we kind of broke some stuff and shit."

I tried to discourage that police captain from interrogating our crew. I told him they hadn't seen anything, had served as ballast mostly. I just didn't want them describing what we'd been up to the past day and a half, all the mayhem we'd been a part of from Arkansas to Alabama. It turned out I didn't need to worry. Those boys mostly giggled and ate nabs.

Cops are provincial anyway. The locals were fixed on all the trouble that Boudrot had made in Tuscaloosa. Tula directed them to a trailer up by Holt where she'd been held. It had been where the dead girl lived, Boudrot's prison girlfriend and a local exotic dancer who me and Desmond had seen him shoot right in the head. Tula told her story to the captain and some detective with a soul patch. Then me and Desmond took turns telling our version of events to those two as well. We knew which stuff to leave out and which items to skip over. We just hit the Boudrot atrocities and left everything else unsaid.

"Whose goddamn navy you in?" soul patch finally asked me.

He shut his notebook. Wafted aftershave my way. Adjusted his nutsack and added, "Huh?"

We rode back over to the arboretum in a couple of Tuscaloosa PD prowlers. The boys and Barbara all piled in the Escalade with Desmond. Tula was still angry enough at me to make like she'd ride with them until she sat in that Cadillac for long enough to get a full dose of the stink. The thing reeked like a locker room on wheels. That was enough to send Tula over to my Ranchero.

"See you back home," I told Desmond.

"Going to order my new Escalade in Greenwood."

What could I tell him other than, "All right."

We were well west of Tuscaloosa, on the far side of Reform, before Tula finally melted a little. I took it anyway for melting.

She punched me in the arm and said, "Gotta pee."

As we approached Columbus, she grew both teary and irritated. I tried to apologize for taking so damn long to reach her, but it wasn't about that anymore. With the Boudrot tension and the Boudrot danger finally overcome and lifted, Tula was letting her wall-to-wall anxiety go.

She came over the console to lay against me. Once we'd finally reached Columbus, she pointed out a Hampton Inn hard beside the four-lane.

"Let's stop," she said.

Me and Desmond, of course, had created a Columbus problem for ourselves.

"Sort of need to blast on through here," I told Tula. "You don't really want to know why."

She could guess well enough. Tula laughed for the first time. I stopped in Starkville instead where we holed up for a day.

TWENTY-NINE

Kendell has the good sense to know precisely what he doesn't want to hear and who he doesn't want to hear it from. Usually that takes the form of explanations and excuses from cracker trash, but sometimes me and Desmond qualify for Kendell as well.

When we got back from Alabama and finally caught up with him, Kendell showed me and Desmond the palm of his open hand. Whatever we thought we had to tell him, he knew he didn't want to know it.

Me and Desmond ended up paying Luther, Percy Dwayne, Eugene, and Dale a flat fee for what they decided to call "professional services."

We reminded Eugene we'd rescued him from an Arkansas jailhouse in a derelict shopping plaza, and we refreshed Percy Dwayne on the trouble we'd spared him at the hands those

Greer brothers, but that only served to get me and Desmond told by the two of them, "So?"

We paid them out of the cash we'd taken off that Boudrot back when he was a meth lord instead of a fuckstick on the run. They wanted twice as much as we gave them, so we negotiated.

Desmond snorted while I told them, "No."

Tula got counseling. Kendell made her. It was in the Washington County P.D. regs or something. After a couple of sessions, she was madder at the shrink than me, so I guess it worked. I developed a new appreciation for therapy anyway.

Pearl came back from Memphis and cooked me a casserole first thing. Green beans and cheddar and mushroom soup, canned tuna and water chestnuts. All of it crusted over with crumbled Wise potato chips. How it came out of the oven stale already was one of Pearl's culinary secrets I hope to never know.

That Boudrot got indicted all over. He stood trial in Alabama. Plead out in Mississippi. They brought him from Tuscaloosa in a jailhouse van so he could get properly scolded and sentenced in a Delta courtroom. We didn't bother to go and hear any of it but decided instead to wait outside. They had the van parked in a side lot, and we just stood where we could see it. Me and Desmond. Tula and Kendell. Dale and Luther and Percy Dwayne. Eugene had come clear up from Yazoo, and he'd brought Barbara with him. She was going shirtless for the occasion and appeared to be well healed.

Two Alabama deputies brought the fuckstick out of the courthouse, and that Boudrot didn't see us at first. Luther was about to shout at him. He had a hand raised and his mouth open, but Barbara beat him to it. She snarled and barked like hounds rarely do. There wasn't any baying to it all. It sounded to me like the canine version of, "Hey, shithead. Over here."

That Boudrot saw us. He saw her mostly and said more hard

things to that dog than even the worst mongrel probably hears in the course of its natural life.

The deputies hustled that Boudrot into the back of the van as he struggled against them and informed Barbara of every vile thing he'd get up to with her if he ever caught her alone. She gave as much back, was dripping foam by the time that van pulled off.

We rode to the Sonic in Desmond's new Escalade, all packed in together.

"What do you think?" Desmond asked me once we were going flat out on the truck route.

"Rides nice," I told him and drew a deep breath. "Smells expensive," I said.

THE POWER OF RECONCILIATION

JUSTIN WELBY

BLOOMSBURY CONTINUUM
LONDON • OXFORD • NEW YORK • NEW DELHI • SYDNEY

BLOOMSBURY CONTINUUM
Bloomsbury Publishing Plc
50 Bedford Square, London, WC1B 3DP, UK
29 Earlsfort Terrace, Dublin 2, Ireland

BLOOMSBURY, BLOOMSBURY CONTINUUM and the Diana logo are
trademarks of Bloomsbury Publishing Plc

First published in Great Britain 2022

A catalogue record for this book is available from the British Library

Library of Congress Cataloguing-in-Publication data has been applied for

ISBN: HB: 978-1-3994-0297-2; eBook: 978-1-3994-0296-5;
ePDF: 978-1-3994-0295-8

2 4 6 8 10 9 7 5 3 1

Typeset by Deanta Global Publishing Services, Chennai, India
Printed and bound in Great Britain by CPI Group (UK) Ltd, Croydon CR0 4YY

To find out more about our authors and books visit www.bloomsbury.com
and sign up for our newsletters

To my mother Jane Williams, my stepfather the late Charles Williams, and to my grandmother Iris Portal, from whom I learned curiosity, presence and imagination.

To the Norton Group and others who pray for me.

Contents

Introduction

God then,
encompassing all things, is
defenseless? Omnipotence
has been tossed away, reduced
to a wisp of damp wool?

And we
frightened, bored, wanting
only to sleep till catastrophe
has raged, lashed, seethed and gone by without us,
wanting then
to awaken in quietude without remembrance
of agony,

we who in shamefaced private hope
had looked to be plucked from fire and given
a bliss we deserved for having imagined it,

is it implied that *we*
must protect this perversely weak
animal, whose muzzle's nudgings

suppose there is milk to be found in us?
Must hold to our icy hearts
a shivering God?[1]

The woman circles the baby in a shawl, enveloping them both. Both faces are barely visible. Her arms and body are the circling not of fear and despair but of love and faith. Were it not for the arms of the mother, the child would be exposed, vulnerable, condemned to die by weather and cruelty. She puts her body between him and the world.

Outside the dug-out where the picture – an ikon of Mary and Jesus – is pinned to a mud wall, the reality is of a frozen hell. It is December 1942, Stalingrad. The German advance of the previous eighteen months had taken them to the edge of the Volga. Here they were stopped and for months the fighting swayed to and fro, until the German forces were turned by Russian advances from besiegers to besieged. The conditions were appalling, the loss of life enormous, the suffering of soldiers and civilians immense, made worse by the callousness of the supreme commanders of both sides.

Yet, amid this frozen killing ground there were some places of hope. Lieutenant Kurt Reuber, pastor and physician with the encircled German army, having drawn the ikon, used it as a place for soldiers to pray and meditate, to find something of the love of family, of their mothers' care. He died in 1944, a prisoner in Russia, together with two-thirds of his companions captured in January 1943 at Stalingrad. The ikon escaped on virtually the last flight out. The original is displayed in the Kaiser Wilhelm Memorial Church, Berlin, while copies now hang in the cathedrals of Berlin, Coventry and Kazan, Volgograd, as a sign of the reconciliation between Germany and its enemies: the United Kingdom and Russia.

Around the margin are included three words, '*Licht, Leben, Liebe*', light, life, love. The light shone in the darkness and the darkness did not overcome it (John 1.5). The butchery of the Russian front, with its tens of millions of deaths, was seen clearly at Stalingrad. In films and books, it is described[2] with scenes of horror that are numbing. The ikon tells of hope, of peace, of God's abundance in Jesus Christ and of human partnership in the ancient dream of swords into ploughshares. It calls for peace.

There is something very remarkable about the ikon. It seems to create a dream of peace in a world of war. It calls from another world, one full of suffering, but one in which a woman and her child could conceivably survive. Its marginal words tell of warmth from light and love and of hope of life. It calls out for help and also reassures because the child is the Christ-child, the baby of Bethlehem, whose existence was menaced from his birth until his death and who yet rose from the dead and decisively changes the world. For me the ikon calls out, 'Have mercy, we want peace' on the one hand, and on the other, 'Have hope, *here* is peace.'

Is this infant fragility really God's answer to the power of war and hatred, to the darkness of sin? Surely God may as well have lit a candle in a hurricane.

The human eye sees a mother in thin peasant clothes cradling a baby who would die so quickly if abandoned, perhaps in minutes: St John tells us this is the Word through whom all things were made.

Yet in the world busy human eyes are too preoccupied and overlook the mother, doubtless walked past each day in every great city on earth, on every battlefield and in every refugee camp. We who are safe avert our gaze from such sadness and suspect a trick: St John says this is an inextinguishable light that reveals the face of God.

That contrast remains true. I ring a bishop in Mozambique after a bitter and bloody attack from ISIS. I speak to another in South Sudan as the refugee camp in which he lives is shelled by rebel forces. I get a message from the wife of a close friend engaging in peacebuilding, Ebola resisting and COVID care in the Democratic Republic of the Congo (DRC), to say he has died from the virus.

I sit by someone weeping at the breakup of a relationship, or the estrangement of a child. I pray by the bed of a woman dying of COVID-19. A letter comes blaming the Church, blaming me, for failing to prevent the abuse of young people.

In all these places it is futile and uncaring – at that moment – to speak of reconciliation. Can there be change amid such suffering? Surely the tide of history will wash away any sandcastles of peace? Surely the darkness will win?

Yet for one very simple reason I turn back to the ikon. For this child and his obedient and self-giving mother, who endured so much more than can be imagined, *is* truly light, life, love. In him God is revealed in all his forceless glory and power. This is the God who draws worship not by compulsion but by fragility that is real and deathless.

The shivering child Jesus – he certainly shivered – and his sheltering mother are God's call to us that he speaks as an adult, 'Blessed are the peacemakers for they shall be called children of God' (Matthew 5.9). God has set the pattern and the means. The pattern is vulnerability. The means is sacrifice. This baby will live some thirty-three years and die on a cross with this mother unable to hold more than his dead, tortured body. This baby will be the cornerstone of stories of peace, the foundation of a community that is more diverse than any other on earth.

It will be a community that rejoices in the abundance of diversity and seeks, because of this child, to learn to love one another and the whole world. It will be an example of failure too often, but sometimes the light of life and hope. That community will be filled with the Spirit of this child so that, at its best, no sacrifice is too great to ensure that God's choice of abundance is poured into the world.

This fragility is reconciliation incarnate, made flesh. Reconciliation must be made flesh if it is going to be real. It must transform the lives of the weak, it must protect and it must go on trying even when it fails again and again. To give up is to accept, as though through scientific experiment, that the will to power of so many people is an undeniable absolute of being human. The will to power, the formation of identity through defining ourselves as what we are not, or by targeting another group as enemies, has become acceptable since the early twentieth century as being what makes for success, satisfaction, virtue.

With the will to power, coming from within ourselves, from pride and desire, there is no space for the ordinarily human, for the good community. Power hates weakness, and boasts that it never explains, never apologizes. It cannot abide reconciliation, which requires listening to another view, even putting oneself or one's group in the shoes of the other. Power will neither offer nor receive forgiveness. As a result, the enemy must be cancelled, perhaps physically, but certainly emotionally and if possible in public esteem.

Sometimes we see the light shine, the life flourish and the love shared. Sometimes enemies destroy each other not through violence but by becoming friends. When that is visible, so is the power and presence of the God of love, revealed in the Stalingrad Madonna.

PEACE AS THE UNIMAGINABLE STRATEGY

There is something a bit clichéd about wanting peace. One thinks of actor Sandra Bullock in *Miss Congeniality* playing an undercover FBI agent in a beauty contest where the only possible answer to the question about your greatest desire is 'world peace'. Yet any account of war makes it obvious that this is indeed what is needed. War can be at any scale, from bullying in the playground, the wars of words and sometime violence in families disintegrating, the vendettas in communities, riots, civil war and insurgency, or the great geopolitical conflicts. In all of them the side effect is destruction of the human spirit, ruination of lives, mental, physical and emotional harm on a vast scale, and a dark cloud of despair and anger, even among the 'winners', if any.

Among what are often called the Abrahamic faiths – Judaism, Christianity and Islam (those that in one way or another trace their history back to the Jewish Patriarch Abraham) – each has a sense of war as normally evil but a sometimes justifiable necessity, even a good. The accounts of Just War theory, or of what makes violence righteous, apply at many levels, including judicial execution and even revenge killing in family disputes. There are also accounts of what justifies the extreme action of going to war and accounts of what constitutes proper conduct in war.

I shall not discuss in detail Just War in this book. However, two things strike me. First, that there is no comparable need to justify peace, a Just Peace theory. Second, that so much effort has gone into defining the ethics of going to war and of conduct in war. International treaties such as the Geneva Conventions have been built on work originating in the Jewish scriptures (the Christian

Old Testament), the teachings of the Prophet Muhammad and subsequent interpretations, and the works of many great thinkers, especially St Augustine of Hippo (354–430) and St Thomas Aquinas (1225–1274). In ancient and modern times, women have been both prominent and essential to peace and as advocates for peaceful ways forward, yet on the whole they are forgotten. More will be said of that later.

There is a communal conscience, a voice within that says that war and killing and violent or destructive disagreement is not good. For it to become good requires justification. Peace, on the other hand, speaks for itself. Reconciliation enables harmonious difference in a way that enables all parties to flourish: reconciliation is the activity that leads towards peace, concord, the common good and well-being.

I have left out the greatest conflict, between human beings and the natural world. Here there is no obvious enemy apart from ourselves. No negotiations are possible except among ourselves. We are the worst enemies to ourselves. It is a newly identified sort of war; with the future, the young and those yet unborn, with each other, with the creation and with God. But, if this conflict is going to end and we are not going to destroy ourselves, we must find a way of living, a means of reconciliation that does not continually diminish what is around us. Climate change and loss of biodiversity constitute long-term mutually assured destruction: the launch button has long since been pushed, and the war is raging.

I've written this book as a practitioner in the area of reconciliation for many years. I do not attempt to hide two things in particular. First, that I write as a Christian and thus the content draws heavily on the

Christian Bible. Second, I do not hide my ignorance, the difficulties, setbacks and failures that are both the most common experience and the greatest frustration of any work involving reconciliation. Both my ignorance and the complexity of the subject mean that no one writer or book can complete the whole subject.

The frustration is one of the reasons for writing. It seems so obvious that it would be a better world in which diversity is a treasure, not a threat, and radically different views could be freely expressed without destructive behaviours. Competition among human beings is good, a gift to drive us onwards and give the desire to excel. Yet to seek not only to do better than a rival but to destroy them is foolishness, for in such a world all lose.

Frustration is true at all levels, from the squabbling families to the peoples at war, where the women and children flee in long, sorrowful procession and the young men and women die in agony, loneliness and fear. At its root is the sin of human pride, which affects all, including those seeking to reconcile. There is even much conflict among reconcilers and much competition for the glory of being peacemakers!

The book is in three parts that relate to each other but can be taken alone.

Part I is a meditation about definitions and difficulties. Here I look at what reconciliation is and why it is so rare. One of the mysteries of human existence is our lack of collaboration. Competition comes naturally to us. There are many reasons, but the way they show themselves in practice is bewildering and often counterproductive for all involved.

Within Part I, Chapter 1 argues that diversity and sin make conflict inevitable. Chapter 2 contrasts the reality of

conflict with the age-old desire for peace, drawing above
all on biblical themes. Chapter 3 looks at the resources
and origins of ideas about reconciliation.

Part II is about juggling the processes of reconciliation.
It draws heavily on the story of Coventry Cathedral in
England,[3] and particularly on the implicit and explicit
approach to reconciliation developed there. I do not argue
for a moment that this is the only approach, or even the
best one, but it is the best I know and is deeply rooted in
the life and teaching of Jesus Christ.

There are six chapters in this part, each of them based
around an action of reconciliation and reflecting especially
on John's Gospel, deeply influenced by Professor David
Ford's commentary.[4]

Part III moves on to the habits of reconciliation. It
uses the pattern of a course for groups of people that
was developed by the reconciliation team at Lambeth
Palace and published in 2020, the *Difference Course*.[5]
The course is held over six evenings, seeking to introduce
the habits necessary for reconciliation within a group.
Originally written for churches and Christian groups,
it is now being piloted among mixed-faith and other
faith groups, as well as secular ones, seeking to provide
a means for people to start on the very long journey
of reconciliation.

At the end of each chapter there is a section for reflection
and discussion. It may well be best to do that with others,
preferably with refreshments (food and hospitality make
a huge difference in reconciliation).

The aim of this book is to encourage peacebuilding
at all levels, recognizing the difficulties but turning the
abstract idea of reconciliation into something that can be
done throughout life, enabling the flourishing of robust

diversity and disagreement without hatred. A society and a world that renews the idea of peace gives a basis for hope of differences being the seed of growth, and not of automatic rejection of all that we disagree with and of hostility towards those who disagree.

Safety for our future is not found by seeking it, but by engaging with those who challenge us. Identity is not made by defining ourselves against others in hatred and by seeking domination: the habits of reconciliation and peacebuilding liberate our identities, preserve our autonomy, increase our safety and show us the common good.

PART I

1

What is Reconciliation?

RECONCILIATION IS DISAGREEING WELL

We need 'world peace' at every level. Like the Stalingrad Madonna it is a fragile dream, never realized but often sought. Let me be clear that I do not mean that this book holds the solution to solving all conflicts and wars, or that I am pretentious enough to think I know the answer. Nor does peace mean the absence of difference, a state of universal and unanimous agreement.

I write about peacebuilding and reconciliation in the sense of seeking relationships at all levels of human life that are resilient enough to have disagreement without destruction, victory without triumphalism, concessions without degradation. Reconciliation is the long drawn-out process, extending sometimes over generations, which seeks to achieve that end.

Peace is not found by avoiding conflict but by disagreeing well.

Where conflicts arise, too often we seek to resolve them with shallow agreements, even if we know that we have only papered over the cracks. At the level of the family that may mean pretending an argument has not happened rather than facing it. At the level of the global struggle over climate change, it may mean finding a million reasons why nothing is possible or a thousand long-term solutions that involve others doing something at some point but nobody making dramatic changes now.

It is very noticeable that peace for most countries is an ideal for the naïve more than a strategic aim for politics. To take a 2021 geopolitical example, the UK's *Global Britain in a Competitive Age: The Integrated Review of Security, Defence, Development and Foreign Policy* (the UK Integrated Review)[1] has only 13 mentions of the word 'peace' in 114 pages and only two of them relate even in passing to thinking about how peace can be built. There is no mention of reconciliation and one of mediation. To put it another way, the idea that the best form of dealing with one's enemies is to make them one's friends,[2] or at least to be reconciled to them, does not appear at any point at all in the UK's 2021 foundational strategy about security in a competitive world.

What kind of story does that tell? It says that we accept a worldview of competitive existence that may lead to violence and our only solutions are defence, resilience and seeking to increase our power. Of course, it would be absurd to argue that all countries and their rulers are seeking peace. Security is an essential and a primary duty of government. However, it is equally absurd to ignore the role of reconciliation in building greater security. Europe is far more secure as a result of reconciliation between France and Germany than it has been for centuries. Merely preserving the capacity and willingness to fight would not have led to the same result.

The same applies at all levels of human life. There is more mediation than there used to be for families and households or communities, but the greatest effort in dispute management goes to litigation. Society is too often structured only for contained conflict, not for transforming the conflict into reconciliation. A historic example of the way in which contained conflict can become a process of reconciliation is in the electoral system, which seeks successfully to enable very robust disagreement to be contained peacefully through the normative – not invariable – assumption that the other side is wrong but not evil. Elections are essentially peaceful struggles for power, civil war by other means. Imagine for a moment how foolish and frightening it would be to settle the drive for power by ensuring that the major parties had militias and enough resilience to frighten the other into submission. Imagine it being normal and acceptable to solve domestic quarrels with violence. Yet both these examples were the case for centuries and still are in many places. In others there has been a dramatic change for the better. Reconciliation is possible when its aims are clear and the means are attainable.

Reconciliation does not imply agreement, but it will demand, at the least, respect for human dignity, patience with difference, and ambition for effective and practical non-violent solutions. Obvious though that may be, it is not what we do. When there is a global problem like climate change, the habit of cooperation is so unpractised globally that potential solutions become alternative competitive forms of power seeking. The same was true in the first year or so of the COVID-19 pandemic. Vaccine nationalism, vaccine diplomacy, accusations and defences – all carried on as if proving that one's own country or group of countries was right and that being right – at least in one's own eyes – would keep the virus away.

All this competition. which is carried on through the veiled or implicit threat of violence or non-cooperative competition at every level of life, seems to come from deep within us. It is part of culture and art, of religious discussion and narrative, and of psychology, anthropology and philosophy. There seems to be a sense that talk of peace and reconciliation is for the naïve, to be laughed at in satirical comedies about beauty contests, for pacifists and for futility. We prefer sanctions to peaceful solutions. Reconciliation seems not to be real enough to be made part of policy, not promising enough to seek to embed in life, not secure enough to build a healthy society. It does not merit a whole paragraph, let alone a chapter or entire section, when considering the future integrated security of a nation like the UK. Even in the household in many places the answer to domestic dispute is submit or leave.

Clausewitz wrote that 'war is the continuation of politics by other means'.[3] One might answer nowadays that reconciliation is the best answer of human beings to every form of war. War is the failure of politics. Reconciliation is the maturity of politics.

That is the heart of the dilemma over reconciliation. It is treated as unattainable, not least because it is so misunderstood. Like many virtues, reconciliation and peace are idealized in imagination, politically unexamined in applied theory and ignored in practice. Reconciliation is treated as a serious solution to destructive conflict when all else has failed and victory is impossible for all involved.

It need not be so. There are remarkable examples at all levels of reconciliation from the geopolitical to the intimate within the household. Most people will know of some among friends and family. At the international level the global violence of the years between 1914 and 1945 led to two attempts to set up a global architecture of peacebuilding. The League of Nations failed, the United Nations progresses with many failures but is still the best forum we have in the world. It has given rise to other groups, such as the African Union, which exist to call for peace and contribute to peace's resilient establishment.

Throughout human history, in most cultures there have been dreams of peace and harmony, but lives have been lived in the muddle, competition and conflict of the world. Unreconciled or seemingly irreconcilable conflict is a daily reality for human beings at every level of their lives, whether in experience or through the news.

WHY DO WE NEED RECONCILIATION?

Identity, politics, relationships between human beings at every level tend to be self-referential. In Christian thinking God's love given to us and known by the gift of God's Spirit liberates us from self-reference by turning us out from ourselves to those who are different and loving them unconditionally.[4] The nature of God's love is seen in the understanding of God as Trinity, three persons in one God, perfect in love. Love not only accepts otherness, it generates otherness[5] through seeing the beauty of the other and through the absence of tying the admiration of that beauty to one's own advantage. In his chapter on Augustine's Christology, Rowan Williams reminds us that Augustine's book *City of God* 'as a whole is a meditation on how desire is judged and reconstructed so as to release us from rivalry and violence'.[6]

Conflict is normal because unreconstructed desire and self-reference are normal in human beings. Reconciliation thus begins with the personal, seeking transformation. The different circumstances of dispute start at the deeply personal, the battle with oneself. So many people carry a sense that life is a constant struggle to be something other than they are. We even have an expression for someone who stands out on account of their inner peace and contentment, saying, 'they are happy in their own skin'. Unreconciled conflict with oneself is among the most destructive, because you cannot escape your enemy except by harming yourself, and many do, directly or through substance abuse or lifestyle. The search for contentment, for inner peace, is a staple of philosophy, drama, art and of religious life.

In the Christian scriptures it is at the heart of the ponderings of the compiler of the first book of the Bible, Genesis, in its early chapters. The story of the fall is not only Paradise Lost, as in Milton's great poem, but also the loss of human harmony and peace, within Adam and Eve as well as between them. Their desire brings wrong action, not enjoying the otherness of God and relishing God's love, but grasping at what they do not have. On being discovered in their guilt they are ashamed, a deep-felt inner reaction. As shame so often does, it leads them to blame each other and then Satan. The loss of peace leads to the first human division.

Very quickly, conflict expands from words to deeds, as their children, Cain and Abel, argue and Cain murders his brother. Death by violence spreads through the generations and contaminates the whole human race. The spread is impelled by desire and self-reference, not by love. Desire is imitated, and develops in its perversion of love.

In these passages, which go on and expand evil into
a world where virtue is the exception, there is a sense of
the writer raising the problem of conflict. Where does it
come from and how can it be resolved? It is no mystery
that animals fight, for they lack the ability to reason and
project forwards in time beyond themselves. When our
dog sees a chocolate biscuit on the floor, she cannot work
out that it is there by accident, that chocolate is bad for her
and will make her ill. It's food now, and no more thinking
is required. If another dog is also going for the biscuit,
the only question is which is stronger (actually our dog is
a wimp so she would leave the biscuit if in competition
with a lethargic mouse, but that ruins the illustration).

Human beings are different. We can reason. We can
see the consequences of actions we take. We can work
out probabilities of something giving us pleasure now but
an ocean of suffering later. To some extent that is often
an attraction in doing wrong; the excitement of seeking
escape from consequences is part of the temporary
delight of sin. At a societal level we are under no illusions
as to the cost of conflict, whether with those around us at
work or at home, or in the community, at a national or
global level. Yet we go ahead, with reasons so weak that
we all know that they cannot carry the weight needed to
excuse us.

At the grandest level we come full circle and find
ourselves confronted with ourselves again, this time
collectively. Nuclear conflict involves mutually assured
destruction, yet at least nine nations in the world have
armed themselves with nuclear weapons knowing that
to use them is collective suicide and in some cases the
end of the human race. Climate change is the other
global menace where our survival is at stake. Even in very

bad scenarios of unchecked rises in temperature, most human beings would survive, but huge numbers would die and large parts of the earth become to some degree uninhabitable. The quality of life for survivors would be greatly reduced. There would be wars as the desperate migrated and wars over remaining resources. Yet there is a perceived first-mover disadvantage (the opposite of nuclear warfare where the first mover might gain a notional and temporary advantage and can convince themselves falsely and fatally it is more) that leads to inertia on a global scale. All rationality is gone.

This picture of conflict is horseshoe shaped. At one wing is the unreconstructed desire within each of us. It widens until, at its broadest, it is some of us against others of us. It ends with all of us against all of us. Both climate change and nuclear warfare are circular firing squads, the proverbial climax of stupidity in conflict.

We all know this, yet whether one is an optimist or pessimist about human nature, most people assume that conflict is just part of the package of life. We feel, if we think about it at all, that human beings have been in violent conflict as long as there have been human beings. That's the way of the world.

Wars of survival are explicable. Changes in climate have always been drivers of migration and thus conflict. Conflict provoked by a justified fear for survival requires enormous virtue to avoid or resolve since it calls for collective sacrifice. We have very little experience of such challenges in the most prosperous parts of the world. As a result, the COVID-19 pandemic exposed a deep desire to preserve ourselves even though most people accepted that the pandemic cannot be halted anywhere until it has been halted everywhere. Rationally, global cooperation is indispensable to individual security. Practically, there is a temptation of 'everyone for themselves' or, as the French saying goes, '*sauve qui peut*' – let the one who can, save themselves.

In smaller groups conflict also occurs naturally. There are obvious parallels between the squabbling seen in groups of apes to those seen in a household. Much of it will be about identity and independence. There are levels of natural competition that in a functional household lead to bickering and irritation but do not go beyond that. The rows are sorted out, affection deepens, respect for difference increases and love prevails. Similarly, in small communities like offices and other workplaces, petty irritations lead to sharp remarks. Usually these are around using the last of the milk in the common fridge or leaving the photocopier without paper.

So far, so natural and so unremarkable. The desire for survival and for adequate resources of shelter, food and water drive some competing groups into violence. Communities bicker. But, beyond the obvious are deep mysteries about the reasons for the self-destructive nature of human violence in conflict, even at the very local level. Most of us have either experienced or know of destructive conflict in the family or household. The same is seen in business partnerships, in voluntary groups, in political parties, in churches and in small communities where it is obvious to all that both the values of the group and the interests of success will be lost by further conflict. Yet many seem to prefer to rule over the ruins of their cause or group than to serve humbly and see it triumph. In Christian thinking the response of God to the sins of pride and self-reference that drive conflict is seen in the great Christian symbols of the cross and the empty tomb. The language of love '*begins* with the primordial "non-worldly" love enacted in Christ'.[7]

The mystery of mutually destructive conflict is at its deepest in our own times, although, as we have begun to see, it occupies the writers of the Bible back to the earliest parts of Genesis and to the last parts of the Book of Revelation. Why destroy what is valued, why engage in destructive conflict when the outcome is lose-lose?

What Things Provoke Conflict?

The question of identity, who I am and who we are (which includes what 'we' means), is core to any understanding of conflict. The search for identity and the means by which it is established are dominant questions around the world. With the advent of social media identity clashes have become some of the main components of social discord. The result is a terrible confusion of quarrels in which complexity gives way to oversimplified binary definitions.

Identity may be given

We accept the identity that someone or something has given us. Historically, that might be slave or free. In the nineteenth century before the American Civil War people of colour in the slave states were assumed to be chattel slaves, which Whites could not be.[8] If you were the child of a slave, you were the property of the slave's master and even those such as Jefferson saw the breeding of slaves as more profitable than the economic use of them. Being a chattel slave was an identity bestowed by birth. There was no choice.

In the middle belt of Nigeria, in many places people are categorized either as an indigene or a settler. The

settlers were often ethnically Hausa, Muslims imported
by the British in the 1930s from northern Nigeria to
work the copper mines. Ninety years later their identity
is still 'settler', with consequential impacts on where
they live and on university places. In India, caste – or
being outcaste or of tribal origin – is still a formative
although not always finally definitive influence on a
person's future.

Conscription in the UK in the Second World War
drew millions into battle because they had inherited being
British. Unless they were very determined conscientious
objectors, they would find themselves serving in one way
or another.

On a far lighter note, in Liverpool when I worked there
at the Anglican cathedral the first question I was asked was
'Are you Red or Blue?' (supporter of Liverpool or Everton
football clubs). When one asked the question back, the
answer would be 'X, my family has always been X.'

At their worst, imposed identities are inescapable and
compel a person to be on a side in a conflict that they
may neither want, nor have the power to change. Under
the Nazi regime of 1933–45 in Germany a person was
non-Aryan if they were one-quarter Jewish and, if so,
would find themselves marked as such on identity papers.
At one-half they were considered Jewish. Their religious
faith, war service, skills and attitudes to being Jewish had
no impact. They were targeted for extermination.

In societies where there is a culture of vendettas, the
imposed identity may compel both taking sides and
hatred of the other. The Nuer and Dinka peoples of South
Sudan have in the past operated a vendetta culture that
could oblige revenge against another clan within the tribe
for more than one generation.

Finally, one may inherit or be born with other characteristics that in the eyes of the outside world determine the answer to identity even today. They may be around sexuality, education, family name, height, even hair colour. Articles about the prime minister of the UK, Boris Johnson, almost always define his character by reference to him going to Eton, implying that his schooling is his identity.

From the breadth of the examples, it can be seen that an inherited or imposed identity has throughout human history probably been the most common way of answering the question 'Who am I?' To be born in a certain place of certain parents at a certain time determined much of one's life experience, not through events that one could choose but through a history one inherited.

We may attempt to choose our identity

That sense of being done to rather than doing – our identity being defined by others – challenges the modern and western sense of having a right of choice as to who we are and what we are like. If the first way is imposed and usually communal, the second is deliberate and often individual or part of a small group resisting larger conformist forces. A phrase often heard is 'I don't want to be defined by …' The defining aspect can be birth or part of how one experiences life or expectations coming from experiences of sexual orientation, race, gender, disability and more other matters than can be described. This second way in which one can find an objective identity is often portrayed as being by choice or by declaration about oneself. There is claimed to be an element of conscious action.

However, one's actions and choices are often no more effective at avoiding conflict with oneself or with others than the act of submitting to the choices of others and being swept along in the stream of historic or cultural identity. The formation of a chosen identity is very frequently on a negative basis. I choose to be x and define x as not y. It may be linked to being in control or regaining control of life. While inherited identity or birthed identity is often a root of the most profound injustice, chosen identity is sometimes experienced as no more adequate in facing the great issues of life.

In 2016 the London *Daily Telegraph* published a long article revealing that the person I had thought was my father was not and that my genetic father was someone else. There was much discussion about the consequences and anxious questions from friends and colleagues about how I felt. My answer was that my identity was not found in DNA but in Jesus Christ. In my own experience, much identity seeking is a search for truth. I may experience myself being different from how I have been brought up. The question then arises as to how I find my true identity, or even create an identity that is closer to the truth of what I really am.

This is where a choice lies. For me, to trust God's love revealed in Jesus Christ was to put myself in the hands of perfect love that knows me perfectly, the good, the bad and the ugly. It is to be accepted by love beyond measure. Another choice is to seek to define oneself.

The group of those who refuse to be defined *by* others too easily becomes a group that defines itself as '*not-the-other*'. The definition of a group of individualists will almost always be negative if it is to enable an alternative sense of identity. The negation of accepted and imposed identities is in itself an identity, but one that is designed to lead to distance and thus to opposition.

The major difficulty with self-identification is that it ignores reality.[9] Our capacity to self-identify comes from numerous influences outside ourselves. It depends on our parents conceiving us, on their nurture or lack of it, on the way in which we are reared. It is found from them genetically. Our culture or faith sets expectations that may be very difficult to break. The radically self-referential attitude of Descartes (I think therefore I am) is behind so much of the modern attitude to my rights to autonomy. It fails, however, to note that I am also because of many others. I exist because a community exists that conceived me, formed me, cared for me, educated me, loved me. No one is autonomous, and thus no one is truly free to form their own identity except within the constraints of community, which will vary greatly in its impact.

Honour or shame may define my identity
This subject is immensely complicated and is different in each culture but common to most. It lies at the heart of many long-lasting conflicts and is a reason for the difficulties that reconciliation poses. It draws in ideas of justice and forgiveness that may become either the greatest possible barriers to reconciliation or its most solid foundations.

Honour is a word that we associate with an earlier era in many parts of the world, and shame is often treated as a sort of psychological condition.[10] Yet even when concealed by other words and concepts, they remain deeply rooted as motivations.

Within Christian understanding, honour and its companion, pride, are meant to be transformed. In St John's Gospel, chapter 13, Jesus begins the last supper he has with his disciples (a Jewish Passover meal) by washing their feet. It was the job of most guests to wash their own feet, of a slave to do so for an important guest only, and was considered an immense courtesy when offered by a householder, reserved only for very special guests. For Jesus to do this was to upturn the ideas of honour and shame and to replace them with sacrificial love-in-action. It eliminates hierarchy. In John's Gospel it prefigures in some ways the summit of Jesus' glory in his being 'lifted up' – crucified, the death of a criminal.

The early disciples in the first centuries of the Church continued to challenge honour as a measure of self-worth in contrast to Jesus' call to humility. However, both before and especially after the Constantinian toleration, which effectively legalized and approved the Church in the Roman Empire, the human desire for status and honour, embedded in classical societies whether Greek or Roman, largely replaced the costly ideas of humility.

Relational identity: the heart of reconciliation

A fourth form of identity is neither imposed nor chosen nor instinctive and cultural, but is one that forms out of relationships with others, including those with whom we disagree and those who are of little account in the public eye. It is at this point that the pessimism of this chapter begins to lift. As we rejoice in love and self-giving, we can begin to see ourselves becoming more than we inherited, more confident in our worth, and more than we could choose by ourselves. Joy and flourishing are the result.

Our identity is capable of changing and being transformed at any point, and neither birth, nor behaviour, nor culture finally fix who we are. Neither adversity nor heritage are destiny.

In Christian thinking, hope is rooted in ideas of repentance demonstrated in action by a commitment to a new way of life and to the resources of God, mediated very often in community. There are strong similarities in other faith traditions.

The monastic tradition in Christianity was, from the sixth century CE, deeply shaped by the Rule of St Benedict, who founded the monastery of Monte Cassino in Italy and is generally considered the pioneer of western monasticism. His short rule sets out a vision of communities in which the members are shaped in their identities by mutual obedience and love, by common ownership of goods, by prayer singly and together, the study of the Bible and daily work. For its time it was a deeply humane document and was so influential that it can be said to have helped rescue European civilization from the Dark Ages. Although other forms of Christian monasticism have grown up over the ages, the influence of Benedict is visible in their form of life.[11]

In 2016 at Lambeth Palace, we began an experiment in community. We opened the Palace to up to fifteen residents from all around the world, all Christians but of any church tradition, and to an equivalent or smaller group of people based in London, who would take part in the community on a part-time basis. They were men and women, between twenty-one and thirty-four years old, who came each September and stayed until the following June. This 'Community of St Anselm' was led by an Anglican dean working in cooperation with brothers and sisters from the Chemin Neuf Community, an order of Roman Catholic monastic communities of ecumenical vocation and experience founded almost fifty years ago.

It has been transformative both for its members and for Lambeth Palace as a whole. The Community has a

Benedictine contemplative aspect, with silent prayer and regular Offices (times of common prayer) in the Church of England form. It is Franciscan in a commitment to working with the poor and excluded in London. It also draws on the Spiritual Exercises of St Ignatius, a process of self-examination.

There have been ups and downs. To bring together Christians from New York and Pakistan or South Sudan is to mix cultures and ways of finding identity on a grand scale. The heart of the Community is a common purpose, to draw closer to Jesus Christ in a way that will create habits that endure a lifetime. No subject is off-limits, but the ways of interacting are guided. The result has been fruitful in love, in depth of spiritual life and in the atmosphere of Lambeth Palace as a place of prayer centred in Christ, not merely an administrative centre.[12] The Community changes our collective and individual identity for the better.

At the heart of this experiment is the desire for a life with God in Jesus Christ. Our identity is to be oneself in encounter with another, jointly serving and worshipping Christ. The Community does not create clones, but embraces and develops diversity, enabling the liberation of identity in reconciliation with others. Conflicts become points of growth.

True community, whether in one place at one time or extended widely across a geographical region, is rooted in the authority of others to summon me to responsibility regardless of hierarchy.[13] Where I acknowledge the other as being in one sense or another part of myself, I find my identity more fully in responding to the other's need.

John Sachs[14] commented that 'the saints are the selves where extreme joy and extreme responsibility converge'.

To put it bluntly, identity is not found in a passive acceptance of how I am born, nor in a passionate rebellion against the fate I have been dealt, or in conformity to self-aggrandizing ideas of honour and shame, but in extreme and joyful acceptance of mutual responsibility with those unlike me, in need of me and whom I need even though I may not be aware of it. It is in such responsibility and joy that we find *reconciliation*.

Releasing the sense of mutual responsibility and joy in relationships of difference, which is implicit within the idea of reconciliation, opens core themes of how we love and deal with diversity, and restores to reconciliation the meaning that is so often lost in a fuzzy fudge of niceness without either joy or responsibility.

The illusions of overspeed and overreach

In secular thinking, reconciliation is an event that takes place quickly and then everyone moves on. It is basically a 'kiss and make up' event, where a gesture, an agreement, a proclamation or a treaty tells everyone that 'we are now in agreement', and we all hold our breath and hope for the best.

Yet this shallow approach seldom succeeds, because it engages either in overreach or in overspeed.

Overreach is the setting of entirely unrealistic goals that are of themselves so frightening in terms of their emotional demands that conflict parties do not feel able to engage even in the beginnings of a process. The potential cost seems overwhelming. They cannot imagine what seems like the possibility of losing something that makes them who they are. At the beginning of seeking to engage with those who have done great harm, or who are perceived as such (I will return to perception and reality in Chapter 5), the pressure of the journey feels overwhelming.

Overreach is usually related to those who are supporting or assisting with reconciliation oversimplifying things. You do not resolve human problems of conflict, whether in a family or at a global level, by pretending that they are simple.

Imagine a family that is experiencing problems between husband and wife. The marriage adviser finds that the wife has committed adultery. As the conversation goes on it appears that the husband is constantly critical, neglectful and goes out with his friends all day every weekend, playing golf. Then it comes to light that a teenager in the family has mental health problems that the husband blames on the wife, which disrupt the times she has set apart to spend with the husband. Further enquiry would show that this pattern of blaming others was the one the husband grew up with and that he was never allowed as a teenager to go out with friends. And so on. Like most people the couple have many different aspects of strengths and weaknesses. The way each finds their identity and value depends on foundations for life that are complicated. Each needs a series of changes in themselves and the other if there is to be any hope of renewing the relationship.

Overreach is to say to the husband: 'Just forgive her for the adultery.' He feels dishonoured by the over-simplicity, she feels abandoned and blamed. Neither may be seeking reconciliation if that is what it means. Simplicity brings everything down to one issue. For the person involved with encouraging and supporting reconciliation, one issue is manageable. As a result they try to simplify the complexity.

Another key cause of failure is overspeed. I remember clearly a leader in Northern Ireland being interviewed on the radio in the early summer of 1998, a few weeks after the Good Friday Agreement. The first questions were as to whether reconciliation had been achieved. I cannot remember the answers, but the idea that something called reconciliation could be achieved in weeks after thirty years of the Troubles and several centuries of bitterness was absurd. Reconciliation takes time, and Part II of this book will look at the process involved, while Part III considers the habits that are required to be developed over time. A UK programme of exercise from the National Health Service is called 'Couch to 5k'. It lasts nine weeks with three 'runs' a week. The first week is very limited, a few minutes walking and running. It has been very popular. If it was called 'Three Marathons a Week from Day 1' nobody would try it.

Yet reconciliation, the emotional and relational equivalent of a marathon, is assumed to be something that gets us from broken relationships in a family, or war in a country, to 'happily ever after' in a short process. It looks unrealistic because it is.

The idea of reconciliation within the Christian tradition is the very cornerstone of Christian faith. Whether in a secular or sacred context it sets a framework for understanding the idea that it must be at the heart of the practices of any functional group.

The living world of reconciliation

Reconciliation is first a lived experience. It takes time, develops habits (see Part III) and turns into a way of life and, above all, of relating. It transforms relationships. The monastic tradition sought to live out this idea in imitation of the lives of the earliest disciples in the Acts of the Apostles. St Benedict, in his Rule (RB) sets out several times that private property is forbidden, as in the last verses of the Acts of the Apostles, chapters 2 and 4. That was only one part of the common life. The monks are to live in obedience to one another, based on length of service and mutual love, as well as to those set above them in the monastery. In so doing they are to find their true individuality through unity and mutuality.[15] Historically, the monastic life at its best set a pattern for the whole Church, both of how to live and of inspiration to do so well.

Living well meant first that Christians must live incarnationally. Jesus' birth and life are referred to as incarnational; the Christian understanding of Christ is God made flesh, living in God's world as fully human. Incarnation is part of God's process of reconciling humanity with God, of reaching across the difference and breaking down the barriers of human failure and selfishness so that human beings can live in this world in justice and equality in the presence of God. The global Church – meaning the body of Christians – is commanded by God to live incarnationally, so that looking at Christians in every culture Christ is made visible. For that to happen, Christians must be reconciled reconcilers. Reconciliation is a visible change.

Second, at the heart of Christian living is the call to sacrifice: as Jesus puts it, each of his disciples is to take up their cross and follow him (Mark 8.34). For Jesus, the way of obedience to God was the surrender of his life, a willingness to sacrifice himself through crucifixion so as to make eternal life possible for all human beings. That sacrifice was an essential part of reconciliation with God on behalf of all humans. Taking place on the first Good Friday, it was followed on the third day by the first Easter, the resurrection of Jesus to life. Resurrection is the reality of the future, of the eternal life with God offered to all human beings. In the Bible there is the promise from God of a foretaste of that life through God's life living in us, the life of purpose and love that is experienced both now partly and completely in eternity. Sacrifice is thus core to reconciliation, something to be looked at more closely in the next chapter.

A key theological idea in reconciliation is its completion. It is a journey, but one with an end in full achievement. In technical theological language, this is about eschatology, the completion of all things and the establishment of God's rule on earth and in heaven. At that point reconciliation is completed, judgement is carried out, justice is done, and all truth is seen in the light of God.

Incarnation, crucifixion, new life, completion – these words in themselves represent a long period of time. Reconciliation must be lived out and grown into. It is sacrificial. It will only be completed when perfect justice rules the earth.

There is a very human and natural use of the word and idea of reconciliation that means a sort of compromise. There is the thought that reconciliation is achieved by everyone meeting in the middle in a sort of huggy and wet mass in which nobody is really happy, and we all pretend to agree.

Nothing could be further from the truth. Reconciliation demands truth and justice, recognition and expression of anger. Forgiveness is only real when freely offered without manipulation, and freely received without compulsion. Reconciliation accepts difference because in God we see difference in perfect unity. It is costly because God won it only though sacrificing Jesus – God – on the cross. It is liberation and joy as the resurrection liberated Christ from death. It will be completed, and all will be well, all will be in the light, and all indignity, injustice and oppression will be overcome in the end. In the meantime we travel determinedly and hopefully

In earthly and human processes of reconciliation all the elements of progress towards justice have to be visible. When we consider the issues of racism, especially against people in or from the Caribbean and Africa, now in the UK and USA, reconciliation is needed. The oppression goes back to the racism of slavery, the indignities and economic control of freed slaves and their descendants through Jim Crow laws and other means. It links in to colonialism in West Africa. The sin includes the practices of racism in Europe and the USA to this day. Such reconciliation cannot be achieved through ignoring the bitter injustices and evils of past and present. It cannot be done by saying to the descendants of victims and to contemporary sufferers today, 'Well, let's just forgive and forget.' That is the position of the powerful and the privileged. It cannot be through turning all the varieties of injustice into one mass and calling it by a single word or expression. Reconciliation will require enormous care.

Reconciliation in this area demands a long period of incarnational living in which the wicked practices of misuse of power and privilege are put aside, confessed and repented. There must be repentance and reparation, the powerful undertaking sacrificial establishment of what ought to be. There must be new life in justice. There must be a vision of a truly just and equal society. In other words, the kind of world of which Jesus spoke when he taught about the kingdom of God is one that must continually be sought in the world, and lived in the Church. Until all that is done we cannot say that reconciliation between races has been begun adequately.

Reflection on John 21[16]

The last chapter of the Gospel of John functions as an epilogue but also as a pointer to the future. It explicitly sets aside any claim to be a complete biography of Jesus, but its strong and vivid three-part narrative structure tells stories of responsibility and joy, among many other things, which engage the reader at the deepest level of emotional and creative imagination.

Following the crucifixion and resurrection seven of the disciples of Jesus are in Galilee and decide to go fishing. They catch nothing all night. The work is that of normal life, with all the frustrations and struggles of wet nets, darkness, and nothing caught. By the morning they would have been tired and frustrated. Suddenly, as they are packing up, a figure on the shore tells them to throw their nets to the other side. Another frustration. Perhaps some memory of previous occasions captures their minds for a moment, and they become open to the possibility of the presence of God. They do as they are asked.

The catch is overwhelming. They realize the presence of the risen Jesus as the figure on the shore and, filled with joy, they take the huge catch to the beach, Peter diving overboard and swimming ahead. When they arrive, they find a fire, Jesus himself, and fish cooking with bread. Here is the reality of Jesus Christ. He is there among the normal, not in a special place but in daily life amid mundane tasks. The miracle of the catch is dramatic but is part of God's choice for his world. Its meaning is profound as it points to their vocations, to their future and to the abundance of the joy that Jesus brings.

But there is shame. This is the Jesus they had let down. This is the risen Jesus whom they had been meeting, but could he still trust them, walk with them, lead them? For Peter there is the warped and misshapen sense of a relationship damaged by Peter's denial. It is morning but the new day seems clouded by regret and worse. And there is ignorance. Why has all this happened? What does it mean? As in their night of fruitless fishing, they have no clear direction. Are they to go back to where they were before he called them?

But they find three things they need. There is a fire, warmth and comfort after a cold night on the lake. There is food, both that they have caught and also already prepared. Their physical needs and low mood will be met. There is the sort of love and conversation that faces any lingering sense of their own sense of failure in the past and shows them, in a sign, the way forward. They are to reach the world. Their life's purpose with Jesus is only just beginning.

These beautiful passages contain a vast richness of meaning. The only other encounters with Jesus they have all had since the resurrection have been in a locked upper room in Jerusalem where he appeared, breathed the Holy Spirit into them and commissioned them. Yet at the crucifixion the other three Gospels and John record that they had run away, and that Peter had denied Jesus three times.

Relationships as close and tumultuous as they had with Jesus during the three years of his earthly ministry have been damaged by their failures. The story of Jesus with Peter shows a level of self-doubt in even the leading disciple, despite the resurrection appearances.

Who would have been confident to meet Jesus at this time? The world is different and so is he. He has died and risen. They have failed. He comes to them where they are most at home. He gives them an abundant catch of fish, so great that it overwhelms their resources. He enables Peter to cancel out his three denials with three affirmations. They are warmed, loved, restored, all by the one who is the more powerful. He demands nothing of any but Peter, and only words from him.

Reconciliation is a gift of sacrifice. It is costly. This moment of revealing a future – for disciples, for the Church at its birth, for the world in the new age of resurrection – follows the crucifixion, the life of God given in humility and pain. Yet that pain opens the way to living in the purposes of God.

Their journey of doubt and failure has ended in a place of abundance and joy. They are at home with Jesus. It is not the entirety of reconciliation; they have their lives ahead of them, which will involve endurance and suffering. Yet the journey has begun. They have a future liberated from their past.

SUMMARY

- Reconciliation involves the transformation of fear and exclusion of others into abundant joy in relishing difference.

- Reconciliation is the transformation of destructive forms of conflict and disagreement into the capacity to disagree well.
- Reconciliation is the experience of a journey of liberation through transformation of where and what we have been. As we see in John 21, its impact comes from at least one party demonstrating that the past need not entangle us for ever. The person or group that is more powerful must be the first to begin the journey, to set aside the power they have and to offer what is needed to the weaker.
- Reconciliation is always a process of gift and responsibility, not just for the outcome but for the flourishing of those involved. It changes the nature of relationships and gives them a way forward. So why is it so rare?

POINTS TO PONDER

- How do most of us understand the meaning of 'reconciliation'? What does it look like in films and stories outside the Bible, in everyday life? Do we have the right morally or freely to reject reconciliation with God, or with others?
- What true stories do you know of reconciliation? What are the key elements that went into reconciling?
- What do you think of as the greatest challenges that need reconciling, at any level, but certainly including yourself or your household and community and certainly including something on a grand scale?

Biblical Reflection

In this and the next two chapters a New Testament biblical passage will be offered as a basis for further reflection. For those of other faiths or those who prefer not to engage in this way please find an equivalent. These are not intended as exam questions! Before doing them, preferably with other people, be silent for a moment or pray aloud for guidance, and be honest about what you think. Don't worry about being right or wrong.

Colossians 1.15-20
This is probably a very early hymn or a statement of belief. In it Christ is described as the agent of creation and the means of reconciliation of all things to God. Creation and reconciliation are thus linked, and it is implicit that there is a conflict to reconcile.

- What does this say to you about the scope of reconciliation? Is there anything outside God's purposes of reconciliation?
- What does it say to you about human response to the possibilities of reconciliation?

2

The Hindrances to Reconciliation

If reconciliation is such a good thing, why is it so rare?

Almost half of all conflicts within countries restart in less than ten years after a ceasefire. Families seem to struggle with conflict from one generation to another. Neighbours find it easier to live miserably rather than make peace. When we get beyond the national to the global the old saying by Samuel Johnson that 'Depend upon it, sir, when a man knows he is to be hanged in a fortnight, it concentrates his mind wonderfully' is proved wrong. For example, climate change is itself a form of conflict between human beings and the planet, one which humanity is bound to lose. In addition, it is a significant driver of human conflict. It is clear beyond any doubt that climate change poses a high probability of catastrophic global impacts in every area of life. Yet far from concentrating the minds of the world, the changes that need to be made are ignored or hidden by unrealistic techno-optimism. That is not a concentrated mind; it is castles in the air.

What makes people act against their own happiness, their own hopes, their own interests so that rather than choose to search for ways to live in harmony, at least in some kind of working relationship across difference, they engage in mutual destruction?

In many parts of the world where resources are adequate or peace has been long established, this will seem to be pessimistic. Yet in other places physical war is the norm, and even in the most prosperous countries culture wars, cyber wars and campaigns of disruption proliferate without attempts at settlement.

In this chapter I want to suggest four areas that delay or destroy hopes of reconciliation. First, as we have seen, reconciliation always involves sacrifice and thus requires a willingness to give something up. Second, reconciliation challenges our explicit or implicit sense of honour and shame. Third, in reconciliation we often forget the impact of long-term trauma and conflict on the whole human being through changes in the neurochemistry, with impacts that are even transgenerational. Fourth, reconciliation is a long-term process and it is natural to look for short-term fixes to problems that will take years or even generations to resolve.

SACRIFICE

In Christian understanding the greatest reconciliation is God's action through Jesus to reconcile human beings and all creation to God. The Bible begins with the breaking of the relationship between the creator and the creation through the disobedience of the supreme point of creation, human beings. That disobedience is attributed to many things, but at their heart is the issue of pride. Human beings, in the story Adam and Eve, wanted the knowledge of good and evil. In other words, they wanted to decide for themselves and to disobey God in order to have more power.

It is a familiar story. One of the most destructive events that can happen in a marriage or equivalent relationship is unfaithfulness, cheating on your partner. Most people know that. Yet even in apparently happy marriages someone will sometimes stray, 'play away from home' as the euphemism goes. It is one of the few nuclear buttons and yet those in marriages press it. As a priest one hears often, 'I don't know why I did it.' Part of the temptation may just be that it is forbidden. Freedom of choice is deeply tempting, even when the freedom will have self-destroying results. Not to exercise the freedom of choice requires sacrifice.

Reconciliation is always costly. It can only begin by one side seeking to break the log-jam that is destructive conflict. Almost invariably that will need to be the stronger party. Morally, it should be in most circumstances one can imagine. The need for mercy and for a willingness to give something up in order to be reconciled is spoken of by Jesus in a parable in the Gospel of Matthew (18.23-35). Jesus is telling about the just rule of God, what he calls the kingdom of Heaven, and describing what it is to experience such rule. He tells of two servants. The first owes their mutual master a vast sum of money, more than he could ever repay. The master is sorting out his finances, sends for the slave and tells him that if he does not repay his debt he will be put in prison with his family. The slave begs for mercy and the master relieves him of the debt. The second slave owes the first a pitiful sum. But, after having been forgiven the huge debt by the master, the first slave proves to be merciless and has the second slave imprisoned. The master hears of it, and reverses the mercy shown to the first for failing to follow his example.

There are many ways of looking at this story and many meanings to it. Within it there is a pattern of reconciliation. Debt is a burden, for many an intolerable one. It is another way of translating the word used for trespasses in the Lord's Prayer, so that it would be perfectly valid to pray, instead of '*trespasses*', 'Forgive us our *debts*, in the same way as we forgive those *indebted* to us.' The paying off of debts to someone is one way of making a relationship more even. Right through the Old Testament, debt is seen as a loss of liberty, and the creditor who is ruthless in demanding repayment or foreclosing on security taken from the poor is seen as deeply wicked. Those to whom I owe a debt have power over me. Being a creditor is powerful, being a debtor involves taking on weakness and worry.

Many of us have experienced these pressures in our own lives. The day a home mortgage or loan is paid off is a day of liberation. One of the greatest burdens in many societies is debt slavery. In the UK it can come from losing a job and racking up debts to a high-interest lender or on credit cards. In many countries subsistence farmers borrow money to pay for seed and repay it from the proceeds of harvest, at high rates of interest. Natural disaster or family illness preventing work leaves them literally enslaved, unable to make any decisions for themselves. In its turn that leads to the breakdown of community relationships with lenders, often themselves farmers with more land or capital.

Who can start the process of forgiveness that leads to reconciliation? It must be the more powerful person being willing to make a sacrifice. In Jesus' story it starts with the master, who sets a pattern of reconciliation through debt forgiveness. The first slave cannot be reconciled to the master by his own efforts because he has no equivalent resource. The first slave commits the sin of not himself sacrificing his power and exercising the same justice so as to be reconciled to the second.

Both the master and the first slave need to make a sacrifice. Until they have decided to do that, the situation is only resolvable by destructive conflict in which the weaker party must lose, and all future relationship is impossible. Of course, the sacrifice by itself is not the end. It starts a process. Self-sacrifice without genuine and equal relationships leads to another form of debt: a sense of resentment at being helped.

This parable opens the way to thinking about two aspects of reconciliation. First, it is liberation for all involved. Liberation may not change the fundamental situation, but it transforms the potential. In the parable the slaves remain enslaved, the reality for about one-third of the population of the time. The parable is not about the evils of slavery. Yet their enslavement will be changed over time by the fact that they should have had an opportunity not to be debtors.

A modern historical parallel is in the outcomes of the peace process in Europe in 1919 at the Treaty of Versailles and in 1945 after the unconditional surrender of Germany. Both were complicated and the second was not completed until the Charter of Paris for a New Europe in 1990, which effectively ended the first Cold War. The largest question in 1919 and 1945 was what to do with the defeated Germany, by far the weakest power.

In 1919 the decision was to impose severe demands for reparations and to take many other steps to ensure that

Germany remained weak. After four years of world war the desire for revenge was understandable but its impact was disastrous. The German economy of the Weimar Republic remained hobbled by debt in a way that damaged its society. John Maynard Keynes began his celebrated career by resigning from the UK Treasury staff working on the treaty and writing *The Economic Consequences of the Peace*, in which he forecast disaster as a result of the economic and social impact of reparations.

By contrast in 1946, led by the Americans, there was a clear intention on the part of the western allies to enable Germany to remain united and to minimize or avoid reparations. The Soviet Union took a different view. However, after much struggle the decision of the western powers at least was to readmit Germany (or West Germany, at least) to the family of nations. The debts of the Third Reich were written off. Reparations were relatively slight. There was no revenge taken except in judicial terms for war crimes. The result, when combined with the establishment of an iron and steel pact and then the Common Market, has led to the longest sustained period of peace in western Europe since the fall of the Roman Empire.

That does not mean competition has ended or that friction has stopped. It did not mean that hatred evaporated overnight. It did not provide cover for the atrocities committed by Germany in the Second World War. In brief, it did not make everything 'all right' as though conflict can be reconciled as easily as a child can be stopped crying by being picked up and cuddled.

The process of reconciliation, which is almost eternal and needs constant renewal, required vast sacrifice by the victors in the war. They had to surrender the desire for revenge. They had to resist the urge to break up and deindustrialize a nation that, in the case of France, had been their opponent in three appalling wars within seventy-five years, in each of which France had suffered terribly. In the case of the USA the sacrifice involved the Marshall Plan to prevent the final collapse of the German and western European economies. The UK needed to find the means to forgive and to aid its former enemy.

Reconciliation is costly economically but also psychologically and, again, it is almost always the more powerful party that must sacrifice the most psychologically, above all their sense of domination. Christian understanding is that the source of reconciliation, the spring from which it flows into all the world, is the boundless and generous mercy of God revealed through the birth, life, suffering, crucifixion, resurrection and ascension of Jesus Christ. The key point is that almost every understanding of divine reconciliation involves the notion of some idea of sacrifice.[1]

In other words, for God to be reconciled with human beings, God needed to initiate reconciliation and to demonstrate that God is serious about it. The 'seriousness' of God's sacrifice reveals at the same time the abundant love and determination of God and the abundant peril of living without reconciliation. In John's Gospel 3.16 either John or Jesus says: 'For God so loved the world that he gave his only Son, so that anyone who believed in him should not perish but have eternal life.' It is because reconciliation matters so much that it requires sacrifice, a principle in both divine and human practice at all levels.

Sacrifice is a problem first, because most people are often in favour of the nobility of other people's sacrifice but not their own. That is especially true when the impact of sacrifice is very rarely effective unless it is by the stronger person or group. Take, at one extreme, the issue of the proliferation of nuclear weapons. If the UK or France forewent owning them, or even committed to a no-first-use or sole-purpose condition on their use, the international impact is unlikely to be more than marginal. If China, Russia or the USA did the same then there would be a very high chance of a breakthrough in new treaties.

In litigation between unequal parties, for example a shop that uses a name, and has used it for a long time, which is being sued for trademark infringement by a major international company that has a similar brand, the generosity of the latter will bring reconciliation, whereas concession by the former will simply be seen as bowing to the inevitable.

The difficulty is that the powerful have become so by avoiding concessions when they are in a position of advantage. Sacrifice demands that they take a different attitude, even acquire a new heart towards the weak.

Sacrifice is a problem, second, because of timing differentials: the fruits of reconciliation take time, the costs of sacrifice are immediate. Jesus had to die before he could be raised. The early apostles were martyred generations before the Church became a force to be reckoned with. Sacrifice takes risk and requires faith. In a bitterly fought divorce, the husband might be advised that, as he is wealthy and his wife not and as he has a strong legal position for reasons to do with the case, he should make it clear that he will fight every inch of the way in the courts. Yet, if he wants reconciliation, which may not involve the continuation of the marriage but may possibly leave the relationships able to be healed and the children less traumatized, he might decide to offer to submit to mediation. The risk is immediate, the probability is that he will do less well in the short term, but in the long term it may be that the children, even his wife, will feel a deep sense of gratitude for the sacrifice. It is a hard choice.

HONOUR AND SHAME

We don't talk much about honour in the Global North nowadays, although shame is still a word much in use. However, honour and shame remain influential in the way we relate to others individually and collectively.

Football is a classic example, much studied by sociologists. In cities like Liverpool, which has two historic and stand-out teams, the mood of the whole city is lifted or lowered by the results of the teams. Some signs are sinister, domestic violence rises sharply after a defeat. The same happens nationally when a country's team is defeated. Others are inspiring, the whole community becomes a better place when one team is doing well, and when that's true of both there is magic in the air. It may be that the word respect is substituted for honour, but the impact is the same. Collectively there is a sense of honour. When the team loses there is a sense of shame.

Shame brings anger, a turning inwards and a blame culture. 'Shame is the experience of one's felt sense of self-disintegration in relation to a dysregulating other.'[2] In Lucie Lunn's and other papers it is argued that, first, all human beings are somewhere on a spectrum of shame and that there is not an opposite, although dignity is what might be described as an antidote. Second, she sees shame as intrinsically linked to language. Third, that the experience of corporate shame is linked to individual experience and that empathy from a member of a group that has had shame projected onto it through the use of language may result in anger at perceived injustice even if perpetrated by a person's own group, rather than joining in corporate shame.

The first view is very much that of many psychologists. Shame is not guilt. Guilt in Christian thinking opens the way to repentance and forgiveness and thus to reconciliation with God. It implies responsibility, accountability or even personal action or omission. Guilt and shame are often blurred, but the latter tends to be destructive, alienating us from others and leading to lies, not reconciliation. The former turns us outwards to see the victim or object of our wrongdoing and to desire reconciliation and reparation for the harm done. It is summed up perfectly and economically in the Church of England's Book of Common Prayer confession:

> Almighty and most merciful Father, We have erred, and strayed from thy ways like lost sheep, We have followed too much the devices and desires of our own hearts, We have offended against thy holy laws, We have left undone those things which we ought to have done, And we have done those things which we ought not to have done, And there is no health in us: But thou, O Lord, have mercy upon us miserable offenders; Spare thou them, O God, which confess their faults, Restore thou them that are penitent, According to thy promises declared unto mankind in Christ Jesu our Lord: And grant, O most merciful Father, for his sake, That we may hereafter live a godly, righteous, and sober life, To the glory of thy holy Name. Amen.

In the Communion service according to the Book of Common Prayer the congregation acknowledge their sins and say, 'the burden of them is intolerable'. Bunyan's *Pilgrim's Progress* pictures guilt as a great backpack of enormous weight that hinders all that we do. In his book, the Pilgrim takes the burden up a steep hill topped with three crosses, and at the foot of the central cross, when he kneels, it falls off his back and rolls down the hill.

Shame is different. It comes upon us unawares, externally or internally. It is more like a hidden cancer that weakens us, hindering like guilt, but without the same objective and healthy incentive to seek forgiveness.

Shame is a weapon used very often by the strong against the weak. Whether it is through being gaslighted,[3] through harassment and bullying, through sexual or other forms of abuse, or through collective social action in dysfunctional organizations and societies, shame may be imposed. Victims may know that they are not to blame yet feel shame.

In this view shame is always destructive and negative as well as being mainly individual. In most levels of reconciliation one of the hardest barriers to break down is the individual against the collective.

The question is, does shame have a role in triggering reconciliation? There is an argument that it creates space by enabling a group to identify itself more clearly and to respond to the identification by collectively seeking reconciliation to mitigate the shame. In this view, collective shame is more like guilt and exists as a trigger to do the right thing.

Here the psychology and sociology differ. The former tends to look individually and the latter collectively.

I will come back to the issue in reconciliation after looking at honour.

Honour historically and in the Bible enhanced risk taking, gave courage and hope, led to flights of imagination and joyful generosity. Honour was something perceived externally, applying mainly to men and received by the individual: 'they shall learn I am just the man they take me for'[4] was a characteristic ambition. The weight of preserving honour for women was very heavy. In patriarchal societies they were expected to demonstrate virtue, and even when they were victims of sexual violence they were perceived as shamed. That legacy continues indirectly today even in countries like the UK but very much so elsewhere.

What makes us respected? For many it is honour. What enables our names to live on beyond our bodies? Again, honour. For thousands of years that has been one of the priorities in human existence, especially among men in positions of power. There are more than two hundred mentions of honour in the Bible. In the Psalms, kings pray for honour from God, they honour God with worship, they trust that God will honour them.

One book, that of Esther, is in part a description of competition for honour. The king in Babylon divorces his queen for failing to show him honour. After a search by courtiers, he finds a new queen – a Jewish woman called Esther, of great beauty – who becomes his wife. One of the king's advisers, Haman, plots to have the Jews massacred across the Empire. Esther's uncle, Mordecai, persuades her to intercede with the king, a risky undertaking, as to approach the king without invitation was to risk the sentence of death. However, after some hesitation she acts and invites him to two banquets, using food and beauty (it is a story of great humour, almost slapstick, and political intrigue). The tables are turned. The wicked Haman is shamed, Mordecai is honoured, and the Jews are saved. The events are still celebrated at the feast of Purim in the Jewish calendar.

The theme of honour is particularly relevant to the men. The king has honour because he is king, although the story shows him to be a bit slow of thought and open to manipulation. Haman seeks honour by serving the king. He aims to shame the Jews and gain honour for himself. Mordecai is humble, sitting at the gate, but a decisive leader with a clear sense of the providence of God. He is faithful in protecting the king and seeks protection for the Jews through the protection of God indicated by the high favour in which Esther is held.

Honour is not the same as pride, nor shame as humility. Haman is proud but without honour from the king and ultimately is executed. Mordecai is humble but receives honour when his service is recognized by the king.

This sort of bestowed honour/shame culture has been predominant in most societies in most periods. Even in the UK to this day, the awards given to distinguished people are called 'honours' and at the award ceremony the monarch 'honours' the recipient.

In past times, until certainly the early period of the twentieth century, honour was a legitimate reason for pride. An ancient name, a long-standing title, great wealth inherited, gave honour 'with no damned nonsense about merit' as the British prime minister Lord Melbourne remarked about being made a Knight of the Garter.

Honour is indeed often unlinked to merit. In many societies important people have honour that they cannot lose unless they are caught out in ill-doing in a way that is shameful. Bribery and corruption may be prevalent, but if they are linked to historic and cultural approaches to honour, such as support of dependants, clan or tribe, the support given enhances honour. Abuse of wealth for purely personal gain rather than as a sign of collective honour for those associated with the leader may bring shame and anger, but if it demonstrates importance and wealth it is a matter of praise.

In Homer's *Iliad* the origin of the Trojan War is the slight to the honour of King Agamemnon when the Trojan prince, Paris, steals his beautiful wife, Helen. War was considered by the ancient Greeks as a way of gaining honour, and perceived cowardice in war brought shame on the person, on their family and on their army if they were a leader.

The issues of honour and shame are still with us, although often in countries like the UK they are implicit. To some extent they are being revived through social media. Shaming is easy through anonymous posts. The power of the written word can circle the globe faster than Puck in *A Midsummer Night's Dream*.[5] Honour still carries a leader far even when unmerited; shame can topple a saint and not be revealed to be false for years. Shame can cripple the will and turn the mind inwards. It can divide a group that is able to do good and remove the courage to act at all. One of the great dangers to free speech and honest expression of views is the fear of being attacked and shamed with accusations impossible to disprove.

Courage and honour are linked. Shame has the psychological effect of triggering depression and undermining courage. To say or do anything becomes impossible. Being honoured restores courage and courage leads to acting honourably.

Neurochemistry and Remembering the Body

The third hindrance is what happens other than in the thinking process. We are not minds alone, but bodies, and even our minds are driven to some degree by chemistry and hormonal reactions with the release of chemicals in response to stimuli. The sight of a threat or the sense that one is about to emerge stimulates the fight-or-flight response. Had you been a hunter-gatherer thousands of years ago that might have been useful, but if you are sitting in a meeting seeking to negotiate a way forward it is likely to provoke unhelpful responses.

Yet we forget this so easily. I am aware that the surroundings in which a mediation is held will have a material impact on the outcome. A windowless room with poor air conditioning will lead to arguments and obstinacy. A good view, adequate refreshments and breaks to get energy back opens minds to new possibilities. The reading list at the end of this book explores the neurochemistry more adequately than I am able to do. It is clear that prolonged exposure to conflict, especially to violence that can be perceived as risking life, alters the entire way in which the mind and body work. Illness is more frequent. Rationality diminishes. Impulsive behaviour becomes more likely. At some point even the DNA is changed.

Worse still is when the experience of fear-filled lives passes from one generation to another. This may be the experience of those in countries like the South Sudan where no generation has lived in peace since the 1950s or even before. Or it may be in a family or a community where habitual dysfunctionality becomes part of the way things are done and the experience of new generations is long-term impacts on mental health for physiological as much as emotional reasons.

The pattern of the ministry of Jesus is of body, mind and soul. When he raises to life the dead daughter of a synagogue leader in Mark 5, he ensures her privacy, treats her gently, and ensures that she is given something to eat.

In a meeting in June 2021, one of the presenters started memorably with the phrase, 'remember the body'. Reconciliation is deeply hindered when we forget that we are bodies and minds, wills and reactions. This section is short, because I am not sufficiently scientifically qualified to write adequately on the subject. However, it is indispensable to consider the psychology, the neurochemistry and the bodily aspects of reconciliation. As will be seen in the next part of the book, handling the issues raised by the body is part of the reconciling process. It is another area that demands partnerships to work on reconciliation, as discussed in Part II.

Always Complete the Course

Most people who have regular access to antibiotics are aware of the instructions on the label, 'always complete the course'. Normally, with most routine infections, after a couple of days one feels much better. The temptation is to stop taking the tablets. But the result of doing so before the course is complete is that the infection is likely to return in much greater strength.

Reconciliation takes a very long time and to some extent is treatment for the chronic diseases of power seeking, of relationship breakdown and of the desire to dominate that so easily becomes part of the human condition.

Reconciliation is a combination of treatments. Mediation may enable a ceasefire or calm a community quarrel enough for longer-term work on meeting, rebuilding relationships and further mediation focused on the underlying issues.

The greatest danger is to think something is complete and to cease to pay attention to the issues that make differences so hard to handle. The *Difference Course*, described and discussed in Part III, is focused on habits, not meetings. It is through cultivating the characteristics of being a reconciled reconciler that long-term means of facing disagreement well can be built.

Summary

- Reconciliation is hard because of the hardness of the human heart and the immediacy of the challenges it offers as against the delayed but far greater rewards it brings.
- It requires sacrifice by those who have an advantage and can thus see the hope of victory as more attractive than the hard work of reconciling relationships.
- It is generally hindered by feelings of shame, but helped by a transparent recognition of guilt. Honour and shame are often unhelpful in that they are not always built on virtue and vice but frequently on perception.
- Remember the body.
- Take time, complete the course.

Points to Ponder

- Think of a conflict you know, anything from family to climate change. Who is the stronger party? What sacrifice would move things forward a little? What can you do to help?
- Is honour/shame an issue in your life or those around you? What does it look like in your own culture or society?
- What physical conditions makes you prone to destructive quarrels? What are the ways in a community or parish of remembering the body?
- Think of an example of reconciliation. Is it ever finished? If so, what would finished look like and how could you tell?

Biblical Reflection

1 Corinthians 1.10-18 and 2 Corinthians 5.17-21. Two letters to the same church, a church that gave Paul much heartache.

- From 1 Corinthians 1, what do you imagine the life of the Corinthian church was like? Is it the sort of church you would have been pleased to go to? What was going wrong? What was Paul's first response?
- From 2 Corinthians, what is the call of God to Christians? What does an ambassador do? What does it tell us about God and ourselves that such a muddled church can still hope to be ambassadors?

3

Changing the Heart

If the obstacles to peacebuilding and reconciliation are so severe, what hope is there? Where is it possible to find the resources to overcome the inertia, the wickedness, the rackets and power games, the deep-set structures of evil – the principalities and powers as St Paul calls them in chapter 6 of his epistle to the Ephesians – that come together to overwhelm the weak, the unthinking and the negligent?

As in looking at the obstacles, this chapter does not pretend to be the volumes-long work that would be necessary to explore all the resources for peacebuilding. I will try to look at some examples and pick up some attitudes that provide a grounding. Parts II and III of this book will develop that thinking and apply it.

THE MORAL IMAGINATION

In the early 2000s I was invited to facilitate a gathering in Bujumbura, the capital of Burundi, where government and opposition military and politicians would discuss reconciliation. The long civil war in Burundi that had started around the time of the Rwandan Genocide, more than ten years earlier, had died down to some extent as a result of ceasefires. Travel was still complicated, and flare-ups were frequent.

The meeting was held in a hotel. Around thirty attended for three days of discussion, all in French. There was a very suspicious atmosphere as long-term enemies met. On the third day a senior government military officer pointed across the room and said, 'That man's militia killed 30,000 people. How can I be reconciled?'

We were near Lake Tanganyika and I pointed out of the window to the beautiful sight of the lake and hills.

> 'If you go out in a boat and fall into the water, what do you do?'
> 'Swim!' came the answer.
> 'And if you can't swim?'
> 'Then you drown.'
> 'And if you do not find a way to reconcile then you will all die.'

The last chapter set out just a few of the issues of reconciliation. It is easy to conclude that peacebuilding is impossible. At its heart is the need for a leap of moral imagination[1] towards a possibility previously unimaginable, a structure for peaceful and reconciled disagreement that is radically different from the experience of destructive conflict. This is the point where an outsider may help. Peacebuilding in many conflicts at any level may seem so impossible that the only response is to continue fighting.

John Lederach comments:

> The moral imagination proposes that turning points and a journey towards a new horizon are possible, though based on perplexing paradoxes. The turning points must find a way to transcend the cycles of destructive violence while living with and being relevant to the context that produces those cycles. A horizon, though visible, is permanently just out of touch, suggesting an epic journey, the pursuit of which in peacebuilding, is the forging of new ways to approach human affairs with an enemy.[2]

That is what is meant by moral imagination: it leads to a change of heart. In all sorts of conflict, the aim becomes more and more towards winning, even when winning is an empty dream. Whether it is a family arguing over an inheritance, or a group seeking political power in a country, once the conflict – within its own context – becomes destructive then only change of heart and a new imagination gives the strength to move forward. The very act of planning victory is itself one sort of imagination that energizes and motivates those involved even where the consequences of victory, let alone defeat, would be terrible.

In March 2021, the UK government published a review of the outlook for security, defence and development in the 2020s.[3] It is a powerful and comprehensive document, probably the widest ranging of its kind in very many decades, possibly ever. Yet in many places it suffers from a lack of moral imagination, especially in dealing with world-changing threats like nuclear war. It includes an approach to nuclear warfare strategy, but never asks the question about consequences. If there was a nuclear war and the UK deployed and used its weapons, what happens next? It comes in the category of 'too difficult, ignore'.

Such a failure of the necessary imagination of the moral consequences of proposed actions are typical of conflicts that pursue a single, straight road, well paved with good intentions. Its underlying assumption is that 'we can control events', 'we will win', or 'it won't happen'. Yet all the history of wars reveals that they are times of chaos and error, where often the side that makes the fewer mistakes wins.

The same is true of domestic or community quarrels. Where the whole resources of imagination are taken up with seeking to win and with mulling over the horrible nature of the enemy, no space, no bandwidth, is left for the moral imagination. The long, straight and well-paved road is never looked at afresh with the question, 'Can I or we imagine an alternative, a fork in the road that takes us on the hard and stony path of peace?'

Lederach quotes his researcher as writing: 'In our context of thirty plus years of the Troubles [in Northern Ireland], violence, fear and division are known. Peace is the mystery! ... Peace is Mystery. It is walking into the unknown.'[4]

The first and indispensable resource for overcoming a sense that conflict is inexorable, unavoidable, conquering all the best intentions, is the moral imagination. The moral imagination is the responsibility of leadership. It is perhaps *the* example of leadership that most clearly sets great leaders apart.

In the twentieth century there are many examples of such moral imagination. In Chapter 1, I have already referred to the leadership of those who sought to bring western Europe together after 1945, to provide a pathway for peaceful competition and to end the centuries of terrible wars that had killed so many, especially since 1870. There are many more examples. After the Nigerian Civil War of 1967–70, President Gowon of Nigeria declared, 'no victors, no vanquished', and thereby started a process of reconciliation that has endured to some extent for half a century. After the fall of the Berlin Wall in 1989, Germany was reunited, and other countries in the former communist-ruled centre and east of Europe adjusted in largely peaceful revolutions. In what was then Czechoslovakia, President Václav Havel, a former political prisoner, led the country into peaceful adjustment (the Velvet Revolution of 1989) and then into the 'velvet divorce' when in 1993 Slovakia separated and received independence. In February 1990, following his twenty-seven years of imprisonment, soon-to-be-president Nelson Mandela navigated the transition to Black majority rule in South Africa, along with President de Klerk.

There are many quibbles and many serious objections that can be raised with every example. None of them demonstrates a process of moral imagination that is eternal or that became part of the DNA of a country or a movement. Time goes by, the vision of the founders fades. Others replace them, the pain of conflict is forgotten as the generation that lived it grows old and dies. Moral imagination, like forgiveness, is a fragile plant that needs constant attention. Moral imagination never will be in human DNA: our desires for power, our capacity to find enemies, our pride and foolish self-reliance, all prevent such a deep change in human nature.

But when it flowers, miracles happen. That fragile plant will, for a few years or even a couple of generations, shelter nations from war and turn human hearts to love for those with less resources than them. Its flowering can be renewed with the right leaders and the right inspiration.

Inspiration matters at several levels. It is far more than emotional. It affects perception and influences imagination. It can change the attitude to outgroups by members of an opposed ingroup. It works across the whole human being,[5] including in the neurochemistry that has a powerful influence on emotions, on decision-making capacity, on ethical attitudes. Inspiration changes perceptions of challenges or, to put it another way, it can nourish or restrict the moral imagination. Studies have shown that perceptions of a challenge, such as climbing a very steep hill, will be improved if someone has a positive and confident companion – the hill, in the case of the climber, then being physically perceived as less steep. Perceptions of threat are appropriate when facing someone violent or for a fighter in battle, but they pose dangers to peace negotiations. Inspiration may nurture a different attitude.

The first and most important resource in peacebuilding is the moral imagination described above: nobody will retain that imagination without being nurtured and inspired by leadership and by functional and mutually supportive communities. Reconciliation is seldom, if ever, the choice of a lone individual and even if they make that choice, they still need the resilience and persistence that comes from community.

A Holistic Focus

The second key resource is a holistic approach to building peace. Peacebuilding is very often seen as those things that capture the headlines. Prime ministers and presidents come and go in convoys of armoured vehicles and howling sirens. They are surrounded by people in dark glasses with curly wires coming out of their ears who talk to their shirt cuffs and are always looking for threats. Exhausted spokespeople talk of honest discussions, slow progress, hope of a breakthrough or the achievement of settlement. Signings are held in large halls with people passing documents from one to the other and pens being exchanged. Polling figures are consulted to see what the impact has been on re-election chances.

Then the caravan moves on. Three or five or seven years later, the struggle re-emerges, perhaps a little different but always the same basic virus of violence. Nobel Prizes are not returned, the politicians may have moved on, but the people, the sufferers, the women raped, the men ignored, were never touched. They had a few courses on job finding, but their hearts and intentions were not treated as having the same intrinsic value and independence as those of the leaders, and their moral imagination was neither inspired nor nurtured. The struggle begins again and this time it is worse.

In the sixteenth century, during the French religious wars, a leader on one side commented that 'in the first war we fought like men, in the second like animals and in the third like demons'. Conflict does not improve with age, nor does it decay and become less dangerous. It rots. The rot is poisonous to the body, mind and spirit of the individual and of the society.

Yet there is as much problem with the hidden work that happens. Grassroots groups may work intensely and intelligently. Local efforts may bring local peace. Yet regional conflicts overwhelm as does the pressure of others with a dog in the fight or who are just observers with bias and interests. The leaders call their followers to arms and out of peer pressure and desire for honour the middle-rank leaders and the people at the most local level respond.

Peacebuilding in every situation must be top down, middle out and bottom up, all at once, all linked and all inclusive.

The illustration of the need for a holistic approach is a failure that taught me a lesson. In the early 2000s, the group with whom I worked at Coventry Cathedral was invited to support work on peacebuilding in an area of an African country. It was a border area where historic expansion of Christianity and Islam met. It was also a border between farmers and pastoralists as well as two ethnic groups. Several thousand people had died during clashes. The area was remote, and police and army groups could not reach threatened towns and villages in time. I remember walking through burned-out settlements one Ash Wednesday, the dust and ash rising into the air from the ruins and the humps of shallow graves in the ground. Hostility, deep hatred, were all around.

The process was long but for a while it was effective. Influential people in different villages were given satellite phones so that they could communicate. They were trained a little and had a very few numbers programmed in. Some training on conflict management was given to local police units. If a person with a phone heard that there was trouble brewing, they could phone the equivalent elder in the nearest village from where the trouble might come, or might be going, and warn them. They would also call the police, rather than walking for hours to a place where they could call.

The results were dramatic for a while. There was a good deal of peace and collaboration. Then, at a higher level, the whole region erupted into new violence and in a short period all the progress was swept away. We had supported the real reconcilers who were local, and the next level up, the middle. But the top remained untouched. The result was failure to establish sustainable non-violence for long enough to change the moral imagination towards peace.

PARTNERSHIP

Everyone wants the glory. Everyone wants, being human, to be recognized for what they have done. NGOs, whether local or international, rely on attention to maintain access to funding streams. Having led an NGO within Coventry Cathedral, I remember well the pressure. It is not corruption or greed, merely the normal reality that any institution seeks to preserve its own life, and, in most institutions, 'life' is represented by money to carry out work. Without money, staff cannot be kept and new projects cannot be completed. In one sense this is right. A good organization, with visionary ideas, comes into being and grows. Sooner or later, however, its initial vision and sharpness of aims and values are blurred as people come to work for it who were not there at the beginning. As it gets larger, more time is spent on finance and function and less on the front line.

Equally, no institution is capable of doing all that is needed. Those with skills at mediation may well not be so good at running refugee or IDP[6] settlements. There may be very severe problems of security that require working with peacekeeping or peacemaking organizations. Epidemics will need medical support. Displaced and disturbed children will need education and stability. Many of all ages and types will require trauma counselling. There will be the need of resettlement, of rebuilding an economy with microfinance and other support. The list is endless.

Perhaps the most difficult and most valuable part of putting together an effort in reconciliation is assembling a team and having the humility or ethos among its members to be willing to share the way forward.

In the UK a town was divided by prospects of a new motorway running close by. The route would divide it from other, smaller villages in the community, and there would be more noise and a disturbance to the view. Many of the older and more conservative households were against it. They had settled in the area towards the end of their working lives, mostly professional and white-collar elite, and they resented the change to the character of the area. For exactly the same reasons, a minority of the older people, those who had grown up there and to quote someone I knew, 'their grandparents are in the churchyard', were in favour because their children could not afford the increasingly expensive housing and would have to move away. For some others, who came from families in the area for up to seven generations, this felt like the end of the world.

The community needed better facilities and affordable housing, not a road.

The priest of the parish rather naively invited people to an open meeting at the church to discuss a way forward. Ahead of the date both sides, who had representatives on the town council, agreed who would speak and a line to take. The meeting quickly turned not into a debate but into an exchange of explosive-filled speeches that did not attempt to address the fears of the other but were aimed at rallying hard-line support for their own view.

The parish priest put aside her fantasies of being loved by everyone because she had put the community back together, and with considerable courage picked herself up and got advice.

To cut the story of a couple of years very short, she found partners and, with a group, mapped the conflict. They saw who had what interests, who led them and who encouraged them. They listened carefully and built relationships with different groups, not least with church services tailored for every different group. They worked with small groups, trained people in listening skills and in having difficult conversations. They understood some very physical needs, such as for improved surgeries, a bigger school and better and cheaper shopping. By the end they had enabled the majority, but not all, of the community to accept that the motorway could go ahead, and negotiated with developers that the new jobs it would bring as transport links improved would open the way to new housing that was appropriate for the area and affordable for those who would work there. There would be more shopping, a sports centre and a new secondary school.

They did not live happily ever after, and the priest was not loved by everyone, until the next one came, when, of course, the previous one was seen as a golden age, but the community grew in diversity and functioned as a place of welcome and hope. And that is good enough.

Think about what was needed for that outcome. Mediation and reconciliation were only part of the problem. There needed to be social understanding, training, developers, lawyers, educationalists, doctors and loads of volunteers. Scale it up to a violent conflict over a region and the complexity grows enormously. Scale it globally and face an issue like climate change and it is orders of magnitude more complex still.

It is obvious that at almost no level can things be done alone. Even a single household may well need mediation, counselling, financial advice, support for a bullied child at school and help to get a leaking roof repaired. The key issue for anyone involved in mediation and reconciliation work is to know what they can do and to ensure that the right team is assembled. We will look at how this is done more carefully in Part II.

A Commitment to Truth and Transparency

At UK schools, textbooks in history usually describe the Battle of Trafalgar as the key naval engagement of the Revolutionary and Napoleonic Wars in which the Royal Navy defeated a stronger Franco-Spanish force after a dramatic chase across the Atlantic and back. It is set out as the moment that stopped Napoleon's 'Army of England' mounting an invasion. The next passage will usually say that the army at Boulogne then broke camp and marched across Europe to defeat the

Dual Monarchy at Ulm and Austerlitz and in 1806 the Prussians at Jena. Nelson's death is always painted in heroic colours. The Royal Navy celebrates Trafalgar Day (21 October) with dinners and a toast to 'the immortal memory'.

A French history textbook for schools described Trafalgar as a naval engagement off the Spanish coast in which the British admiral was killed. End of story.

Both statements are true, but neither is the whole truth. The understanding of history is seldom precise. There is always a myth that somehow 'truth' in a dispute exists somewhere. The reality is that the nature of conflict at all levels of our lives makes us perceive reality differently. There is a letter in our family from someone who was part of the Charge of the Light Brigade in 1854 at the Battle of Balaclava in the Crimean War. It was written to his mother immediately after the battle. He tells of the charge, of friends who were killed or wounded, and of his horse having been hit by a shell splinter. Surely this would be accurate? It certainly is, but it is only one aspect of the battle and contradicts other accounts in some important ways. There is a true account of the battle, but no single person could tell it and no history will get every detail right.

We all have the experience of listening to friends whose marriage or relationship has broken down. It is painful and sad. It is also confusing. Sometimes there is a sort of resigned defeatism, 'it just was not working', which cannot be explained. Sometimes there are flat contradictions. The outsider cannot tell which is true and often even those involved don't know or convince themselves of truth that has no relation to what happened. Finding the truth is a difficult process, and the bigger the conflict the more complicated the truth. It takes time and often a process of enquiry.

The Truth and Reconciliation Commission (TRC) approach was most famously applied in South Africa after the fall of the Apartheid regime. Chaired by the Anglican Archbishop of Cape Town, Desmond Tutu, it achieved a remarkable success in enabling the hardest of stories to be told by victims and perpetrators. Not only did this result in a far clearer understanding of truth, but in some remarkable cases it opened the way to reconciliation between individuals and symbolized the beginnings of reconciliation for the nation.

TRCs have been tried in many places. The key to their working is a deep commitment to transparency by individuals and organizations. They must have official support and a willingness by all significant figures to be open and not simply to use a TRC as a forum for putting their own case. Truth is only found by transparency that listens as well as speaks. It requires the humility of being able to accept that wrong has been done. Above all, TRCs require leadership that is trusted in the way that both President Mandela and Archbishop Tutu were.

Truth and transparency are painful and costly. A commitment to both is essential but needs help through skilled and trusted figures in a TRC or through good facilitators in other methods. What matters is developing habits of facing conflict in a way that always leaves space for changing of minds. 'My truth, right or wrong' does not lead to progress.

The sign of a commitment to truth and transparency is the seeking of a joint understanding at best, or at least an understanding of the position of the other. To be able to tell the other's story and to give an account of their view, even when disagreement is profound, is a major step on the journey of reconciliation.

EMBRACE COMPLEXITY

I love simplifying things. To look at a complex problem and be able to extract the key elements in a way that is simple feels like a great achievement. I hold strongly to the adage 'KISS', 'keep it simple, stupid!' Complicated problems end up with untidy solutions.

In some areas of work, it is a good rule. The organization of companies or other institutions is better kept as simple as possible. I once worked in a company that relied on matrix management. The theory was fine: that junior employees like me had more than one manager so that all those above knew what was going on. The result was at best disorder and at worst an opportunity to play off one boss against the other. Paper proliferated as people like me tried to tell all those who we thought might be one of our line managers everything they needed to know about everything we were doing.

However, there is no simplifying the human heart. We seldom understand all our own motivations. The wonderful film *Bridge of Spies* with Tom Hanks and Mark Rylance (2015) is about the Cold War in the 1950s. Mark Rylance plays a Russian spy in the USA who is caught and sentenced to death. His lawyer is played by Tom Hanks. Hanks says to Rylance on several occasions, 'You don't seem worried', and the Rylance character replies, 'Would it help?' Most of us are not quite like that. People annoy us and even when we do not show it, we are unsettled by conversations with them. Often, we cannot quite explain it.

Put our own internal complexity into a group and multiply it by the number of people. Add in the soup of not-quite-understood history and the impact of historic myths and legends. Add a garnish of fear and anxiety for the future, of apprehension for one's family and stability and the ambitions of many leaders. Combine with the influence of those who gain from conflict at all levels. Don't forget the impact of pride and unwillingness to agree one is wrong and the strength of greed for gain and the fruit of victory. Even then one is not anywhere close to the complexity of many conflicts.

Imagine you end up in hospital after you have had a bad fall. You are wheeled into the emergency department. A doctor takes a very quick look and says, 'You have a bruised head; take some paracetamol and lie down until you feel better' but ignores your broken leg. You would not be impressed. You would certainly not get better.

Simplifying the genuinely complex leads not only to misdiagnosis of the problem but also to the wrong treatment and thus no recovery.

A clear example of this is the use of religion or immigration or another single issue as a political hook, on which politicians often hang much more complicated problems. Religion and immigration are easily identifiable differences between people. News and media will often present a conflict as 'religious', or 'tribal', or a similar term. The reality will be a very complicated mixture of history, economics, ethnicity and numerous other causes. For a political leader seeking office, simplification enables more followers to be found. For a reporter in a war zone, who usually understands how intricate the problem is, the pressure of condensing a report into less than two minutes makes complexity impossible to communicate. For someone facilitating the process or for the parties there are no excuses: complexity has to be faced. You cannot heal what you have not identified.

In 2002, I had the privilege of being the note taker at a meeting in Jerusalem chaired by the then Archbishop of Canterbury, George Carey (now Lord Carey). It was a gathering of religious and political leaders who had signed the Alexandria Declaration on religious peace in the Holy Land. There were about twenty-five people present in a brilliantly chaired and fiercely argued meeting. The discussion covered the situation of the *intifada* (the uprising) that was currently happening, the issue of bombings, Jewish and Christian and Islamic theology, as well as a multitude of historic events as far back as the destruction of Herod's Temple in 70 CE. I was sitting next to the British Consul General in Jerusalem, who at one point muttered, 'I hope you understand all this, because I don't.'

No simplification could do justice to the complexity of a dispute that in some readings goes back to the time of Moses. Lord Carey's remarkable ability to hold the subtleties delicately enabled a good outcome to the day. He recognized and embraced the complexity.

SUMMARY

- In some ways the keys to progress come down to character.

- Humility enables partnerships to work, complexity to be embraced and the unknowable and undiscernible aspects of truth to be left on the table where they can be examined over time. Pride seeks self-glory, wants partners only as subordinates, simplifies to show sharp insight and is impatient.
- Openness to others stimulates the moral imagination. A gentle manner and a confidence when needed, another way of saying courage, combine to make it possible for the moral imagination to be spread and taken on board by those in a dispute.
- And I would say faith enables us to call out to the God of peace for blessing on the journey of reconciliation and the miracle of roadblocks circumvented and barriers overcome.

POINTS TO PONDER

- Do you believe reconciliation is possible? Looking back at Part I, are the obstacles too great? List some disputes you have known, locally, in families or on a wider scale. What proportion have been fought out and which ones have shown some fruit of reconciliation? What made the difference?
- What is most discouraging and most encouraging about this Part? Why?
- In your own faith tradition or non-faith tradition, what are the stories that call you to reconciliation?

Biblical Reflection

John 13.1-20

A famous passage. Spend time talking about the reaction of those involved. What would a foot-washing church look like at every level? Try washing each other's feet, if everyone is happy with that. Then share how you feel. Then pray.

PART II

INTRODUCTION

Peacebuilding is about the heart. There is never a *technique* that provides all the answers, but there can be systematic approaches that improve the chances of the people involved in a dispute finding a way forward towards a better outcome. There are also innumerable side-tracks, red herrings and blind alleys that can bring things to a halt.

This Part II is not a method, it is a pattern of working at any level of dispute. It is not exhaustive. It has been helpful. I first came across this pattern when working with Canon Andrew White in Coventry between 2002 and 2005. Later, Canon Paul Oestreicher, Andrew's predecessor in leading the work at Coventry described earlier, confirmed that, although he had not put all of this into words, it was the way he worked.

In the world of peacebuilding and reconciliation there are many very good approaches, often with scientific names and much system. I am not pretending to that. The question is always, 'While lovingly respecting the dignity and autonomy of those in the conflict, what helps them most to find a way to transform destructive conflict into healthy disagreement with diversity and unity held together?'

The Coventry model is based around six words beginning with R. They are not sequential, you don't do one and then the other, but like a juggler you start with one and end with all going at once. That is essential to any peacebuilding. Each R deals with an aspect of being human and struggling with conflict. To drop or forget one is to become mechanistic, which always leads to failure.

The underlying principles of the Six Rs are those of Part I. They are designed to encourage the development of a holistic approach that draws in partners in the work of peacebuilding and enables the parties to a dispute to reimagine the possibility of the 'Mystery of Peace' when they are accustomed to destructive conflict.

This Part involves the figure of the facilitator, peacemaker or peacebuilder. I use these words interchangeably to mean the person – more usually the group of people and organizations – who seek to enable the parties to find a way forward in disagreeing well and in rebuilding resilient and sustainable relationships amid deeply held differences.

In Christian understanding the foundational breakdown in relationship is that between the creator God and the human beings who were created and exist to relish and enjoy relationship with God, each other and the creation, in a world in which love, righteousness and justice reign. God's answer is out of love to reconcile human beings who seek to go their own way, to live independently, to be autonomous from God. That was done by God becoming fully human, living a fully human life, dying a fully human death, in the person of Jesus Christ. He was fully God who makes all things well, fully human in being tested and tempted in all things as we are, yet without sin.[1] The core of Christian belief is that God in Jesus Christ lived with human suffering, died and rose again to new life, and calls all people to know God in joy and liberation. In so doing they find that same new life and the power of God's Spirit at work in them as the Spirit is already at work in the world.

For Christians not only is the history of Jesus Christ an example and a pattern to follow, but he also opened the way to peace with God and to the calling to live as those who make peace, to be reconciled reconcilers. He is alive and known, dwelling in us by the Spirit of God given to us.

It was Jesus who said to his disciples, 'Blessed are the peacemakers for they shall be called children of God.'[2]

All very well, but what does a peacemaker look like? This part looks at what a peacemaker does, but it also makes assumptions about character.

At any level of conflict peacemakers are those who stand in the middle and extend their arms to all, in the way that Jesus Christ extended his arms on the cross. They become bridges for people to cross over to embrace those from whom they have been separated, even hated and in many cases sought to kill.

Builders of peace are seldom favoured by those with whom they engage. They are often the lightning conductor for the rage, fear and despair present in every conflict. Therefore what are the qualities required?

As this part begins, I will offer two from within Christian teaching and the pattern of Jesus.

The first is transparency. Peacebuilders are called to be known. The beautiful passages of the call of the disciples (John's Gospel, chapter 1) have several questions and descriptions.

The first is that Jesus is light and in him is no darkness at all. A characteristic of light is seeing. The great Christian renewal that began in the 1930s in East Africa had as one of its rules 'walk in the light' – especially with those around us. To walk in the light is to be seen and to see truly. In John 1 the first disciples ask questions of Jesus, such as 'Where are you staying?' Jesus replies: 'Come and see.' Nothing is hidden. The implicit and underlying question addressed to Jesus that runs through the whole chapter and indeed the whole Gospel is equally simple: 'Who are you?'

Any facilitator of peacebuilding must be knowable and transparent in who they are. Without knowing the facilitator in depth, the participants in a conflict will not be able to trust them. The suspicions of manipulation are almost always so great that the facilitator is assumed to have a hidden agenda in favour of the other parties. Peacebuilders must walk in the light with regards to their own history, their funding and their motivation.

Second, peacebuilders must work in the background. They come to serve; glory is for others. One of the very oldest hymns of the Christian faith is found in the letter to the Philippians, chapter 2. It speaks of Jesus, who did not count equality with God a thing to be grasped, but humbled himself, taking the form of a servant.

The reality is that the people who take the biggest risks in peacebuilding are those who are in conflict. They risk credibility, loss of honour with their followers, being seen as naïve by those siding with them, and so much more. In armed conflicts they risk death at the hands of the more radical. Facilitators do take great risks. For example, the Anglican Communion commemorates every year the Melanesian Martyrs, a group of Melanesian Anglican monks who went to the camp of a warlord in 2003 after a peace agreement ending much of the fighting in the Solomon Islands around the year 2000. They went to plead for peace but were tortured and murdered. In that death for peace is seen the true image of Jesus Christ. They went to serve and were willing to give all.

The temptation to be the hero who makes peace, the centre of the story, is common to many of us. Peacebuilding and facilitating discussions seek something else: the transformation of conflict.

4

Researching or How to Become Consciously Ignorant

We were driving through a swampy area in the Ogoni region of the Niger Delta. It was the original area of oil production in Nigeria, with the first flow in 1956, the same year as my birth. The result of oil is something often referred to as 'the natural resource curse', in which the huge wealth under the ground leads to conflict, to inequality, to corruption and to violence. In the case of Ogoni, to those demons can be added pollution of soil and waterways, destruction of fishing and crops, and deterioration of air quality from the almost uninhibited flaring of the gas that was produced with the oil.

The people who had scarcely – if at all – benefited from the oil that had been produced for fifty years were the local inhabitants. A region that should have looked like Abu Dhabi was still desperately poor, with high underemployment or unemployment, low incomes, short life expectancies and insecurity. Along with militia groups and banditry, life was (and is) insecure.

The outcome has been very understandable unrest. A charismatic leader called Ken Saro-Wiwa founded, with others, the Movement for the Survival of the Ogoni People (MOSOP). In 1995, during the tyrannical, military dictatorship of General Abacha, and with Ogoniland seething with discontent, Ken Saro-Wiwa and some of his colleagues were arrested and then executed by hanging. The company operating the production was Shell. They were accused by MOSOP of collaborating with the government, something they forcefully denied. Additionally, many among the Ogoni people saw the production as the theft of the natural resources and wealth that they should have owned. The unrest meant that oil production had to be shut down. In the early 2000s, Coventry Cathedral's International Centre for Reconciliation was invited to help with a process of reconciliation.

By this time of the closure of the oilfields in the 1990s, Ogoni oil production was somewhat depleted. If oil was to be lifted, each well would produce for a while until the internal pressure dropped and oil stopped flowing. Then the well was closed until the pressure built up again. It was all a bit like the plumbing in old houses.

On that day in Ogoniland, as usual when someone else is driving (I should pay tribute here to my wonderful driver, who went into all kinds of bad places and kept me safe) I was dozing in the hot and humid air blowing through the open windows of the car. A colleague pointed out a steel object rising above the grass at the side of the road. We stopped to take a look at what was a well-head, the kit on the surface of the ground through which oil can be produced, often called a Christmas tree. The metal was in fairly good condition, and despite having been theoretically unused for over ten years, there were fresh, shiny scratches on the top where spanners and wrenches had been used to open it for production. Clearly, oil was being lifted by someone.

As we were looking, we heard voices. A group of about a dozen young men, with machetes but not guns, were standing around the car. They were talking in Ogoni, but when we got near, some began to speak English. They thought we were from Shell and were angry and threatening, speaking of taking us prisoner and asking what we were doing there. They had seen petrol tankers in the area in previous weeks, and assumed Shell were producing oil despite their promises not to. Ogoni could produce, at that time, about 30,000 barrels of high-value crude oil a day and with the price of oil around US$100 for each barrel that was worth doing.

After a while they began to calm down, and we spent quite a long time listening to their stories and their sense of despair at the endless conflict and hopelessness of their lives. Their great refrain was, 'Where has the oil gone?' They also wanted to know why they had not benefited. The conversation ended with a prayer together, and we moved on to the next village and next appointment to listen to others. I was very grateful for the unplanned stop. It offered the chance to hear some voices who were not pre-programmed to lobby us, but spoke from their hearts, albeit very embittered hearts.

The first R is Researching. It is a straightforward list of things to do. Desktop analysis is the beginning: read as much useful information as you can find, which was much less at the time of this story, with the web in its infancy. Look at Twitter feeds, Facebook pages, Instagram, TikTok and the rest. Then interview everyone you can get hold of who is willing to talk. Try and do so in a systematic way, taking notes, and without simply doing a check-list of questions, seeking rather to get things in a shape that enables comparison of stories and discernment of different perspectives. It is much better to do this in pairs. One point to note is that, if at all possible, in cultural areas where that is a sensitivity, women should interview women.

As you interview and listen, the third step is to begin to populate a map of the conflict. This is not a moment of judgement, but simply of analysis. Who are the key parties? Since when have they been involved? Who are and have been the leaders? What is the timeline? What are the key environmental, cultural and other contextual factors? Who are the shadow players with influence but less obvious presence? Who are the spoilers who have a vested interest in the conflict continuing or even getting worse?

I am not going to be prescriptive about tools. This is a book at a general level and specialist publications will be more helpful. An online search will show many different tools for mapping. Like all tools they are only as good as the data that goes into them, so the key to a good map is having covered the ground, metaphorically but preferably sometimes physically. In other words, the map quality depends on the building of a good rapport with those involved directly and listening well. We will look at this more closely in Part III.

Which tool to use will depend on the complexity of the conflict. A tool that could adequately map the Second World War is likely to be a little over the top in a community or family confrontation. At this point I always struggle to hold two things at the same time. The first is to keep the tools used as simple and accessible as possible. There is a well-known but likely apocryphal story from the terrible, long drawn-out struggle in Iraq after the 2003 invasion. The new American general was in place and had asked for a proper conflict map. After some days, there was a presentation with all the possible links and networks. The result covered an entire wall in lines and arrows. The general is said to have remarked that if anyone could understand the map then they would have no trouble with the war.

The best tools will help shape the questions you seek imaginatively but not constrain a flexible response to emerging shapes and patterns that may take the facilitators in new and unexpected directions. In other words, in Lederach's beautiful phrase, they will liberate 'the moral imagination'.[1] Nothing is more important. The experience of researching is often deeply depressing. The move to conscious ignorance is one of recognizing one's position as an outsider, without the same emotional sensitivity as those most closely involved to culture, fear and history. The complexity grows and grows until one's head begins to spin. At first in such situations, I tend to see numerous occasions when it was 'obvious' that the conflict could have been avoided, solved or at least mitigated. As I learn more, I usually feel that there is no solution at all, and that my first reaction left out the emotions of those involved, treating them only as purely rational beings able to separate themselves entirely from emotions. The third step is a more balanced view, aware of ignorance, but also aware of the signs of hope and sensitive to any movement. Humility is an essential.

The moral imagination has to contain room for identification with people who are different, feeling what they feel, even where one disagrees. It cannot be purely distanced and objective. The former is a statement that we are all human beings, the latter is paternalistic. The heart of conflict, whether in a marriage or a war, is an intensification of isolation: those involved think that nobody else can understand and, worse, that nobody else cares. The outsider knows that the first of those two is true but the second can be overcome. There are certain journalists who seem to be able to report well, but always with passion. They do more than tell a story; they conscript the emotions of the hearer. The moral imagination starts with that deep passion for peace, for the well-being of those whose lives are in pain.

The leap of moral imagination is costly and hard, and needs wings on the feet. For example, in the last twenty years the work of interfaith dialogue has been transformed by the use of scriptural reasoning. This involves a group of people learning to study each other's scriptures together. Pursued over time it is not aimed at a syncretistic soup of 'we all really agree' but, through engagement with sacred texts of others, being given the impetus to develop deeper understanding and profound friendships. The sacred writings give wings to the moral imagination.

In any conflict or confrontation, whether it is within a church or school or community, between faiths, or armed struggle at different levels, the facilitator is hearing people's dreams and fears and memories. The loss of a relative in an extrajudicial killing, or the fear that comes from being threatened if one looks too closely at the wrong data or asks the wrong questions or goes to the wrong place, or the despair from seeing one's homeland torn apart, are all areas of emotional horror. One must weep with those who weep.

Even in utterly non-violent situations, dreams and hopes, security and expectations will be in the course of destruction and that leaves people very vulnerable. The worst form of premature judgement is that which says implicitly, 'because this does not much matter to me, I will not allow myself to feel the pain that you are suffering'.

I described a visit to Ogoniland at the beginning of the chapter. That trip was the first step in researching. Much research in a conflict is undramatic. On that occasion we had more drama than usual. We were flown across part of the Niger Delta by Shell, in a helicopter, as they explained to us *their* view of the situation. We spoke to senior managers and those in the middle ranks, a few from Holland, the UK or USA but the vast majority from Nigeria. The conversations were very revealing. Many of the Nigerian staff had family links in Ogoni and felt deeply torn. Some of the expatriates were terrified by their experience of seeking to deal with the problems. We listened to village leaders, women, youths, NGOs, to the very intelligent and passionate Ken Saro-Wiwa Junior and to Ledum Mitee, the man who had succeeded to the leadership of MOSOP after Ken Senior's death. We spoke to people with links to militias, and to crime and corruption. We spoke to Government at numerous levels. The list was very, very long indeed.

What all those meetings did was to reveal complexity. Learned articles by experts in the area spoke of the destruction of the environment and the resulting socio-political impacts. The history of relations with neighbouring ethnic groups and the impact of the Nigerian Civil War (1967–70), where different groups were on different sides, added to the recent historical uncertainty. Then there was that natural resource curse.

Most of the trouble came back to oil and gas. Some of it was linked to the perceived actions of Shell, or their perceived lack of actions. Lawsuits had been started by MOSOP and other groups.[2] There was also significant division among groups in Ogoni and others across the whole oil-producing region, which had resulted in fighting in three states at least. Politics in the region had used oil money gained illegally to fund militias and they had in their turn become drawn into large-scale criminal activity involving kidnapping, drugs and the stealing of vast quantities of oil. Corruption was and remains endemic. Amid it all, those who suffered and suffer the most are the poorest and most vulnerable.

As discussed, earlier researching could be easily termed enquiry. It enables the move from unconscious to conscious ignorance. There are further steps, whether to partial understanding, good understanding or an intuitive grasp of the situation. The reality is that the last of these takes generations. I was listening to a friend who has spent more than forty years in the Democratic Republic of the Congo. He commented that he is beginning to grasp how little he grasps.

Unconscious ignorance is to repeat what 'everyone knows to be true', but almost never is. It is also to take one conflict and project its solution on to another. Unconscious ignorance is the staple fuel for manipulative leadership and for rackets and power games. It is also the staple deception amid well-meaning but damaging intervention, as has been seen in many wars such as Iraq.

Researching muddies the water, or perhaps, to be more exact, it enables one to see that the waters are very muddy indeed. Working through 'what everyone knows' produces simple answers to complicated questions, answers that in reality do not tackle the question at all.

Ogoni is a very good case study. Unconscious ignorance looks at the characteristics of extractive industry conflicts and says, 'It's all the fault of [in this case] Shell.' Or, from another point of view, 'It's all the fault of corrupt government' or militias.

Alternatively, mediators and facilitators of peacebuilding may come in and try to apply the lessons they have learned elsewhere. That sounds sensible but is usually a problem. They may have worked on, or learned from, community/company disputes in Australia, or Papua New Guinea or Latin America. There will of course be lessons but all who work in this area are in danger from time to time of making the problem fit their toolkit rather than getting the tools for the job.

Researching is an interrogative process, not an accusatory one. I make a practice of taking detailed notes of every meeting, so long as those I am meeting give permission. They should be allowed to see what has been written. Taking notes gives a clear sense of being present, and of learning rather than somehow being above those caught up in the situation. Good facilitators are never parachuted in as those who solve, but arrive humbly to serve and assist.

The process of researching is to some extent value neutral. That means that judgement is suspended, at least outwardly, until further stages have been reached. One of the major difficulties is that one deals with bad people. Conflict (even in what is seen as a just cause) brings out the worst in people. It does not matter whether it is in a household or family, or somewhere like Ogoni. All involved are running on their nerves. As was discussed in Chapter 2, the impact of confrontation, especially involving violence and threat of injury or death, is something that builds up responses in the human body. The longer the conflict continues, the stronger those responses become and the weaker the collective impact of moral decision making.

Moral neutrality poses its own dangers. Some of the wickedest people can be the most capable of appearing attractive and helpful, not always deliberately. In many professions, supervision is obligatory. The facilitator or mediator needs accountability to others disconnected from the conflict, in order to see where they are being affected by their contacts. The practitioner shares their experiences and views with someone else, or better still a group. Are they getting too close to a client? Are they being manipulated? Are they allowing proper emotions of humanity and sympathy to colour their approach to others involved? Wise peacebuilders will always have supervision and accountability.

A few years ago I was with a group of very experienced and wise English clergy in Northern Ireland. On one day we met the eloquent and articulate spokespeople for one side. All the clergy came away committed to justice for the oppressed, those that they had heard that day. The next set of meetings was with the other side. All the clergy became confused. As we drove off in the evening, someone called out to me: 'Archbishop, I know what you are doing. You're messing with our heads.' It was a wise comment, recognizing that contact with people in conflict always affects our perceptions. It is to identify and reflect on the impact of perceptual change that makes supervision necessary.

Many people will be very familiar with some conflict in which they have found themselves caught. Perhaps they know a couple whose marriage is facing a bitter collapse. They meet friends of the wife and are told that the husband has been totally unreasonable for so many reasons. They meet friends of the husband who talks of the way the wife controlled him and spent money so fast. In each conversation what they want to say is, 'but it's more complicated than that!' The friends have simplified things to the point where one side is to blame. The truth is deep and historic, sending out roots in all sorts of directions that are to do with everything from the model the couple inherited from their own upbringings to the way in which they communicated. There will be times when there is some simplicity; for example, violence or emotional abuse where safety demands separation. The aim of reconciliation in such cases may very likely not be restoration of co-habitation but rather the capacity to move on towards personal healing and hope, or in the case of an abuser, to repentance and change.

That being said, and with all due precautions, there are some questions where the answers are very often decisive to the future hopes of any kind of reconciliation. They are very often not questions put directly, because that always invites the answer that the interviewee thinks is wanted. Many interviewees will be glad to talk and want the facilitator to see it their way.

The key ones are about dreams and objectives. Is it possible to sense a war weariness? What would a good outcome look like in their own minds? How deep is the bitterness? Can the other side have any merits? Something that is extremely rare but is also a sign of immense hope is when one hears the view – or the echo of the view – of the other put across, not as something to be agreed with, but with even the smallest level of mutual understanding or empathy.

The great strength of the facilitator is that they need not pretend to knowledge that they do not have. Asking foolish questions is not foolish when you are an outsider. Asking apparently foolish questions is often a way of giving agency and respect to those involved.

In John's Gospel, chapter 5, John tells of Jesus going to the Temple in Jerusalem for a big festival. He visits a pool at Beth-zatha, which was believed to have healing properties when the waters stirred. Many sick people were there, and Jesus approaches one who had lain there all his life: 'When Jesus saw him lying there and knew that he had been there a long time, he said to him, "Do you want to be made well?"' (verse 6, NRSV). The reader's first reaction is often, 'What a daft question!' He had been there for thirty-eight years. Yet it was the opposite of daft. It gave the man choice, provoked self-reflection, and meant that the sign Jesus performed to heal him was done with him, not to him. There is always a question in the back of one's mind: 'What do the participants in this struggle want? Do they want peace?' It is rare that the question is put so bluntly, but as we will see further down the line, there are many ways of getting to the answer and there will have to be a point where the challenge of desire is faced.

DANGERS

As discussed earlier, throughout the process there are dangers, in particular those deriving from *overspeed* and *overreach*. Researching will prepare facilitators to anticipate those dangers, to avoid them or to have plans ready to face them.

Overspeed. In all conflicts that have reached a level of maturity and where there is genuinely a sense that it is necessary to try something new if the struggle is ever to end, there is a desire for speed. Peacemaking tends to have two speeds: stationary and rush. Both are dangerous. The latter is often encouraged by those around, by circumstances and in public situations by the media.

The mystery of peace is not only that for those in conflict it is hard to imagine but also that its coming seems to take either for ever, or far less time than one might fear. In one case, patience is lost and with it progress. In the other, opportunities are often not taken because peace has slipped in by surprise. The Middle East has a long history of overlooked opportunities. By contrast, in one African country a handshake at church between two leaders who could have torn the country apart led a few weeks later to them spending a day together alone, and to the establishment of peace. They had the wisdom to grip the unexpected opportunity, and broke conventional approaches to do it.

In a conversation while I was writing this chapter in the summer of 2021, I was invited to get involved in a relatively large-scale peacebuilding process. I was very doubtful, but the doubts diminished enormously when the person with whom I was talking said, 'Of course, the first stage of design, mapping, planning and research, is going to take a long time.' The sense of that comment showed a great deal of realism.

In Ogoni the research became a very important part of the process and to my surprise did lead to a slight change in the mood – although I am not in any way claiming that I made much difference. The start made at the time I was involved was followed up by more skilled, more local people who achieved much more significant progress. The most effective facilitator was Bishop Matthew Kukah (now Roman Catholic Bishop of Sokoto). Having already played a key role in numerous Nigerian disputes, up to and including national level, he renewed the momentum of the reconciliation work in Ogoni. His book, *Witness to Reconciliation*, to be published in 2022, is a magisterial account of both the stories and the approaches. Fifteen years later the list of those who have been involved is long, but the credit for the small change made goes to the people of Ogoni.

Overreach and *underreach* are two sides of the same coin. An overreach of imagination leads to the illusion that great difficulties can be overcome in the twinkling of an eye and bitterness will evaporate with a touch of sense. Underreach is the problem of looking at the gaps and not the potential bridges. The first is a sign that the lessons of the research are not sinking in with the facilitator and the second that the pain has become overwhelming.

Both happen easily. In the difficult discussions within the Church of England over the question of ordaining women as bishops, the biggest step was to imagine that a way forward could be found. In some of the conversations, several groups were involved. In one of them the facilitator was obviously pushing a solution. It led to all sides digging their heels in. The facilitator was not arrogant or bad at their job, but they were desperate for progress and sought to take things faster than was the mood of the participants.

By contrast, earlier in the process, after a major setback, all and sundry spoke of needing five years at least to chart a way forward that ended taking less than two, owing to the desire by all concerned to find such a way. The setback opened the way to progress.

The third crucial error is leaving out those participants who matter, and its twin, giving any group too much profile and thus a disempowering veto at the wrong moment. Most conflicts have someone or some group that, like Voldemort in Harry Potter, cannot be named. It may be a powerful militia or an important and shadowy government figure. In Ogoni there were constant rumours about who was lifting the oil. There was also clear evidence of criminal gangs who were very willing to threaten violence.

The identification of those who matter is one of great political sensitivity. If a person or group is left out, they will very often seek to become disruptive. On the other hand, including a genuinely marginal figure gives them influence and importance and further complicates the process. Embracing complexity is one thing, adding to it without genuine need is quite another. The arithmetic of the relationships is worth recalling. Two groups and a facilitator mean that the process has three relationships, the parties to each other and each to the facilitator. Go up to three groups and a facilitator and the number of relationships becomes six. Go up to ten and it becomes forty-five.

At this point scale poses its own questions. In a civil conflict everyone seeks to show that they are the most valid representatives of the people. The very act of accepting the claim and giving them a seat at the table means that they acquire far more legitimacy. They also set up their post-conflict trajectory to power. In other words, the stakes are very high indeed. Excluding those with a claim that has validity may drive them to attention-seeking violence.

There are many opt-outs from these types of decisions and many ways round it. The opt-outs are too easily cop-outs.

The researching should give benchmarks for testing the validity of claims to participation. History will show the extent to which they have taken significant risks, mobilized large numbers of people, or in places where elections have some substance, where they have been successful. Research and attentive listening also reveal those who have been marginalized and need to be heard. What is not said, or what is dismissed, is as important as what is said.

Three groups are very often forgotten. First are women. The harsh reality is that whether it is at community level or in war, the significance of women is usually forgotten until too late. They matter for many reasons. They are at least half the population and, as human beings, of equal dignity before God to men, whatever the culture says. They are remarkably vulnerable in armed conflict, especially to sexual abuse. They are the ones who find themselves driven from the homes where they farm, without support, and living in IDP or refugee camps. They bury the dead, whether spouses, children, siblings, friends or parents. It is almost unknown for an effective peace to be made and for a process of peacebuilding to become embedded unless women's groups are centrally involved, and their voice is heard.

Women will perform very central roles in peacebuilding if given the opportunity. In more patriarchal societies, the need to understand what they can do without undue risk is a major task of researching. The spouses of leaders are often given significantly large roles without the training or education required. They will frequently be highly educated but much neglected. Researching should reveal both the most gifted and the requirements in every group for training in building peace.

Second are youths. The definition of youth varies from the western culture, where it will typically mean teenage and early twenties, and in some other places anyone less than forty. Youths are often forgotten, although in most wars they are the main combatants and thus have the most interest in ending or occasionally in continuing the struggle. They may be drawn into fighting as children, with resulting intense trauma. They will have the ability to end the war if they can be brought into a position where they are willing and trained and equipped not to participate.

In community disputes they remain very important as, like women, they will often be done to rather than doing. In families that are in difficulty they will often be the ones longing for settlement and stability, with an equal interest in and love for the disputing parties and no desire to be manipulated into taking sides.

Third are traditional mediators. There is a remarkable arrogance in some outside facilitators that consists in assuming that because there is conflict in a society, it contains nobody with reconciliation skills. Most societies have developed ways of facing conflicting ambitions for power, issues around land ownership and boundaries, conflicts between herders and farmers, neighbour disputes, community breakdown, and marriage and family divisions. They will also very likely have customary law that supports answers. In Rwanda, after the genocide of 1993, local village courts were essential to holding accountable those who had committed crimes and enabling those who had suffered to hear their story. In Burundi there existed a tradition of wise mediators. This group was suppressed in the colonial period lest they become community leaders against the colonial government. Researching must show whether such traditions work or not, so as to go with the grain and not against it.

In many, even most, communities there are equivalents. There may be a church or other religious group that operates as a mediator. There are often individuals who are known as peacemakers.

At the heart of researching is understanding what the weave of the conflict is and of the group and groups in which it is set. Above all, research seeks to enable facilitators to develop confidence in knowing their own ignorance and in being able to know those involved and be known.

Mapping should reveal those who do not seek to participate but prefer to work in the shadows, not in some conspiracy theory imagination but in hidden reality, undermining progress. This has been discussed earlier, and shadow figures and spoilers are among the easiest to miss. Their significance is that their power is real but not evident. Many of those who claim participation in a process will have power that is evident but not real. In armed conflict it is essential to know where the arms and logistics come from, who pays, and how and from where they get the money. In a community it matters if groups are part of an outside network with a wider agenda. In a church where there is a deep divide it is always possible that broader groups are seeking to expand their influence within a denomination.

The danger in looking for shadows and spoilers is that people can become caught up in conspiracy theories. However, even hearing false ideas is useful in the process of research as an indicator of mood. The volume and attraction of conspiracy theory in a group or society is very frequently an early warning of more violent conflict.

Knowing that the Research is Bearing Fruit

The move from the first to the second R, Relating, should be seamless. Researching goes on throughout the entire journey as all involved need to be able to expect that they will gain a better understanding. So how does the facilitator know that it is time to start spinning the second plate?

The most important sign is that they can tell the story of the conflict from the different perspectives of those involved in the process, in a way that each of them can recognize. Thus, in Ogoni a good sign would have been for Shell to hear the local community tell the story from Shell's point of view in a way recognizable to Shell. More importantly still, given the power of Shell, MOSOP leaders, women, youths and civil society observers who had been helping the Ogoni people should recognize their own view of the conflict when Shell told the story from the local as if from the community's point of view.

Research does not bring solutions; it brings out the next plate, with its deepening relationships.

Summary

- Researching is a long process that continues right through the journey of peacemaking.
- Researching takes the peacebuilder from unconscious to conscious ignorance.
- It should enable mapping of the conflict and recognition of complexity.
- It goes from desktop analysis to interviews and meetings in the field.

- It must include women, youths and traditional peacebuilders, whether in a family or a war.
- It should enable discernment about the roles and categories of different people.
- Supervision matters to avoid being traumatized or misled.
- It will reveal the problems and may reveal ways forward.

POINTS TO PONDER

- If you know of a conflict, how much do you really know? Have you decided that you know everything before you really do? Does that happen if you are caught up in a dispute?
- Look at some quarrel, dispute or conflict you know about. Whose voices are not heard? Who is forgotten?
- Try getting together with someone and exchanging the story of a dispute familiar to you, four times. Twice tell the story from one side, and then twice from the other? Can you do it? (It is not unusual to answer no.) What are the biggest challenges?
- Read John 5. If reading the Bible is not part of your normal life don't try to understand everything but ask some questions. Who are the key people involved? How would you describe the quarrel? How does Jesus treat the man who is healed? Before and after? How does he treat Jesus?

5

Relating – the Power of Love

A young woman – an economic migrant – arrives in a village belonging to an enemy. She is accompanied by her mother-in-law, who had grown up in the village. For the latter it is reverse migration. She had gone to the enemy country, also as an economic migrant perhaps twenty years earlier, with her husband and two sons. The men had died after a few years, leaving two daughters-in-law and no grandchildren. In desperation, one daughter-in-law goes back to her paternal home, and the other joins in the frightening and dangerous process of travel.

It is a love story. The young woman and her mother-in-law love each other. The time is a little over three thousand years ago. The region is what we now call the Holy Lands. The story is that of Ruth, a most beautiful book in the Old Testament. But it could have been today. We have economic migration, refugees, ancient hatred and wars, the travel of desperate people to places they do not know. They support each other on the way; they often die. Occasionally the ending is happy. That is the case in the case of Ruth and Naomi, where Ruth meets a man, they marry and have children.

The story is so much deeper than that, of course. It is a love story where, as in all the best love stories, the main characters cross boundaries, show courage, are imaginative and see solutions that are not visible to anyone else, and in this case everyone is kept and held in the love of God.

That is the link to two of the best-known and most overwhelming of the statements on love in the New Testament. In John's first letter he says baldly, 'God is love.'[1] Earlier on he has made it clear that the letter is a witness and testimony to what he has experienced and seen in meeting Jesus and following him for three years. The second overwhelming statement is in John's Gospel, 'For God so loved the world that he gave his only Son, so that all who believed in him should not perish but have eternal life' (John 3.16, NRSV). These verses speak of the love of God as boundary busting, leaping over the gap between God and human beings. The leap is made by God and it is a leap of reconciling love.

The action of Jesus breaks all boundaries and dissolves the barriers that reinforce those boundaries. In John 3 Jesus is in conversation with a Jewish leader and teacher. In John 4 he engages first with a woman from an enemy people (a Samaritan) and then with the child of a senior official for the king of the region that included Galilee. In John 5 he heals a man on the Sabbath, breaking the barrier of what the leaders interpreted as work, expressed in God's commands not to work on the Sabbath.

That is still the work of God today and the Church is at its glorious best when it seeks to demonstrate the pure and holy love of God in breaking barriers and when with courage it stands with those whose experience is of being barred from leading a full life, what Jesus calls an abundant life.

Because it is the work of God it is also the best way for the world. Reconciliation is not the exclusive possession of the Church or of the religious. Ruth is not from Israel yet God's work of reconciliation is active in her life and character. Peacebuilding and the desire for peace is hardwired into the desire of most people. To make it happen is to act well. To make it happen well requires relationships founded on love, whatever more they also need. The reconciliation that God gives through love is more abundant than we can imagine. It is not just barely sufficient, a sort of just-about-enough love for reducing conflict, but when shared, reconciliation grows and expands and overflows. In John 6 Jesus feeds five thousand with a few loaves and fish, and twelve baskets of food are left over. In this act we see the meeting of physical need, but much more than that the super-abundance of the provision of all that is needed. So it is with reconciliation. It can never run out when it is what we aim for.

As it is presented in the Bible, love is far more than an emotion. It is something of great activity. God does not sit in heaven saying soppily, 'I love people'; God acts, and it is through God's action that we perceive God's love. It was God's love that carried Ruth and her mother-in-law, Naomi, through the agony of bereavement back to Bethlehem, Naomi's home. It was God's love that brought Ruth into contact with Boaz, the landowner and cousin of Naomi. It was God's love that opened Ruth and Boaz's hearts to love for one another and it was God's love that meant that the resulting child was King David's grandfather.

In other words, God's love broke down every barrier in order to ensure that Israel's second – and model – king was partly Moabite, an enemy. The Book of Ruth is many beautiful things, but it is centrally a book about reconciliation.

In doing so it points forward to Jesus, the ultimate, absolute, definitive reconciler, and shows that love is not just what we feel but is true when it is what we do.

The second 'R' is relating, and it is founded on love.

All reconciliation work deals with the bitterest and most powerful of human emotions, emotions very often justified by the terrible circumstances faced. A family quarrel of great bitterness has a capacity to penetrate the hardest emotional armour and hurt deeply. A church that is riven by disagreement has a toxicity that is the opposite of what its members hope for and seek. Community quarrels are hard-edged because the participants are continually with each other or seeing each other. As for violent conflict and struggle – the mixture of terror, pride, hatred and ambition is an emotional cocktail that historically has led to the greatest courage and the greatest cruelty.

The only force that can cross the boundaries is love. The role of the people and groups that facilitate reconciliation is not a functional and mechanical one characterized by technique, but a relational one characterized by love. Of course, love is not all we need (sorry, The Beatles), but any action not based in love and driven by love is, to quote St Paul in 1 Corinthians 13, nothing but a sounding gong or a clanging cymbal. It is noise without substance.

One of the most effective peacebuilders I have met is Canon Andrew White, with whom I worked for almost three years when I was at Coventry Cathedral. He is a controversial figure, larger than life, physically as well as everything else. Having watched him in action, one thing that is overwhelming is his gift for relating to people, because they know he loves them.

It was that love, and the risks he took to see people, that enabled Andrew to play a key role[2] in gathering those who signed the Alexandria Declaration, which sought to undermine the religious blockages in peacemaking. Many of the signatories were bitter enemies; his friendship was a common factor to them all.

For several years he had visited Jerusalem and the other parts of the Holy Lands continually. At times in places of heavy fighting, he had done the research that enabled him to see who needed to be involved. All this time the situation was deteriorating, but that did not cause unreasonable rush. Eventually he had built relationships strong enough to get permission to hold a meeting in Alexandria, supported by the UK Foreign Office, in which the traditional enemies came together to call for peace and commit themselves to work for it. The final, three-day negotiation was chaired superbly by the then Archbishop of Canterbury, Lord Carey of Clifton as he now is.

The impact of the Declaration had the potential to open a door that had been neglected in the Oslo peace process: that of religious leaders. It illustrates the need to get the right people involved.

The Muslims included a Grand Mufti (a very senior judge) as well as a number of sheikhs and imams, religious teachers with a strong political and juridical role. The Jewish figures included an Israeli government minister and rabbis, including from a settlement in the Occupied Territories. They had already been building links across the barriers of conflict, and one of the most important parts of everyone's research was to identify which of the apparently hard-line figures behaved in a way that opened opportunities for peacebuilding.

The meeting exhibited partnership. Apart from the Archbishop of Canterbury, there was involvement by diplomatic groups and other organizations with whom relationships had been built. All were crucial, including the ones who had done invisible preparatory work but got little or no credit in the final outcome.

The research demonstrated what could and could not be done. A declaration was possible but not a peace settlement; the latter would need a more comprehensive process. The necessary time was taken. The signatories were in a place to go on working together.

Working with Andrew demonstrated that he loved genuinely but was also realistic about those he worked with. They were not remotely all 'good people'. A number had been involved with violence. The various regional governments that had some involvement were not all being helpful out of mere goodwill. There was a desire to instrumentalize the process for their own reasons, many of which were more about gaining advantage than making peace.

These behaviours are part of being human and part of the corrosive impact of conflict. It undermines all that is best and most selfless, and draws the mind, morals and emotions into a place where personal power seeking and advantage gaining, by any means, are not just temptations but normal ways of living. It is not a criticism of the Oslo process; the focus in Oslo was on the central, political issues. However, if the old slogan and wisdom of peacebuilding – 'top down, middle out, bottom up – is to be the aim, then the religious actors will need to be involved in most countries in the world. Nowhere is that more important than in Jerusalem, Israel and Palestine. Religious actors will seldom bring the 'top down', but they may ease the way for political leadership, and they tend to be part of networks that go from grassroots to presidential mansions. Moreover, for those whose faith is more than skin deep, loyalty to God and faith will matter more than anything else and is the most powerful possible force for good, or evil.

Relating love-in-action. To return to John's Gospel, the gospel of the holy love of God, the way that Jesus loves, shows the true nature of reconciling love.

All four Gospels tell us that on the night of his betrayal, arrest and trial, Jesus held a Passover meal, a celebration of the liberation of God's people, the Israelites from Egypt under the leadership of Moses. According to John, chapter 13, before the meal he took off his outer clothing, wrapped a towel around himself and washed his disciples' feet, including those of Judas, who he knew was planning to betray him. John says, 'Having loved his own who were in the world, he loved them to the end.'³ The Greek word for 'end' can be translated in a variety of ways, but has the sense of completely, to the finish, to the limit.

Together with going to be crucified, this is the central demonstration by Jesus of the nature of God's love and of the way he wants human beings to love one another: we are to love to the limit. The Church above all should show this love. The leaders of this world should show this love. I remember a remarkable moment in the concluding service of a gathering of the senior leaders of the Anglican Communion from around the world. At the end of a very difficult meeting, full of conflict, we washed each other's feet. It is more difficult to receive than to do, for it requires one to submit to being loved, to having something done for you by someone who you feel is at least your equal and very often your superior. Yet it is a channel for the healing of relationships when done properly.

The proper response of love is temporarily to suspend judgement but not wisdom. Judgement in this sense, the sense of Jesus' command in the Sermon on the Mount,[4] is a pretence of objective and virtuous distance. The basis of the incarnation, of God taking flesh and being fully human in Jesus, is that identification with human beings is complete. We do not have that ability, but we can be creatively imaginative.

On one occasion, in the Niger Delta I visited a remote town, at that time only accessible by boat through the creeks of the wetlands. There were three of us in the group. When we arrived, we were taken to see a gang leader. He was slightly drunk and very threatening. He declared that we should be killed – a statement that was delivered all in the local language and that he was persuaded not to carry out by our local companion. We were 'invited' to stay overnight in a local guest house.

The next morning, he reappeared and took us on a tour of the town. A couple of miles away was a flow-station, a centre of oil production with the local field producing more than a hundred thousand barrels per day of very high-quality crude. Its generators gave it twenty-four-hour, reliable electricity for the plant and equipment, as well as for air conditioning, light and entertainment. Its helicopters could whisk people in and out and provide easy access to medical facilities. There was clean water and good food.

By contrast the town was a place of tragedy. It sat above the oilfield, a source of enormous wealth but only to others. Sewage ran down the main street, where children played. There was no regular electricity. Food was terrible, clean water absent, education for the next generation non-existent, medical care a mere dream. Malaria was endemic. Violence was constant in order to gain control and seek income from local contractors and others. It was at the very gates of hell.

Our 'host' was not a good man by most standards and was probably very bad indeed in many people's eyes. Yet he had grown up there, comfort and wealth in sight in the near distance, and filth and violence his normal life. To judge would be to say that if I were him, I would have been better. To show wisdom would be to empathize with the sheer misery of his life and prospects but not to collude with the decisions he made.

So perhaps love *is* all we need (spot on, The Beatles): but we need to reimagine love.

Many people know the Apostle Paul's beautiful hymn to love in 1 Corinthians 13. It is often read at weddings, which puts a sweet, fluffy coating of sugar on it. When the words are taken and applied as they are meant, it is a soaring vision of foundations in peace for the world around us.

If I speak in the tongues of mortals and of angels, but do not have love, I am a noisy gong or a clanging cymbal. [2] And if I have prophetic powers, and understand all mysteries and all knowledge, and if I have all faith, so as to remove mountains, but do not have love, I am nothing. [3] If I give away all my possessions, and if I hand over my body so that I may boast, but do not have love, I gain nothing.

[4] Love is patient; love is kind; love is not envious or boastful or arrogant [5] or rude. It does not insist on

its own way; it is not irritable or resentful; [6] it does not rejoice in wrongdoing, but rejoices in the truth. [7] It bears all things, believes all things, hopes all things, endures all things.

[8] Love never ends. But as for prophecies, they will come to an end; as for tongues, they will cease; as for knowledge, it will come to an end. [9] For we know only in part, and we prophesy only in part; [10] but when the complete comes, the partial will come to an end. [11] When I was a child, I spoke like a child, I thought like a child, I reasoned like a child; when I became an adult, I put an end to childish ways. [12] For now we see in a mirror, dimly, but then we will see face to face. Now I know only in part; then I will know fully, even as I have been fully known. [13] And now faith, hope, and love abide, these three; and the greatest of these is love. (1 Cor. 13, NRSV)

PATIENCE

Peacebuilding requires patience in love. The nature of conflict is to generate suspicion. Facing suspicion and the irrationality that comes with it requires a deep love and understanding in facilitators as they seek to untangle the belief that they are taking sides. Part of the suspicion will be born out of years of being tricked and deceived. At the Congress of Vienna in 1815, ending the Revolutionary and Napoleonic Wars, it is reported anecdotally that when the Chancellor of the Austro-Hungarian Empire heard that the leading French representative, Talleyrand, had died (he had not, in fact), he said, 'Now what does he mean by that?' Talleyrand was notorious for changing sides, and for his duplicity. Conflict involves deception, and deception breeds suspicion.

Patience is seen by time given. It is represented by long-term commitment. More than that, the commitment must be organizational, not just individual. There is something deeply addictive about being seen to be indispensable, but it is only of any benefit to the person concerned, never to the cause they support. Too often in facilitating peacebuilding there is dependence on a star figure. The more of a star they are the less they are able to give time and patience to one place.

The Alexandria Declaration depended to some degree on the skill of Canon Andrew White. When he became caught up in other equally important areas momentum failed. Relationships need nurturing. No individual can manage the commitment and be sure to be available as much as required. However, it is possible to create institutional links where trust is created over time by a consistent and patient commitment through a group.

The nature of institutions is, however, bureaucratic. A clear example is the United Nations Organization. Created in 1945 it has grown into a vast network of specialist groups within the UN family. At its centre sits the Security Council (UNSC), served by the Secretary General. Almost all who work in it know and see its faults and the inertia that develops because of the rivalries among the P5, the Permanent Five members of the UNSC, who are able to veto or otherwise block UN activities in peacebuilding.

It is easy to criticize, and there is plenty of valid criticism, but nobody has come up with anything better. The UN has built up great skill in intervening in conflicts and has both an unrivalled view of what is happening in confrontations around the world and wisdom in how to approach them. The agendas of its members may frustrate it plans, but that is not its fault. Most of all, it avoids the star system.

The single hero figure and the UN represent the two ends of a process of peacebuilding. One end struggles with patience and resilient long-term commitment and thus initiatives run out of steam. The other is prone to being unable to act in time while its members work out their interests. The first can build good relationships with an individual. The second has the methods but misses the personal approach.

Peacebuilding and reconciliation facilitation includes the necessity to hold the two together. Earlier on in this chapter we looked at John 13 and the account of Jesus washing the feet of his disciples. He had been committed to them for three years or so, and the moment was approaching when he would go, and they would remain. Their capacity to take over and to live as they were called to by him was essential to the whole of God's plan for the world. As in so much in the Bible, God's love is shown in patience and in partnership with human beings.

Jesus has built a community and in the washing of the feet was setting a pattern for its life. It is an act that ensures that the community is people- rather than task-focused, and this is achieved through obeying his command to 'love one another as I have loved you'.

Those who are going to be involved in facilitating reconciliation must therefore be committed to working in a team, with no stars among them and a long-term vision in which their contribution may well never be recognized. They will need love that patiently suffers setbacks and yet continues, perhaps from a different approach. They will need to see those involved in the conflict not as resources to be managed and manipulated but as human beings to be liberated from the struggles in which they find themselves.

LOVING AND KEEPING DISTANCE

Where are the limits in love? At what point does wisdom say, 'Do not meet such and such a person'?

In the 1950s a Dutch Christian, using the name Brother Andrew, began to reach out to Christians behind what was called the Iron Curtain.[5] He carried out this work for many years,[6] but after he had stepped back he continued to visit terrorist groups in order to build relationships with their leaders and to speak to them of peace. He did all this without publicity, public funding or self-advertisement. Its impact cannot be measured yet the risks were very considerable.

First was the risk meeting the people he did. Second was the risk to his reputation. To meet people who are known to be involved in violence, or in a domestic situation, in abuse of one kind or another, is often seen as collusion. It risks being shut out from speaking to those on the other side on the grounds that if you have met the bad person you must be their friend, and my enemy's friend is my enemy. Third, it risks losing the wisdom of seeing the reality of those you deal with (as discussed above in Chapter 2). One terrorist I met was in appearance and manner a sort of Father Christmas. He was small and round, smiled the whole time and told jokes. He also killed a lot of people, but his charm somehow seemed to overshadow the evil. Another, a former Head of State, spent an hour explaining that the rumours of the number of people he had killed were very exaggerated. So charismatic was he that I caught myself thinking, 'Well, that's not too bad.' It was only later that reality sank in more clearly when I compared notes with others.

Evil is attractive in a horrible way. The villains in novels and plays are often more interesting than the heroes. Look at Satan in Milton's *Paradise Lost*, or at Shakespeare's *Richard III*, *Macbeth* or *Coriolanus*. Fiction reflects reality. Where then are the limits and how does a facilitator avoid being sucked into collusion?

Love should not be blind. Researching will have demonstrated the character and history of the main parties to a conflict. To emphasize what has been said already, humility in the facilitator, when with colleagues or a supervisor, will enable them to be aware what their motivations are. Some participants in a conflict are deeply committed to power seeking and active hatred. Recognizing who those are will seldom be the role only of one person.

There are some obvious rules. If there is a family where the breakup of a marriage is linked to abuse of children, or to substance abuse that is not admitted, or to violence where there is an attempt at self-justification, then reconciliation will almost always mean seeking to find the least damaging parting possible.

The same may well be the case with regard to racist activity or other systematic and calculated oppression of minorities or the vulnerable. One test as to limits is the possibility of one party being willing to repent and make reparations. This was the test imposed by the South African Truth and Reconciliation Commission.[7] Those who participated in acknowledging their crimes could hope to share in the amnesty only if they were willing to be honest (Truth) in front of victims and to demonstrate that they understood what they had done wrong.

Talal Asad,[8] in a very powerful examination of the sociology of suicide bombing, saw this most extreme and irreconcilable of violent acts as requiring a violent response from law enforcement that says 'some humans have to be treated violently in order that humanity can be redeemed'. Love is not infallible but must be held in a moral framework so that 'being loving' cannot become an excuse for behaving wrongly or ignoring injustice. Temporarily suspending judgement must not become the toleration of injustice. Love wrongly expressed may lead to great evil and require violence to be faced. There are some people who, in police terms, need to be removed from a conflict if there is to be hope of reconciliation. That removal is a demonstration of a love for the majority whom they may influence by fear or favour. To bring them into reconciliation the worst of the spoilers may have to be faced and not included in the process.

SUMMARY

- Love is of the very nature of God, and it is in love for human beings that God opens the way to reconciliation with God and also with each other.
- Reconciliation is a fruit of abundant love and is itself abundant.
- Relationships of love-in-action are the foundation of reconciliation. The love must be genuine.
- However, love-in-action is characterized by the words used by Paul in 1 Corinthians 13, above all patience. Reconciliation takes time.

- Love in reconciliation will often need to suspend judgement, but never to lose wisdom. It must discern where evil lies in individuals and structures and avoid being drawn into collusive and co-dependent behaviour.

POINTS TO PONDER

- Think of the best examples you know of love-in-action. It may be family, or community, or more widely. What are its characteristics, compare them with 1 Corinthians 13.
- How do you avoid being taken in by charming villains or fascinating structures of evil? What would be examples you have seen, perhaps just in one person, or in history?
- Where have you seen the best examples of care that are emotionally committed but still wise and discerning?

Exercise

Your local primary school, St Thomas, in the Diocese of Barchester, is on the edge of town, between a series of small villages and an outer estate. It is a Church of England school, where the vicar chairs the school governors. The estate has high unemployment and considerable deprivation, made worse by the closure of a local shoe factory about three years ago. The local church, St Thomas the Pompous (a lesser-known Barchester saint of the sixth century), has a very strong tradition of involvement with the community. It runs a food bank in partnership with other churches and a mosque, has a debt-counselling centre and a job club. It also is part of a group with churches in all four of the local villages, which are traditional country settings, with strong communities and ancient buildings. The town church was built in the 1960s.

Two major social changes are going on. First, a large number of asylum seekers are being sent to the estate and housed there. The town has one part with a significant, mainly South Indian population. Community relationships have been very good. However, the asylum seekers are from numerous other places, especially Syria, parts of Africa caught in war, and Afghanistan. School places for unaccompanied children are stretching the facilities of the school, food bank, social care and local doctors' practice. Funding cuts have meant the council is very short of money. Waiting lists for housing are growing, affecting the children of people on the estate. There is ethnic tension that has shown itself in the church feeling less welcoming and some comments that 'they should go somewhere else'.

In order to raise money, the council is selling some land it owns between the town and the nearest village. It is doing this in partnership with the Diocese of Barchester, which also owns land in the same area. The bigger development is attracting a lot of bids from developers to build executive housing for commuters at a new railway station connecting to Barchester itself, a financial services hub.

The vicar is caught. Interfaith relations are beginning to struggle. The villages are up in arms at being 'joined' to the town by the new housing. The school has gone down an OFSTED (quality assessment) grade, which is felt by the staff to be very unfair considering the pressure they are under. The vicar and her colleagues want to see the village churches rise to the new challenge. The churches are very keen not to.

The staff team have asked you, as the Diocesan Reconciler, to help.

Can you start by mapping a little of the various conflicts? In a group of three or so, look at the research you want to do, and invent the answers (keep it relatively short!). Second, who do you need to build relationships with? How will you overcome the problem that you are from the diocese that is contributing to the issues?

Warning: this story is going to extend through Part II. Feel free to adjust the jargon for a non-Anglican situation or reimagine the case in terms of your own circumstances, but with the similar challenge of large-scale change in a conservative area with a religious institution that seeks to serve the population.

6

Relieving Need – Love Made Visible

The Democratic Republic of the Congo is enormous. To fly from one side to the other is a journey of around 2,000 kilometres (1,400 miles). Much of it is forest. Its historic main highway is the river. Transport other than by river or air is very difficult indeed.

Its history over the last 150 years is terrible. It was for decades the personal property of the King of Belgium, whose colonial rule was appalling even by contemporary standards and a source of scandal before the First World War. Joseph Conrad wrote a book about a river trip called *Heart of Darkness* (turned into a film set in Vietnam and Cambodia by Francis Ford Coppola, *Apocalypse Now*). The DRC was then a Belgian colony, again badly run until it was given unprepared independence in 1960.

Civil war and strife combined with corrupt and tyrannical government have been two of many plagues in the DRC much of the time ever since. Since the mid-1990s more than four million people have died directly and indirectly from war. In the east there have been severe outbreaks of Ebola, measles is rife, as are most tropical diseases. More than 130 militia groups operate under warlords.

Goma is a city on the Rwandan border, set amid remarkable beauty, like much of the country. Lake Bukavu is on one side. Mount Nyiragongo, a very active volcano, on another. The city is often shaken by earthquakes or threatened and damaged by huge flows of lava. The lake contains vast quantities of methane in solution, which might escape, covering the city. In surrounding forests there is a national park with gorillas.

My friend Désiré Mukanirwa was an Anglican parish priest when I first met him in 2005, at a conference in Geneva. He was training in international development. In 2009 I visited him in Goma, in his parish. The city was under siege and many of the NGOs had been forced to go home. We spent time training people in reconciliation at a local level. He took me to a refugee camp, one of a number with a total of about a quarter of a million people in the region. Appalled, I asked him, 'But what can you do?' 'We do what God enables us to' was his calm reply. His church building, damaged in an earthquake and nearly destroyed by a lava flow, was rickety but full of people. His home was full of women, most of whom had been raped in the conflicts, expelled from their communities and now receiving medical help, pastoral care and food from Désiré, and his wife Claudeline, who taught them a trade in clothes making.

I kept going back, introducing him at the UN, also to a UK government minister leading on international aid. His goodness, cheerfulness and faith caught everyone's imagination. About four years ago he became the first Anglican bishop of Goma. Unchanged by all this, he worked everywhere, travelling into conflict zones where militias threatened to kill him. He organized football competitions, bringing together teams of young men from opposing groups, vulnerable to being recruited as soldiers for the militias. In the morning they played football, then they were fed, and in the afternoon he taught them peacebuilding. The girls were taught and trained by Claudeline.

I last saw him in October 2019, when I spent time at some Ebola centres, in towns in the midst of the conflict, with other remarkable bishops and faith leaders. At the same time another English bishop, Michael Beasley, a skilled epidemiologist, taught a three-day course in Goma to local church leaders, 'Faith in a Time of Ebola', translated into Swahili and French. In the summer of 2020, Désiré died of COVID, after yet another trip into the forests. His funeral was attended by many; he was mourned by most of Goma.

I have told his story and its context at some length because it is a shining example of the holistic nature of peacebuilding, and of reconciliation. Désiré was remarkable, but not exceptional, among effective peacebuilders. His reconciliation work was aimed at relieving needs, all needs, in partnership with numerous NGOs – some, like Tearfund, faith based.

Relieving need is the third R of the six. It is what makes relationships solid. For most of us friendship means something tangible. We talk with friends, enjoy their company, share thoughts and opinions, play sports. But we also turn to them when we find ourselves in trouble. We visit them in hospital, offer them hospitality when they in turn face trouble, even go and see them in prison. The love expressed in true friendship is holistic; it relieves need.

In almost every society on earth, weddings are great occasions for friends and family. The way people get married varies, but it is a rare society where there is not a party of some kind. In many parts of the world the food is special, and very often there is wine or something equivalent. Certainly in the ancient Middle East, weddings were major community affairs. In John's Gospel, chapter 2, Jesus attends a wedding in Galilee, along with his disciples. The wine runs out, his mother prompts him, and Jesus turns the water set aside for rites of purification into wine. Only those serving the wine – Jesus, his mother and the disciples – know about the miracle.

Jesus prevents the public shaming that would go with inadequate supplies of wine. The village would remember such a failure for years. The wine is very good quality. The sign is revealing Jesus as the one who brings radical difference, transforming the water of the Old Testament law into the wine of the Spirit. There is much that can be said, but one obvious point is that there is a huge amount of wine. On a rough calculation it is not far short of two thousand standard bottles. John is not just having fun in telling this, nor is he simply making the point that Jesus was a great guest who really would be welcome at a 'bring a bottle' party. The central points are overwhelming abundance and decisive change.

God's love is expressed in super-abundance. Everything God does is more than just the barely essential. The creation itself is almost literally infinitely wonderful, complicated and beautiful. The love that is the offer of God covers every part of our needs, including the 'luxury' of abundant pleasure in one another and in the great events of life. The purpose of the work of Jesus, in his own words in John 10.10, is that human beings may have *life* in all its abundance.

That abundance is made available through God choosing to work with human beings as partners in prayer and in the actions of demonstrating the love of God. That is the most essential partnership. It is to work with God, to cooperate with God's love in order to be God's hands and eyes, and ears and feet and heart. That is the pattern of Jesus, who says that he only does what he sees the Father doing (John 5.19). Without that partnership with God the church is an NGO with some old buildings. With that partnership it is the channel of God's love.

We know that God is love because God acts in practically loving ways. God's action with and for human beings is normally, although not invariably, through the agency of human beings. The Church is called to be God's image in its partnership with God, love for one another, in learning to forgive and to be a global community of immense diversity united in faith by Christ and living out abundant life in the power of the Holy Spirit of the Creator God.

God's abundance and partnership reaches far beyond the Church. We see love expressed and blessing for human beings through all sorts of agencies, who act in God's ways without being aware of it. The sharing of support through official aid, the innumerable charities in every field of life that work around the world in the places of greatest need, the free gifts given at times of crisis: all these are part of abundant life. Abundant life is declared in John 10.10 by Jesus as the reason for his coming into the world, The finding of abundance is at the heart of God's purpose in reconciling humans to God and, by extension, to one another. It is not enough merely to stop fighting and quarrelling. Abundant life is seen as a vast diversity of character and nature and custom, a diversity that is negotiated in our world through the expression of love and a constant sense of curiosity about others, compassion for them in need, and attention to every need they have.

As has already been seen, Jesus breaks boundaries. In his time the barriers between Jew and non-Jew (the Gentiles) were immense. On one occasion recounted in Mark's Gospel, chapter 7, he was away in a Gentile area, probably to get some time in peace with his disciples. A Syrophoenician woman comes to see him, begging him to help her daughter who is possessed by a demon. Jesus refuses, saying that the 'bread' – of his ministry – is for the family (the Jews), not for the dogs (the Gentiles). She responds with a spirited and deeply biblical riposte, saying that dogs eat what falls from the table, that God's loving mercy is for all the world. In the Old Testament the Gentiles received abundant blessing out of God's abundance towards the people of Israel. Jesus sees the woman's faith and her recognition of him and heals her daughter. He has broken the boundary, acting not on the basis of merit but in an abundant overflowing of God's love expressed in action.

Love Means Love-in-action

Throughout the Christian Bible, and in Jewish understanding of what Christians call the Old Testament, God's love means the knowledge of love through God's action. There is no such thing as passive love, because love expresses itself in action. A friend of mine has worked in hospital chaplaincy in the Midlands for many years. Recently the NHS has agreed to develop the outreach work he has led into a new area of work called 'Compassionate Community Development Across Coventry & Warwickshire'. It's one of those excellent titles that says what it does (as opposed to the Archbishop of Canterbury, he might reply). Compassionate means suffering with and bringing support for people, alongside them, rather than doing things to them. The department recognizes that healthcare includes spiritual care but that the whole human being must be reached. It is an expression of the love of God, from within the NHS, and with the far-reaching aim of bringing abundant life. It is 'love-in-action'.

God's love means action. God is not seen in the Bible as sitting on a remote cloud feeling loving and generally benevolent. The Bible tells of God's love and faithfulness through the experience of people who encounter God directly and indirectly, from Moses as an exiled Israelite and Egyptian leader, meeting God in dramatic miracles, to Esther, caught up in political machinations and finding courage and faith amid God's absence, to Ruth the refugee and throughout the New Testament, especially and supremely in Jesus. Yet even Jesus lived 90 per cent of his life in normal obscurity, with a trade. God's love is not found only in great miracles, but in a day-to-day living presence expressed through the Church and through actions of people in the world. We know God loves us because we experience care and compassion in the world.

Love to the Limit of Capacity

Again though, we have to ask about limits. Bishop Désiré in Goma was at peace with himself and with God because he did what he could, what God enabled him to do, and trusted God for the rest. At its peak the number of refugees in the area he covered went over one million. Yet he still cared and served as much as he could.

Love given and received is an expression of our sharing in the needs of others. In this chapter and before, there has been much talk of partnership, with God and with others. Part of the third R of relieving is that it calls us to *reconciliation in the form of partnership* with others who are seeking to relieve need, and to humility in seeking for each partner to do what they do best.

The absence of such partnership has been a serious problem in many disaster relief operations, although there have been significant improvements in recent decades. A major influence in the work of the armed forces of the UK has been a brilliant book by General Sir Rupert Smith, published in 2006, *The Utility of Force*. Smith starts with the challenge that force continually fails to bring peace or reconciliation in areas of conflict. His argument leads him to the conclusion that peacebuilding, of which he had much experience as a commander of NATO forces in the Balkans, requires extensive partnerships and a team approach, drawing in civil society groups and NGOs. It is a process of partnership.

The obstacles that are usually encountered are in the unwillingness of many institutions to work in partnerships unless they are top of the pack. Peacebuilding requires attitudes of humble collaboration in which every partner seeks to contribute what they can.

The eastern part of the DRC has been a good example, especially during the Ebola crisis, where many of the lessons of the earlier outbreak in West Africa were shared and acted on. In the Ebola treatment centres various NGOs and local health officials worked well under the leadership of the Congolese government and the result was that despite the immense insecurity of the area the outbreak was brought under control.

However, the same collaboration was not seen on the battlefield, where there were poor relationships between regular army and UN forces, and the integration of local groups on wider health and security problems was not pursued. The result is that the disorder and often severe violence has continued.

The same lessons apply closer to home, in normal circumstances of community difficulties. One issue I worked on for a short while in a very diverse UK city involved rising violence between two gangs within the same, recently arrived ethnic group. Working with a – much more knowledgeable – local community leader we interviewed a significant number of people seeking to build up a picture of the problem and to map the conflict. The next stage was for local leaders to form relationships at street level with those from that ethnic group. However, the gangs were also involved in predictable sorts of crime, such as protection, exploitation of sex workers through people trafficking, and low-level but disturbing violence. One part of the response required police action in order to remove the key offenders from the scene. They would otherwise be spoilers and were shadow influences on the more local difficulties. There were also needs for education and job-finding skills, learning English as a second language and work with families. It can easily be seen that such a fairly basic problem would require expertise from those who worked with refugees and asylum seekers, including on legal matters of settlement, schools, education support for adults, jobcentres, debt planning, as well as police and local faith-based groups who could increase the sense of security in a deeply unfamiliar environment for those involved.

Finally, partnership with skilled community mediators was essential in order to create a capacity for working together and giving people the tools to take control of their own destinies through access to other agencies.

Writing it this way makes it all sound very obvious. However, these ingredients were mixed in with funding uncertainty, people who were very busy, varying priorities, and individuals moving from one place to another for work reasons. Continuity of relationship, sharing of knowledge and lack of resource were barriers to effective action. Bringing together such a varied group, who all had their own problems elsewhere, can be close to impossible. For that to happen community leadership is essential from within, and thus the cement that will be necessary to hold the bricks together is likely to be found with those in the community, locally, not from outside.

The need for partnership means that every agency and person does only what they can, but the combination is effective. Yet the difficulty of pulling together disparate teams leads to spending all the time in meetings about how to work together and combine better, rather than on the ground working together and combining well. That can often cause busy people to give up and either work less effectively on their own or simply not participate. It is an opportunity for perfection to be the worst enemy of action. The motto must always be, 'Do what you can, not what you can't.' What you can do may leave huge and glaring gaps, but it is better to try something than to do nothing.

Love is Simple to Express, Complicated to Arrange

As has been seen in Chapter 4 on researching, we must accept and embrace the complexity of the problems discovered. At the same time, it is essential to keep the answers focused and as simple as they can be. Partnerships exponentially increase the number of relationships required to be maintained. Not only does the complexity of a conflict increase with more parties involved, but so does the complexity of the response. When the complexity of the response begins to be as great as that of the conflict, the result will be a sharp reduction on what we can do, and a very large increase in what we cannot do.

The essence of simple structures is trust. Mistrust leads to complicating oversight dramatically. Meetings end up much larger because every partner needs to be at everything. Often to show that they are needed every partner will feel a need to give a report. One arrives quickly at that point in a meeting where everything has been said, but not everything has been said by everyone.

Trust without accountability is gambling. There is always a need for a route by which people can express concerns about standards or behaviour, especially where large numbers of volunteers are involved. For facilitators who are at best consciously ignorant, the fear will be that the process of reconciliation is being used to bring advantage. Some of that will be inevitable, and missing it happening is part of the 'only doing what you can' principle. At the same time, keeping the initial two plates, 'Researching' and 'Relating', spinning securely will not only reduce the level of ignorance but also provide good bases for feedback about one's own failures and about manipulation.

IDENTIFYING THE NEEDS

It might seem that this particular 'R' does not always apply. However, it always matters. It may be better camouflaged in places of high resources but the need will still be great. It is just that its shape changes.

At one point I worked with a church in the middle of a university area.[1] The minister (church leader) had been in post for about four years, was very different from his predecessor, and had changed a number of things at the church, including the form of the morning service. Relationships had deteriorated within the church, to the point where it seemed about to split and damage its ministry severely in the process.

Two of us worked together meeting lay and ordained members of the church individually, researching, and spending time getting to know people a little (relating). My instinct was that in this wealthy and very highly educated community of faith, with a strong tradition of large congregations, we could mentally skip the third 'R'. What could a place like that need in terms of physical support?

Thankfully, my colleague was more sensible than I was. Several issues began to surface as we got to know people better. Being curious and being present, listening hard and attentively, began to bring out some common themes.

One was isolation and loneliness. The church abounded with activity, but it was all about doing things. There was little opportunity for its members to form close friendships that would weather the normal storms of life and strengthen them in hard moments. Many families had moved into the area for work and for the very good schools, and found themselves financially very stretched, with consequent strains on their marriages and households. Drugs were easily obtainable and the church youth group for teenagers did not seem to the families to address the issue.

The presenting issue was that the minister had changed the services to make them more student-friendly, seeing the call of that church as being towards the university. He spent a great deal of time on this sort of work. As a result, as one person put it, 'those of us who have been around for a long time feel that we are only valued for what we give'.

Listening to the other group (for the sake of keeping it short I am somewhat simplifying) the story was very different. The minister had felt bullied from the day he arrived, with both he and his family not being welcomed into people's homes, something they were used to at their previous post, where they had been for a long time. It seemed obvious to the generally younger part of the church that the students needed to hear the good news of Jesus Christ, and that the people in the church already were prone to be an obstacle to what they felt was God's call. The list went on and on, and the regional head of that denomination was at her wit's end, worrying about the health of the minister and the future of one of the flagship churches.

Even in such a well-resourced church there were needs for help, physical demonstrations of love. One example was to bring in experts in debt counselling. Another was to encourage home groups to have time to eat together and pray for each other, as well as reading the Bible.

On the other side there was a need for welcome to be symbolized, done in this case through a visiting programme and bring-and-share suppers in groups of twenty, with a town-hall-style question-and-answer session with members of the Eldership group and the minister.

The minister was given access to coaching and further training on leadership, and there was a service of repentance and recommitment, based on the beautiful Methodist Covenant service.

Resources used were thus psychological, time, hospitality, counselling in areas of pressure, and an open acknowledgement of where things had gone wrong.

Everyone has needs, even if they are intangible. Peacebuilding demonstrates love in paying attention to needs. The facilitator may not be able to do everything – in the church example, neither I nor my colleague were anywhere near doing so. But we did what we could, and sought to liberate the resources of the church to make their own reconciliation work.

SUMMARY

- The nature of God's provision is abundance, with generosity to a lavish extent. In the ministry of Jesus, especially in the 'signs'[2] in John's Gospel, abundance often plays a role, particularly in the miracle of the water into wine and the feeding miracles. The abundance is gracious; it is not earned but is a gift of love. Imitating Christ, consciously or not, points us towards relieving need with abundant generosity.
- The actions of meeting need by Jesus are usually in dialogue with the person concerned or with those who can speak for the person concerned, for example Mary and Martha in John 11 when Lazarus is raised from the dead. In this way people are given respect; not treated as objects on

which to demonstrate magic tricks but rather as
people of value.

- Love is demonstrated by action. For those
caught up in the insecurities of conflict, at
any level, proof of love matters and is found
through action.
- Relief is not to be guilt inducing. We do what
we can, not what we can't. That will, however,
be sacrificial and costly.
- Meeting needs with relief will drive us to
partnership, and that is always a test of character
and values. Are we willing to wash feet, to be
obscure and in the background, and see someone
else get the credit if that means real progress can
be made?
- The central partnership is with God, sometimes
unconsciously.
- However complicated the conflict, seek to build
trust in the partnership supporting and facilitating
and thus to keep that group simple, but enable
accountability. Very often the first reconciliation
will be among the facilitators and other partners.
- Everyone has needs that will need relieving. In
all situations, always. If we can't see them it's
because we are not paying attention enough, not
researching and relating properly (I speak from
foolish experience) – not because they don't exist.

POINTS TO PONDER

- Look closely at one or more of Jesus' miracles, for
example the Marriage Feast at Cana in John 2, or

the healing of Bartimaeus in Mark 10.46ff. There
will be surprises but see how agency and dignity
are maintained and abundance and generosity
is demonstrated.

- Try and think honestly and write down how you
feel about working hard and sacrificially and
not getting the credit. In a situation you know,
would you be attracted to help in peacebuilding
on those terms?

- Thinking of a dispute/conflict with which you
are familiar, in a club, church, at work, in the
community or more widely, what are the needs
on every side that require relieving to enable
people to be freer, to have more of life in all
its fullness?

- Regarding the same issue you just thought of,
what can you do, and what can't you do? If you
are someone who prays, write it down and make
a promise to God to do what you can and not
feel guilty about the rest?

- If you worked with someone else, could you do
more? Who might they be?

Case Study (continued)

Go back to the case study at the end of the previous
chapter. Looking at the situation, what are the needs
that require relieving that you, as the facilitator, can
identify? What kind of groups need to be involved?
Who is likely to want to lead? Who do you need to get
onside first?

7

Risking

Judgement is a word that has all sorts of uncomfortable connotations. One of them is that it involves risk. God's judgement is risk free because God is truth, but human judgement is all too fallible.

Even the idea of judgement involves division. It may be the ultimate division at the end of time, or it may simply mean that we have a choice, with different risks in each way forward.

Every journey of peacebuilding and reconciliation has innumerable judgements and choices. It does not matter whether it is at the family level or in war, there will be moments where a choice lies ahead. It will usually include whether to continue or whether to try for a settlement. In the film *Darkest Hour*, set in May 1940, Winston Churchill struggles to keep the British War Cabinet committed to continue the war even after the defeat of France and the triumph of German armies across Europe. One of the lines he is given is: 'You do not negotiate with a tiger when your head is in its mouth.' The Foreign Secretary, Lord Halifax, was arguing that the possibilities of a negotiated peace on poor terms were better than the prospect of complete defeat.

Both arguments convinced some people. Churchill was generally seen to have been right, but even he had grave doubts. The road forked and neither potential route had many attractions; there was no risk-free option.

The role of the facilitator in reconciliation and peacebuilding has been seen to start with Research, to continue while adding the building of deep and resilient Relationships, and third, to add to the first two, commitment to Relieving need, good in itself and a sign of the genuineness of the love in the relationship.

The first three steps are usually the easiest. By the third there are three plates spinning and there is probably a group of partners in peacebuilding, formal or informal, small or large, depending on the level and scale of the dispute. Much research and learning has had the effect of moving from conscious ignorance to partial knowledge. As time progresses, the need for the moral imagination grows and grows and the role of the facilitators becomes increasingly to enable the participants in the quarrel to reimagine their choices. In other words, they must see that there are numerous possible forks in the road and have the will to take the ones leading to peace.

This is a moment when the issues of risk become more and more evident. There is nothing new about the idea. Jesus spoke of it in one of his best-known parables, that of the Two Sons, often called the Parable of the Prodigal Son.[1]

[11] Then Jesus said, 'There was a man who had two sons. [12] The younger of them said to his father, "Father, give me the share of the property that will belong to me." So he divided his property between them. [13] A few days later the younger son gathered all he had and travelled to a distant country, and there he squandered

his property in dissolute living. ¹⁴ When he had spent everything, a severe famine took place throughout that country, and he began to be in need. ¹⁵ So he went and hired himself out to one of the citizens of that country, who sent him to his fields to feed the pigs. ¹⁶ He would gladly have filled himself with the pods that the pigs were eating; and no one gave him anything. ¹⁷ But when he came to himself he said, "How many of my father's hired hands have bread enough and to spare, but here I am dying of hunger! ¹⁸ I will get up and go to my father, and I will say to him, 'Father, I have sinned against heaven and before you; ¹⁹ I am no longer worthy to be called your son; treat me like one of your hired hands.'" ²⁰ So he set off and went to his father. But while he was still far off, his father saw him and was filled with compassion; he ran and put his arms around him and kissed him. ²¹ Then the son said to him, "Father, I have sinned against heaven and before you; I am no longer worthy to be called your son." ²² But the father said to his slaves, "Quickly, bring out a robe – the best one – and put it on him; put a ring on his finger and sandals on his feet. ²³ And get the fatted calf and kill it, and let us eat and celebrate; ²⁴ for this son of mine was dead and is alive again; he was lost and is found!" And they began to celebrate.

²⁵ 'Now his elder son was in the field; and when he came and approached the house, he heard music and dancing. ²⁶ He called one of the slaves and asked what was going on. ²⁷ He replied, "Your brother has come, and your father has killed the fatted calf, because he has got him back safe and sound." ²⁸ Then he became angry and refused to go in. His father came out and began to plead with him. ²⁹ But he answered his father, "Listen!

For all these years I have been working like a slave for you, and I have never disobeyed your command; yet you have never given me even a young goat so that I might celebrate with my friends. ³⁰ But when this son of yours came back, who has devoured your property with prostitutes, you killed the fatted calf for him!" ³¹ Then the father said to him, "Son, you are always with me, and all that is mine is yours. ³² But we had to celebrate and rejoice, because this brother of yours was dead and has come to life; he was lost and has been found.""

The story speaks for itself. The context is that Jesus was being accused by the religious leaders of mixing with bad people. In response he tells three stories, of which this is the longest. In each of them there is a process of something very valuable being lost, and of the key figure (here, the father) seeking the thing that is lost. As in all the parables, it is a story that will have had his listeners oohing and aahing, taking one side or the other, laughing in places, shocked in others, but having a sting in the tale. The sting is that God is like the one who seeks; God reaches out to the lost, even the lost who are wicked.

You may like to read the story again, see what strikes you and what surprises you. It is worth noting that we do not know the conclusion at all. The younger son has come back, but does he stay? He is not getting the slight independence of being a hired servant living in the village, able to get a job elsewhere; he is bound to the family as a member of it, indebted to his father's forgiving love. That may be very uncomfortable. The elder son is left making up his mind as to whether to go into the feast or not. Will he accept his proper role and restore his brother completely, or will he stay outside?

As with all of Jesus' stories there are an almost infinite number of ways to read it. In this case, taking the story as one of reconciliation and peacebuilding, I am going to analyse the risks being taken as a trigger to stimulate a sense not only of risk, but also of possibility.

Risks in most journeys of reconciliation can often simply be divided into two main categories, each with a number of sub-categories.

Risk for the Facilitators

The first is the risk for the facilitators. Any kind of reconciliation, especially mediation, brings the risk of much psychological and emotional pain and occasionally the risk of physical harm.

The latter is more dramatic but unusual. Canon Andrew White, of whom I have already written, was present at the siege of the Church of the Nativity in Bethlehem in 2002. The church had been seized by an armed group, with up to two hundred monks and priests in the building. The siege lasted thirty-nine days and was resolved by negotiation. Canon White was present for the vast majority of that time, supporting the negotiations. There was occasional shooting and much confusion, during which time he was under fire.

Subsequently, while working in Baghdad, he was attacked and frequently threatened.

Andrew is something of an exception, as anyone who works with him will tell you, and his experience is certainly more remarkable than that of most facilitators except for people like Terry Waite.

However, one risk affects all those who stand in the middle, which is the pain of being mistrusted, abused and insulted and even hated by all those involved in the conflict. While working in the Niger Delta I was accused of being in the pay of Shell, of the State Government and of the Federal Government by one group. The other group said that I had taken the side of the militia groups. One of my predecessors at Coventry Cathedral, Canon Paul Oestreicher, was at one point accused of being a CIA agent by the intelligence services of the German Democratic Republic (better known as East Germany, the very undemocratic satellite of the USSR in the Cold War) and of being an agent of the Stasi, the intelligence service of East Germany, by the CIA. He joked about it, but it was painful.

In the Parable of the Sons, we see the risks being taken by the father.

The first is that he continues to hope and to look, risking disappointment and public shame (in a strongly honour-/shame-driven culture). He had been terribly ill-treated by his younger son, who in asking for his inheritance has effectively said, 'Dad, I wish you were dead.' Then and now it was an act that would have become the talk of the community and diminished the father in the sight of neighbours. Even though he is evidently rich and respectable, with servants and lands, he would have been shamed.

For the community, his looking out for the son would have made it worse. You can imagine his neighbours saying to each other, 'Have you seen that silly old fool, hanging around looking for that useless son of his? Hasn't he learned anything? You would have thought he had more self-respect.'

When the son comes back it all gets worse. The father runs, something that important people are often too dignified to do. He embraces the son.[2] He honours him with a ring on his hand, a sign of familial authority, with a cloak, a sign of wealth, with shoes, a sign of status, and above all with a top-class feast for all. When Jesus was telling the story, it is possible to imagine that the crowd – on hearing that the father was looking out for and ran towards his son – would have expected the story to continue something like: 'He beat him, kicked him, rebuked him, but out of great kindness offered him a role in the house as the lowest form of slave.' How much more astonished would they have been at the way the story unfolded.

Many of us have a sneaking sense of sympathy for the older brother. What he says is true. He has done the right thing and yet he has not been rewarded for it. Capital has been taken out of the family farm that could have been invested and was instead squandered. His father has been moping around on the road in a probably fruitless wait for the return of the prodigal. And when it does happen the old man throws a lavish party, so loud that the elder son can hear it as he comes in from the fields. It is no wonder that he is furious.

With the older brother there is the same sacrifice of dignity by the father. Instead of ordering him to come in, join the party and at least try to look pleased, he goes out and begs him to come in. It was the older brother's job to reconcile, but he does not. It was his role to set an example of respect for his father, but he does not.

Jesus is speaking to two groups. He is saying to those who have wandered from God, 'Come back; whatever you have done, you are loved by God, not just as servants but as children.' He is saying to the religious leaders, 'Come in and feast on the goodness of God, of which you already know, but seem to have forgotten. You too are loved; receive that love and with it these prodigals who have found their way back to God.'

Biblical approaches to reconciliation are decisive and clear, based in actions that both symbolize and enact reconciliation. The process takes time and sometimes fails, but begins with a marked point. In the Prodigal Son passage, both the speech and the acts of the Father are powerful testimonies to his forgiveness. The psychological subtleties are not overlooked but the order of events and symbols is different from our more gradualist approach in the Global North, where forgiveness is at the end of the process. God starts with forgiving.

In most disputes the greatest risk to the facilitators is being insulted, mistrusted and disliked. Motives will be doubted. Actions will be second-guessed. It requires resilience and the moral imagination to continue and through love to demonstrate to all parties that the objective is peace, and that true, just peace is a feast worth anything.

In situations of armed conflict, taking physical risk is also essential. No facilitator or peacebuilder going into a conflict area takes the same risks as those who live there all the time. Usually, it will not even be the same risk as to the diplomats stationed in the area, or the relief personnel from NGOs and multilateral agencies such as the UN. But to go there makes all the difference. It gives credibility that when many have gone the opposite way someone came to be alongside, even if only briefly. The unique significance of Jesus Christ begins with God taking flesh, incarnation. Fully God and fully human, Jesus endured all the troubles of living in a very troubled part of the world. He came to share our humanity so as to make it possible for us to share his eternal life.

Risk for Those in the Dispute

Yet if we love those in the dispute and seek their flourishing, the aspect of risk that weighs most heavily is the one that they face.

This is the risk of the consequences of decisions. Actions and omissions have consequences, and once past the events of the action or omission, the consequences will come in one way or another. They may be mitigated or changed, but other things will have to happen as a result of what we do and don't do.

The actions of the industrial revolutions and of the growth in economies, energy use, global wealth, technologies and populations over the last two hundred years or so have the consequence of global warming, loss of biodiversity and threats to the circumstances and even in some cases existence of those who will be alive in the late twenty-first century. Some of those consequences are already very present indeed. We cannot undo the actions, and as each year passes, we cannot undo the inactions that have been allowed.

It seems obvious but it is easily forgotten. As I mentioned in the Introduction, a UK strategic outlook in 2021 spoke of the policy around the use of nuclear weapons. It never said anything about the policy for the aftermath of using nuclear weapons. But there would have to be one. Actions have consequences, but it is very human to avoid thinking them through.

In armed conflict a risk of beginning a process of reconciliation is the loss of impetus in seeking victory. A second risk is loss of confidence in the leader's commitment. What Churchill felt in 1940 is that any politician who sought terms of peace would be thrown out of office on the spot and replaced by someone with greater determination.

There are some circumstances where resistance, even armed resistance, is the only possible response to forces so evil that no negotiation is possible. Most people see 1940 as one of those. However, we must bear in mind that the early steps towards conflict begin with demonizing the opponent. That happened in 1914, with terrible results. In George Orwell's *1984* the enemies are all demonized, without challenge. The result is eternal conflict and tyranny. We have to acknowledge that few – but some – groups are intrinsically evil. Most are mixtures, hence the need for research and relationships.

The moral imagination of alternatives to conflict will often be a crucial part of the work of the facilitator, but it must be offered as a gift, not imposed, and it must be done in a way that builds on research, relationships and relief work. Yet the consequences of the exercise of the moral imagination increase the risk levels in the process. At the same time, the absence of any exercise of moral imagination almost certainly condemns the process to failure. The facilitator is on a road where a new map has to be drawn, a map that itself helps to create the topography through which the participants journey. However, once started, the option of stopping and ceasing to move while the map is drawn is not usually a possibility. The consequences of starting a reconciliation process is to follow the road either where the participants were going or on a new route that they themselves imagine: there is rarely a third option. Actions have consequences.

I have always found that two equal and equally unpalatable risks present themselves at some point during every facilitation. One is to meet and the other is not to meet.

Of course, 'meeting' is a concept with many shapes.
Bringing together those who were in dispute used to be a
process of literally sitting in the same room. The advent of
new forms of communication offers far more choice and
opportunity for a sliding scale of risk in the encounter.
This is yet to be proved, but increasingly facilitators are
reporting that a video conference meeting can be much
more carefully calibrated than physical presence. It is
also harder to walk out of. I once did quit a meeting on
video conference, making a dramatic exit, as I thought.
The drama was diminished and my sense of foolishness
rightly increased when it turned out that half the meeting
thought my connection had gone down.

Meetings may either be remote, which removes the
difficult negotiations on where and how to meet, or
adjoining but separate. In this case there is a sort of
shuttle diplomacy in which the facilitator goes from one
group to another. It is less confrontational but also very
significantly less effective.

In the end the day has to come when real human
beings in dispute meet in the same physical space to
seek to imagine a new future. Unless it is a form of
dispute in which the settlement will end all contact
definitively, the outcome of a successful start to the
process will be growing contact and the need to live
with one another as the parties develop the future they
have begun to imagine.

As an example, let us return to the issue of climate
change and global warming. The paradox of meetings is
that they involve huge numbers of people flying around
the world in exactly the forms of transport that contribute
to the thing they are seeking to prevent. As a result, and
because of the COVID-19 pandemic, the proportion of

meeting being done online has gone up enormously. Yet their impact is limited. Whatever steps are progressively put in place, or not as the case may be, the world will have to live together with the consequences. This conflict between the climate and the human population is by far and away the most complicated one to resolve in human history. Yet it *is* a conflict, and one reason for the long delays in confronting it is that it is only now being recognized as such. I have deliberately included the question of reconciliation with both climate and the innumerable parties to the conflict as an example, because reconciliation is required for necessary action to be taken.

First, one party is not human: the climate and the biosphere. It is the weaker party in the short term, suffering the consequences of human acts and omissions. Yet, in the long term the climate will dominate. What happens to it is in the end a matter of science, but it is science that is not understood in its detail. It is now generally accepted that global warming is caused overwhelmingly by human beings. It is not known exactly how, or to what extent, the process may have other influences, and whether self-reinforcing feedback loops are already playing a role. Even definitions of targets such as 'zero-carbon' can be argued about. So, although we have mainly moved as a human race from unconscious ignorance, we are still in many areas in conscious ignorance or at best very partial knowledge.

Second, the conflict map is incomplete in identifying the different interests and needs of all the millions of parties involved. The map has vast blank areas where it is hard to assess who the actors are, who the spoilers are and who will shift from being in one category to another owing to extraneous or short-term issues relating to other conflicts, to trade, to political change or to entirely unforeseeable impacts of economic collapse, wars or events like the pandemic.

Third, questions of ethics arise as to who can carry a burden – and how – the size of which we cannot yet accurately measure. Yet, the choice of pausing and waiting does not exist, because inaction is itself a decision with consequences that we do know, and that we are aware cannot be supported by a significant proportion of the world.

Fourth, there is not yet agreement on relief needs, nor on how to meet them. Disasters are handled ad hoc, whether it be flooding, storms or droughts.

The risk of meeting is therefore huge. A failed meeting would be a colossal setback that might in the end derail the whole process. Yet not to meet regularly, albeit that the meetings' outcomes are exceptionally difficult to manage, would be the greater disaster. At the meetings, the rich look the poor in the eye and hear first-hand the tales of struggle and suffering. The heart can be touched as well as the mind. The sciences can be assisted by the graces of compassion and fellow feeling.

The same pattern of analysis can be made of anything from family disputes to wars, community struggles to commercial litigation. Both meeting and not meeting are each a risky choice.

MITIGATING RISK

Risk raises key questions. First, who is best able to carry the risk? And second, how can it be made less severe?

There are a number of approaches to the first question, but one model put forward is the Risk Allocation Matrix (RAM).

Let us use an imaginary case. The Diocese of Barchester[3] is in great difficulty. The dean of the cathedral and the bishop have fallen out badly and both brought complaints against each other. The dean accuses the bishop of sexist behaviour, of sexual harassment and of bullying the dean's staff. She (the dean) has been off work with stress, and the cathedral congregation, which is very disconnected from the diocese, is sympathetic to her. The bishop has a pattern of falling out with staff. Nevertheless, he inherited a diocese that was on the edge of financial insolvency, where numbers of those attending church were collapsing, where recruiting clergy was nearly impossible, and where only a very small minority of the ones in post thought prayer and worship to be of any significance. The average Diocesan Synod was like the House of Commons without the same level of charity.

The Archbishop of Wessex is in despair (although to be fair he is such a long streak of misery on a good day that it is hard to tell the difference). He has asked for mediation and reconciliation work to be done.

The facilitator and team have begun work with nearly a hundred meetings across the diocese, collated on the church equivalent of Scotland Yard's Holmes system for managing complex cases and linking up disparate areas of evidence. In this case it is called Father Brown (FB) after Chesterton's detective.[4] As a result, they have discovered a pattern of bad and autocratic decisions and lack of communication leading to a breakdown of trust going back to the nineteenth century and a bishop's chaplain called Slope.

Having gained the confidence of many people at the grassroots and in the leadership of diocese and county, and with the help of FB identifying common themes, they have begun to meet certain needs, with the help of central church funding. The diocese has received a grant to pay salaries, there is an internal communications expert on loan, the dean is receiving counselling and the bishop is getting coaching. It is time for the senior staff and the key leaders to begin a process of cascading meetings to see a way forward.

What if it all goes wrong? Here is a very simplified form of the RAM.

	Bishop	Clergy	Laity	Cathedral	Central Church Funds
Loss of confidence within diocese	Too autocratic to deal with it	With encouragement and help can renew prayer life and inspire laity	Wonderful but need good inspiration. Local lay ministry?	Too fragile	Irrelevant to risk
Insolvency	Able to talk to Central Church Funds	Can manage locally but cannot all handle raising money for stipend payments	Pandemic has cut giving	Broke	Has reserves for this purpose
Public disagreement worsens	Persuadable to share in an event of repentance and reconciliation	Too dispersed	Too dispersed	Willing to try as a place for a renewal of common life	Not relevant
Senior staff breakup	Archbishop of Wessex would need to deal with bishop	Big danger of splitting	Big danger of splitting	Unable to respond	Can find and support interim staff

Of course, Barchester is not part of the Church of England or any other church group at all, and any appearance of similarity to any diocese outside the nineteenth-century books of Anthony Trollope is purely coincidental. In addition, this is very simplified. Most people would see it differently.

The aim of the RAM is that, before meeting, the principal foreseeable risks are set out and there is an analysis of which party or which outsider will be most influential for good or ill and how that risk will be faced. Who can handle the consequences, who cannot? The RAM can be made more and more complicated but is best kept to the point where it does not give answers but does ask the central questions about how to manage the risk of meeting. There can be a lead RAM that summarizes and there can be sub-matrices for different areas. Actions to be taken can be added. It is a flexible tool.

Mitigating risk involves developing resilience among those involved in the dispute, so that the process is not toppled over by a setback. Resilience will come from the moral imagination, from relationships and from developing a sense of hope. It is above all a question of confidence and the facilitation team must all be as one in expressing publicly the expectation that there is a way forward, however difficult.

Risk is also mitigated by the way meetings are set up. I remember missing this point some years ago and arriving at a meeting to address the claims of a group that they had been left out. The meeting was conducted in the normal way (a serious error) and the unhappy group were sat on one side and told they should only speak if spoken to. The whole set-up confirmed that they were being left out and it was a serious setback.

Generous hospitality and humility by the hosts is essential. As was written in Chapter 2, remember the body. Adequate ventilation, clear sight-lines, a space for the acoustics so that everyone can hear easily, suitable food, and comfortable chairs that do not encourage sleep will all help. If people have travelled, give them time to recover. Beautiful surroundings, good music, a regular timetable that is kept to, and a capacity to be in touch with others will quieten nerves. If the conflict is centred in a place of different faiths, make equal room for prayer, contemplation and silence for all, in a way that is appropriate to them. Do everything you can to respect the different faith communities' habits or dietary rules. Care for the details. That shows love.

Above all, do not spring surprises. People will need to know exactly what to expect, from the largest to the smallest aspect.

The next chapter will bring in some of the absolute essential values in peacebuilding, most importantly truth and justice.

SUMMARY

- Creating a fork in a road that otherwise leads only towards deepening hatred and further confrontation requires the moral imagination of which Lederach writes so powerfully. Normally a reconciliation process will require many such forks in a road that is otherwise heading only for confrontation.
- Each fork is a place of meeting or decision or both, and thus of risk.

- There are risks for the facilitators. These will involve emotional and psychological strains, the acceptance of not being trusted and, in some situations, physical dangers. All must necessarily be faced.
- There are even greater risks for those in the confrontation. A failed process is a huge blow and often makes things worse.
- It is essential to see what the risks are for all involved, who is most capable of carrying them and who is least capable.
- Risk mitigation is a question of detailed work as well as careful thinking. It comes down to making people feel deeply secure and equally valued.

POINTS TO PONDER

- What are the issues in a conflict that make you most uncomfortable? Is it raised voices? Silence? Threats? Being mistrusted? Or any other things? How will you find resilience to cope with these discomforts in any area of reconciliation and peacebuilding?
- When you look at conflicts and disagreements about which you know, at any level, what are the risks you identify with an absence of progress in reconciliation or attempting reconciliation?
- Consider from your own experience what makes you most able to relax and be open about what is on your mind. Think about the physical, the emotional, the psychological and the spiritual factors.

- Finally, ask yourself how those sorts of things can be applied in tense situations. What will set a meeting on the road towards feeling sufficiently safe?

Case Study (continued)

See if you can develop a RAM for the St Thomas dispute (see page 118). Enter 'Risks' in the left-hand column, the names of groups or individuals across the top. The key questions are about developing a sense of who is strong and who is weak, who can bear which risks and who can't. The conclusion that you are seeking is: 'What meetings might I have; with whom, and how?' Who is not in the story who should be? Who do you need to get onside? Which VIPs locally might help as conveners? Put yourselves in the shoes of each group and use your imagination to empathize. There are few simple right or wrongs here.

8

Reconciling – the Long Journey

Having Researched, built Relationships, begun a programme of Relieving need with partners suited for whatever the need is, taken a deep breath and, after careful thought, Risked the beginning of meeting, the long journey of Reconciling can now move into the next phase.

It is worth going back to what reconciliation is and is not. Reconciliation is a portfolio word meaning the gathering together of all the processes and skills necessary to transform destructive differences and conflicts into constructive and imaginative acceptance of difference and capacity to disagree well.

Reconciliation is not a series of compromises to reach a weak middle ground on which all stand, equally unhappily and with no basis for action together. That is kicking the can down the road, or into the long grass or wherever. Fuzziness of that sort is the evasion of the challenge of difference. What should be sought is a transparent and clear-eyed blessing and welcome of diversity so that all, without exception, may have an equal opportunity to flourish as individuals and groups. Reconciliation is also, especially, not the signing of a peace agreement or some other kind of accord, and assuming 'that is that, deal done, problem solved'.

If we compare the last two paragraphs it is easy to see why reconciliation, properly understood, is so difficult and takes so long.

At its heart is the transformation of every part of a person and group.

There will be a need to see some opponents differently, at least the ones who are themselves willing to be involved in the process. Seeing people and groups differently is not necessarily seeing them as good but, at the least, as people with whom to engage if possible.

There will be a need to forgo some aspects of the conflict, especially violence or its threat and other forms of deeply destructive behaviour. The process will have to lead to a change of heart as well as commitment to the journey. Changing hearts takes a very long time even in the simplest of cases. It is difficult and demanding for all involved.

There will need to be a fresh approach to justice, and a realistic search for truth. Myths will be exposed. Long-held assumptions will be progressively changed by continued contact and relationship building. A dispute that has naturally focused on what was objectionable about the other may well begin to change into a more or less friendly partnership looking outwards to the world around and seeking to bless it.

It is an uncertain process. It has moments of failure and despair and success and elation. It is prone to fits and starts, to forgetfulness and to recalling its importance. The further away in time that the destructive confrontations become, the less urgency there is in reconciliation. It may collapse altogether for a while, or look as if it has collapsed.

So once the engagement with the other has started, what are the key elements?

The most important question is about how to approach the demands of conflicted parties for truth and justice. They are also the most controversial parts of reconciliation. That is why handling those issues comes at this point and not earlier. They come later because they are so important that there has to have been a solid establishment of relationships evidenced by taking risks in meeting, the relief of need, and founded in good and continuing research. Otherwise, both truth and justice become weaponized by one side or the other or both.

The very action of introducing these areas will raise the risk level a great deal more, but ignoring them is the kiss of death. There can never be reconciliation unless it is clear that the journey involves addressing injustices and seeking to find a common understanding of events. However, how they are handled is itself very difficult to manage.

OPENING TRUTH – REVEALING MYTH

The hunt for any sort of knowledge begins with asking the right questions and using the right approach about what is being hunted. You do not look for new stars with a microscope, nor is a telescope of much value in seeking the answers to the makeup of the ocean floor.

Each conflict will have its own myths, and the longer they have gone on, the more embedded they become. 'Truths' that were recognized as convenient myths when first put forward end up as articles of dogma in the hands of supporters of one view.

That is very clearly seen in responses to the conflict in the UK and USA over racism, and in the UK especially over the legacies of slavery. It is one of the most necessary issues to face and will need long work, probably over decades. It reveals itself in different views of history, particularly that of the British Empire, and in rapidly accepted statements of so-called truth. For example, the title of the violence within the army of the East India Company (EIC) beginning in 1857 together with many simultaneous conflicts within Princely States is referred to very often in the UK as the Indian Mutiny, but in India it is called by a variety of other names including the First War of Independence, or the Uprising. For many years these later titles were rejected as it was argued that India was too disparate to have a single war of independence at that stage and that the British-ruled area was an oasis of order. However, that view is widely challenged by contemporary evidence of letters gathered by Indian and British historians, and indeed the demonstration that the British were seen as a common menace, a source of economic destruction and far from benevolent, dates back as far as the late eighteenth century.[1]

That may seem a long time ago. Yet, for any process of building relationships between modern India and the modern UK, the question of a serious search for the truth will be essential. Memories matter and symbols change thinking. Visiting Amritsar in 2019 I was taken to see the site of an infamous massacre of Indians by British troops in 1919, at a place called Jallianwala Bagh. The killings were the result of the troops opening fire on an unarmed crowd at close range when there was nowhere for the crowd to flee. It was a horrifying atrocity. When I came to the memorial to those who had died, I prostrated myself before it. That caused much fuss in the UK, but in India it was seen as a gesture of deep sorrow, owing to the historical significance of prostration.

Another very current example is that of the island of Ireland. During a trip to Dublin, also in 2019, I was astonished by the impact of a state visit there by Queen Elizabeth II in 2011, as a contribution to reconciliation after the Troubles of the late twentieth century in Northern Ireland. Every detail was recalled to me, particularly the recognition by the Queen of the troubled history between England and Ireland, her speaking in Irish at the beginning of a speech, her visiting memorials to Irish Republicans, and other apparently more mundane but for the Irish very significant gestures, including the bright green of her dress.

Her visit had a huge impact at the time. Its perceptive use of symbol reflected a step forward in the discussions of historical truth, and an acknowledgement that the past was much more complicated than it was often allowed to appear.

It is a good example because the truth in Northern Ireland remains highly contentious. In July 2021 there were exchanges in the UK Parliament about the legacy of the troubles and the very difficult issue of accountability for such events as the Bloody Sunday killings in Londonderry/Derry (even the name has very significant political connotations arising from history). The history even of the extremely well-documented recent past is contested on nearly every point.

The reality of every dispute is that the truth that is sought will always be affected by the point at which one starts and the lenses one has.

This can easily lead to a sense of despair or of relativism in which the rightful assumption that an absolute and agreed sense of the truth in a dispute is impossible to reach leads to the wrongful conclusion that no search for truth is worth undertaking.

Truth in terms of telling a true story can be progressively uncovered by many small steps. Like the buried cities of Pompeii and Herculaneum, continued excavation reveals more and more and enables a clearer picture of the overall pattern of life.

One of the best examples of progressive and helpful truth telling was in the South African Truth and Reconciliation Commission. Detailed examination of testimony was both politically illuminating and enabled the culture of the Apartheid state to be revealed.[2]

The nature of conflictual relationships is that there is always a fear that facilitators are falling for the stories told by others. In a marriage dispute, one will often hear that the mediator, the judge, the lawyers, the social workers all believed the other party, for example the husband. Yet all the wife's friends believed her, and one is told that thus everyone else was fooled. Even in the terrible cases of the abuse of children and vulnerable adults there will be passionate defences of the perpetrator, not just when suspicions first arise, but also after they have been formally accused, and even after legal and police action.

The facilitator's approach to truth will therefore always be cautious but persistent.

First, in any large-scale dispute the reconciliation process must include truth discovery by people who have no skin in the game. In a community, this may well be the mediator in the dispute, who listens carefully. In a relationship, the relationship counsellor will do it. As the scale becomes larger or more complicated it will become necessary to build up partnerships, with anything from forensic accounting, where large sums of money are at stake, to specialist historians who are known in the relevant field.

Three examples illustrate the point about the difficulties.

In the Ogoni example and in the wider conflicts in the Niger Delta, already described, good progress was made long after I had moved on by the use of environmental programmes to assess the damage caused and to oversee the discussions about reparations. One Commission in Bayelsa State was led by the then Archbishop of York, now Lord Sentamu, with powerful effect. The clarity brought to the different accounts of environmental degradation contributed to the possibility of setting up a fund and commissioning work in the wetlands.

Second, in one area where I worked, historical enquiry indicated that a very serious outbreak of violence, which was initially described as Christian vs Muslim, had significant roots in ethnic rivalries. For some time, there was an improvement, which has now been reversed as a result of more general conflict in the country concerned. This is an example of where truth is strongly contested. For those involved, the issue of Christian against Muslim is easy to understand, mobilizes internal support and generates external sponsorship from overseas observers in one way or another. Religion certainly plays a significant part, but there are also historical rivalries and the introduction of a new factor in terms of climate change driving people movements.

The reaction from those whose external support depended on the religious conflict message was understandably to deny any complexity beyond the

Christian/Muslim factors, and allege either persecution by Muslims or persecution by Christians. In any peacebuilding process, participants must be listened to as perception is almost as important as reality. In the first place, perception *is* the reality they feel that they experience, and, second, no peace will be built unless there is the beginning of a process of movement towards a common story. In other words, start where people are in terms of truth, not where the facilitator feels they ought to be. Recognize that statements of facts are necessary but far from sufficient, and will be challenged, even irrationally. The impact of narrative on brain chemistry, emotions and thus responses is also foundational. Movements to change the narrative affect the whole physiology of individuals and thus groups, especially those in leadership. They respond with flight or flight, and the handling of truth discovery thus must 'remember the body'.

Incidentally, as so often, in the case just described the mention of factors other than religion earned the facilitator a great deal of abuse from everyone. Other factors were threatening to all sides in that they undermined their self-identity as victims. In a study of the issues of shame and honour in Palestine and Israel a powerful comment was: 'Without the expectation of vindication, the role of the righteous victim risks losing its face-saving function. It could easily take on qualities of the weakling, the deserving victim or, worse, one who condones wickedness.'[3] We cannot forget the intense importance of shame and honour in conflict.

Third, in the UK the issue of racial justice, especially as it affects people of Caribbean and African heritage, is one where truth is hard to pin down. Cover up of the terrible abuses of the Windrush scandal,[4] a lack of welcome in churches and other institutions, institutional racism and many other failings obscured the realities of life for Black people in the UK.

After the murder of George Floyd in the USA in the middle of 2020, the challenge of institutional racism and Whiteness or White privilege resurfaced, especially among the Black population and among young people of colour more than in other groups. At the same time there was pushback from White groups and a number of highly confrontational and even violent clashes in London and other places across the country.

Within the Church of England other incidents spiralled to cause a great loss of confidence by not only Black but other ethnic minority members, especially those who are ordained or in the process of training or of discerning a call to ordination. Memories of past experiences were reawakened.

A leading member of the Black Majority churches (mostly Pentecostal in tradition) in the UK organized a series of online conferences with Black church leaders, youth leaders and young people from across the Christian tradition. It was attended by four of the presidents of Churches Together in England, including myself.

The encounters were remarkable and testing. The experience of the young Black leaders was of continually being stopped and searched, of a sense of profound alienation in a White country where Whiteness is the controlling dynamic in most institutions, including churches. I spoke at the same time to a remarkable and exceptional Black priest in the Church of England. They confirmed the impression of racism, which held despite that particular person being in a senior role and being widely recognized for their work. Their perception was of a 'cultural disorder' where Whiteness is in everything that is done. They saw change as involving both power and truth. They were utterly demoralized by their experience.

While I was hearing this, I was also talking to senior police officers of different ethnic backgrounds and to politicians in government and opposition. Again, there was no agreement on truth, although they saw the issue as very important and believed strongly in the idea of truth. More than that, they were convinced that their view was true. The police were not, as a number of officers saw it, harassing young Black men; they were seeking to stop knife crime, which had a disproportionate number of Black victims. They were aiming to protect, not persecute.

The argument continues to sway to and fro. That is for further along in this book. The reality of the disagreement among most people cannot be put down to malice but is a question of different perceptions that are related and believed – genuinely, sincerely, deeply and without malice – as being the whole truth; not a part of the truth that their opponents refuse to accept. There may be a minority that seeks confrontation and trouble, but it is not the general rule.

Progress will take time but needs to be made. It cannot wait until, as if by a miracle, everyone wakes up one morning with the same perception. The capacity to own a narrative, or to live with multiple narratives and yet be in relationships, albeit with grave and painful struggles, will be a mark of the transformation of reconciliation. It will be very far from the finished product, but it will help.

Even in reading that last paragraph we each come to it with different eyes. For the minority communities, the struggle to get to the truth is not just painful, it is existential. Many, not all, feel dehumanized, dismissed as a reality in society. It is immensely important to recognize that reconciliation begins with sacrifice, and sacrifice is the responsibility of the stronger, majority, groups, not the obligation of those who are already victims. For many White people, who are themselves ignored and marginalized by economic, educational and social circumstances, to speak of them as privileged is rightly heard as patronizing nonsense. The complexity of the fragile human condition and the myriad characteristics we hold mean that life is not a simple binary or a game of snakes and ladders. While we may not always be vulnerable to marginalization and oppressive conditions by virtue of a particular condition, this does not make us invulnerable in other spheres.

Embracing complexity means precision. Black Lives Matter is not all Black people against all White people. White people are not a single category, any more than those of UK minority (but global majority) ethnic heritage. They are all first and foremost people, human beings, to be treated with equal dignity and not to be patronized, ignored or put in a category. That is a good place to start.

JUSTICE DELAYED CAN BE JUSTICE AFFIRMED

It is a great gift to live in a place where the administration of justice is genuinely intended to be neutral and unswayed by political considerations, albeit with very human failings. The corruption of the courts, or their capture by one group, is the first and most necessary step towards ending democracy and freedom of speech.[5] In mid-2021 severe riots broke out across South Africa after the imprisoning of the former president, Jacob Zuma, for refusing to pay attention to the courts. Although it was very disruptive, cost many lives and damaged the economy, the ability of the court to prevail was widely seen as a good step for democracy. By contrast, the Chinese Communist Party declares that independent courts are a threat to party rule and thus to the good of the country.

The need for an independent and apolitical judiciary is based deeply in the realities of human beings. The use of power almost always leads to the abuse of power. Those who wish for an outcome to their policies will sooner or later begin to see that outcome as the just result and any other as unjust.

Yet justice is fragile; it flourishes in strong light but wilts in darkness, and is easily killed in times of conflict. Victor's justice is always a great fear. The winners of a war apportion 'justice' against the losers without giving attention to proper representation, and when the 'justice' is in the midst of conflict, violent or not, it will be far more likely to have the characteristics of revenge.

Justice must therefore be independent and must wait for the moments when people are confident that it is being done calmly.

Institutions are especially bad at the administration of justice within their own systems. The nature of an institution is to seek to preserve its life. Those who end up leading an institution are likely to see survival of that institution as best guaranteed by their own survival as leaders.[6] One might imagine the Bishop of Barchester channelling the future head of General Motors and saying to himself, 'What is good for me is good for the Diocese of Barchester.' A state of co-dependency is created that can only be broken by independence in justice, and yet the sense of self-protection is so great a power that almost any reason can be found for preserving internal control.

To be bad at justice within one's own system will lead to being bad at justice wherever one has power. Add to the human desire for power the stresses and tensions of dispute, let alone violent conflict, and there will be an overwhelming tendency towards injustice.

The slogan (and title of an NGO), 'No Peace Without Justice', is thus accurate only with a series of provisos. They include that the justice must be independent of the most powerful, and committed to impartiality, and at the right time, which will almost always be once conditions of the dispute have calmed, as a means of avoiding a new flare-up. Theologically, Christianity claims that sometimes good justice will only be found before God and is beyond human reach. That may be the case where a perpetrator cannot be found, or the truth seems unfathomable. It is not a reason for human effort to end: it is a source of eternal hope.

John's Gospel, chapter 21, has an aura of peace and of resolution, but that is a surprise. It takes place only a few weeks after the chaos, betrayal and cowardice of the disciples at the arrest and crucifixion of Jesus. The disciples are still coming to terms with the idea that he rose from the dead and has appeared to them. Resurrection life, which he has given them through breathing the Holy Spirit into them, is to be lived in the ordinary. It is not living on a continuous elevated plane slightly disconnected from the world. Food needs buying, families and friends need feeding. Peter tells his friends that he is going fishing in the Sea of Galilee. This is not, as some commentators suggest, an attempt to return to his life before meeting Jesus; it is getting on with things.

Yet, even among the disciples and certainly with Peter, there must have been a lurking cloud. They had not stood by Jesus. Jesus has not mentioned this to date, but it is there, an elephant by the lake, to misuse a cliché. After a fruitless night of fishing without catching, the power of the narrative comes in waves of ever deeper love from Jesus, waves that ever more powerfully commission them for the rest of their lives.

First, a stranger on the shore calls out instructing them where to place their nets. The voice will have been clear in the early morning stillness. The net is filled with fish. All of them will immediately have remembered, as we do as John's readers, the story of the great catch of fish at the beginning of the ministry of Jesus.[7] They have been recommissioned, reconciled after their failure, not in some messy compromise but in the power of the grace of God catching them and reimagining their futures.

Then, when they have all got to the shore, they find breakfast made. Again, this takes them back to the feeding of the five thousand and, through there, to the feeding of the Israelites during the Exodus by God in the wilderness. Jesus' reconciliation relieves their hunger and assures them that his promise that those who follow him will not hunger – spiritually – is true. The reconciliation has moved on from renewal of relationship in hospitality, the meeting of need and the security of being in God's hands.

Finally, Peter is taken aside, and in three questions his denial of Jesus at the time of Jesus' arrest is reversed. Justice is done, truth is revealed. Peter does not have failure swept under the carpet but rather it is clearly exposed, truthfully addressed and justly dealt with, by the perfectly just God who has shown Peter what it is to fail and be restored.

Truth and justice are met in love, and the result is healing and a future.

TRUTH AND JUSTICE – SOURCES OF HOPE

Truth and justice are central to the character of God in what we see by God being revealed through Jesus. Wisdom in timing, in place and in manner of dealing with sin and failure puts them in a context of safety and security, not a context of uncertainty and revenge. That has to be true of any process of reconciliation, even more so once we take account of the fragilities of human nature, of our proclivity to confuse justice with what we want, and truth with what we perceive.

The facilitator – however large and complicated or small and simple the dispute, whether it has the violence of guns or the savagery of words and hatreds – has to take as a central aim the establishment of a 'Galilee beach': a place of peace and security where truth and justice are seen and recognized.

MAINTAINING THE MOMENTUM

All that having been said, the issue of maintaining the momentum and excitement of the journey of peacebuilding will continually come back.

I have been using the metaphor of a journey. In 1977 or so two friends and I walked across Scotland from the Kyle of Lochalsh to Montrose, sea to sea. It was a long and beautiful walk across the Highlands, camping in remote valleys. It was also very enjoyable apart from the midges and blisters. When I look back more than forty years on, there are various moments that stick in my mind, milestones that enable me to see how we kept going (a fourth person did drop out).

The journey of reconciliation is a very long walk indeed. I remember a married couple I knew whose marriage disintegrated. They separated and began the process of divorce. In a series of remarkable events, they got back together, despite one having found a new partner, and cancelled the divorce at the very last moment.

There will be many who would have loved that to have been true for themselves, but I am not holding this couple up as especially virtuous, any more than they claimed to be so. That is not the point of the story. Some years after they got back together, I was chatting to one of them and asked how they were. 'It takes a lot of working out,' was the reply. Long journeys take a lot of working out. On our Scottish walk we had Ordnance Survey maps and compasses (no satellite navigation in those days). Milestones were important – they gave a lift – but the dogged hard work was reading the map, getting the direction right and putting one foot in front of another on agonizingly steep hills where it felt as though some nasty person had added several bricks to the backpack.

Much reconciliation and peacebuilding work is patiently sitting in a hot room trying to get the direction right. I want to suggest a number of ways of keeping the momentum in the hard work as well as in the high moments.

TELL THE STORY FORWARDS AND BACKWARDS

In Part I the two dangers of overspeed and overreach were discussed. One of the methods of containing them is to set realistic and achievable targets while maintaining as a final aim the vision of the sunny uplands that are the ultimate destination.

A way of forming the vision and getting the general direction established uses working together to develop the moral imagination of a world without the conflict, the imagination of a 'golden age' and then the development of a backwards history process to look from the future and see how you got there.

At its heart it is an attempt to draw people into a common story and permit the surfacing of what they see as ideals. If a secure enough environment can be created in the discussions, by small groups and lots of preparation and briefing, those involved are asked to look forward perhaps five or maybe ten years, to two imagined scenarios.

One is a dark age when everything has gone wrong. They are asked to describe it and to set out in some detail what it is that makes it so bad.

The other scenario is a golden age when their best hopes are fulfilled. Once again, they are asked to describe it and say why it is so good.

The second linked exercise is to take the future situations they have imagined, and to fill in the intervening time with the actions and omissions that happened to get to those places. This is the history backwards. Stand in the future scenario that has been imagined and tell the story of how it happened, year by year.

These exercises work best in lower-level and informal disputes, in a community or a church setting. At the level of conflict, they may come in useful later, but the expectations of face-to-face negotiation will be very high. It will almost certainly be necessary to mix and match different approaches as the exhaustion of face-to-face talks often leads to a loss of the sense of direction and desire for the future, and participants become intransigent.

To do these exercises properly will take days for a complicated situation and much less for a simple one. It needs to wait until those in the different groups are sufficiently relaxed with each other to be able to risk a level of openness. The exercises should be repeated occasionally to enable participants to see the progress that is being made and to refine their ideas.

Probably there will be little interaction between the different sides at the beginning. It may be necessary to do the first round entirely separately so that they can each discover more about the others. The expectation and experience are that they grow into an ability to work together in their imaginations, as a first step to working together in reality.

These exercises are sensitive and difficult to time, to design and to moderate. There will always be objections to 'playing games' and part of the facilitators' skills are going to be shown in the pace, the layout and design of the process, and how to ensure that its use is communicated and accepted.

Facilitators will also introduce the very serious questions for consideration. The history backwards exercise will need to include the ways in which truth and justice were established and by what mechanisms.

The underlying purpose of the exercises is to make space for the moral imagination. The question for each side is: 'What would a truly good society look like?' At the beginning, the answer from every side is very likely to be: 'One in which we are in total control.' The introduction of further questions, the mixing in of direct talks and time spent in imagining the future and the ways forward will remind participants of what they are seeking, enable unrealistic goals (e.g. complete victory) to be challenged, and open the way to non-binding discussions of what is good, preparing the way for the decisions emerging from negotiations.

RUNNING ON PARALLEL LINES

The idea of truth and reconciliation commissions almost always appears at some point. Like the exercises just mentioned, they are enormously powerful tools, but seldom of value by themselves. They are the best known of a wide range of approaches, the timing of which is very delicate, and if used either too early or too late will become useless or even destructive.

Imagine a railway line, single track. If there is a blockage everything stops. The blockage can be a broken rail (easily repaired), a landslide (takes time to deal with but not complicated), a bridge down (major problem). There may be traffic coming both ways, meaning one has to give ground (not at all easy). A simple answer is to run more than one track, but with points to connect them. There will still be blockages, but there will be a great deal more flexibility in dealing with them.

A community dispute is likely to involve many people. There will be leaders, supporters, encouragers, opponents, some elected, some informal, some belonging to organizations with community power such as residents' associations, schools, hospitals and churches. The dispute might be over access to community facilities, or their absence, or new housing, or a bypass, or any number of other questions.

Facilitating such a dispute in one gathering is likely to be very difficult. Blockages will result from groups feeling left out in a big meeting. There will be discrimination against more vulnerable groups that have difficulty in expressing themselves. The strong will dominate. The development of parallel tracks in which blockages that could affect the main line can be dealt with before they become serious is a way both of managing a difficult level of complexity and a wide variety of levels of power and of keeping a sense of momentum. There will always be something happening. In this approach the biggest and highest-level meeting will focus on key issues and should arrive with a good level of participation and many potential tangles already straightened out. Communication of all that is going on will be essential, for the suspicions of a community that is locked into a dispute will always be of deals being done and fixes being fixed behind the back of other people.

The number of tracks will vary very considerably according to the number of groups that have opposing views, and that need to be able to sort a way forward. Each track requires facilitation, and each track will gain expectations of being important. The balance between creating inclusion and adding superfluous complexity is very difficult to manage.

Inclusion matters. Deals done on high without a top-down, middle-out, bottom-up approach will lack approval and thus fail to gain a social licence to operate in practice. Grassroots deals will be subsumed in overall, elite-based conflict. Those who can wield a power of veto and have an interest in the dispute continuing will do so unless there is significant grassroots pressure that overwhelms obstructions.

Truth and Reconciliation Commissions (TRCs)

These have been discussed in principle elsewhere. The questions in practice are simple to ask and very hard to answer. The answer to the first question must be no and to the others must be yes.

- Is a TRC being looked at as a magic wand that will make everything suddenly better?
- Are there the right people to lead it? They must have widespread confidence.
- Does it have very clear terms of reference?
- What will be the outcome of its actions? What are the criteria that will give great advantage to telling the truth, and how will that lead towards reconciliation?
- Will it be tied into other parts of the process?

Summary

- Reconciliation is a very long journey. To accomplish anything the travelling must ensure variety of pace, of activity and of content. There must be a mix of milestones with celebrations and steady travelling.
- The structure of a process should be kept as simple as possible. The complexity of the dispute must always be embraced and respected.
- Keep the other Rs going at the same time. The different Rs are cumulative, not successive.
- Ensure that different tracks are used to keep support for the process at all levels, not just the top.

- Use the partnerships required for the job; for example, skilled mediators are specialists.
- Fit the activities to the people, not the people to the activities. But find ways of keeping vision and necessary direction something they reflect on constantly.

Points to Ponder and a Case Study

- Try telling the story of a dispute or conflict from both sides. Do a history backwards exercise; it can take thirty minutes not a day! If not a real one, use the St Thomas case (see p. 118).
- What are good examples of truth being revealed that you know? Whose truth is it? One side? All sides?
- What are the best examples of justice after conflict? How was it done, and does it now seem fair?
- Look for examples of reconciliation you know. Describe the time, the extent and what transformation was needed. What were the key milestones, the moments where things changed? How did they get from one to another? What has been the outcome?
- If there is time, in the working case of St Thomas, ask yourselves how the different groups would imagine a moral and beneficial outcome. What will need to be looked at?

9

Supplies for the Journey – Resourcing

Reconciliation is a process, not an event. Dispute and conflict are addictive drugs. Societies become hooked on them. Research has shown (as mentioned in Chapter 1) that prolonged exposure to conflict literally alters the DNA and has an impact on subsequent generations, especially when the conflict is intergenerational.[1] A group that is always resolving disagreement with destructive forms of confrontation, even when they are violent, can only see solutions in terms of destruction of the other. As the last chapter said, reconciliation is a process of transformation, especially of the moral imagination.

That takes a very long time indeed. The aim is to create habits of dealing with diversity through collaborative endeavour, not simply trying to win. At this point many people will give up and think, 'How naïve!' Sometimes I do myself. Yet history gives us examples of change that demonstrate something far from perfect, but nevertheless offer hope.

Two examples have had a profound impact on the United Kingdom.

The first is the change in Europe since 1945. The European Union may arguably have failed the vision of the founders in some ways but in one respect it has succeeded. France and Germany have not fought each other. Northwest Europe has not been a battleground since 1945, the longest period since the fall of the Western Roman Empire. That peace has been achieved by a sustained and deliberate policy of reconciliation and the Franco-German partnership remains the key grouping of the EU 27. For the rest of continental Europe, whether members of the EU or not, that success has altered the way of life. The EU has stabilized democracy in former dictatorships on both sides of the former Iron Curtain. It has helped economies grow rapidly. It has in many ways brought a freedom that is unrivalled in European history. The discussion of what its vision should be now, and whether it can be more than material wealth for some, is for a different place and probably does not include contributions from the UK.

The second is within the UK. From time immemorial the border with Scotland was a place of conflict. The Lords of the Marches, including the Bishops of Durham, had as their first duty the protection of England, and their equivalents north of the border had the task of protection from the English.

The possibility of Scottish independence is very real, something that in other countries might be a cause of war. Yet although the arguments are severe, the reconciliation between Scots and English – except in sport – is so robust that the idea of a war is absurd. Many will find it bizarre even to use that as an example, but for centuries the idea of war being out of any question would itself have seemed utopian in its turn. That is true transformation. Differences remain essential, even encouraged. School systems, the law, Scottish regiments, social policy, the established church, the flag, all differ. We are united but not adversaries, except, as I say, when it comes to sport. Even if the countries divide, it is taken for granted that the process would be by consent, not by war.

Reconciliation happens eventually, even in the most intractable conflict. War-weariness sets in, new leaders appear and what holds people together becomes more important than what causes them to hate. However, we also can point all too easily to conflicts that one can trace back through the ages, whether in the Holy Lands, Afghanistan, parts of Ireland, the Balkans or many other places. Transformation matters. Just because certain types of behaviour are customary and cultural, that does not make them right. Violent solving of disputes should always be a last resort that comes from failure in other approaches, and even then in Christian terms will almost always be wrong.

For example, resorting quickly to violence to resolve disputes is habitual in certain groups, where vendetta is linked closely to honour and shame. Failure to take revenge for an incident in a previous generation brings shame on a family or clan. It is still wrong, but it illustrates the need for transformation and not just peace agreements or a casual hoping that something new may turn up. It is also worth noting that the concepts of honour and shame are very present in all societies, as are vendettas and revenge, even if they are disguised in different clothes.

Very deep transformation is not something done to people by outsiders, but is a heart change, a change of spirit, a change towards an entirely different future. There is nothing new in this dream; in the eighth century BCE the prophet Isaiah wrote of a time when God's rule would come: 'nation shall not lift up sword against nation neither shall they learn war any more'.[2]

In a marriage it can take weeks to recover from a bad argument lasting a few hours. In a community or a church, wounds and disagreements badly handled become part of the folklore and often have very long-term effects. In a nation, or between nations, violent conflict can do damage in a week that takes generations from which to recover. In the UK the legacy of the bitterness of the Brexit campaign of 2016 was still experienced and showed itself in 2021 directly and indirectly, on social media and in political controversy.

The final plate to set spinning is the R of Resourcing the future. No facilitator or group can commit to decades, even generations of involvement, and even if they could it would not in any way be desirable. The presence of outsiders provides opportunities to shift responsibility for a good process to someone else. It creates dependency and it prevents transformation. Those in the conflict need to develop new ways of working, the capacity for moral imagination, the instincts that create possibilities of disagreeing well. They need changed hearts.

It is necessary to recall continually that reconciliation does not seek clones who work together in unanimity. It seeks human beings who grow in diversity and bring all their rich differences together for the common good. The vision of the global Church is that people from every nation should be united in love for Jesus Christ and for their neighbours, meaning in this case, their own locality, as well as further off.

The heart of Jesus' teaching, signs and prayer in John's Gospel is often seen as found in chapter 17. Whole books are written on this passage, which some see as the most profound of the Bible.[3] It is a prayer by Jesus in the minutes before his arrest. In it he prays for his disciples and for those who believe in him because of the testimony of his disciples. The prayer is all-embracing. It begins with prayer for himself, affirming God's authority and his own over the entirety of the creation. It embraces all things and all people, overwhelming every boundary that could exist in the human mind. Jesus prays in this section for the completion of all he is doing as a demonstration of God's glory (vv. 1-5). In the second section he prays for his disciples and their purpose. He prays for their resourcing and for their protection as they carry on the work of Jesus (vv. 6-19). In the last and climactic section (vv. 20-26), Jesus prays for those who will believe through the testimony of his disciples. The theme is the union of all things with God in love, and of the unity of all those who desire God in that unity in love. The vision is breathtaking, impossible to absorb in all its depth and beauty. Described utterly inadequately (who could describe it adequately?), it sees a new humanity abounding in diversity in a world conformed to the love of God and seeking and desiring God with every part of human existence and every last ounce of strength.

In 20.19-23, Jesus comes to the disciples after his resurrection, and in verse 23 he breathes the Holy Spirit of God into them. The Spirit is their equipping to carry on the work of testifying to Jesus, of transforming the world, of cooperating with God in the work of reconciliation of all things.

This sense of the Church (the people of God through time and space) being equipped to become what they are called to be and to carry out the works of God is one that sets a pattern for the whole way in which we treat each other.

It is a vision that is to be a foundation of a new heaven and new earth, where truth, peace and justice reign and all creation rejoices a unity that is made more wonderful by holding together such diversity.

The vision is collective, not individualistic. The prayer and the gift of the Spirit is for all who believe in the name of Jesus, not for all those who believe AND qualify in some other way. God's resourcing is gracious, generous, abundant, overwhelming and transforming. The gift of the Spirit breathes into the receiver the sense of the parenthood of God by adoption. The Holy Spirit creates a new people described in Peter's first letter (2.9-11, NRSV) as 'a chosen race, a royal priesthood, a holy nation, God's own people'. The church is to be a global nation without arms, borders or police, united in love, called by grace, living in peace with all, sent to do the work of God.

This is a vision of complete reconciliation that will take all of human history to reach. It is also a process of equipping those on the journey to travel, to be renewed in their determination and vision and to take responsibility for what they do. God does not give us the option of leaving it all to God in a quietist or fatalistic way, nor does God leave disciples without the necessary means to do the work of being those through whom reconciliation flows to all, and who find the reconciling work of the Holy Spirit already at work.

For facilitators the greatest temptation is to seek the buzz of being needed and to pursue it by moments of high drama and not through the long, undramatic, grassroots work that is of the essence of peacebuilding. For those in senior positions, drama is the way to the possibility of prizes and recognition. Resourcing is about stepping back in a way that enables the journey to go on and grow and deepen in effect and skill and develop its own character, entirely without the presence of the facilitator. Best of all will be when those who are involved in a reconciliation process become peacebuilding facilitators themselves, take the skills they have learned and adapted, and, in their turn, give them away repeatedly.

This process of gift, and the quiet withdrawal, should be almost invisible.

For resourcing to happen, it must be a genuine objective of the facilitators, yet at any level of dispute involving a process of reconciliation, there is a temptation to remain and control, and, with the parties in the dispute, a desire to keep someone else around, if only to blame them for difficulties and to avoid responsibility.

One of the most obvious areas for such dependency is in marital or relationship disputes. Reconciliation can only work when the couple have decided to make it work, when they are clear that they want success in reconciliation, but they may feel that the only safe place for discussion of the most sensitive areas is with a relationship counsellor whom they know. That is fine for a while, but in the end, reconciliation cannot be said to be making serious progress until they are able to handle difficult discussions routinely by themselves.

At the other extreme end of conflict, the presence of UN forces as peacekeepers is both a support and resource, but the sign of serious progress in reconciliation is their withdrawal. In places like the Democratic Republic of the Congo they can become part of the problem if they are there too long.

Reconciliation is a normal part of life. Most people deal with it unconsciously day by day without the slightest need for advice or support. It is made up of apology, of good manners, of letters to clarify and explain, of telephone calls to settle a sense of unease. Sometimes it needs a cup of coffee to clear the air, but mostly we are unaware that we are reconciling; it seems that all we are doing is listening, deepening friendships, helping, hanging out together, sorting things out. It is perhaps over-simplistic, but the list in this paragraph could be called Researching, Relating, Relieving, Risking, Reconciling.

However, when relationships break down seriously between individuals or groups, then we find out whether our relational DNA inclines us towards destructive conflict or towards reconciliation. Where we have grown up and been formed in an aggressive and conflictual style, it is often the case that we lose the capacity to make agreements that work for all, to oil the friction points between groups, to heal hurts and defuse resentments and desires for revenge.

In the days when I was still in the oil industry, I remember one company that appeared incapable of having a discussion without aggression. They were an enormous organization and dominated by a culture that had formed the character of their employees and that went back to the 1920s. On one occasion, I asked someone with whom I had been negotiating why they behaved in such a way. His answer was one of surprise that I had noticed: 'I thought everyone did. It's the way we are trained.' Not only did he behave that way, but he assumed it was the way the world works and should work. The result was that as a company they had more expensive and time-wasting litigation than most of the rest of us combined.

The Coventry Way

The aim of Resourcing is to begin a culture of reconciliation and leave it with the potential to become the natural way of handling things. That is transformation and it is also transformative for the people involved.

Coventry Cathedral, as I wrote earlier, is a worldwide symbol of reconciliation through the message of its rebuilding, the genius of its architecture and sacred art, and its continuing ministry as a place for training and developing in reconciliation. Yet, like all institutions, it has many ways to have arguments and for people to disagree very strongly with each other – that is because it has human beings attending and participating in its ministry.

Very early in its life after rebuilding, one of the clergy staff sought to address the issue with a structure of groups and of spirituality. That was updated in 2005 as the Coventry Way.[4] It suggests a spirituality of reconciliation based on three concentric circles of relationship, widening out like the ripples of a pond.

Each circle is divided into sub-sections. They are typically about how we learn to deal with different aspects of living in reconciliation, and they vary in each of the three circles.

The **first circle** is about personal spiritual life.

It starts with prayer and scripture. This part is about reconciliation with oneself, the recognition that in Christ we are forgiven, born again and able to begin to live his resurrection life. That involves the hardest reconciliation of all, the acceptance of who one is, the recognition of and repentance and reparation for sins – where possible – and the freedom that comes with the complete forgiveness of

God. It grows in us through our encounter with God in all the intimacy of solitude.

The second part of the first circle is study. Since the time of St Benedict in the sixth century CE it has been understood that Christians need to think long and hard, and to learn from others. For Benedict and the monasteries that obviously involved books and manuscripts; today it will be podcasts, films, TED talks and many other ways of learning and growing in faith through the testimony and understanding of others.

The third part of the first circle is in what the original writers called the Foyer. A foyer in this context is a small group meeting in homes for hospitality, deeper learning and walking together, the practice of extended community, prayer and the study of scripture. These groups must be diverse, for it is unity in diversity that is sought in reconciliation, not unity in identical ideas. The foyers are and should be places of challenge.

The fourth part of the first circle is that of the church congregation, of worship and life together as the body of Christ in a locality or an institution, cathedral, parish, chaplaincy or other local Christian gathering. Relationships will be more distant in any larger church, even of over thirty or so people. Yet this is where it is easy to settle into cliques of the like-minded, identifying most strongly with those with whom one agrees on everything important, even if the most important agreement is one's disagreement with another group. It is important to note that the intimacy and trustful openness of the first two circles is very unlikely to be achieved in a larger group. However, this fourth part is essential for the learning of reconciliation, of love-in-action beyond the natural group of intimates or even of the often hard-earned intimacy of the foyer.

The four parts build on one another. Those who cannot accept that they are loved and forgiven by God (itself a long and progressive journey of reconciliation, but where starting opens the way to transformation), and in that security face the consequences of their sin and deal with it, are unlikely to find it easy or even possible to deal with others in a small group. Those who cannot cross boundaries in a small group will cling to the security of the familiar in the larger circle and exclude others.

The fifth part of the first circle is where the Church reaches out into society through its membership. This will typically mean in the sort of place that Archbishop William Temple described as intermediate institutions.[5] They may be schools, clubs, places of work, almost anything that comes between the central state and the individual or household. The outreach of the Church in such places and institutions is part of normal life. Christians live in retirement homes, or go to work somewhere, or meet others. Here is where the reconciled person who has grown to be a reconciler begins to find themselves encountering disputes and conflict. In the first circle we are called to allow ourselves to be known to be Christians, and in life and love to demonstrate the transforming work of Christ in our lives.

The **second circle** focuses on the way in which a local worshipping community builds up and encourages habits of reconciliation within itself and its life in the world. In this circle the community is called to consider its role in God's world. It is to be a community that is outward-looking locally and globally. It should pray for issues around the world as well as down the street. It should speak and campaign for the common good of its area, and join in the call for justice around the world.

The community should do all these things out of the overflow of the love of Christ, so its own internal reconciliation, worship and prayer life is essential to its lived-out love for those who encounter the community. It will be local as well as global. It is easy to speak clearly about issues over which one has no control and from which there is no fear of retaliation. It will self-audit as to its own standards of justice and listen to its own voiceless, those within its own life who are overlooked and ignored. Depending on the context they may be children and young people, or older people. Often they will be those with a more liberal or more conservative theological, social or political view than the fashion. It may be a group that challenges accepted behaviour and power structures. Essentially, this is where 'love one another' is made real, and it is often very tough. It must pay a living wage to its staff, safeguard the vulnerable and be conscious of exclusions and of imbalances of power.

The local community of worship is the very heart of the work of reconciliation. If it is not active in this way, no one else has the capacity to stand in for it. There is no Plan B.

The **third circle** is about engagement with the world around. From the first circle being the individual, to the second being the worshipping community, the third looks entirely outwards. It is here that a community of reconciled reconcilers, who deal with issues inside their own institution, equip each other to be active in reconciliation wherever their daily lives take them.

Once again, the ministry of reconciliation will start with prayer, but as suggested in Chapter 6 on Relieving, it will develop quickly into the formation of partnerships. Study and research will have revealed local and regional needs, and global prayer and the connections built to pray more knowledgably, through websites and other ways, will mean that different people in the community and in the group of communities that is the wider Church, in partnership with all of goodwill, of all faiths and none, will lead to deep and passionate concern to see transformation in God's world.

One of the greatest examples of such engagement was in South Africa with the fall of the Apartheid regime. The Coventry Cathedral-linked Communities of the Cross of Nails (CCN) were involved, the leadership was interfaith, the basis was seen in the moral standing of President Mandela and Archbishop Desmond Tutu, and all sorts of people around the world were drawn in. The image of the Rainbow Nation grew out of spiritual vision, the avoidance of civil war out of Truth and Reconciliation work, and the outcome continues to be messy, unsatisfactory, but better than it could have been. This is paradigmatic reconciliation work.

It sounds idealized but the examples are numerous. In each of them reconciliation is practised in different ways through the engagement of a worshipping community with areas of need that lead to alienation from society or the embedding of deep structures and powers of injustice and thus division.

Since the financial crash of 2008–09 and the very deep economic recession that followed in the UK, churches have gone into partnership to provide shelter for those sleeping rough. Seven churches will get together during the winter months in order for each one to do so one night a week.

Churches and other groups have also partnered together in providing food banks for those referred to them. Provision is often done through national organizations like the Trussell Trust, which ensures learning and development of best practice.

In many towns and cities, churches have got together to provide night-time patrols on Fridays and Saturday to provide care for those in the night-time scene at clubs and pubs, ensuring their safety, defusing trouble and caring for those who have taken too much of one substance or another. Street Pastors has become a national movement and the police are open and affirming about the reduction in crime and incidents where street pastors are operating.

At a national and international level, reconciliation hubs have set up more local centres to bring groups together, particularly around gang- or militia-controlled areas, and to help broker better ways of life. They have campaigned for nuclear disarmament, as part of protests against economic injustice or racial injustice, and above all in the area of climate change, especially at the major conferences.

At a national level, the Church of England is involved in a project called /together, which seeks, in many different ways, to challenge the deep differences that have grown up in society over the last decade or so. Almost forty different organizations are involved at a variety of points, including polling groups, media, the NHS, and many others. Events may be local or national, but in all cases, they are based around careful research and an effort to reimagine a future with more capacity to disagree well.

The /together project is in many ways the heart of reconciliation and illustrates the model set out in Part II of this book.

It is based on very extensive research, which continues, with large numbers of consultations on the views people of the UK have on what holds society together and where and how serious the divisions are.

It is aimed at deepening relationships at every level from the steering group to the local.

It is based around relieving needs in many ways, especially through existing work of those involved, which covers nearly every aspect of life, and on working in partnerships, avoiding any attempt to reinvent the wheel.

It does not impose views but seeks to take the risk of events and gatherings where relationships are developed, and that may fail.

It is a very long-term process of seeking unity in diversity, of fostering national reconciliation not by overcoming differences of opinion such as Brexit or nationalism, but by changing the way in which disagreements are negotiated.

It is at an early stage of looking at how to resource the way in which we look at difference.

When it comes to the most global of all required reconciliations, of human beings with the natural environment, there is not the time to take generations. Change must happen quickly, certainly by 2030 in terms of policy and some severe action. By 2050 there must be a decisive fall to near net-zero carbon emissions to avoid the climate change that will drive severe and damaging effects on weather generally. Habitability of coastal and of tropical areas in particular will be compromised and will become a driver of many other conflicts as a result of people movements.

The obstacles to the necessary steps are formidable. While most countries admit the problem, the capacity of political elites to lead on a solution appears to be nominal at best. It appears that little will be done if the short-term political cost is high. Here there is a need for internationally approved leadership that can continue not merely to advocate but to advance negotiations at speed. In addition, research needs to continue on necessary costs and a fair balance of burden sharing agreed.

These are uniquely demanding tasks, and it is difficult to see who will lead them. Outside Hollywood films there is no single nation that will save the world, nor is there, rightly, any appetite for such. Countries value their national history and autonomy, often achieved with great struggle. Even if the right leadership can be found, the task of potential mediation is vast. Here we see that the Risking is the point at which there is a danger of the global process being blocked, not by lack of Research, but by inadequate Relating so that love-in-action is missing and thus Risks are too big to contemplate.

The blockage is only resolvable by general political agreement on principles and commitment of political capital now for the generations yet unborn. The prize is a legacy of gratitude for centuries, but much struggle and political cost today.

These conflicts are open to reconciliation, but only with profound commitment politically and a foreswearing of seeking temporary advantage from them. There are many spoilers whose interests are against any reconciliation at all. The mood must change, and that is essentially a grassroots issue. Part III will carry the move from the theory of Part I through the principles of Part II to a grassroots resource for individuals and groups.

SUMMARY

- Resourcing reconciliation means providing the means for those in conflict to be persistent in seeking a way forward.
- In Christian thinking the purpose of God in creating the Church was to have a body that represented and carried on the work of Jesus of reconciliation with God, with creation and with other people.
- The Church and the world are energized and resourced by the gift of God's Holy Spirit, changing hearts, renewing hope, giving strength.
- The divine pattern of reconciliation, as well as a sense of human weakness and forgetfulness of the pain of conflict, leads to the need for deep works of reconciliation to be resourced, perhaps for generations.
- Resourcing involves facilitators being willing to give away their skills, to render themselves superfluous and to fade away, leaving the participants in a conflict who have begun the journey of reconciliation to develop the process in their own way, to add to the skills they have received and themselves to facilitate others.
- For that to happen they must develop a culture, a DNA, of reconciliation. A Christian example, the Coventry Way, is given. Every place, religion, culture will develop its own pattern. At the heart of the Coventry Way are principles of locality, of renewal, of practice in safe settings and of a commitment to going out.

Points to Ponder

- What are your memories of serious and violent conflict like war? Are they first-hand or through friends and relatives? Does it seem to you a distant memory or a recent event?
- How will you pass on to future generations the ideals of peace?
- Within your own circles and organizations or voluntary bodies of which you are a part, do you seek to cross boundaries or stick with those you get on with easily? This is not suggesting that natural friendship groups or common interests are wrong. It is asking where and when – if at all – you form links across boundaries.
- What are the natural boundaries for you? Race or tribe? Age? Social background? Work type and interests? Other things; if so what?
- What are the resources and skills you need to make the effort to form close relationships across natural boundaries?
- Do you know any institution, faith-based or other, that challenges you to make the considerable effort to work at reconciliation?

A Case Study

A couple of years have passed. St Thomas is a better place, the community is stronger but still very fragile. What resources does it need in all the different areas in order to keep going? How can it celebrate progress and the journey still be completed?

PART III

INTRODUCTION

Part I of this book was a meditation on the mystery of reconciliation, asking the question, 'What is it and why is it so difficult to achieve?' Part II looked at a very generalized but practical pattern for approaching issues of reconciliation. This part is the shortest and asks the question, 'What can I do about it?'

The book now seeks to complete the move from the theoretical to the highly practical.

Chapters 10–12 look at the *Difference Course*. *Difference* was first piloted in 2019 and its fifth iteration was published in September 2020. It was designed by the reconciliation team at Lambeth Palace.

The reasons I am focusing on *Difference* are, first, that it has had a very good response in its pilot and beta phases in the UK, South Africa, Hong Kong and the USA. Second, that it is simple, adaptable and down to earth. Third, that it is flexible and accessible. There are many courses of all sorts, but this is the one I know best. I did the course afresh myself, during preparation for writing this book.

Any theoretical structure for reconciliation must answer some questions:

- 'How do I/we start?'
- 'What is a facilitator or reconciler like?'

- 'How do I develop attitudes that make me better at it?'
- 'What difference might this make to me, my household, my group, my church or workplace?'

Difference is a beginning of an answer to those questions.

10

Difference Should Make Us Curious

The *Difference Course* ('the Course', or *Difference*[1]) is designed in its first form for churches. Its aim is enabling people to think for themselves about their attitude to those who are considered by the individual or society at large to be other. As time goes by it will be rolled out in adapted form for secular, other faith and interfaith groups, and in more culturally appropriate ways around the world.

The Reality of the Other

Our capacity to deal with difference is probably no less than it ever was, in many ways it is much better, but the scale of the challenge now appears vast as it is magnified by social media. However, our capacity to do so privately has gone downhill. At a recent Church of England meeting there was discussion about a phrase used by someone in a lecture that could be understood to imply that clergy were unnecessary. People phrase things badly the whole time. I should know as I do it myself. There are a number of rules for dealing with it that used to apply. The first was to ask yourself, 'Did she/he really mean something so bizarre?' and assume the best rather than the worst. The second is that one used to tell the speaker privately what one thought, get it off one's chest and move on. Now people tell the world via social media. Instantly.

There is nothing new about dispute; what is new is the capacity to globalize it. A Convocation (the ancient gathering of clergy and bishops in the Province of either Canterbury or York) in 1689 went on for months, so bitter was the wrangling. But they did not have social media, which was a mercy.

The challenge of dealing with outsiders, or those within the group one belongs to whom one makes outsiders through disagreement, extends around the globe, through much of the natural world, and is not restricted to recent years and issues of racism. It is so much part of being human that for many people it is taken as a virtue, or at least a reality that cannot be challenged. 'They're not like us' is very often a sufficient explanation for antipathy towards incomers.

When I was a parish priest, the wonderful and wonderfully dry-humoured parish clerk said to me once, 'You're not really local until your grandparents are in the churchyard.' I must have looked nonplussed because she went on, 'But you're all right. You may just have arrived as Justin, but as Rector you have been here for 750 years.' It was certainly the way it worked. Dates were sometimes set by reference to when Rector x was here, rather like the time of particular Consuls of the ancient Roman republic were the means of remembering a year.

The point was insiders and outsiders.

On a larger scale, the Church of England has its own gangs. They go by more sophisticated names, such as Evangelical or Traditional Catholic, or Liberal Catholic or Charismatic. There are ways in which one fits into the tribe. Many of these will be very friendly to other tribes, but they are still tribes. One training course run by the Church of England had good reviews, which included the comment from several participants that it was the first time they had worked with Anglicans from a different tradition.

To a large extent such diversity does not do much harm on the surface, and the historic reasons for it is important as well as the fact that each tradition brings value to the Church, but the underlying problem can be a deep sense of competition for control of it. The question often being asked is whether 'they' – whoever they are – obtain more senior appointments and greater control of things. At the extremes it becomes about unchurching people, treating them as outsiders entirely. At that point it becomes even more like political parties and less like the people of God.

Move a step further to political life in the public square and the problem becomes more complicated, and in recent years more damaging. Again, it's an old reality. In *Iolanthe* Act II, a late nineteenth-century comic opera by Gilbert and Sullivan, a sentry on duty during the night at the Houses of Parliament sings,

I often think it's comical – Fal, lal, la!
How Nature always does contrive – Fal, lal, la!
That every boy and every gal
That's born into the world alive
Is either a little Liberal
Or else a little Conservative!

Today we would have to write socialist rather than Liberal, as Labour would not scan, but the reality of the two-party system in England (and the USA) still exists as firmly as ever. Again, the different views are not a problem – but the hatred of one for the other can be.

In 2021 my mother, in her nineties, was admitted to hospital in London. The care she received was wonderful. But when I arrived to see her, she was cross. The excellent Nigerian doctor who had cared for her was told by another patient that she wanted to be seen by an English (i.e. in her mind, White) doctor. Both my mother and I said how sorry and ashamed we were. The doctor took it in his stride. He was highly qualified, patient in attitude, caring in his values. Why would anyone prefer delayed treatment to being treated by him purely on account of his colour? The answer was simply that he was 'other'. If we are easily capable of othering those we see and know – even those we need – how much more easily do we do so for foreigners far away? Asylum seekers, refugees, people in far-off countries of which we know little[2] – all are easily forgotten and ignored.

The list can go on and get broader. Racism, factionalism and other ethnic differences remain among the most pervasive, most deadly and most challenging forms of othering. It may be regions of a country that refuse to let 'settlers' from another part of the same country attend university for both religious and ethnic reasons. In another democracy it may be steps taken to make voting more difficult or to gerrymander constituencies so as to pack all the opposition voters into a smaller number of seats. Either way the othering leads to attacks on human dignity.

It is the slide downwards from recognizing difference to fearing and then hating those who are different that becomes the corrosion that destroys a community or society. The call of Christ is revolutionary in this regard. It is to love God with everything we are. Second, we are then to love one another, those who are 'one of us'. Third, we are to love our neighbours, those with whom we have the common connection of humanity. Fourth, we are to love our enemies.

The revolution goes further than that. We are to love others more than we love our lives. Neighbour is redefined in the Parable of the Good Samaritan (Luke 10.25-37) to be those whose need we see regardless of their otherness. In other words, the Christian community is called to turn away from all hatred. The capacity of Christians to love like this, when it is carried out, is so radical that it reveals the reality that Jesus Christ is God, coming from the Father (John 17.21). The global Church, should it learn so to love amid all the realities of rivalry and distance and desire for power and influence, would turn the world the right way up.

In a book published in 2021, Gordon Brown,[3] the former UK prime minister, discusses global approaches to great problems that threaten large parts of humanity. Reasonably, the first chapter is about the COVID-19 pandemic. He points out that the return to the wealthy countries on money spent to enable a global response to the pandemic is almost US$5 for every dollar spent.[4] In other words, it is an immensely good investment. If someone offered me an investment like that, I would probably turn it down on the grounds it was too good to be true. But it is true. Why then do we not invest as much as we can rather than cutting back on overseas aid? The return would pay the aid budget for years.

The answer is that it is always more difficult to feel a concern for those further away, and that the larger the group of which we speak the more we become consequentialist (what are the outcomes) and even indifferent to moral obligations. The late Rabbi Lord Jonathan Sacks, in his last book, *Morality*,[5] makes this point powerfully. He puts it in a moral context where the moral obligation reaches beyond ourselves and 'home' – as in 'charity begins at ...' – to the common good.

The first step in responsibility for others and thus participation in reconciliation is thus the question of distance, which is effectively where *Difference* starts.

The key response to distance and consequent lack of concern is *curiosity*. Whether it is our neighbour next door who comes from a very different background, the people moving into a new estate on what was the edge of town, immigration pressures or a foreign war, our curiosity is easier to engage nowadays because of good information and it offers a way of shrinking distance.

When encountering those who are other, the most important foundation for overcoming the sense of distance that comes from them being new or different is to listen to their story. The impact of story on who we are is huge. History is not destiny, but it is certainly very influential. The questions about behaviour or attitudes are answered not by seeking to know 'What's wrong with you?', but by the much more open question: 'What is your story; what has happened to you?'

A close relative of ours was a police officer. She was on a call with other officers to deal with a situation of an asylum seeker behaving oddly. He had crawled under a

bed and was resisting all attempts to get him out. She lay
down so he could see her and asked him about himself,
his faith and his history. It turned out later that he had
been arrested in his home country and severely tortured
by the police there. The sight of police uniforms triggered
a reaction. Telling the story enabled the police here to
understand and see him as someone who had been a
victim of abuse, not a problem.

Being curious brings people nearer as we begin to
engage with them in order to understand their concerns
and their priorities. Far more than that, it puts them in
the category of those whose good we seek.

In the Old Testament in the Book of the Exodus, the
Israelites are settled in Egypt where they have been for
generations. Having originally gone down from Canaan
in order to avoid a famine, they had been welcomed and
settled through the agency of Joseph, who ruled Egypt
for the then Pharaoh. Exodus 1.8 starts a new part of the
story, saying: 'Now a new king arose over Egypt, who did
not know Joseph.' The Pharaoh looks at the strength and
numbers and prosperity of the people of Israel and sees
them as a threat. To be ignorant of a person or a group
is to leave space for fear. In some cases, knowledge may
justify fear, but in almost all circumstances it reduces it
and makes space for reconciliation.

The result of the ignorance of Pharaoh is, first,
oppression of the Israelites, the long-standing descendants
of economic immigrants; second, their ill-treatment; and
third, outright war against both them and God. Ignorance
settles us into hostility.

Exodus is the story of the liberation of God's people
by God's supreme power. Reading other texts alongside
Exodus, Egypt becomes the symbol of several aspects

of Israelite existence. It is the place of slavery. It is the place of refuge, as with Jesus himself as an infant. It is a place of betrayal, a hope for Israel when oppressed by others, but a hope that always fails, as with the exile when Egypt's help is sought against Babylon, but Egypt does not deliver. Egypt contrasts with God, who is trustworthy and faithful, the place to turn for help. Finally, however, Egypt, like every other nation, will be called faithfully to turn to God in repentance and obedience.

All these stories are the stories of Israel. They define who they are, and thus how they are known, by the stories they tell about themselves. To keep them faithful they recount the story of the Exodus at the Passover. They are to teach their children, who are to be curious. In being curious they will meet the greatest 'other' that exists, God, and in knowing the story of God with God's people they will hear the call to turn to God and be faithful.

The greatest reconciliation is between human beings and God. God is revealed in God's story, through the life of Jesus Christ. Being curious is not just a means of overcoming ignorance and thus fear; it is the means of discovering the depths of love that are possible across difference.

The *Difference Course* applies the habit of being curious in five sessions, as with the other two habits of being present and reimagining.

The first session is about God's command to be peacebuilders and reconcilers. How does our being curious show itself overall in our ways of living? Where do we get information from? Is it only one source or does it include those with whom we disagree?

I listen to podcasts and read publications that make me feel good because they agree with me and say that what I am doing is right – well, I have never found one of those, but one day, somewhere? – but I also read things or listen to podcasts that keep my blood pressure up, at least metaphorically. I look for intelligent criticism, out of curiosity about the views that I do not currently accept. Over time some of them change my views. I also try to mix with a variety of people who have very different views and to listen carefully.

We are all aware that the tendency of social media is to draw us into bubbles of the like-minded. Many people will know the somewhat illicit satisfaction emotionally that comes from hearing a good speaker telling them how right they are and how wrong their opponents are. Its known as preaching to the choir.

One of the most striking features of the debates around sex and gender and transgender is that, according to some, to disagree is not only to be wrong, but to be evil. Similarly, the questions about the levels of racism in the UK institutionally lead not merely to very robust debate, but to death threats and profound abuse of the individuals concerned.

The stirring-up effect of social media is critical in this area. Try doing an audit of those you follow on social media, of the podcasts to which you listen, of those you follow on Instagram, TikTok and all the other forms of media that spring up and die down. What proportion are those with whom you disagree?

The second session of *Differences* is called 'Crossing Divides'. There are, speaking as a clergyman, certain ways of encouraging a congregation to take a Sunday off church. One is to announce that you are going to preach on giving. Another is to share a service with a different church, or to do a pulpit swap. There is nothing malicious about people being away; they like what they know, the familiar.

In John 4.1-30 we read how Jesus met and talked with a Samaritan woman at a well in Samaria. That encounter shocked his followers as he crossed gender and ethnic boundaries. He demonstrated the spiritual insights of curiosity-in-loving-action, which is far different from nosiness. It was a curiosity that spoke to her of hope and a future, of a better life than she had known and of one that could be lived by her whole village. Yet the first step for Jesus was to ask for a drink of water.

Where are the places that offer the chance to cross boundaries? It may be a local meeting of the Council of Christians and Jews. It could be visiting another church. A friend in the USA was aware of Dr Martin Luther King saying that Sunday morning is the most segregated two hours of the week in America because Christians all go to churches full of people like themselves. He therefore visited all the churches in his part of Virginia, of all denominations and all ethnicities. At the Black Pentecostal churches, he was very warmly welcomed. His own church was Episcopalian and very White. He tried, mostly unsuccessfully, to get the ministers to visit other churches, and then members of the congregations. Yet they all felt it would not be safe, and that they preferred to be where they had always been, not hating each other but not in unity-within-diversity either.

We are commanded to cross divides because you cannot build bridges without being on both sides of a divide. We are commanded to be boundary breakers, because you cannot bring reconciliation without crossing boundaries.

The third session is on disagreeing well. 'Disagreeing well' is a controversial phrase. Shortly after I used it for the first time (I have no doubt it does not come from me in the first place, but I picked it up somewhere), I was firmly criticized on the grounds that Christians should not disagree. To which my answer is, 'But they do! Incessantly! And who says they should not?'

Paul is always dealing with disagreements in churches to which he was writing; look at 1 Corinthians 1, Romans 12-15, and the stories about Paul personally (e.g. Acts of the Apostles 15.36-41, but cf. 2 Timothy 4.11). He tells the church to be of one mind or to have the same mind in Philippians 2.2, but the context is to avoid destructive divisions of jealousy and anger.

Disagreeing well requires being curious about the real thinking of the person with whom you disagree. Instead of trolling, or cutting off contact, or ignoring and effectively cancelling, it is worth asking, 'Please would you explain your reasons for what you think?'

The fourth session concerns practising forgiveness. All Christians are called to be forgiven forgivers, reconciled reconcilers. In the way that a doctor practises in their identity as a doctor so should we practise in our identity as forgiven forgivers. At the same time, we are generally very bad at it and thus practice is important in every part of life.

One of the schools that our children attended taught the very small pupils to say sorry when they had fallen out and then for the wronged one to say, 'I forgive you.' It spread, with some difficulty, into our family. Forgiveness is harder to give and receive than apologizing, saying sorry.

Sorry is a powerful weapon of passive aggression. It is also a well-established way of conceding with a non-concession. In a satirical political sketch, one of the leading politicians says words to the effect of, 'If you feel offended by my accusing you of fraud and treason, then I am sorry.' A genuine apology would be: 'I accused you of fraud and treason, I was wrong. Please forgive me.' Yet the 'non-apology apology' is the most frequently used. Anything that begins with 'if' and puts the blame for being offended on the victim is a non-apology. Anything that leaves the more vulnerable trapped into being manipulated towards forgiveness is not an apology.

Forgiveness is one of the toughest parts of reconciliation. It is often manipulated and usually misunderstood.

The manipulation comes, as I have said, through putting the pressure on the victim. For example, with regard to the need for racial and ethnic reconciliation in the UK there is often the explicit or implicit suggestion that Black people should forgive so that we can all move on. In the safeguarding of children and vulnerable adults, perpetrators have piled abuse upon abuse by requiring forgiveness or by using sacraments such as the confessional and saying that the victim/survivor is required to keep it secret. In a recent case the survivor was told that the perpetrator had sought the forgiveness of God and therefore the survivor must treat it as past. That is a blasphemous misuse of forgiveness by the perpetrator.

In these and many other ways the notion of forgiveness is distorted and the most precious of gifts, the greatest treasure, is soiled in the hands of the manipulators.

God calls us to be forgiven forgivers. Forgiveness is, however, not the same as forgetting the consequences. We can forgive someone who still is sent to prison for a crime against us. The indescribably awful national sins committed through slavery, through Empire and in war, by many nations, may by grace and goodness be forgiven by those who are the descendants of the victims and whose lives are still affected by what happened, directly and indirectly. Yet the offer of forgiveness is not the same as waiving justice. It will still be necessary to show repentance and make reparation, not to earn forgiveness but as a real sign of a change of heart. As I wrote earlier, actions, even of those long before us, have consequences. That is part of what the great Conservative political philosopher Edmund Burke[6] meant by his speaking of the social contract as a covenant with those who have lived, those who are alive today and those who are yet to be born.

To be curious opens the way to practise forgiveness. It is to enquire into the state of mind of a perpetrator, to seek to understand their thinking, to sense their guilt and desire for change. It is also to understand one's own feelings. I know the desire, when I have suffered wrongly, for the perpetrator to be made to regret deeply how wrongly they have acted. I wanted them to feel what I felt. It took time to set that aside, to battle with God in prayer in order to see my anger and to find his love. Psalm 137 speaks of the Jewish exiles in Babylon cursing their captors who saw them as entertainment: the exiles wanted their enslavers to see their own children murdered as they had murdered the children of Jerusalem. I have sat with Christian leaders in the ruins of their town by the mass graves of their families listening to them speak of their inescapable pain and desire for revenge.

The Quentin Tarantino film *Django Unchained* (2012) is a revenge story, full of blood and violence. Although the escaped slave Django kills many, one cannot help but empathize with his anger at the cruelty of his White oppressors. To be curious is not to reject justice. To be curious must mean that one seeks to enter the feelings of those who suffer and those who oppress, while also seeking justice. Archbishop Desmond Tutu was a passionate advocate of the oppressed, but sought to love their oppressors so that they might see their wrongdoing. He was never neutral between perpetrator and victim, but neither was he consumed with a desire for revenge.

Forgiveness frees the victim from the chains of hatred. It enables the victim to seek justice and campaign for righteousness. It is a liberation, it is a gift to us from God, but it is never a tool with which to oppress further the already oppressed, the abused, the weak and the vulnerable. It is a key to freedom, not a club for the powerful to impose settlement.

The final session of *Difference* is about hope. It is called 'Risking Hope' because it sets hope clearly in the context of offers made and expectations arrived at, but with the risk of neither being fulfilled.

As the epistle to the Romans says in 5.5: 'hope does not disappoint us because God's love has been poured into our hearts through the Holy Spirit that has been given to us'. The *Difference Course* says: 'we need to know that we are called to be part of God's story of restoration in the world'.[7] In C. S. Lewis's book *The Great Divorce*, hell is full of those without hope and with regrets, and heaven is a place of ever-growing joy in an ever-greater place, journeying together in forgiveness and hope to an ultimate destination. The journey begins in pain, with the reality of heaven making even grass as sharp as glass, but eases as progress is made. Lewis paints a similar picture in the final part of his Narnia Chronicles, *The Last Battle*.

Hope is, however, often unexpressed and in short supply. To be curious is to ask yourself about your own hopes and to ask your community about theirs. The curiosity will be fed by the act of crossing boundaries, of practising forgiveness, of disagreeing well. All these build community and communities are built to grow on hope. Churchill's speeches in 1940 were great for many reasons, but chief among them was that they gave hope. His capacity for great errors was huge, but his capacity for inspiring hope was even greater. In any community, reconciliation will be strengthened by hope, but hope must be made known, declared and owned.

SUMMARY

- The first of the key habits of reconciliation is curiosity, being curious.
- We need a lively but not busybody curiosity in order to build bridges and cross divides, so as to understand the stories of others.
- We need a curiosity that listens carefully to those with whom we disagree so that we may disagree well and be able to tell their story and put their argument as well as we can our own, even when we disagree.
- Being curious about our own feelings and the reality of the motivations of others will enable us to practise the hard work of forgiveness. Forgiveness is not the same as allowing injustice.
- We need to be curious about our own and others' hopes, so that in community we may grow in faith and love.

Points to ponder are to be found in the *Difference* resource and website.[8] The only one I will mention now is whether you know of a group that would like to try the *Difference Course* together.

11

Being Present

The temptation to save time by multi-tasking is hard to resist normally. Why not have the mobile on the kitchen table during family meals? Why not do emails during some kinds of conversation? When there is a telephone conference call, or even a video conference, if my laptop is below the camera's reach, do something else as well, it saves time later. And it's not only multi-tasking. Politicians in long and doubtless boring meetings are regularly caught playing games on a smart phone, or texting or using social media.

Yes, but ... It tells everyone that you are *not present*. It tells the family that the caller at a meal is more important than they are. It tells people they do not have your attention. Above all, it means that you are not listening properly, engaging creatively, exercising the double hearing of listening to the people you are meeting and to the Spirit of God. Love-in-action means being present, and being present is the second of the habits of the *Difference Course*.

It begins with theology. We should be present to others as a commitment of love because God was, is and always will be present as a commitment of love to us.

God sees and knows everything. The consistent celebration of the Psalms is that God sees, except in a very few psalms of lament and protest where the psalmist calls for him to look. That theme of lament and protest is also picked up in many modern theologians of the Global South. It is a theological theme that emerges from suffering and injustice. Yet the presence of God in the Old Testament and the New is seen as deeply dangerous. Where God is visible it is either in a form of possible incognito (as with Abraham before the condemnation of the cities of the plain, Genesis 18) or as a cause of fear (with Gideon, Judges 6.22; the calming of the storm in the New Testament; the announcement of the birth of Jesus to the shepherds; and many other places). God's presence is so awesome that it may lead to death. In the New Testament the coming of Jesus is God's presence in a way foretold through the Old Testament but drawing into God all that is human by taking on the form of a servant, fully human, and in that extraordinary mystery suffering with all human beings. Presence in the incarnation is presence to everything in life, and to death.

In John 14.16, Jesus promises his disciples that he will send the Holy Spirit to be present – a promise fulfilled after the resurrection – and to this day, in the gift of the Spirit of God, to make all alive in Christ and to carry on the creative and sustaining work of God in all the world and all of creation.

The Church – in the sense not of the institution but of the people who are Christians – makes many mistakes about the presence of God through the Spirit.

Too often we try and confine the Spirit to God's areas of work as *we* see them, as if God had a job description and we had to monitor it properly. At worst there is in some churches and traditions the sense that though God may be at work everywhere, God is especially at work in 'our congregation' or 'our church or denomination'. It will seldom be put like that, although I have heard it, but it is often implicit in the way certain groups speak. It is often a tool of control by manipulative church leaders, or a sign of a deep arrogance.

Slightly less bad, but still an implied caging of God the Spirit, is the sense that God is only at work in the Church universal and not outside it. There is a feeling that God would not want to be contaminated by dealing with people who are not like God, as if God did not have enough practice. It reveals itself in pietism, where involvement with the things of the world around us is wrong. It sees areas like reconciliation as only the real deal when they involve the Church. I remember being asked when I worked at Coventry Cathedral why I bothered with reconciliation involving people who were not Christians? Should I not be preaching the gospel to them? My answer now would be that I was preaching the gospel and that I worked in those circumstances and places, and still do, because when I get there I find God at work, and I join in to learn.

To put it less informally, the creative and sustaining work of God is revealed in Jesus Christ, the Prince of Peace. In Colossians 1.15-20 St Paul speaks of the cosmic Christ in whom 'all things hold together' (17, NRSV) and 'through Him God was pleased to reconcile all things, whether on earth or in heaven, by making peace through the blood of his cross' (20, NRSV). 'Everything', 'all things', the piling up of words indicates Paul's passionate proclamation of the truth of Christ. The human ministry of peacemaking is, consciously or unconsciously, worked out in the day to day, by human beings imperfectly and partly, seeking the glorious reconciliation of all things that is the purpose of God.

The presence of the peacemaking Christ is thus always and everywhere. The pleasure of God in reconciling all things (as in Colossians) is in a cosmic reconciliation, of all of creation, for God is the Creator. It is not just with human beings, or even this planet. Those who are involved in peacemaking, who are seeking or supporting reconciliation, have therefore to be present because God is present. Being present, as I admitted in starting this chapter, is often difficult.

As with being curious, the five sessions of *Difference* each have some thinking and challenge on the habit of being present.

God's Call

When I was training for ordination, I had a work placement with the chaplain of the local hospital. His main feedback was that I needed to learn to be more present with those I was visiting. I did not like hospitals. I was unsure of my role and found the process difficult, and it showed. He was quite right, and the lesson stuck in my mind. During the COVID-19 pandemic, during 2020 and 2021 I have had the privilege of supporting the superb senior chaplain at Guy's and St Thomas' Trust in London. This involved regular time spent in the hospital, with the critically ill in COVID-19 wards or others. I have tried to put the lesson of those many years ago into practice in this recent experience.

We all have encounters we do not like. For many people they involve confrontation, or difficult conversations.

Most of us will be familiar with the sinking feeling of waking in the morning, thinking through the day, and knowing that there will be an event or a meeting that we dread. It may not happen often, but we avoid it.

It is always easier to be with people you like and get on with naturally. One of the lessons that both my wife Caroline and I have had to learn in my role as Archbishop of Canterbury is how to work a room. That is, when there is a reception or gathering, to ensure that time is spent with everybody. It is a discipline because you always come across people with whom you want to chat. They may be old friends, and it is just easier. They may be complete strangers, but utterly fascinating.

Being present is a habit. It needs self-awareness like all habits. God's call is to be present across the range of people, to be not only present but a presence that people know and trust. *Difference* encourages us all to see who we choose not to mix with; how we use the opportunities to be present.

It is worth breaking down your time into those different aspects of life, like leisure, work, family, church, friends. You may be part of a club or sports group of some kind, or of an association that does things together. Who is avoided and who is easy to be with?

How we are present can be a very important sign of the health of significant relationships. Sometimes people will spend more time at the office or more time outside the home because their marriage is difficult. An audit of what we do and what we avoid doing will show us where the lights are flashing a warning. Absence is often not a way of making the heart grow fonder but of avoiding the reality of a heart that has grown less fond. Reconciliation requires being present.

CROSSING DIVIDES

Every year there is a service in a cathedral or major church for police officers who have died in service, whether in the line of duty or any other reason. The service rotates around the different nations and regions of the UK. One year it was at Liverpool Cathedral and the Prince of Wales attended, as he always does. After the service there was a reception for him with the families of officers who had died within twelve months. There were around a hundred and twenty present, with the most recently bereaved having lost a partner about three weeks earlier.

It was a deeply moving occasion. I was struck that the Prince was 'present' to each family he met as if they were the only ones there. I learned a great deal just watching. The impact of his interest, focus and compassion was healing for all.

It was not just because he is the Prince of Wales, although that was very significant. Added to that was the way in which he engaged. Being present is much more than physical. It means engaging the whole of oneself.

As was written earlier, 'remember the body'. In a hospital, where it is appropriate for the person, touch, holding a hand, matters greatly. The body's sense of touch is very significant both positively and negatively. Some people dislike personal space being invaded in that way, some who are isolated find it comforting and full of meaning.

Eyes are important. A person at St Thomas' was gravely ill in critical care. I remember above all their eyes. They had COVID-19, could not speak, were exhausted and quite possibly not far from the end of their life. But their eyes held mine and spoke volumes. Not only in those very extreme circumstances or those of someone bereaved, but also in mediation, the engagement of look and attention is significant of presence.

Of course, everything needs calibrating. When we meet someone for the first time, normally we do not want a deeply intense encounter. There are people I have met who fix me with their eyes and say, 'How are you really?' My normal answer is 'Fine, thank you', although sometimes I want to say (but never do), 'That's my affair.'

Being present can be just as simple as showing up. Look around at your neighbourhood, at other churches, at different religious communities. Find out what can be done together by going to be with them. Go to places and meet people you normally are distant from. Cross boundaries.

DISAGREEING WELL

Being present when bored in long meetings requires discipline. Being present when having a disagreement is another thing altogether; it requires courage.

There are many ways in which we seek to avoid being present in such circumstances. One is to be physically absent. I am aware of one colleague with whom I worked who always had a reason for being somewhere else when it was clear that there was going to be disagreement. It was always polite, always reasonable, and always happened. The result was too often that the can got kicked down the road and the disagreement, when it was properly faced, was much more difficult to deal with and often led to disagreeing badly.

The skills of facilitators and of mediators – they are not exactly the same thing – have an overlap in that they involve enabling those disagreeing to be present to each other and for the deepest reasons for the disagreement to be faced. As a result of these skills, the use of facilitation and mediation is growing so that some organizations almost never have a meeting without an outside leader.

That in its turn leads to another way of not being present: hiding behind the process of disagreeing well. To be truly present means to develop the skills of disagreeing and to do so without being defensive. We are all aware of having heard defensive answers to interviewers on current affairs programmes. A public figure leading an organization has acted badly themselves or the organization for which they are responsible has done so. Their answers to probing questions begin with explanation or with a negative. 'You don't understand' or similar phrases abound.

It is the same in disagreeing. We may be present physically, we may be curious, but our presence needs to be undefended. We are truly present when we listen and reflect on what is being said, when we enquire (being curious) to understand better.

It is a severe test. No one likes to say that they are wrong. Yet we will not disagree well unless the whole of us, including our vulnerabilities, is present.

PRACTISING FORGIVENESS

My own experience of forgiveness, forgiving and being forgiven is mixed and human. A severe wound from someone almost always leads to a desire to be away from them. The nature of relationship breakdown – whether with a friend, a lover, a spouse, child or parent – is above all one of absence. In my own childhood, like so many children I had the experience of a family where parents were not together and there was, in one household, much anger. The means of dealing with that complicated relationship as very much the weaker party was to withdraw emotionally, even when present.

So many of us do that. Cut our losses, sever the relationship, don't speak about the person any more.

Yet that understandable way of dealing with emotional pain as a child needs to be grown out of if we are to become whole adults. Forgiveness is a necessity for a functional society, however much it is a challenge for individuals. We must recognize – I have already discussed this but it bears repetition – that when encountering one person or a group that have been the victims of cruelty, sometimes on a vast scale, the imposition of an obligation to forgive can easily become more abuse.

Yet at a societal level there needs to be institutional presence. The habit for the powerful of being present to those who have suffered from their power is one essential component of developing into a society that is capable of forgiveness. The importance of being present and risking pain is an essential to arrive at a place that is honest about forgiveness and that gets past manipulation. Even more powerful is the presence of those who have suffered, who are so often not asked for permission for the powerful to be there, or the terms on which the powerful are there.

That sort of institutional presence is a severely endangered species. Presence may be very rare, for example, between police and groups like young Black people that want to challenge with a sense of victimization or between different groups who hold clashing views on the nature of the rights of transgender people. The lack of presence may be fear of confrontation, often based on past experience; it may even be the arrogance of power. Whatever the causes of not wanting to be present, those meetings, if presence is genuine, will have to take the chance of including space to ask for and to offer forgiveness for past wrongs. The alternative to presence is to remain in trenches lobbing social media grenades at each other to little or no effect.

RISKING HOPE

Being present is a huge risk. To be present implies hope, above all hope that progress can be made amid difficulty in relationships or in conflict. In Part II, Chapter 7 looked in some depth at the whole issue of risk, and especially the risks involved in meeting. To take those risks and then be physically but not properly present is a certain route to failure.

Yet to be present feels like betting everything on a very uncertain outcome. In John's Gospel, chapter 6, Jesus – among many other things – deals with being present. In the chapter there are two miracles, or signs in John's language: the feeding of the five thousand and walking on water. Jesus makes himself present to the crowd when the disciples want to avoid presence by sending them away to get food. He then absents himself from the crowd and his disciples when they seek to use their numbers to make him a king. Instead of being with them, he, like Moses on Sinai, goes up a mountain and is present with his Father, God. He comes to the disciples on the waters of the windy lake and remains with them (a key concept in John is remaining, staying). The crowd are seeking him, another key word, linked to presence. When he challenges them as to what they seek – are they genuinely present to him because he is the bread of life, or only as a high-value grocer with miraculous logistics? – they leave.

They will not be present on Jesus' terms but only on their own. Presence goes with curiosity, and as we will see, with reimagination. The crowd's presence is quite unlike that of Jesus' disciples. The crowd know what they want, and will only be present for what they want. Presence in that way avoids the risks of disappointment. It is not making oneself vulnerable, which true presence does.

Then Jesus turns to his disciples and asks them (vv. 67-69, NRSV): "'Do you also wish to go away?' Simon Peter answered him, 'Lord, to whom can we go? You have the words of eternal life. We have come to believe and know that you are the Holy One of God.'"

Jesus is challenging them to be present. Peter's response is to say, plaintively, that in Jesus is hope. They must be present with him because that is the risk to be taken for that hope to be fulfilled. They do not know what is going on, but they know that in Jesus is hope. In that way their presence is genuine; it commits to mutual relationships amid the fog of not knowing.

Summary

- Being present is an obvious habit to develop because no relationship can be built without it.
- To be genuinely present, especially with those with whom we disagree, is very difficult. We long to run away from the challenge.
- Being present at a shallow level is insufficient to build unity in diversity.
- Being present is something that happens with groups and institutions as well as individuals. It enables systemic reconciliation.

- The culture of avoiding those with whom we disagree is one that leads to more and more fracturing and less and less of an abundant life for everyone.
- Jesus was not afraid of being present, including to God. To be hopeful requires us to be present at greater depth, especially when our hope is in God.

POINTS TO PONDER

- In prayer are you present to God entirely, or only those bits of you that you think God will like?
- Are there a few simple rules you can set for yourself to be more present to family, friends and work colleagues or others? How does your use of electronic gadgets affect you being present?
- Are there people from whom you have drifted? What are the options to renew a mutual presence?
- Are you good or bad at difficult conversations? Can you decide to have them AND decide not to be defensive but to be present?

12

Reimagining

As we all know, the imagination works in bizarre ways. What we imagine in our sleep, as dreams, is wildly beyond anything we could imagine while awake. Some people have a disciplined, practical but unimaginative approach to challenges. Others have flights of fancy that are amazing but lack all capacity to turn them into reality. In most areas of life there are the occasional geniuses whose imaginations enable them to forge new directions in hopeless situations or new ideas in a time without ideas, and who also have the knowledge, skills and discipline to make it happen.

Examples abound throughout history. In recent times we can think of Captain Sullenberger landing a crippled aircraft on the Hudson River in New York without losing a single life. He had no engines, no height and no space, but he both imagined and performed the landing. We can think of J. K. Rowling imagining a world with witches and wizards who hide in plain sight and writing seven volumes of coherent narrative that grips people of every age and contains a profound morality. She imagined, but then she wrote something that makes sense in its own terms. We can think of Václav Havel, a political prisoner of the communist government of Czechoslovakia, or Nelson Mandela of South Africa, prisoner of the Apartheid regime, imagining freedom, gaining freedom without a collapse into civil war and then building a nation on a basis of seeking reconciliation. Of course, things went wrong, but skill and imagination kept them on course as long as they were alive.

The list is endless. We can list names like St Hildegard of Bingen correcting and challenging emperors in the Europe of the Middle Ages, Elizabeth I, Jane Austen, Florence Nightingale, Churchill, or Washington, or Augustine of Hippo. It goes back to Homer, Dido, Cleopatra, Aristotle. Athletes like Jesse Owens at the 1936 Olympics, Lewis Hamilton in motorsport, Emma Raducanu at the 2021 US Tennis Open, are all a mix of ambition, determination, imagination, and skill forged in practice.

We are used in music, the arts, sport, politics, and every area of human endeavour to the idea of imagination. It is an indispensable part of success and nowhere more than in situations where conflict and disagreement have reduced hope and eliminated expectations of a better world. It is one thing to be imaginative when all is going well. It is quite another to be able to reimagine a future that is different and to develop the tools for bringing it into reality.

One of the supreme examples of imagination is the famous speech of Dr Martin Luther King Jr on 28 August 1963, at the Lincoln Memorial in Washington, to a vast crowd who had marched for civil rights. One of the most often-quoted parts is: 'I have a dream that my four little children will one day live in a nation where they will not be judged by the color of their skin, but by the content of their character. I have a dream today!' Not only was it rhetoric of an extraordinary skill but it gave a crowd and a nation, weighed down by racial division and oppression, a vivid idea of possibilities that they themselves had not imagined. It put deep hopes into tangible form, something to aim for, a vision not only for dreams, but also for practical ambitions. Even unknown people may, by an act of courageous reimagination, change the course of events. Seven years before Dr King's speech, Rosa Parks, in Montgomery, Alabama, refused to give up her bus seat for a White man. It was a major step in the struggle towards justice and civil rights.

Imagination is not a one-off moment after which the serious work begins. It is a process that is twinned with the use of skills and that leads to reimagination as progress is made or as setbacks occur and new ways forward need to be found.

In November 2012, the General Synod of the Church of England (a sort of church parliament) declined to support proposals that would have permitted the ordination of women as bishops. The mood in the days after the vote was very dour. The approach that would make it possible had been thrashed out over a great many years, decades even, and endless reports and periods of prayer and deep theological reflection. There was contempt for the failed process expressed in Parliament and in many newspapers. The general opinion was that it would be five years before another attempt could be possible.

However, in the immediate aftermath of the vote a group of people, both women and men, began to reimagine the possibilities of a different way forward. Much hard work was done on the legal detail and many conversations took place between people of differing views. To cut a very long story short, in July 2014 a simpler form of the legislation was passed and the first woman to be nominated a bishop was announced before the year end, a bare two years after the failed vote.

That was an example of reimagination, along the lines of 'if this does not work, but its failure had an impact, let's try a new approach, building on the new mood'. Reimagination has to happen again and again and that is why it is the third of the habits that the *Difference Course* seeks to inculcate. It links, obviously, to Lederach's moral imagination, discussed in Part I.[1] It is more than a practice, or a discipline, it has to be a habit. Imagination is not always spontaneous; in my case, very seldom. My default is to plod on. The habit of reimagination needs to grow to the point that it is always there, as part of the character of the group, or nation, or individuals.

The Bible is full of reimagination that opens the way forward to new developments and finds a way to deal with potential serious conflict. In the Acts of the Apostles 10.1-11.18 (Acts) there is one of the most significant reimaginings of the call and purpose of God for the people of this world. From very early in his public ministry, Jesus encountered Gentiles who were seeking help or advice. Earlier in this book we looked at the story of the Syrophoenician woman whose child was possessed by a demon. Jesus challenges her as to his mission but her answer in faith leads him to act. There are many other examples of boundary crossing, both by Jesus and by the apostles after his ascension. In Acts chapters 10 and 11 and thereafter the mission of the Church is pushed by the Holy Spirit of God into taking a decisive turn to the Gentile world.

As a result, over the following decades Gentiles of a huge variety of backgrounds and cultures became the dominant groups among Christians. The first reaction of Jewish believers was shock. In Acts 11.1-18 Peter tells believers in Jerusalem the story of his encounter with a Roman centurion (the events are recorded in Acts 10), after Peter had seen a vision, and of the centurion and his household receiving the Holy Spirit in the same way as the Jewish believers. From there the Gentile mission spreads to Antioch, through Asia Minor, to Greece and to Rome and beyond. It is the moment at which Christianity turned from being a Jewish group to a potential worldwide religion.

Throughout Christian history the response to radical change in circumstances has been a process of reimagining theologically the mission and actions of the global Church. With the fall of the western Roman Empire in the fifth century CE, Augustine of Hippo rethought the shape of a church in a western world without a centralized and powerful empire, but a Church surrounded by anarchy. In Ireland, northern England and Scotland, long before Augustine of Canterbury came in 597 CE, Celtic missionaries reshaped the way the Church worked, with few or no bishops and with bases in monastic communities. At times of great decline and division in the Church, figures like St Francis of Assisi, St Benedict and St Teresa of Ávila have emerged with a reimagining of the transformation and reconciliation of the gospel. Where the institution was willing to be inspired by reimagination, the Church found purpose and renewal, was reconciled to God and to each other, and recovered a missionary zeal and a commitment to Christ. Where they refused, most notably for all sides in the Reformation, division occurred.

Reimagining is the means of retaining a vision when circumstances have altered.[2] The events in Acts 10 and 11 were in the context of growing persecution, the murder of some of the Christians in the Holy Land and the scattering of believers all over the Roman world. Reimagining is both collective and individual but is usually much more effective in a group. It is not the unthinking acceptance of a new direction, but, as in the passage from Acts, a carefully tested and examined set of proposals that seems good to the consensus of those concerned.

GOD'S CALL

The source of all good imagination, of vision and of hope, is God. The test of genuine reimagining is that it reflects the love of God revealed in Jesus Christ and testified to by the Bible. The limits of reimagining the extent of reconciliation are the limits of God, which is another way of saying that there are no limits. When we combine the work of God through Jesus Christ in reconciliation, we find that the call to be peacebuilders is a call to imitate God. It is not the work of specialists and technical experts. It is a call to the whole Church of God, every Christian person, and on every occasion on which each of us falls short of that call we fall into sin. Yet God knows our weakness. My own experience is of constant falling and failure, but also of the love of God who picks me up and gives me a fresh start. That is the constant tension all Christians live with.

Holiness is seen in many ways. For the wounded and oppressed it may be simply that they call out to God. Paul speaks to slaves in his letters, telling them just to try to work well. So does Peter in his first letter. God knows us, our sufferings, our weakness and our failures. To go back to my friend Désiré in eastern Congo, 'Do what we can' – the rest is God's problem.

At a global level, holiness calls us to seek to reconcile the creation with human existence, even if the cost is very great, and our contribution very small. The creation is not ours; it is God's. We are the stewards and our reconciliation with creation, including climate and biodiversity, is also an essential part of holy living in reconciliation with God.

At a global, national and community level, the reconciliation of race and ethnicity, as well as class, gender and sexuality, nationality and other differences, is a holy call. It does not mean that everything wanted by everyone is right, but that finding out what is right depends on a foundation of living in a reconciled disagreement that enables us to search for the will of God. We cannot live in holiness and hatred, or holiness and enmity. They are incompatible.

As a global Church we must not rest comfortably among our divisions and rivalries. Ecumenism grew up in the 1920s out of a desire for unity. That unity must be our constant desire and to the extent that it is not yet possible to find a common voice of unity institutionally we must do so by cooperation through love-in-action.

As a global Church we must seek to find ways of relating well to other faiths. Christians have always lived among other faiths, but have too often been tyrannical when in the majority. The intense need for interfaith engagement becomes stronger as the proportion of the world's population in one faith or another grows and as faith becomes, in many countries, more and more a tool of politicians to define who is 'us' and who are our enemies.

God's call is shown by God's example in Jesus, who gave up heaven to become poor in this world for our sakes, to die for our sakes, for our sakes to rise and for our sakes to give the Holy Spirit so that a new body may emerge that crosses every boundary and exists in love and freedom and light in a dark world.

At the most local level we seek to be known as reconcilers and peacemakers in our families and communities. That is what is to be reimagined: not being blocked by the possibilities that we see but inspired to hope by the possibilities God sees and that we hear in solitary and collective prayer and study of the Bible.

Crossing Divides

I wrote earlier about my friend in America who visited the other churches in his area, not just the ones that were like his own. I also wrote about Brother Andrew, crossing the boundaries of the Iron Curtain with bibles and bringing hope to Christians being persecuted, later crossing other boundaries to meet terrorist leaders. In both cases they reimagined the situation with hope injected into it and with contact and humanity as part of it.

Not all of us, or even many of us, will have such dramatic opportunities as Andrew. However, the beginning of crossing a boundary is to try and imagine what everything would look like if that boundary were not there. After that comes the hard work that is described in the rest of this book. The six plates of Part II need to be spun and kept spinning. We need the habits of curiosity and being present. We need to know and understand the barriers. Most of all we will want our reimagined vision to be seen, even in small ways, so that it is caught more and more widely.

Crossing divides cannot be about us. It is easy – I have often seen it and even more often been tempted by it – to want to be known as a peacemaker. The recognition looks wonderful from the outside. Yet when you meet the winners of Nobel Peace Prizes, often they see it as slightly embarrassing to have been treated as the hero. They also know the cost.

A few years ago, I met a doctor who works with the huge number of women in eastern Congo who have been raped during the war. Denis Mukwege treats them physically and psychologically. His faith and work are utterly inspiring. He does not seek attention for himself but for them. He took the Nobel Peace Prize for them and he takes the death threats made against his work for himself. That is the reality of someone who saw the condition of the women and reimagined what could happen to them. Before he received the prize, he was almost unknown. He crossed the boundary to those who were excluded from their communities, unvalued by their attackers and without hope, and brought all those blessings of value, inclusion and hope with him. He also knew that he had not acted alone. In his acceptance speech he spoke of those women who had served with him at immense risk, and paid tribute to the survivor of sexual violence in conflict, Nadia Murad, who was honoured equally with him, and is equally remarkable.

The question when facing a boundary, whether it is resistance to global action on climate change, or to new patterns of interracial relations, or to reuniting a community that has fallen out, is what reconciliation would look like. It will very seldom if ever be in our image. It will even less often look like overwhelming victory for one side and the complete destruction of the other – evil ideas may need to be destroyed, but not people.

The second question is to reimagine the steps by which things could change. What relationships could be different? How could there be a way of dealing with the particular causes of division that put justice front and centre and gave dignity to all involved?

The third question is to imagine who I would like to work with, and then to ensure that the imagination is disciplined by an intention of diversity. To cross boundaries well we need to be in relationship with people on both sides of the boundaries, so that the collective decision making has the benefit of good navigators on both sides. Perhaps it is worth beginning by asking what you are praying for, and who.

Disagreeing Well

'On some things we will never agree.' So spoke one friend in Liverpool about another who was and is a 'Blue', an Everton supporter, as opposed to a 'Red', a Liverpool supporter. And they don't. But they are friends. Those who come from Liverpool and are football supporters will understand that a friendship like that can be noticeable.

In their case it did not take a major effort of reconciliation. After all, they each married one of two sisters and are the closest of family as well.

Disagreeing well, in most circumstances, is very much more complicated. It may be over a fundamental point. I have several Muslim friends with whom I disagree on the most basic of issues: the very nature of God. Yet we are friends, we seek each other's company and enjoy it when we meet.

Even that, though, is not disagreeing well enough yet, because disagreeing well is tested by the circumstances of disagreeing over something very important, and doing so with passion, and yet maintaining a relationship. Within the Church of England and the Anglican Communion, among the many people I deeply admire and whose example inspires me are a whole group of bishops who form close relationships with others with whom they disagree profoundly and publicly. They meet annually, in 2020–21 on Zoom, of course. They focus their discussions on the questions of human sexuality, same-gender marriage and a host of related issues. It is a very practical approach to reconciliation within the Communion.

At the Anglican Consultative Council of 2018, in Hong Kong, there was a motion put forward about human sexuality. Different people spoke with powerful views and different approaches. It was heated and difficult. Among them were some of those who had met in the group I had just described. They did not minimize the differences, hide their passions or settle for fuzzy compromise. They did speak to each other afterwards, listen to each other well, be present with each other and continue to meet. That is disagreeing well. They recognized that the subject being discussed was of immense importance, so much so that feelings and tempers would be touched. It was also recognized that those who disagreed might be wrong but were not evil. They were part of the family.

Practising Forgiveness

If disagreeing well is a steep hill, then forgiveness can be a vertical cliff face. The number of global and irreconcilable or deeply intransigent conflicts there are is a major subject of academic discussion on peacebuilding. We probably know of or experience relationships where forgiveness seems beyond reach under any circumstances. Many people simply cannot forgive themselves.

Forgiveness is not achieved by grovelling when one does not believe one has done wrong. It is often a way out of an argument. Metaphorically, you cross your fingers while saying sorry, in your mind feeling that you are right. All that does is store up a sense of bitter self-righteousness that will explode even more damagingly in the end. The same thing can happen at a national as well as an individual level. Feeling forced to admit blame in which one does not believe was behind much of the deep resentment in Germany after the Treaty of Versailles in 1919. It leads to a desire for revenge, in the individual as well as the community.

There are many other ways, but they require reimagining as well as the other habits. It is necessary to ask oneself, and often others, what forgiveness would look like. An objective but loving and accepting view will help see one's own responsibilities. The TRC in South Africa led many participants to a proper sense of their own participation in evil deeds and the need for them to accept fault and seek forgiveness. Conversely, hearing and seeing such transformation permitted forgiveness in some of the most unlikely of cases.

Reimagining forgiveness is a hard task as either perpetrator or victim. It is so easy to make it a duty that abuses the already abused. Survivors of abuse often rightly push back vehemently against cheap views of forgiveness or the immense pain that forgiveness will often cause to the forgiver.[3] There are many ways of getting to the place of forgiveness far more slowly and circuitously in which the victim begins to see themselves in a new light and to sense that their power to forgive or withhold forgiveness is very great and in some cases puts the perpetrator within their hands. As has already been said, there is a big difference between forgiveness and forgetting the consequences. The statement 'I forgive you, but you must still carry your punishment from the law' is perfectly coherent. It recognizes that crimes and oppression are communal and not purely individual, even the dreadful ones of abuse and discrimination, even the most terrible crime of murder.

Reimagining forgiveness begins within oneself, in complete honesty with God and complete openness to learning to know that one is loved. That is a first step of many, but a strong one.

RISKING HOPE

Horses are not my favourite thing. They are lovely to see, some of the most beautiful animals, and I deeply admire good riding. Purely personally, however, I notice that they have teeth at the front and powerful hind legs and hooves at the back. They are intelligent enough to know what they want and big enough to choose it. As a child, when I fell off a horse, rather than getting back on I decided to go sailing in small, tippy dinghies. No teeth, no hooves, no brain. Less fear.

Getting back on is very difficult even in something as unimportant as a riding lesson. Getting back on is a wholly more difficult thing when you have fallen away from hope and risked everything in hope of reconciliation.

For exactly this reason most reconciliation work, or even mediation work within it, is better done in pairs or teams than by oneself. Recent work in South Sudan has involved remarkable teams from numerous agencies. There have been no solitary stars. Reimagining hope is a joint exercise. It is also a systematic one.

It starts with acknowledging the problem and the failures. It does not use euphemisms like 'challenge' or 'opportunity', as in 'there is no such thing as a problem, there are only opportunities', to which one of my work colleagues replied to our mutual boss: 'in that case we are facing an insurmountable opportunity'. Honesty starts with finding reality because hope grows out of reimagining starting with where you are, not where you would like to be.

It continues with a reminder about the end vision. What is it you are trying to achieve? If it is for the COP conferences on climate change it might be world net-zero carbon emission by 2050 on a basis of just sharing of costs and benefits. There may be setbacks very early on but there will still be many other ways of getting there. The failed Copenhagen COP[4] of 2009 was followed eventually by the success of Paris in 2015. Holding the end vision in sight enables one to see the whole countryside and not just the immediate roadblock.

It may be that in a family dispute the end vision needs rethinking. Perhaps, rather than putting the marriage back together, it may be parting well and with care for all those affected.

It involves essentially a great deal of trying of ideas, of thinking, and starting with what should be rather than with the resources. Imagine first, then look for the resources to get there, and only if that fails imagine again on a different basis.

Risking hope requires the highest level of reimagination because reimagination's greatest enemy is despair. In the

most intransigent disputes, hope is formed by coming
back to my friend Bishop Désiré's adage: 'Do what you
can, what God resources you to do, and leave the rest to
God.' In that way, bit by bit the reimagining will rekindle
the hope.

SUMMARY

- Reimagining is hard and seldom purely solitary.
- It is perspiration and detailed work as much as it
  is inspiration.
- It is a foundation for vision, which in turn feeds
  new and stronger vision.
- It is a habit, not an event. Every setback is met
  by it.

POINTS TO PONDER

- Are you imaginative? Who do you know who is?
  How does it happen?
- Looking at disputes of which you are aware, try
  the exercise of seeing afresh what the vision for
  success looks like and work backwards towards
  the reimagining needed to get there.
- If you are in despair, or caught by bitterness
  because of suffering, do not surrender; imagine
  who can help you and seek support.

13

Three Examples for Reflection

In this chapter we are going to look at three cases, at a very high level, but seeking to apply some of the lessons of this book to potential avenues for exploration. I am aware that in none of the three is there detailed discussion, and they are not included to give answers but to suggest humbly some examples of the very beginnings of application of some of the ideas of this book. I am equally aware of the huge complexity of the issues, and that vast numbers of people do nothing but work on them. I am not for a moment feeling that I know better!

There are two conflicts that are both universal and local. The first is climate change and the second is racism and ethnicity. Within the western democracies there is a third: the issue of populism (used here in the sense of manipulating genuine fears and grievances for the end of political power, not in order to find their solution. Of course, the issues are very often, even usually, genuine and need dealing with in genuine partnership and giving power to those who endure them.).

This last challenge of disagreeing well also exists in all other countries, including Russia, India, Pakistan, much of the Middle East and in many countries in Africa. However, the social situations underlying these countries are so radically different that they are not possible to consider here except in widely generalized form.

CLIMATE CHANGE: HUMAN CONFLICT WITH THE PLANET

In the case of climate change the research is very well developed. The vast majority of scientists agree, and the objective evidence supports, the idea that the climate is changing and biodiversity is threatened, to a degree that will threaten the future habitability of large parts of the earth, especially in low-lying areas and in the Tropics.

It is also very widely agreed that these enormous changes are to a large extent human driven. There have been very many extreme changes before, but never at this speed and never with such a clear and unprecedented externality, human economic development, and its consequences in the emission of pollutants and carbon or other gases linked to global warming.

Since 2016, it is also widely agreed that the target for the twenty-first century should be to limit global warming to 1.5°C above pre-industrial levels. The present outputs from human activity seem more likely to result in more than 2°C – perhaps 2–3°C, or even higher.

The mapping of the conflict is less clear, but some key features are easily seen.

- As discussed earlier, it is possible to see two major sides: the creation and the human race. However, that is a terrible over-simplification.

○ Human beings range from massive contributors per head both to a loss of biodiversity and to global warming, to those whose contribution is insignificant. In general the former are from relatively rich countries and the latter from the poorest, including people groups who are essentially non-contributors and thus are victims of the changes.

○ At the same time there is uncertainty about the impact on the climate in specific areas. Some places may become easier to inhabit and do relatively well. For example, the UK and especially its northern parts may become more open to new forms of agriculture where it is currently not warm enough. Whether this is true or not, the overall effect is likely to cause people movements of extraordinary size, the political impact of which will only be manageable with huge sacrifice or immense inhumanity.

○ 'Spoilers' are also identifiable by many. They are not a single block. Some disagree with the majority of scientists. Some agree but feel that morally it is not right to limit economic growth now for the sake of those yet unborn and that the discounted cost of future climate warming is less than the current cost of its prevention. Some have a vested interest in the economic rents and returns from economic activity that drives climate change. This includes companies, political parties, nations and individuals. They are in different moral as well as political categories. The first group

may widely be seen to be mistaken but it helps
no one to categorize them as wicked. Spoiler
is thus a bad term. The other groups have a
more dubious role. Finally, there are significant
shadow influences, especially in international
politics and in politics in the democracies.

- Risk capacities range vastly, and a RAM (Risk
Allocation Matrix; see Chapter 7) would be a
book in itself. Essentially, though, the strongest
players in the short term are human beings in
geographical areas that are less likely to be heavily
and adversely affected, and that also happen to
be, in some but by no means all cases, the richest.
In the short term the poorest in any country
are the most at risk, and the poorest countries
have the highest risks. In the long term, human
beings are likely to be the weaker party, and the
creation the dominant force, in the absence of
something extraordinary turning up in scientific
and technological aspects of climate control.

However, the adequacy of work breaks down when it
comes to relating.

- There is no universally trusted group to act
as a convenor and facilitator among the 197
states and far more people groups, lobbies
and interests.
- The human side is bitterly divided, at odds
with each other to the point of war on other
interests, and divergent in capacity. The creation
side is impersonal, a thing that is not open to
negotiation or discussion. It simply responds

to inputs in a way that we do not understand
adequately. It could be argued that the conflict
is within the human side, but that ignores the
consequences of failing to act.

- The sense of responsibility for creation has been
diluted by millennia of activity that did no
permanent harm, by religious teaching of various
traditions, and the huge extent of groups having
an impact so that everyone feels the problem is
someone else's.

- The mere fact of a common need does not seem
to break down the individual wills of nations
and groups.

The common good is thus not recognized and needs
establishing. At the same time the danger threatening
the planet should give a great incentive to every human
being, provided they have hope of some progress in their
lives and of adequacy of food, shelter and security.

The relating is therefore going to have to work hand
in glove with the relieving, and reconciliation to reduce
conflict and increase security must be a priority in
order to enable longer-term thinking and minimize
the possibilities of wars that prevent any further action
on climate.

For all human beings, the imminent threat of death
or the destruction of society will outweigh all longer-
term issues.

The urgent need is therefore to relieve need.

- The restarting of trade that is fair and open
will give huge incentives to innovation and will
reduce extreme poverty very rapidly indeed,

as has been seen in the last fifty years. The World Trade Organization is therefore a central structure for the necessary developments that will open the doors to better work on climate and biodiversity.

- In some places, this can only be done with aid offered at the UN's recommended 0.7 per cent level of Gross National Income. The giving of such aid to parts of the economy where the economic return is too long term for thinly capitalized and poor countries, such as infrastructure, health and above all, education, will ease the pressure towards a world climate change agreement sufficient to limit the temperature rise. Aid needs reimagining and political leadership must enable the richer parts of the world to be curious and present to see the impacts.

- Peacebuilding needs to be of the highest priority and enabled by every nation with good armed forces and the skills to enable local populations to be reconciled. Key areas to tackle must be, first, the arms trade, which must halt the flow of weapons and ammunition to conflicts. Second, anti-corruption and tax evasion is indispensable, and tax havens and lack of transparency must be ended. The largest financial centres, in particular London, the EU, Europe other than the EU, Singapore and the USA, together with those areas of dependency, can tackle this question. Legislation on an international basis needs to make tax evasion and money laundering even harder than now.

- The UN must have the capacity to stop conflicts, intervening early. This would need more cooperation from the permanent five members of the Security Council, the strengthening of regional and multilateral partners such as the African Union, and the embedding of mediation and reconciliation hubs in national and international security structures.
- But relieving must also be done at the most local level. Basic improvements are indispensable in green spaces within communities, in recycling even at household level, with incentives to alter behaviour. Added to that must be a huge effort in education. Excellent local practice will deepen the commitment to excellent national practice (middle out) and thus in its turn to global progress.

The risks involved are huge.

- The very large political risks of the sacrifices necessary by the currently rich to enable the poor to grow sufficiently to take their own steps against climate change are risks of a monumental nature. The major problem is pain now in exchange for survival and flourishing in fifty years. Those risks can only be decided by people voting, but must be encouraged by politicians and others leading. One essential is for the weight of sacrifice in each economy to be borne by the wealthy in the same way as globally it must be borne by the wealthiest economies.

- The role of faith groups, which account for over 80 per cent of humanity, is essential. Their leaders must take risks: of being responsible for teaching on the sacred relationship with creation, of meeting and leading, of taking responsibility for the errors of those who claim to follow their faith. Christians have to be the global foot-washers, by their service and example enabling others to be liberated to serve well. For church leaders, this will often mean the risk of laying aside prestige, partition and inter-church quarrels for the sake of God's call to be stewards of creation and lovers of the poor and suffering.
- One way of mitigating the pain of the sacrifice is through green technology, fiscally encouraged. Expertise cannot be allowed to be monopolized by one country. What benefits only a small group will never motivate the vast majority. If the vast majority is not motivated, the future is lost.
- The struggle to combat climate change is going to be one full of setbacks, with the outcome visible only after more than a century. Maintaining the impetus will be a great risk. Finding milestones that can be celebrated is a huge challenge.
- The risk of meetings failing, and of major economies taking a short-term advantage, and the risks of terrible diversions such as wars, make the need to cooperate in this area on which all should be able to share a vision a potential huge mitigator of risk in other areas of competition.

Reconciling, with all these challenges, offers great hopes and great difficulties.

- It will bring hope to see nations agree on objectives. The relationships built may enable other dangerous areas, such as nuclear weapons proliferation and use, to be addressed with greater mutual confidence.
- The endless meetings and necessary campaigns are a long road without much beautiful scenery or interesting diversions. What progress can be made to encourage resolution and resilience?
- Reconciliation must be at the three levels: top down, middle out and bottom up. On such a scale of issue as this, the top is the global, the middle the national/regional and the bottom the local. To reimagine at each level, to make the struggle present at all levels, to encourage presence and participation without elitism, all these habits will be necessary.

Resourcing is where it hurts.

- The sharing of costs is the largest problem of the day. Sacrifice, suffering and altruism are required.
- Resourcing must include the development of adequate scientific, mathematical, technological and cultural skills to enable civilizations to develop and grow in a way that is committed to the common good. This can only be done at a national level; any form of international paternalistic or imperialist top-down approach is utterly wrong. Yet it must be resourced to

give every person in any economy opportunity
to aspire, to compete, to be ambitious and yet
to serve.

In all these areas we have the skills. There is a need for a
trusted, diverse, transparent and effective global secretariat
to coordinate and advocate. The UN is made for such
things. There is also a need for brave leadership. That we
must see in the years up to 2030.

RACIAL AND ETHNIC DIFFERENCES
AND DIVISIONS

Racism and ethnic divisions are invariably born out of a
common fiction, which is summed up for the British in
a satirical poem by Daniel Defoe, who wrote *The True-
born Englishman* in 1701, when Britain had a Dutch king,
sandwiched between previous French, Welsh and Scottish
dynasties and our present German line:[1]

Thus from a mixture of all kinds began
That het'rogeneous thing, an Englishman:
In eager rapes and furious lust begot
Betwixt a painted Briton and a Scot ...
In whose hot veins new mixtures quickly ran,
Infus'd betwixt a Saxon and a Dane ...
Fate jumbled them together, God knows how;
Whate'er they *were* they're true-born English *now* ...
A true-born Englishman's a contradiction,
In speech an irony, in fact a fiction ...
Since scarce one family is left alive
Which does not from some *foreigner* derive.

Or to put it more bluntly, Professor Mary Mwiandi, former chair of the University of Nairobi's History department, said at a 2009 historians conference, 'We're all immigrants and we're all here.'[2] The loss of that reality is fertile ground for racism across the world.

In the case of climate change the biggest weakness is in the R of relating. In the case of race and ethnicity, including the challenges and suffering behind BLM, the areas of failure are much wider.

Researching is prolific but not agreed.

- In terms of the habits of reconciliation in the *Difference Course*, the effective segregation in many parts of many countries reveals the absence of curiosity, betrays the failure of presence and prevents reimagining.
- By failing to see the distinctions, there is radical over-simplification of failures that are different in different societies. The problems in race relations in the USA are very different from those in the UK or in France, to take three examples. For example, the UK has not since the end of serfdom had *legal* slavery in the way that many states in the USA did until the mid-nineteenth century. However, the prosperity of many English cities, especially Bristol, Gloucester and Liverpool, but indeed of the whole of what is now the UK, was built on the slave trade. In addition, the entire UK economy gained hugely from not only trading in slaves but also the related trades in the Golden Triangle of shipping goods to West Africa, slaves across the Atlantic, and sugar and other goods to

British ports. It is also worth remembering that
the legacy of slavery in the UK is so profound
that the compensation for the abolition of
slavery in the British Empire only stopped being
paid to the descendants of former slave owners
in 2015.

- The British position is enormously complicated
  by the legacy of Empire, which has led to great
  diversity of religious and ethnic backgrounds
  since 1945. The simplification of all these
  factors into one category of BAME, when there
  is immense diversity within that grouping,
  also provides for lack of clear thinking and a
  recognition of proper responsibility by some
  among the White majority. As was discussed
  much earlier, many White people in the
  richest parts of the world are themselves
  deeply excluded from the benefits of economic
  growth and do not experience privilege in any
  meaningful sense.

- Another example is France, where the history of
  empire is very different and thus the minority
  ethnic groups tend to have a much higher
  proportion from North Africa. In the case of
  Black people in the UK, a high proportion
  of those who came from the Caribbean, and
  were and are so ill-treated, are of Christian
  and not Muslim tradition. Those of a Muslim
  background often come with the legacy of the
  British Empire more than that of slavery.

- There has also been a tendency for debate
  to become focused on highly controversial
  areas such as Critical Race Theory, as though

disproving it would somehow show there is
no problem with racism. Such self-unaware
approaches to the genuine issues of racism reveal
a lack of willingness to be present, to be curious
and to reimagine.

Thus, researching has done much, more than in almost
any other area of dispute and conflict, but has not resulted
in an acceptance of a basis of truth that reflects perception
and real experiences.

Relating has been alluded to in discussion of the issues
of the 'two hours of segregation' on a Sunday in the USA,
and in equivalent separated living in many other places,
including parts of UK cities, schools, housing and so
on. In France the suburbs of places like Paris reflect this
problem very significantly.

- Relating starts at the local. It must be the
  responsibility and vision of local groups, of
  intermediate institutions, to work hard with
  programmes like *Difference* and then seek in every
  possible way to encourage local gathering. Where
  this happens the results are superb, as can be seen
  by schemes in England like Near Neighbours.[3]
- Once again education must play a large role. Key
  issues to be addressed at local and regional levels
  must be differentials of health and education
  outcomes, standards of housing, language
  proficiency, and opportunities for high-quality
  higher and further education.
- There are increasingly good role models where
  relating is demonstrated. In many countries these
  are seen specially in sport. That is true in the UK.

- Challenges around public health and housing give a very good opportunity for building relationships within local government areas. So do local politics.
- One of the biggest challenges is the quality of relationships and not just the quantity. Do they permit the raising of genuine areas of concern and differences of perception? This is where the habits matter of being curious, being present and reimagining.
- A genuine area of controversy is free speech. The danger of facing the issues of racist behaviour is that fear of experiencing racism again, or of being called racist, lead to self-censorship. In that sense people are not present to each other and dare not be curious. The reality of the problem is handled in the USA by the First Amendment rights, and in other countries by tight restrictions. They represent two ends of a range. Truth is something that needs to see the lie in order to challenge it. Better to hear racist language and answer than to be unaware of lurking thoughts is an approach that has much to commend it. All that being said, encouragement to violence is always wrong.
- At the heart of relating, to quote a friend from an African British background, is that the issue of 'Whiteness' is a cultural disorder in everything we do. In other words, the whole way of living assumes being White (or, for that matter, male). I have heard this comment from many people who never speak of Critical Race Theory. The point being made, from a strongly

Christian and biblical view, is that change
requires a shift in power, and a clearer sense
of truth. In the conversation there was a very
interesting metaphor, which I am still thinking
about, involving Old Power in our society and
New Power. Old Power is institutional; you
have to fit. New Power is participative; you have
to join in. Old Power is *Tetris*, New Power is
Minecraft. Both forms of power are needed, but
both need each other in order to balance the
other's weakness.

Relieving need is a huge issue and very weakly addressed.

- The largest challenge is that of reparations. The
  historic legacy of slavery, Empire and racist
  attitudes linked to both has in many ways
  led to systemic discrimination. The question
  about reparations will have to be faced, and
  an answer found that is a sufficient sign and
  symbol of genuine relief of the needs caused
  by past actions. It cannot be right to say that
  the policies of past generations are not our
  fault, and thus should not be the subject of
  reparations, while on the other hand enjoying
  the results and fruits of those policies in terms
  of global power, of privilege, and of position
  internally and externally to our country,
  whichever it may be.
- The danger is that reparations will be so difficult
  to agree that at a national or international level
  the search for the right answer will take so

long that it will lead to no answer for several generations. Once again, the local matters. For example, Virginia Theological Seminary has a programme of tracing and seeking to support those who are the descendants either of those enslaved at the Seminary or of those who were employed there in the time of the Jim Crow laws. That can be done in many places.

- A clear area of reparations will be in working with countries that were affected by the slave trade to improve education and opportunity.

The issues of risking and reconciling will vary from country to country. There will never be a universal settlement, even in one society, because it is rightly impossible to work out who represents whom. Reconciliation in all these areas will be sociological, long term, local, and above all will require sacrifice by those who are in power. Each discrete area of discrimination will need looking at to ensure justice and truth. In some cases, this will be by a panel. The scandals of Windrush and associated racist actions come to mind. In other areas the key question will be representation in leadership. It is very noticeable that in the UK the Home Secretary in August 2021, the Chancellor of the Exchequer, the Business Secretary, the Health Secretary and the Cabinet minister who was president of COP 26 in Glasgow were all from a minority ethnic heritage. That would have been impossible even thirty years ago. Progress can be made, but it requires a continued determined effort, a vision and a fixed aim to see greater justice for all human beings, for all are made in the image of God.

Hatred as the Great Good

The third and last of these reflections is on the divisions we find among ourselves, sometimes called populist, or nationalist, but realistically each label misleads to some degree. These divisions are as old as human beings for they are founded on desires for power and desires to retain power. Those who stir up these hatreds seek to enable people to find their identity by finding their enemies.

In 2 Samuel 15, King David's son Absalom, returned from exile, carries out a textbook *coup d'état*. The first step is to stir up latent discontent within the kingdom. This he does by supporting those who felt excluded and 'thus Absalom stole the hearts of the people of Israel'. It is a classic approach, which culminated in a swift military strike that capitalized on the popular support he had. The pattern is equally familiar in modern times. Conversely, the pattern of Jesus Christ and of his Church when it acts rightly is not to seek power but to serve. The revolutionary nature of all that Jesus did and all that God does today is found in this rejection of the classic means of taking power.

The extreme opposite characterizes many populist rulers and leaders today, whose ability to gain traction in their campaigns arises from using existing divisions, not only some magic in the way they campaign or speak, or in their policies.

The impact of divisions unreconciled – that is to say, without the capacity to disagree well – is to open a society and large groups of people to manipulation. By contrast, the justice and goodness of God, in the words of Mary the mother of Jesus in Luke 2, is seen in equality, the humbling of the proud, the satisfaction of the needs of the poor. To put it infinitely less poetically than the *Magnificat*, God is present and shows us a reimagined world of justice, of forgiveness and of love. A church that does not identify with that vision but rather seeks its own power loses its soul.

In the UK, the USA and many countries in Europe and around the world, great changes have taken place, often through democratic votes that did demonstrate the voice of the people, such as the Brexit referendum vote in the UK, but leaving behind a deeply fractured and angry society. On 6 January 2021 a crowd stormed the Capitol Building in Washington DC, claiming that victory for their candidate in the US elections of November 2020 had been stolen. The claim of a rigged election is very often the cry of those who lose, but to see sights such as occurred on that day and to experience the bitter divisions that continue was deeply shocking to many with no personal interest in who was elected.

What can be done about this anger? Is such a thing as a reconciled society possible to imagine?

The strength of populist leaders is considerable as a result of political skills of a high order. In a way that mimics the *Difference Course*, but with motives of power rather than peacebuilding, they begin with listening, a habit of paying attention, being present to those whose voices are not normally heard. The contrast was often seen, and still is heard, among so-called elites, who openly, or behind closed doors, appear to be contemptuous of the voices of large groups of people.

Virtues such as patriotism are too often derided or ignored as old-fashioned and out of date. There is contempt for many who are genuinely concerned about the changing nature of the country, whether through social change, immigration, economic impact, the financial engineering of international capital in the City of London, Wall Street and a thousand other centres, and above all the sense that they exist to be the objects of other people's manipulation. In the words of the UK Brexit campaign, people want to take back control.

What is seen above all is an absence of research and relationship. To put it simply, many of those with money and power don't know what the struggle is for those without it and don't care. Whether genuinely or not – it is too easy to judge over hastily on that question – many populist leaders, for want of a better description, do 'get it'. Or, at the very least, they sound as if they do. They channel the anger that is felt in communities that for generations lived in one way and that, through no fault of their own, have seen their ways of life changed. In the north-east of England in the 1960s there were more than eighty thousand people employed in the mines. Today there are none. In Liverpool, at the same time, up to forty thousand people worked in the docks and related industries; today it is less than one-tenth of that figure.

Anger and discontent are reasonable and proper reactions from people who find their world changing and whose leaders do not appear to be paying attention. To combine rapid economic change with rapid social change only adds to that sense of insecurity as communities feel disrupted.

The relieving of need, in the absence of a genuine understanding of those needs, does not make a difference, even if done with the best of intentions. To use the language of the habits encouraged in the *Difference Course*, being curious leads to understanding, being present to relationship, and those two enable a reimagining.

The risks in such divisions are on one side from those who seek to use disrupted economic and social conditions to gain power, and who point to perceived and often real injustices. On the other side, the risks are accentuated by distanced and mechanical systems of care and mutual support. The impersonality of government actions is a direct result of the fact that they are not mediated through the local. Archbishop William Temple pointed to the essential nature of intermediate institutions, those that exist between the state and the household, that are sometimes voluntary and in other cases small businesses, social clubs, churches, schools, hospitals and an infinite number of others. Those in them know their areas, recognize needs and are capable of meeting them.

The infrastructure for meeting needs exists, through everything from parliamentary, political constituency associations in the UK to local mayors in France and to very strong faith communities and other local charitable groups in the USA. Local governments, when properly funded, are accustomed to meeting needs.

One of the earliest and most crucial developments in epidemiology took place in the Soho area of London in 1854. A severe outbreak of cholera was in full swing. The local curate, the Revd Henry Whitehead, working under the leadership of Dr John Snow, and with support from Florence Nightingale, mapped and identified the source of the infection as one water pump. Although removing that pump helped, the more significant change was in the understanding of the causes of cholera as being waterborne, not airborne.

The point of what happened was that it was local, as public health is to this day. Local actions based in local knowledge and relationships are critical for the national or global changes required.

Reconciling divided societies is the ultimate test of whether we can find the will and determination to overcome issues of privilege and power and work simultaneously from the bottom up, middle out and top down.

Reconciling happens when there is a level of trust created by the previous Rs, when people see genuine curiosity based in love and care, when they experience relationships, when needs are met and when people take risks. To map the conflicts of our societies is too large a task, and the different local levels are too varied. Yet some things we can see, based around inequalities and injustices. Resourcing reconciliation requires a shift in the way government works in divided societies, from doing to changing to doing with.

As mentioned earlier in this book, one area of work going on is the /together campaign. That includes a vast range of groups of all sorts and opinions in the UK and is designed to demonstrate that there is much in common. It contains the potential for work at all levels. It is only one of numerous possibilities.

There is nothing inevitable about societies divided by hate. It is possible to disagree well. Yet, as in other areas, it requires the empowering of the local, not the distanced actions of an impersonal state. It is an economic process, but it is very far from being only that. It also requires moral imagination, deep relationships, profound risk taking, thoughtful research, adequate resourcing and long-term work. What it offers is not a society that has conquered all its problems, but one that has the structures and trust to face anything with resilience.

14

Conclusion

Reconciliation is a work of courage, not so much from the peacebuilder but supremely for those caught in conflict. The image of the Stalingrad Madonna is an image of the courage of God. God has chosen to be entrusted to a woman who is poor, helpless and in a country full of conflict. The living God is the lamb of the poem, fragile, vulnerable, dependent on someone who herself cannot keep them in safety. The setting of the Madonna is in the frozen terror of Stalingrad, the place of the consequence of the evils of power seeking and war. That is the most appropriate setting for the Lamb of God, who is the source of hope, life, liberty and light.

This is our true image of who God is. This is the reality that revolutionized us and the whole of creation. Our response to this 'light of the world' decides on what we are; in our response we judge ourselves, make our plea before God, and with our plea show by our choice of attitude to this fragility the evidence that our plea is true. The judgement of God is the perfect justice of giving us what we have chosen. To choose this helpless figure cradled in the arms of the helpless mother is to choose courage, the courage to receive love, hope, life: it is the courage to choose reconciliation with God and the journey of reconciliation with the world.

It does not matter whether it is the unknown sorrows of a life caught in a noxious relationship, or of workplaces surrounded by contempt and bullying, or the great decisions of life and death in global struggles. The will to peace is the will of courage, for it begins with seeing the humanity of the ones who hate us and whom we hate. Reconciliation offers the gift of overcoming ourselves, to listening attentively to others, seeking a reimagined humanity. Reconciliation develops our moral imagination in order to find other ways to disagree, ways of disagreeing well.

RECONCILIATION AS THE SOURCE OF HOPE

Imagine for a moment a world where the processes of politics were full of alternatives that included peacebuilding with our enemies. This is not a world where evil is easily overcome. Reconciliation requires the will to be exercised. The desire for power is so great in individuals and in nations that it will be taken by some at all costs.

The first point of conclusion is thus the least hopeful. There are some situations where reconciliation is not possible. Either one person involved is too proud, or too evil, or both. When we encounter genocide, the perpetrators must be stopped by any means necessary. We do not sit down to talk first, we seek a cessation of the carrying out of the evil. If it does not stop then action must be taken at once. The Rwandan Genocide could have been stopped very quickly. Even the Second World War could have been stopped by determined action in the mid-1930s. It is easy to judge in retrospect and hard to see clearly at the time. The moment a war starts, even in a righteous cause, all control of the future is lost. Yet sometimes it must happen.

The same is true at the most intimate level. Removing a parent where there is good reason to believe abuse is occurring in the home is drastic, irreversible and with a terrible long-term impact. Yet sometimes it must happen.

However, in most circumstances reconciliation is possible. This is where hope begins, provided we know what we are talking about.

First, a reminder of the definition: reconciliation is the transformation of destructive conflict into disagreeing well. The impact of disagreeing well may continue to be disagreement. It may be a state of well-contained hostility. It may mean the end of a marriage. But it will always open new possibilities of mitigating the harm, at the least, and of bringing genuine healing, at most.

Second, there is hope because reconciliation, over a lengthy period, offers the possibility of forgiveness, of the victim being liberated from the perpetrator's control, whether that is exercised through power or through the lingering hatred of the perpetrator. Either way, they remain a presence. Forgiveness is the most final form of revenge. It is often desperately hard. It cannot be used against a victim to blackmail them into waiving the right to justice. It is something else apart from justice, it is the chance of freedom and a future. In Christian understanding, in some extraordinary mystery of beauty and love, God on the cross brought together justice and mercy, opening not only the gift of forgiveness to all who accept it but their own forgiving of themselves, and even others.

Third, reconciliation is a way of hope because it requires the stronger party to make the sacrifice of choosing to live with the weaker and not to control, dominate and rule them. It is a sacrifice made by God out of the purest of love, love so pure that it sent a beam of light through the whole of creation: the light of Christ. It is also a sacrifice called for if the strong recognize their own need of reconciliation. Whether it is with the creation, with ethnic minorities, with those who are different, with the fragile and weak in a community, the sacrifice opens the way to build beautiful places in which to live. It is the way, at its best, to destroy enemies by making them friends, and at the worst to remove fear and anxiety from the places we live and the relationships we have.

Fourth, reconciliation opens the way to justice and truth. When sacrifice is made, then truth can be told. When truth is told, justice and mercy can meet and can be seen to be real. Justice before there is the beginning of reconciliation is almost always suspect, either because it is justice imposed by the strong or because the truth is not clear.

PRE-EMPTIVE RECONCILIATION A NECESSITY FOR ALL OUR FUTURES

A world of power seeking and dominance by the strong depends for its future on the flimsiest of foundations. It depends on the consistent benevolence of the strong, caring for the weak. That only has to be said to be unbelievable.

At present there are approximately fifty significant conflicts in the world. At the same time, in many areas the circumstances of economics and challenges to historic sources of power are leading to talk of a second cold war. Some see the activities of cyber conflict as already a form of that war heating up. Nuclear proliferation remains a serious threat and the impetus towards disarmament has been lost. Climate change will accentuate the threats and dangers of the next fifty years.

It is easily forgotten that the world now possesses the capacity to kill every living thing, including every person. The nuclear strategies have no after-plan, for what happens once the buttons are pressed? The obvious answer is: 'Then we are all dead.' The idea that such an approach can be called a strategic move would be called insane if put forward by an individual, but is taken for granted when advanced by a government.

National and civil conflicts are taking place in the context of a world with an unprecedented capacity for destruction through nuclear, chemical, biological and cyber weapons and with an unprecedented threat caused by its normal economic activities and their impact on the creation. Conflict is always profoundly dangerous and usually deeply wrong. For it to happen amid such other dangers is beyond any degree of foolishness. Reconciliation is an essential.

In the face of all these threats, very often reconciliation will be impossible. So it is essential that there is pre-emptive reconciliation. Every nation should see reconciliation as a routine part of diplomacy, not a fire hose to put out an existing inferno. Pre-emptive reconciliation acts in a way that most will not notice. I remember a primary-school joke I heard as a child. A person stands by their gate. A neighbour asks, 'Why have you painted your gate pink?' 'It keeps the elephants away.' 'But there are no elephants round here!' 'You see, it works.'

Even if we are willing to spend scores of billions of dollars on armed forces, which we do, then some precautions make sense to reduce the extreme cost of their use. If we are willing to risk the future of the planet with nuclear arsenals, then working out how not to use them is obvious. Nations, communities, churches should all invest in developing pre-emptive reconciliation. It saves pain, time, money and, in the end, it saves life. The use at national level of mediation and peacebuilding units within every diplomatic service should be as routine as having a police force, or a health check-up.

Even in what we all hope is the more likely scenario – that the nations of the world learn to mitigate and contain conflict, that no nuclear outbreak happens, and that climate change is faced and dealt with – reconciliation is indispensable.

The capacity of human beings to disagree well has never been good, but the damage done by our failure to do so is vastly amplified by modern communications. On the day I write this, in mid-2021, there are reports of midwives having their lives threatened because they advocate vaccinations against COVID-19. The disagreement is tolerable, its form is evil.

In some places there are suggestions of near censorship to control forms of communication about the vaccines and the COVID-19 virus. A correction will always lead to censoring truth as well as lies.

Reconciliation offers the hope of vigorous and free differences of opinion without fear, of truth challenging lies without lies retaliating violently. It is the example of God. Even for the atheist it is the call of wisdom.

In this book the training suggested, the pattern set out and the needs described are a beginning. The *Difference*

Course has many alternatives, and it is my hope that further and more advanced training will follow quickly.

This book has tried to look at the reasons for reconciliation, to describe one – among many – patterns for it to happen, and to encourage the habits that make it possible. My prayer is that many will seek their own route to share in reconciliation, to start groups that will advocate and train others, and that will seek to make disagreeing well part of how we live at every level from household to global.

Acknowledgements

Too many people have been involved in this book to thank them all. To start with there are those who took part in seminars early in 2021 and while I was at Trinity College Cambridge, in the summer of 2021, where the research and first writing was done. Professor Anthony Reddie, The Very Reverend Dr Mandy Ford, Dr Gary Bell, The Baroness Reverend Maeve Sherlock OBE, Bill Marsh, The Reverend Canon Stephanie Speller, Alex Evans, Professor Miroslav Volf, Professor (or Father) Emmanuel Katongole, Pádraig Ó Tuama, Mariam Tadros Lord John Alderdice, General Sir Adrian Bradshaw KCB OBE, Roxaneh Bazergan, Irenée Herbert, Dame Karen Pierce, Professor Alasdair Coles, Professor Pumla Gobodo-Madikizela, Professor Simone Schnall, Professor Manos Tsakiris, Professor Miles Hewstone, Sofia Carozza (PhD student and Marshall Scholar Cambridge University), Revd Dr Tim Jenkins; Revd Catherine Matlock, Onjali Rauf, Canon Sarah Snyder, Dr Zaza Elsheikh, Dr Mukulika Banerjee, Dr Fenella Cannel, Dr Carlton Turner, Dr Ibram X. Kendi, Ebonee Davis (PhD student at Howard University), The Most Revd Michael B. Curry, Dr Catherine Meek, The Reverend Canon Cornelia Eaton, The Reverend Canon Stephanie

Spellers, Dr Kristopher Norris, The Revd Dr Katherine Grieb, Dr Nalini M. Nadkarni, The Reverend Canon Peter G. Kreitler, Martha C. Franks, The Reverend Gwynn Crichton, The Reverend Melanie Mullen, Dr Robert P. Jones, The Reverend Dr Molly F. James, The Reverend Gregory O. Brewer, The Right Reverend Martyn Minns, The Reverend Dr Canon C. K. Robertson, The Reverend Valerie Mayo, The Right Reverend Dr George Sumner, Amber D. Noel.

I am especially grateful to Professor Emeritus David Ford, for wise advice and wonderful encouragement over many years, and to his wife Deborah, similarly. Also to Dr Robert Heaney, whose book on post-colonial theology is so inspiring, and to the Reverend Professor Michael Banner and his wife Sally for yet more hospitality and for organizing the sabbatical term.

I thank Trinity College Cambridge, Master, Senior Tutor and others (especially the Fellows' Eight that kept me exercised) for their gracious and generous provision of space to study.

The first readers whose comments were invaluable were Katherine Richards, Joanna Alstott, Amelia Sutcliffe, Revd Dr Flora Winfield, Martha Jarvis, Kiera Phyo, Revd Dr Isabelle Hamley, Peter Welby, Chris Cox, Keziah Stephenson and Christopher Long.

Over the years I have learned from so many people. The reconciliation team at Lambeth Palace and Coventry Cathedral have taught me greatly, so I thank them especially.

The number of people I encountered who inspired me is huge. I owe especial thanks to Anglican archbishop Josiah Fearon and to Roman Catholic bishop Matthew Kukah. I add also Pastor James Wuye and Imam Ashafa (the Pastor and the Imam) in Kaduna, Archbishop Emmanuel Egbunu, Archbishop Benjamin Kwashi, Claudeline Mukanirwa and so many more that I cannot count them. Above all have been the huge numbers of women who have sought peace and pursued it, whose names, in the old expression from the First World War, are known only to God, but whose courage has transformed those around them.

My colleagues in the office have done a huge amount, especially David Porter, Emma Ineson, Tim Thornton. The hard work of organizing, sorting and making diaries work was through Joanna Alstott and Katherine Richards, as well as Amelia Sutcliffe.

I am very grateful to Robin Baird-Smith, a kind and thoughtful editor, and to Bloomsbury for patience, support and probing questions. Also to Nick Fawcett for his careful copyediting of the manuscript.

The cover is a production of the very remarkable artist, Timur d'Vatz.[1] His pictures are influenced by iconography and medieval art. I find them profoundly moving and his creation of such depth of art on the cover is a treasure.

And, of course, most of all, the family! In every way they educate, train and support, especially Caroline, my wife, whose own ministry of reconciliation with women leaders is so inspiring.

Reading List

In addition to works referred to in the Notes, you may find the following helpful:

Azevedo, R. T., S. N. Garfinkel, H. D. Critchley and M. Tsakiris, eds (2017), 'Cardiac afferent activity modulates the expression of racial stereotypes', *Nature Communications*, 8 (13854).

Baer, T. and S. Schnall (2021), 'Quantifying the cost of decision fatigue: suboptimal risk decisions in finance', *Royal Society Open Science*, 8 (201059).

Baez, S., E. Herrera, A. García, et al. (2017), 'Outcome-oriented moral evaluation in terrorists', *Nature Human Behaviour*, 1 (0118).

Barton, M. (2005), *Rejection, Resistance and Resurrection: Speaking Out on Racism in the Church*, London: Darton, Longman & Todd Ltd.

Brendtro, L., M. Brokenleg and S. Van Bockern, eds (1990), *Reclaiming Youth at Risk: Our Hope for the Future*, Bloomington: National Educational Service.

Brett, Mark G. and J. Havea, eds (2014), *Colonial Contexts and Postcolonial Theologies: Story-Weaving in the Asian-Pacific*, New York: Palgrave Macmillan.

Bruneau, E. G. and R. Saxe (2012), 'The power of being heard: the benefits of "perspective-giving" in the context of intergroup conflict', *Journal of Experimental Social Psychology*, 48 (4): 855–66.

Carlson, J. and A. Dumont, (1997), *Bridges in Spirituality: First Nations' Christian Women Tell their Stories*, Etobicoke: United Church Publishing House.

Carvalhaes, C., ed. (2015), *Liturgy in Postcolonial Perspectives: Only One Is Holy*, New York: Palgrave Macmillan.

Charleston, S. and E. Robinson, eds (2015), *Coming Full Circle: Constructing Native Christian Theology*, Minneapolis: Fortress Press.

Clarke, S. (2014), 'World Christianity and postcolonial mission: a path forward for the twenty-first century', *Theology Today*, 71 (2): 192–206.

Coates J. M. and J. Herbert (2008), 'Endogenous steroids and financial risk taking on a London trading floor', *Proceedings of the National Academy of Sciences of the United States of America*, 105 (16): 6167–72.

de Sousa Santos, B. (2018), *The End of the Cognitive Empire: The Coming of Age of Epistemologies of the South*, North Carolina: Duke University Press.

DeYoung, P. A. (2015), *Understanding and Treating Chronic Shame: A Relational/Neurobiological Approach*, London: Routledge.

Douglas, I. T. and K. Pui-lan, eds (2001), *Beyond Colonial Anglicanism: The Anglican Communion in the Twenty-First Century*. New York: Church Publishing.

Fanon, F. (1967), *Black Skin, White Masks*, New York: Grove Press.

Fanon, F. (1967), *Wretched of the Earth*, Harmondsworth: Penguin Books.

Gobodo-Madikizela, P. (2003), *A Human Being Died That Night: A South African Story of Forgiveness*. Boston: Houghton Mifflin.

Gobodo-Madikizela, P. (2015), 'Psychological repair: the intersubjective dialogue of remorse and forgiveness in the aftermath of gross human rights violations', *Journal of the American Psychoanalytic Association*, 63 (6): 1085–1123.

Haidt, J. (2012), *The Righteous Mind: Why Good People are Divided by Politics and Religion*, New York: Allen Lane.

Heaney, R. S. (2019), *Post-Colonial Theology: Finding God and Each Other Amidst the Hate*, Eugene: Cascade Books.

Horsley, R. (2002), *Jesus and Empire: The Kingdom of God and the New World Disorder*, Minneapolis: Fortress Press.

Jewett, R., ed. (2011), *The Shame Factor: How Shame Shapes Society*, Eugene: Cascade Books.

Joh, W. A. (2006), *Heart of the Cross: A Postcolonial Christology*, Louisville: Westminster John Knox Press.

Lederach, J. P. (1997), *Building Peace: Sustainable Reconciliation in Divided Societies*, Washington DC: United States Institute of Peace Press.

Lederach, J. P. (2010), *The Moral Imagination: The Art and Soul of Peacebuilding*, Oxford: Oxford University Press.

Lederach, J. P. (2014), *Reconcile: Conflict Transformation for Ordinary Christians*, Harrisonburg: Herald Press.

Malina, B. (2001), *The New Testament World: Insights from Cultural Anthropology*, Louisville: Westminster John Knox Press.

Marzouk, S. (2018), 'Famine, migration, and conflict: the way of peace – a reading of Genesis 26', in D. Schipani, et al. (eds), *Where Are We? Pastoral Environments & Care for Migrants: Intercultural & Interreligious Perspectives*, 3–18, Düsseldorf: Society for Intercultural Pastoral Care and Counselling.

Merz, J. (2020), 'The culture problem: how the honor/shame issue got the wrong end of the anthropological stick', *Missiology: An International Review*, 48 (2): 127–41.

Milevska, S., ed. (2016), *On Productive Shame, Reconciliation and Agency*, Berlin: Sternberg Press.

Nash, S. (2020), *Shame and the Church: Exploring and Transforming Practice*, London: SCM Press.

Neyrey, J. (1998), *Honor and Shame in the Gospel of Matthew*, Louisville: Westminster John Knox Press.

Owen, D. (2011), *In Sickness and Power*, London: Methuen Publishing Ltd.

Pattison, S. (2000), *Shame: Theory, Therapy, Theology*, Cambridge: Cambridge University Press.

Pettigrove, G. and N. Parsons (2012), 'Shame: a case study of collective emotion', *Social Theory and Practice*, 38 (3): 504–30.

Reardon, S. (2018) 'Columbia: after violence', *Nature*, 557 (7703): 19–24.

Reddie, A. (2019), *Theologising Brexit*, London: Routledge.

Reddie, A. and M. Jagessar (2007), *Postcolonial Black British Theology: New Textures and Themes*, London: Epworth Press.

Rossall, J. (2020), *Forbidden Fruit and Fig Leaves: Reading the Bible with the Shamed*, London: SCM Press.

Rowe, N. and S. Marzouk (2014), 'Christian disciplines as ways of instilling God's shalom for postcolonial communities: two reflections', in K. H. Smith, J. Lalitha and L. D. Hawk (eds), *Evangelical Postcolonial Conversations: Global Awakenings in Theology and Praxis*, 224–41, Downers Grove: InterVarsity Press.

Schnall, S., J. Haidt, G. L. Clore and A. H. Jordan (2008), 'Disgust as embodied moral judgment', *Personality and Social Psychology Bulletin*, 34: 1096–1109.

Schnall, S., K. Harber, J. Stefanucci and D. R. Proffitt (2008), 'Social support and the perception of geographical slant', *Journal of Experimental Social Psychology*, 44: 1246–55.

Smith, K. H., J. Lalitha and D. D. Hawk, eds (2014), *Evangelical Postcolonial Conversations: Global Awakenings in Theology and Praxis*, Downers Grove: InterVarsity Press.

Strathern, M. (2000), *Audit Cultures*, London: Routledge.

Sugirtharajah, R. S. (2001), *The Bible and the Third World: Precolonial, Colonial, and Postcolonial Encounters*, Cambridge: Cambridge University Press.

Sugirtharajah, R. S. (2002), *Postcolonial Criticism and Biblical Interpretation*, Oxford: Oxford University Press.

Swinton, J. (2007), *Raging with Compassion*, Grand Rapids: William B. Eerdmans Publishing Co.

Swinton, J. (2012), *Dementia: Living in the Memories of God*, Grand Rapids: William B. Eerdmans Publishing Co.

Swinton, J. (2018), *Becoming Friends of Time*, Waco: Baylor University Press.

Tajfel, H. (1970), 'Experiments in intergroup discrimination',
    Scientific American, 223 (5): 96–103.
Tsakiris, M. (2020), 'Politics is Visceral', *Aeon*, 18 September.
    Available online: https://aeon.co/essays/politics-is-in-peril-if
    -it-ignores-how-humans-regulate-the-body (accessed on 21
    June 2021).
Turner, C. (2020), 'Could you be loved? BAME presence
    and the witness of diversity and inclusion', in C. Ross
    and H. Southern (eds), *Bearing Witness in Hope: Christian
    Engagement in Challenging Times*, London: SCM Press.
Turner, C. (2020), *Overcoming Self-Negation*, Eugene: Pickwick
    Publications.
van der Kolk, B. A. (2014), *The Body Keeps the Score: Brain,
    Mind, and Body in the Healing of Trauma*, New York: Viking.
Volf, M. (1996), *Exclusion and Embrace: An Exploration of
    Identity, Otherness, and Reconciliation*, Nashville: Abingdon
    Press.

Notes

INTRODUCTION

1 Part of the last poem (*Agnus Dei*) in a six-part 'agnostic Mass' entitled 'Mass for the Day of St Thomas Didymus' by Denise Levertov, *Candles in Babylon*, 113–15; also in *The Collected Poems of Denise Levertov*, 677–8. Found in David Ford's Theological Commentary on John's Gospel.

2 See *Enemy at the Gates* from 2001 for an example of a powerful film. *Stalingrad* by Antony Beevor (1998) is a superb history of the battle, traumatic to read.

3 For those who do not know the story there are many sources, starting with www.coventrycathedral.org.uk, The medieval cathedral and parish church was destroyed in a great bombing raid on 14 November 1940. The Provost of Coventry, Richard Howard, established it as a centre of reconciliation from the end of the Second World War, symbolized by a cross of nails that fell from the burning timbers to the floor of the cathedral. A new cathedral was completed in 1962, at right angles to the old, and linked by a great window so that the two go together as a symbol of death and resurrection. The Community of the Cross of Nails is a worldwide association of over two hundred centres that have crosses of nails or a non-Christian symbol, which work at reconciliation in their own contexts.

4 David F. Ford, *A Theological Commentary on the Gospel of John*, Baker Academic, a division of Baker Publishing Group, Grand Rapids, MI, 2021, (hereafter Ford, *John*).
5 Difference.rln.global.

1 https://www.gov.uk/government/publications/global
-britain-in-a-competitive-age-the-integrated-review-of
-security-defence-development-and-foreign-policy.
2 Attributed to many people, including President Abraham Lincoln, Mark Twain and Dr Martin Luther King.
3 *On War*, Princeton University Press (date unknown), p. 87.
4 For developed discussion see Rowan Williams, *On Augustine*, Bloomsbury, 2016, Chapter 12, 'Augustinian Love', especially page 192. (Hereafter RW.)
5 RW, p. 185.
6 RW, p. 149, footnote 11.
7 RW, p. 55.
8 *Critical Race Theory: The Key Writings that Shaped the Movement*, ed. Crenshaw et al., The New Press, 1995, pp. 276–90.
9 Discussion with Revd Canon Dr Isabelle Hamley was very valuable here. She quotes Luce Irigaray as saying that Descartes seeks to 'give birth to himself', an act of 'astonishingly arrogant solipsism'.
10 Seen as a signifier of PTSD in the *Diagnostic and Statistical Manual of Mental Disorders*.
11 A powerful examination of the nature of monastic identity and its relationship to the world and cultures around it is found in Rowan Williams, *The Way of St Benedict*, Bloomsbury, 2020.
12 More details on the Archbishop of Canterbury's website.
13 See discussion on Ricoeur's Oneself as Another by Henry Venema in *Literature and Theology*, Vol. 16, No. 4, December 2002, around page 418.
14 Review of David Ford's *Self and Salvation* by John R. Sachs in *Theological Studies*, Vol. 6, No. 1, Washington, March 2001.

15 Williams, op. cit., especially Chapter 7, pp. 106ff.
16 Ford, *John*, pp. 416ff..

CHAPTER 2

1 *The Political Dimension of Reconciliation*, Ralf K.
   Wüstenberg, Eerdmans, 2009, especially Part III,
   pp. 197ff.
2 Revd Lucie Lunn, private paper quoting DeYoung (2015).
   *Understanding and Treating Chronic Shame: A Relational/
   Neurobiological Approach*, New York: Routledge. The next
   paragraphs arise out of a personal conversation, 7 June
   2021.
3 Using language to create a sense of low self-worth and/or
   deep personal insecurity about anything from one's abilities
   to one's sanity.
4 Conrad, 'Nostromo', commented on in 'Conrad and
   Masculinity', PhD thesis by Emma Fox, 1995, p. 56.
5 'I'll put a girdle round about the earth in forty minutes',
   Act II, Scene I.

CHAPTER 3

1 *The Moral Imagination: The Art and Soul of Building
   Peace*, Oxford University Press, 2005. Professor John Paul
   Lederach is a key writer in peace building. It is superbly
   written by one of the wisest and bravest of facilitators and
   thinkers about peace.
2 Lederach, *Moral Imagination*, p. 29.
3 *Global Britain in a Competitive Age: The Integrated Review of
   Security, Defence, Development and Foreign Policy* describes
   the government's vision for the UK's role in the world over
   the next decade and the action we will take to 2025.
4 Lederach, *Moral Imagination*, p. 165.
5 Neurosciences Roundtable, Cambridge, 4 June 2021; see
   notes for further reading.
6 Internally Displaced People. Technically, a refugee has
   crossed an international border while an IDP is still within

their own country. It tends for those who have fled to be a difference without a distinction but has a major impact in international law, which governs the two categories differently giving more protection to refugees.

INTRODUCTION TO PART II

1 Hebrews 4.15.
2 Matthew 5.9 (NRSV).

CHAPTER 4

1 Op. cit.
2 One lawsuit on pollution concluded in the Dutch Courts as recently as January 2021, holding Shell liable, https://www.bbc.co.uk/news/world-africa-55853024.

CHAPTER 5

1 1 John 4.8.
2 Of course, nothing is ever exclusively the work of one person; Religions for Peace, Bill Vendley and many others were also central and only God knows who was the most important.
3 John 13.1 (NRSV).
4 Matthew, chapters 5–7, especially 7.1-5.
5 Because of a speech by Winston S. Churchill, 5 March 1946, in Fulton, Missouri: 'From Stettin in the Baltic to Trieste in the Adriatic an iron curtain has descended across Europe.'
6 His own account is in a book called *God's Smuggler*.
7 For a detailed examination see *The Political Dimension of Reconciliation*, Ralf K. Wüstenberg, trans. R. H. Lundell, Eerdmans, 2009.
8 Talal Asad, *On Suicide Bombing*, Columbia University Press, 2007, pp. 62–3.

CHAPTER 6

1 Identity carefully camouflaged, including nationality and denomination.
2 In John's Gospel, Jesus' key miracles are referred to as signs; in other words, actions that reveal the nature of Jesus and thus the nature of God.

CHAPTER 7

1 Luke 15.11-32 (NRSV).
2 Dr Isabelle Hamley, formerly Chaplain at Lambeth Palace, commented in a note: 'interesting to note that this is a very different approach to Western-centred models of justice and forgiveness, when we want offenders to make contrition (often multiple times) and victims to be able to go over their grievances repeatedly. The model here (as virtually everywhere in scripture) is of beginning with a willingness to embrace, from which other things follow.'
3 A diocese in England is a geographical area within which the churches are overseen by a bishop. The dean runs a cathedral, which is the main church of the diocese. The archbishop oversees a group of dioceses. A diocesan synod is a gathering of elected clergy and lay people led by the bishop to help decide on policy.
4 Sadly, it is yet to be invented.

CHAPTER 8

1 For example, *William Dalrymple*, 'The Anarchy', Bloomsbury, 2020 edition, p. 246.
2 *The Political Dimension of Reconciliation*, Ralf K. Wüstenberg, op. cit.
3 Glen Pettigrove and Nigel Parsons, *Social Theory and Practice*, Florida State University, Vol. 38, No. 3 (2012): 526; a very powerful and useful article.

4 Where the earliest Caribbean migrants to the UK were systematically deprived of their rights and even of their identities, being sent back to the Caribbean decades later.
5 *Financial Times*, 13 July 2021.
6 See *An Ethic for Christians and Other Aliens in a Strange Land*, William Stringfellow, Word Books, Waco, Texas, 1973.
7 Luke 5.1-11.

CHAPTER 9

1 Please see Chapter 2 and the Bibliography for further sources in this area.
2 Isaiah 2.4 (NRSV).
3 Ford 2021, op. cit., p. 297.
4 Appendix x, reproduced with permission.
5 *Christianity and Social Order*, 1942. For an updated approach, *Reimagining Britain*, Justin Welby, Bloomsbury, 2nd edition 2021.

CHAPTER 10

1 Found at difference.rln.global, +442078981016, hello@rln. global.
2 Prime Minister Neville Chamberlain used a phrase like this about Czechoslovakia in 1938.
3 Gordon Brown, *Seven Ways to Change the World*, Simon & Schuster, 2021.
4 Op. cit., p. 57.
5 Jonathan Sacks, *Morality: Restoring the Common Good in Divided Times*, Hodder, 2020.
6 *Essays on the French Revolution*, 1793.
7 *Difference: Your Guide*, 2020, p. 14.
8 Difference.rln.global.

CHAPTER 12

1 Another example of reimagining is that of Dr Sara Schumacher at St Mellitus College.

2 For an attempt at this please see Justin Welby, *Reimagining Britain*, Bloomsbury, 2018.

3 See a very remarkable examination of this: Dr Stephen Cherry, *Healing Agony: Re-imagining Forgiveness*, Bloomsbury, 2012.

4 Conference of the Parties, on facing climate change.

CHAPTER 13

1 Quoted by Professor John Lonsdale in an unpublished paper of 2021. The paper is a profound and superb reflection on the pre-colonial ethnic influences in East Africa. John goes on to say: 'So I make a serious if impractical suggestion: that the Ministry of Education award an annual prize, perhaps to be called the *Karibuni*, "You are all welcome", prize, to the high school student who best illustrates the multiple origins of her or his ethnic group in the style of Daniel Defoe.' One might suggest the same for the UK.

2 Lonsdale, op. cit.

3 Government-financed and often church-/faith-group-led interaction of different communities at local levels, administered by the Church of England Church Urban Fund.

ACKNOWLEDGEMENTS

1 www.timurdvatzstudio.com.

Index